FACE THE NIGHT

OTHER BOOKS BY LANI FORBES

THE AGE OF THE SEVENTH SUN SERIES

The Seventh Sun
The Jade Bones
The Obsidian Butterfly

ANTHOLOGIES (CONTRIBUTING AUTHOR)

It's All in the Story: California
Warriors against the Storm

Face the Night

LANI FORBES

BLACKSTONE
PUBLISHING

Printed in the United States of America

First edition: 2023
ISBN 979-8-212-03091-5
Young Adult Fiction / Fantasy / General

Version 1

Blackstone Publishing
31 Mistletoe Rd.
Ashland, OR 97520

www.BlackstonePublishing.com

FACE THE NIGHT

FOREWORD

What would you do with a glimpse into your future? A preview that gave away the next few moments?

Lani Forbes and her protagonist Cat both foresaw the near future.

I have the tremendous honor, while filled with sorrow, to write this foreword. I am Lani's husband. I had a front-row seat from the very first thought to the final word as Lani wrote her last tale, *Face the Night*. She sat on the hospital bed, holding our two-day-old baby, when she was told she had stage 4 neuroendocrine cancer. While neither of us said it out loud, we both knew deep down, it was just a matter of time.

I accompanied her to hospital beds to get chemo, drove her across states to various hospitals, and rode planes with her across the country to speak with some of the top cancer specialists in the world. She fought for every possibility, and at the same time, she wrote with abandon, knowing her time drew near.

If you were with her, you would have heard her phone clicking with every letter of this wild adventure.

Everyone who watched Lani's journey saw her bravery. She instilled in our children that being brave does not mean you are not afraid. Being brave means that despite being afraid, you still go forward. The main character, Cat, has plenty to fear from her checkered past—those that want to steal what is hers, those that want her dead, and perhaps love itself. However, Cat battles forward, never giving up, even in her darkest moment, just like Lani.

The characters are full of love, attachment, betrayal, guilt, and shame. Their individual stories will compel you to read "just one more chapter."

Lani wrote her own strength, humor, determination, and fears into *Face the Night*. She weaved together magical and spiritual elements, including lore, into this brave new world. To those that read the Age of the Seventh Sun series, this will be no surprise. Lani's ability to build worlds won her many awards. I would open the mailbox to awards for which I didn't even know she was in the running. Sometimes she'd receive two awards on the same day.

Thank you to Samantha Wekstein, Thompson Literary, and Blackstone Publishing for making this story, full of new characters, magic, and adventure, available to the world. Every character written by an author is a shard of themselves, and I'm grateful the shards of the most amazing wife, mother, daughter, friend, teacher, scientist, trauma coach, and author, Lani Forbes, will be out in the world forever.

She faced the night. May we only be as brave.

—*Kevin Forbes*

THE TWELVE PATRON SAINTS OF THE ORDONIAN EMPIRE

NAME:	PATRON SAINT OF:	BLESSING GIFT:
Saint Clementia	Mercy and Gentleness	Healing sickness
Saint Comitas	Humor and Goodwill	Manipulating emotions
Saint Dignitas	Nobility and Self Awareness	Immunity to sickness and poisons
Saint Firmitas	Tenacity and Strength	Unnatural physical strength
Saint Frugalitas	Wealth and Prosperity	Ability to multiply, create abundance from little
Saint Honestas	Respectability and Image	Ability to shapeshift or change appearance at will
Saint Industrias	Hard Work and Grit	Inhuman endurance
Saint Pietas	Duty and Obedience	Mind control, influence over others
Saint Prudentia	Foresight and Wisdom	Predicting the future
Saint Salubritas	Wholesomeness and Cleanliness	Invisibility
Saint Severitas	Sternness and Self Control	Inducing sleep or paralysis
Saint Veritas	Justice and Truth	Discerning truth from lies

CHAPTER

1

The hangman's rope dangled against dark clouds obscuring the sky. Fate had finally come for its bitter vengeance, and for once in her life, Catriona Whitfield couldn't run.

The iron bars across her open window had done little to hold back the recent rains. Lightning from a passing thunderstorm charged the desert air, blowing in a damp smell of earth mingled with sweet sage. The stone walls around her seemed to press in tighter, sparking a fluttering panic. She couldn't breathe.

I need to get the hell out of here.

Her fingers clawed at her throat. The heavy chains secured around her wrists clanked at the movement. The damn sheriff had made sure they were good and tight—a wise choice on his part, even if the rest of him was every shade of stupid.

Her gaze darted to the wall opposite her cell. Beside her faded wanted poster, a pair of perfectly shined six-shooters hung on an iron peg. Her fingers itched for the familiar worn handles. What she would do with them if she ever got the chance to hold them again . . .

There was a long list of charges against her. The last few years with Amos and the Wolves, she'd gone along on cattle raids and coach robberies, even flirted with watchmen to distract them while the Wolves sneaked into the places they were supposedly guarding.

Maybe she did deserve to die, but certainly not like this. What kind of legacy would that leave? To hang as a petty criminal in a foreign nation? No, if she was going to die, it needed to be a statement as grand as the sins she'd committed. As grand as the destiny that had been stolen from her. Fate owed her that much, at the very least. Cat swallowed and clawed at her throat again.

A vision flashed suddenly behind her eyes, zapping into her mind like the bolt of lightning that hit outside the jailhouse last night. A harshly handsome face, angular and young, but still older than her own seventeen years. The navy-and-gold uniform of an Ordonian soldier, accompanied by the sounds of keys jangling and the iron bars of the cell door creaking open.

As soon as the image came, it was gone. Her visions of the immediate future never lasted more than a brief moment. They were a Blessing gift from the Saints, her father had always said. A gift that had always given her the warnings she needed to stay one step ahead.

It's how the revolvers hanging on the wall outside her cell had become as infamous as the hands that wielded them.

Thudding boots announced the sheriff's arrival, but she already knew he would not be alone. An Ordonian soldier would be coming with him today. She nervously fingered the end of her long braid. The faded light trickling through the storm clouds illuminated hints of red in the dark brown strands. A few heartbeats later, the sounds of jangling keys and creaking metal made her look up. Her stomach twisted into a nervous knot, but she quickly stuffed the feeling down. The face from her vision wasn't one she recognized, but that didn't mean anything.

Plenty of folks were hunting her now.

"Here she is," the sheriff said, pushing open the cell door. The old man's thick, gray mustache stood out like a bramble against the rugged landscape of his face. He tucked his thumbs into the pockets of his jeans and tilted up his chin—like a proud hunter with the season's finest catch strapped across the back of his horse.

She looked past him, searching for the smooth-cheeked face from her vision. Whoever he was, he was some kind of threat, or her gift wouldn't have flashed his face.

"Where's the young buck?" She angled her head and gave the sheriff a saccharine smile. The smile that said, *You can't break me.* It was true. You couldn't break something that wasn't whole to begin with.

More thudding boots, and the handsome face moved into the cellblock. It was too handsome, pretty almost. Boys that looked like that didn't have to work for a damn thing in their lives. His military uniform and the light hair under his hat were coated with the dust of a long journey, and his dark, greedy eyes shone like beetles scuttling under a rock. He let out a low whistle, stretching out his words. "*By the Saints.* She actually saw me coming?"

"Told you it's her. Caught her two weeks ago, trying to escape across the border," growled the sheriff. "Stay back though, she's slicker than pig snot and just about as pleasant."

The young man tipped back his hat, exposing a long pale nose. "It's hard to tell under all the grime. But she's younger than I expected."

The sheriff moved a hand to the pistol at his hip. "She's seventeen. Makes her old enough to hang, in Caseda."

"She's an Ordonian citizen. You don't have the authority to hang her here." The soldier's voice rang with subtle power, like he was used to telling others what to do.

"That why you came to fetch her? Take her back?"

"Yes," he said, removing his dusty white gloves. "I'm taking her back to Saint's Landing."

Saint's Landing? Catriona hissed like a feral cat and scrambled back against the stone wall. She hated the godforsaken port city that sat like a blemish on the otherwise unmarred face of Saelum Territory's coastline. The territory's only city, really. The wild desert of northwestern Ordonia was populated mostly by crumbling townships and rugged outposts. And, of course, the sprawling ranches of wealthy cattle barons who fancied themselves the royalty of the westlands. "You're not taking me back there!"

"This ain't up to you, sweetheart." The sheriff patted his gun again. "This man paid a pretty penny to take you off my hands and I sure as heck ain't gonna stop him."

"I'd rather hang, you filthy, greedy son of a—"

A hand whipped across her face. The sheriff chuckled. "You might wanna muzzle her too."

Cat spat blood onto the muddy floor. She lifted her dagger-filled eyes to his. If only she had her guns . . .

"My men are prepared for the transport. We'll get her on the train before sundown. We should cross into Saelum Territory by morning and reach Saint's Landing by midafternoon. I've got laudanum to sedate her if it comes to that."

"If you're not careful, that gift of hers will give you trouble, Captain Freeman." The sheriff narrowed his eyes as if he doubted the captain fully understood the situation.

But Freeman waved a dismissive hand. "My men have handled the Blessed before."

Cat snorted. He really thought he could "handle" her all the way to Saint's Landing?

An irritated muscle twitched in his too-perfect jawline.

"She ain't one of your Blessed, Captain. No Saint in their right mind would've granted any blessings to someone as soulless as this creature. Cursed by the Fallen One, more like. She killed three of my men before we were able to get her in chains."

A shadow seemed to flicker in Freeman's gaze. "How *was* she finally captured?" Though he didn't say it, Cat could tell it chafed his pride. It had taken the authorities of a foreign nation to finally subdue her, when Ordonia had been hunting her for years. *Good.* She liked watching his pride squirm. But Cat knew the truth. It wasn't the prowess of the Casedian authorities that had led to her capture—it had been her own bleeding heart.

The sheriff shifted his shoulders. "There was a family sneaking across the border, couple o' young kids in the group. She was hiding with them in the wagon."

Captain Freeman narrowed his eyes. "I seriously doubt it was as simple as that."

The sheriff hooked his thumbs into his belt, puffing out his chest.

"People don't cross our border without paying the tax. The family couldn't pay, so we followed standard protocol and apprehended them. Somethin' must have triggered her crazy bloodlust, though, 'cause she burst out of the wagon and started shooting every deputy in sight. Foolish choice, considering she was outnumbered. Took quite a few of us, but we got her down eventually."

Cat ground her teeth. Of course he'd leave out the details that made him look bad. That the deputies at the border were trying to charge the family above and beyond the set crossing tax. That they took an innocent father into custody when he questioned them, beating him in front of his wife and young children. She hadn't needed a vision to tell her what would happen after a Casedian deputy put a pistol to the father's head. Her own guns had been out before the trigger was pulled. She wouldn't let those children lose their father. It was the last thing a kind, young family like that deserved—a brokenness that never really heals.

The night before, they had taken her in, given her shelter and food from their own stores. The children had run around the campfire, giggling with a joy that had been stolen from her so many years ago. They embodied what a family was supposed to be. And then to watch them ripped apart . . . maybe the sheriff was right. Maybe she was crazy.

Crazy sick of watching those with power abuse it and take from those without.

"They got in my way." Cat flipped her hair out of her eyes and smiled as big and wide as a sliver of the moon.

But Captain Freeman ignored her. Irritation flared hot inside her chest. She'd just have to push him further to find that seething temper she sensed beneath his cool facade. For all his pomp and swagger, something dark and dangerous festered in his soul. She couldn't explain how, but she could sense it. Light from the single gas lamp reflected off his polished gold buttons as he turned to the cell door. He whistled, and two more men clad in navy uniforms came to join him.

Only two. How interesting.

She lifted her chained wrists and pouted. "You gotta unlock me, unless you plan on taking this wall back to Saint's Landing too." She rattled the chains for emphasis.

The sheriff's frown deepened, but he stepped forward. "Your men ready?"

Cat eyed the keys jangling in his hand with the same kind of lust miners got in their eyes at the news of an aurium discovery.

Freeman settled a hand on his holster, his jaw still tense. "Ready."

Cat held her breath as the rusted key slipped into the lock that secured her chain to the stone wall. She held still, perfectly still.

The flash behind her eyes flickered with the image of where the sheriff would move next. Metal links clinked against each other, and the heaviness pulling her arms down was gone. Though the cuffs were still around her wrists, the chain was loose. It wasn't freedom, but it was close enough.

Just as her vision had predicted, the sheriff took his offensive stance exactly where she knew he would . . .

Faster than the strike of a rattlesnake, Cat jerked the chain down and out of the sheriff's grasp. Another jerk. The end of the chain snapped into her open hand.

She threw it over his head and tightened it around his neck. Her arms and back ached from the bruises he'd given her. The old man fell to his knees, fingers fumbling over his neck. *Brutal bastard.* Let him be the one to look up at her for a change.

"The Fallen One awaits you in hell," she purred in his ear.

A vision warned her of the gunshot before it happened. She saw one of Freeman's men about to squeeze the trigger, the barrel of the pistol flaring with golden sparks.

So they were using aurium bullets? They'd cursed the metal in some way that would stop her?

Cat wrenched the sheriff in front of her to take the bullet, and the pistol fired. Voices shouted in a frenzy as the soldiers scrambled to get a handle on a situation that was quickly dissolving into chaos.

Just how Cat liked it. Chaos was a familiar friend.

The sheriff's body went rigid against her, his muscles tensed tight. A stain of red mingled with gold blossomed across his chest like the spring roses Mama had grown back in Saint's Landing. The bullet would disintegrate the moment its magic was spent, but the damage to his body was already done. And judging by his body's response, it must have been cursed with the tainted power of Saint Severitas to paralyze him. An effective trick to make sure your quarry did not escape. Even if the bullet had just grazed her, she would have been rendered incapacitated.

Aurium looked like gold, but it was infinitely more precious. If you were willing to sell your soul and offer prayers to the Fallen Saint, you could release its corrupted magic—a depraved way for common men to tap into the power of the Saints. It seemed fitting that Captain Freeman didn't mind using it. But she wasn't going to give him the chance to use that depravity on her.

The sheriff's unseeing eyes were wide open, a golden sheen shimmering within their glassy depths. She snatched the keys out of his open hand. The shackles around her wrists thudded to the floor.

Freedom. Glorious freedom.

Mud and the Saints knew what else crusted her trousers and shirt after weeks in this cell. They were stiff and hard to move. Another flash of a vision. A bullet coming right for her head. She ducked, and the bullet bit into the jailhouse wall. Webs of shimmering gold arced out from the impact point, the magic wasted on stone.

"No point having aurium bullets if you can't hit me, Captain." With enormous effort, Cat shoved the sheriff's lifeless body into Freeman's knees, knocking him to the ground. Another bullet whizzed past her head. Adrenaline thundered through her veins.

Cat sprang for the open cell door.

"Stop her!" Captain Freeman yelled from somewhere on the floor. "Don't let her get—"

But it was too late. Her fingers closed around the worn, familiar handles of the six-shooters hanging on the outside wall. A rush of gratitude almost brought tears to her eyes.

She turned, raising her hands and fixing both barrels on Captain Freeman. She flashed him her most wicked smile. "Shouldn't have let the Cat out, Captain." Her thumb clicked back the hammers. "Send my regards to hell." And then she pulled the triggers.

Click. Click.

The barrels were empty. Cat swore violently. The damned sheriff must have emptied them and left them hanging where she could see them just to taunt her.

Captain Freeman's face split into a grin as wicked as her own.

Desperate rage burned through her chest. This arrogant soldier wasn't taking her back. She'd rather die than face Saint's Landing again. Even the mention of the name had loosened the carefully crafted locks she kept on her memories. They bled into her consciousness like the visions of her Blessing gift—not of the future, but of a past tainted with shame and blood.

The light fading from her father's eyes. Her mother's screams. Her father's ring, buried in the desert along with every dream she'd ever had for her future. Her family shattered like a porcelain vase dropped on tile. Knowing it was entirely her fault.

She'd never go back. *Never.*

Cat's muscles tensed to spring. If she couldn't shoot the eyes out of the captain's head, she would scratch them out instead.

A sickening crack sounded through her skull. Light flashed behind her eyes. But this time it was not a vision from her Blessing gift. It was the barrel of a gun smashing into the back of her head.

And all went dark.

CHAPTER

2

"Governor Pickett is *dead*?"

Adrian Caldwell read the headline again. The governor had been in excellent health at the last gathering. And barely fifty years of age. He and Adrian had laughed and discussed the horse trade not even a week ago. All the women had danced, twirling their lace-embroidered dresses like blooming flowers beneath the stars, the men astride their horses looking on. Music swelled through the night amid the savory scents of smoked meats, roasted corn, and freshly baked biscuits. The governor had danced with those same ladies, jovial and full of life. And now the man's ashes were one with the wind.

Saints.

He dropped the paper back onto his father's desk. The office of Baron William Caldwell was as elegant as the man himself, carefully manicured from the gold-embroidered trim of his coat to the highly polished black boots. The wood-paneled walls shone with the reflection of the gas lamps, while the deep-red velvet curtains framed the light from the tall arched windows.

"What happened to him?" Adrian asked.

"It's not important. I have another matter I need you to attend to." Mr. Caldwell shoved a piece of parchment toward his son. Prices scrawled across its surface told Adrian it was some kind of purchase receipt.

Adrian didn't touch it. He frowned. "Not important? Father, the barons are the ones who will recommend a new governor—"

His father slammed a fist on his desk. The thick black mustache above his lip quivered. Adrian immediately fell silent. He knew better than to test his father's temper.

"Let the *real* men worry about politics. I need you to go down to Saint's Landing and ensure that our shipment of cattle from the capital arrives safely."

Adrian stiffened his spine. "Yes, Father."

"Good. If you can manage to get all ten of the beasts here without losing a single one to thieves or stupidity, then maybe we can discuss you sitting in on one of my meetings with the other barons."

Adrian winced at the harshness in his father's tone, but then he clenched his teeth. How his father did not yet see him as a man at *nineteen* . . . But if he was going to be Baron Caldwell someday, he'd just need to prove himself even more than he already had. As impossible a task as that seemed to be with his father—

He took the receipt in his gloved hand and bowed his head. "I won't let you down."

His father barely grunted a response.

Adrian's stomach clenched, waiting for his father to look at him. He cleared his throat. "I'll see you in a few days, Father."

Another grunt.

The older man's gaze remained firmly planted on the other documents spread across his desk. Maps and business contracts, purchase receipts and several wanted posters for well-known outlaws. His father's handwriting was scrawled across one of the posters in thick, dark strokes, as though his hand had channeled an inner tension through the pen and onto the paper. Before Adrian could read the words, his father tucked the poster away. Of all the worries plaguing his father's mind, Adrian appeared to be at the bottom of the list.

Adrian tightened his fist, the parchment crunching in his hand, and strode from the room with what little pride he had left.

+ · · · · ◉ · · · · +

The heels of his boots tapped against the polished tile floors of their ranch estate. Roses and bougainvillea climbed the trellises and stone arches lining the expansive hallway, throwing a scent of flowers and late spring into the courtyard. Somewhere out of sight, a fountain splashed joyfully in the dry heat. It seemed inappropriate in light of the governor's death and the chaos sure to ensue from the vacancy in power. His father seriously misjudged Adrian's ability to understand the intricate political workings of the cattle barons. The emperor of Ordonia had his favorite territories, and he did not care about Saelum Territory beyond what taxes the barons paid him and the beef luxuries they exported. He would want to make his new appointment as quickly as possible before escaping back to the glories of the capital, agreeing with whoever the barons chose as governor to escape that much faster.

Adrian turned to the older servant waiting for him. "Saddle my horse, please, Joseph. And I'll need to take at least two of the ranch hands with me."

The servant bowed his head. "Yes, Mr. Caldwell."

"Thank you, Joseph."

Adrian headed toward his rooms. He'd need to change into his riding clothes. Maybe once he distracted himself with his task, he could shake the sickened feeling in his stomach. He'd show his father what he was really capable of. What kind of *man* he could be.

As he passed a small table covered in fine white lace and topped with a glass vase filled with Ordonian roses, he stopped. The lace at the bottom corner fluttered ever so slightly.

Adrian narrowed his eyes, his intuition flickering.

"Oh, Mr. Caldwell! Thank goodness!" An older woman, as round as a fresh orange and dressed in a simple brown novice dress, appeared out of nowhere and threw herself at him. She pulled at his coat, tears pooling in the corners of her eyes.

"I can't find Miss Edith! I turned my back for a moment and the child was just *gone*."

Exasperation mingled with amusement made him grin despite himself. Adrian gently pushed her off and steadied her. "I'm sorry, I don't think we've met."

The words came out in a rush, heavy with a southeastern accent. "I'm so sorry, Mr. Caldwell. My name is Marta. Your father hired me yesterday to take care of your little sister. I am supposed to—"

Adrian hushed the frantic woman before she dissolved into hysterics. So his father had tried to hire *another* governess for Edith without telling the poor woman about some of Edith's . . . tendencies.

"You have not lost her, Marta. I assure you she's fine. Edith is—uh—" How could he explain? "She is probably hiding somewhere in the house."

The woman's eyes went as wide as porcelain dishes. "Hiding? Why? How will I ever find her in an estate this size?"

Adrian's eye caught the flutter of the lace table cover again. He sighed, long and heavy. *That child.* Edith had been wild before their mother's death, but now . . .

"Why don't you try the library? It's one of her favorite places. I can go check her rooms."

"Thank you, Mr. Caldwell. I had no idea that taking care of a little girl would be so . . . exhausting."

The woman rushed away toward the library, her hands flapping wildly in the air. Adrian, however, turned to the table with his hands on his hips.

"You had the poor woman in tears, Edith. Are you trying to scare *all* of them off?"

The lace twitched.

"Father will not be happy if another one quits."

Silence.

Adrian chewed the inside of his cheek. Another tactic then.

"Fine. I was going to ask what kind of sweets my dear sister wanted me to bring her back from Saint's Landing, but I guess if I can't find her to ask . . ."

A little groan sounded from beneath the roses.

Aha. He was getting closer. "I heard they have chocolate sweetened with oranges. I will have to eat it all by myself, I suppose."

The table cover finally shifted, and a skinny little girl of nine toppled out from beneath it.

Edith straightened and smoothed out the folds of her blue cotton dress. Matching periwinkle bows tipped the ends of her twin dark braids, giving her a look of childlike innocence that Adrian knew better than to trust. His sister was about as innocent as the coyotes roaming the brush in the hills behind Caldwell Ranch.

She tilted her little nose into the air. "You wouldn't dare eat all the chocolate without me."

He cut her a look. "You expect me to share chocolate with you after you scare away another governess?"

Edith crossed her arms. "She hasn't quit *yet.*"

Adrian stifled a laugh. "I bet you two bites of chocolate she's gone before I get back."

"I'm not making that bet. We both know you'll win," she sniffed.

"You know, you could try *not* scaring her away."

Edith grimaced. "She's just like all the others. Everything she wants me to learn is boring, and I don't think she knows how to smile."

Adrian let out a laugh. "I'm heading into town. Don't you want to say goodbye before I leave?"

Her haughty expression crumpled, betraying the smallest quiver of her lip. She hesitated for a moment before throwing herself at him and wrapping her thin arms around his waist. "I hate when you leave. Promise me you'll come back."

Adrian embraced her, resting a hand against her soft hair. "Of course I will. Who would find you if I didn't?"

She squeezed him harder. He patted her head and stepped back.

"I need to go. Head into the library and let poor Marta know where you are, please?"

A dimple formed in her cheek, and Edith scurried off down the hall . . . in the exact *opposite* direction of the library.

Adrian sighed. At least someone in this family didn't care what their father thought.

3

The floor beneath Cat rattled and swayed. Her head ached something awful, and a strange tang coated her tongue. If the motion didn't stop, she'd lose her stomach. Not that there was anything in it to lose. Her head gave a particularly nasty throb, and her fingers dug into the soft fibers of . . . carpet?

Cat groaned and rolled onto her back. Above her, a small golden chandelier jangled in time with the motion of the train. A painted green ceiling matched the rich carpet beneath her. She pushed herself up onto her elbows, a familiar heaviness on her arms. She looked down.

Iron cuffs encircled her wrists once more, attached to a metal pole that ran along the polished wooden wall of the train car.

Damn it.

She growled, shaking the chain.

"Oh good, you're awake." Captain Freeman sat facing her in a plush pink armchair. His wide-brimmed hat hung off the armrest, exposing the sandy hair he kept meticulously trimmed. He casually flipped the page of the newspaper he was reading, his tone bored and detached. "I was beginning to worry that I'd have to settle for the 'dead' reward."

"I thought you *paid* money to get me."

He snorted. "Petty coppers compared to what I'll get for bringing you in alive. Besides, my patron has a particular interest in Black Cat Whitfield, the cat that runs with wolves."

Her heart skipped a beat. But she shouldn't make assumptions. A lot of people were hunting her. His patron could be anyone. She let out a heavy breath. "I don't run with the Wolves anymore." Her chest ached with the piercing truth of those words.

"Obviously." He chuckled and flipped another page. The headline splashed across the paper read, GOVERNOR PICKETT OF SAELUM TERRITORY FOUND DEAD. EMPEROR LAWRENCE TO APPOINT SUCCESSOR. "Did they kick you out of their little ragtag gang? Couldn't run with the big dogs anymore?"

"That, or maybe some of the dogs were as scared of a little cat as you are."

Captain Freeman lowered his paper and exchanged looks with the three other men in the room. Amusement pulled at the corners of his thin mouth. "I am not afraid of you in the slightest. All it takes is a little aurium and your kind are easily subdued, no matter what gift the Saints have Blessed you with. You are only as talented as you are because of what was *given* to you, by whatever Saint was foolish enough to give it."

Cat turned up her nose. "The Blessed are chosen to do the will of the Saints. Those who choose to use magic from a cursed metal are following the will of the Fallen One."

Freeman ignored her reference to the sheriff's death. "So you think you are *chosen*? For what, exactly? Robbing the wealthy landowners of Saelum? Stealing from the hardworking hands of the barons and baronesses?"

Cat snorted. "The barons pride themselves on what gets done by those working *under* them. I wasn't doing anything except stealing from those who stole in the first place."

That muscle in his jaw twitched again. "Perhaps I should get a muzzle like the sheriff suggested."

"The sheriff tried to muzzle me, and look how well that turned out for him." Cat cocked her head to the side.

Captain Freeman did not even rise from his seat. He snapped his fingers, and Cat had a vision of the punch to her gut coming only a second before it knocked the wind from her lungs. There was no way to avoid it, trapped like a chained animal as she was. Another blow and she found herself flat on the floor gasping for breath. Captain Freeman's crony went back to his post behind her. The other two guards sneered.

Cat coughed and pushed herself onto her knees. The iron chain clanked against the metal pole set into the wall. "Why don't you just kill me now and be done with it?"

He picked his paper back up. "My patron prefers you alive. The reward is bigger for me if you are. And despite how filthy and disgusting you look right now, you'll shine up pretty enough for what he wants you for."

A thrill of terror shot down her spine. She should ask who this patron was . . . but she was too afraid to hear the answer. Cat sat back against the wall, brushing her dark auburn braid over her shoulder. The muscles of her stomach screamed at the movement. Her voice came out breathless. "What's the point of that? They'll hang me in Saint's Landing the moment we get off the train anyway."

"No, they won't. You'd sit in prison for a long time before a trial. Every criminal, no matter how foul, receives the same due process. Even in the wasteland that is Saelum Territory, we are expected to follow the same laws as the rest of Ordonia."

Cat rolled her eyes. "Lucky me."

Captain Freeman smirked. "Not lucky. I'd say *blessed*."

She caught the eye of the guard hovering over her and bit back her retort. She didn't need a vision to tell her what would happen if she let another smart comment slip past her lips. So instead, she settled for watching the expanse of gathering thunderheads through the window. Maybe one of the last times she'd ever get to see a spring storm roll in across the desert.

Sometimes she wondered if she really had been Blessed. Either the Saints loved her or hated her, but she couldn't decide which. Maybe they couldn't decide either. Or maybe they just wanted to punish her for her sins.

The Saints—human once but lifted to godlike status by the Creator Mother because of their great deeds while alive—supposedly handpicked certain individuals for specific divine purposes. In order to help their chosen complete their missions, the Saints Blessed them with divine gift-ings. Gifts such as immunity to poisons, given by Saint Dignitas, patron saint of nobility and self-awareness. Or inhuman endurance, gifted by Saint Industrias, patron saint of hard work and grit, or the ability to heal sickness given by Saint Clementia, patron of mercy and gentleness.

The priests and priestesses of the Saints were trained to recognize the Blessed and help them realize their divine missions. Cat, like other rare members of the Blessed, had been singled out at her baptism as an infant, Blessed by Saint Prudentia, patron of wisdom and forethought, with the gift of visions of the immediate future. Whatever her divine mission or purpose was . . . obviously it had been some kind of mistake. Sometimes she felt cursed instead.

She pulled up her knees to soothe the ache she felt in her chest. Even though every once in a while she'd used her gift to help others, she'd made mistake after mistake. Her most recent one had been leaving Amos and the safety of the Wolves. But what choice did she have? Ricky, the smug little rat, had challenged Amos's leadership from the day he'd joined the gang. If she hadn't left when she did, Ricky would have led a revolt within their ranks. He didn't think the favoritism Amos showed her was fair. But Cat had been like a daughter to the leader of the Wolves for years, and he'd stepped in for the father she'd lost. Amos showed her everything she knew, honing her natural skills in horsemanship, teaching her to use her gift to her advantage both on a horse and with a gun in her hand.

He was a leader she had been honored to follow.

But she'd heard the whispers among the men after the last horse raid. Rumors that she was getting more of their earnings than the rest of them. Their portions had seemed small, yes, but it wasn't because anything extra was going to her. Or even Amos. She had no idea what he was doing with the money. It wasn't her business. But she wasn't going to risk Amos's position as gang leader just because of their bond. He'd given her a family again, and the best way to repay him was to protect him.

It was just a fact. People that got too close to her ended up hurt one way or another.

So she'd left a hastily scrawled note and headed into the night with a small bag of supplies. There hadn't been a plan beyond *run*. Getting captured at the border of the neighboring nation of Caseda had slowed her down. Then the weeks in that cell had almost broken her, like a cruelly trained mustang. The thought of another prison stay tightened her throat.

But who was paying the captain to hunt her down? If it was who she feared, she'd be facing a prison of an entirely different kind. Thoughts buzzed around her head like fat flies in the blistering heat of summer. She tried to swat them away, but eventually, she couldn't stand it anymore. She had to know. "So who's your patron?"

Captain Freeman ignored her. Her temper flared. Fine. She'd *make* him pay attention to her. She had to know the answer or it would drive her mad.

"I know the barons sometimes bribe the emperor's soldiers to do their underhanded bidding. So which one is paying you off?"

Captain Freeman still pretended as though she hadn't spoken. He checked a golden watch from his pocket and then snapped it shut. "We're about thirty minutes outside of Saint's Landing. Once we arrive, we'll . . ."

But this time, Cat stopped listening. Her vision flashed with an image she didn't understand. In her mind's eye, the train car appeared to topple sideways, its contents and passengers thrown about as if caught in a twister. She wrapped her hands around the metal bar that ran the length of the train car. The coolness of the metal seeped into her palms, and she squeezed it tight. She only had moments to secure herself before—

There was a rumbling crash somewhere ahead of them. The train car shuddered. A sound of screeching metal rang through her ears. Sure enough, the world around them tipped sideways. The pale dirt of the desert gobbled up the windows as the train car was thrown off the tracks.

Captain Freeman and his guard flew to the opposite wall, their bodies smashing into the glass windows. Captain Freeman's face, contorted with rage, disappeared behind his pink armchair. There were screams and shouts as men were buried beneath toppled furniture. Cat, however, hung on tight to the metal bar that was now part of the ceiling, her bare feet dangling into the open air and her pulse thrashing behind her eardrums. Every nerve in her body thrummed with adrenaline. After several more tense seconds, the vibrating beneath her fingers stopped. The train car must have skidded to a halt.

There were groans from the wreckage beneath her. She choked on the thick cloud of dust pouring in from the broken windows. Her hands slipped slightly. She squeezed the bar to keep from losing her grip. The windows were shattered into jagged points, but maybe she could somehow swing herself up? Her aching arms told her it was unlikely. She'd gone so long with so little food—her strength was gone.

A shadowy figure materialized through the dust above her. A dark, wide-brimmed hat and matching vest. A tanned, leathery face beneath a scrubby black goatee streaked with silver. An overwhelming emotion thickened her throat. Tears burned behind her eyes.

It was the Wolf of the West himself.

Amos Whitfield had come for her.

CHAPTER

4

"This can't be right." Adrian counted the silver coins again, but it just didn't make sense. His father hadn't given him nearly enough money to pay for all ten cows. He counted them a fourth time.

"There a problem?" The rough-faced trader gestured with an outstretched hand.

"Excuse me for just a minute." Adrian gave him a weak smile and motioned to the oldest ranch hand to follow—the same one who had been on dozens of trips like this with his father. They retreated a short distance so the trader couldn't hear their discussion over the bustle of activity around them. The docks of Saint's Landing were busy this time of year. Ships crowded the small harbor, their sails billowing as seagulls swooped between them. Palm trees danced against the darkening sky. The persistent winds hinted that a storm lurked just offshore.

"This can't be all the coins," he whispered frantically. "Do you think any of your men might have . . . ?"

"No, sir. Mr. Caldwell never gives us enough money for the trade. We're supposed to make up some kind of 'scuse as to why we don't have it all. Robbed, lost, gave it to some poor peasant to feed her starving child. Don't matter what you say, just get the trader to believe it. They'll usually take less if they think they'll lose the whole trade."

Adrian pursed his lips. His father *never* paid the agreed-upon price? That was . . . that was . . . He blew out a heavy breath through his nose. He stomped back to the trader.

"How many cows can we get for this much?" He held out his hand with the coins.

The trader took far too long to count them than he should have. "I dunno, I can give you . . . maybe seven beasts for that?"

"Sir." The ranch hand tapped him on the shoulder and leaned close to his ear. "We have to get all ten."

His father's words floated back to him.

"If you can manage to get all ten of the beasts here without losing a single one to thieves or stupidity . . ."

Stupidity. Saints Almighty. This was a test. A bloody test, to see if Adrian had what it took to follow his father's instructions. If he had what it took to get what he needed, no matter the cost. Was that what his father thought was required to become baron of Caldwell Ranch? Cheating and dishonesty?

Adrian may have been many things, but dishonest was not one of them. His integrity was the only thing that set him apart from his father. He wasn't about to sacrifice that now, no matter how weak his father thought his "ideals" made him. Fine—if this was a test to show what kind of *man* Adrian was, then he'd show his father exactly the kind he was.

"We'll take the seven cows then."

Behind him, the ranch hands sucked in a collective breath. "Sir, you can't . . ." said a voice behind him.

"My father signed the contract for that price, and I'm not going back on our word. We'll take the seven," Adrian repeated, his voice stronger. He was so sick of people assuming he was as immoral as his father.

The trader shrugged and threw the coins into a pouch secured around his waist. His bloodshot eyes moved to Adrian's neck, a flare of hunger flashing within them. "That an aurium chain, boy?"

Adrian blinked, confused. "Excuse me?"

"'Round your neck. The necklace. That plain gold or aurium?"

Adrian fingered the fine gold chain that had once belonged to his mother. One of the few things of hers he had left. "No, it's just plain gold."

The greed in the trader's eyes dimmed in disappointment. "Not as valuable, but I'll throw in the other three for—"

"No."

The trader tipped back his hat. "You sure?"

Irritation flared hot in his chest. Did his word mean nothing? "Yes, I'm sure."

He didn't like that this trader was willing to trade for aurium either. What did that say about the man's morals? The metal was valuable, yes, but it was cursed for a reason. And forbidden to use, if you followed the way of the Saints. If you sold your soul and offered specific prayers to the Fallen Saint, you could corrupt the aurium by imbuing it with the power to poison instead of protect from poisons, paralyze instead of ease sleep, control the emotions of others, even sicken instead of heal. Once it was cursed, all someone had to do was touch it and the magic was released. The magic would fade, but so would the aurium, crumbling to dust as the magic was spent. The more aurium, the more magic . . . and the more depraved your soul.

Another frantic whisper behind him: "Sir, *please*. If your father . . ."

Adrian was done with this whole ordeal. Done with everyone questioning every decision he tried to make. "Bring the seven cows around. We are heading back to Caldwell Ranch tonight."

"Wouldn't recommend that," the trader said, glancing at the purple clouds churning overhead. "Storms this time o' year can get pretty nasty. Might end up with no cattle if you get stuck in a flood out in the desert."

Adrian didn't know why he was feeling so stubborn. He clenched his fists, heat rising up the sides of his face. "We'll be fine."

Calm down. It's not this trader's fault your father is an ass.

"Suit yourself, kid."

Kid? The heat in his face spread down his neck. He turned his attention to the older ranch hand, who was wringing his hands in front of his chest. "Get the cows and meet me at the stables."

The ranch hand nodded, but his mouth opened and closed with words he was obviously itching to say. Adrian noticed the fear in the man's eyes. Shame burned a hole in the pit of his belly. What was wrong with him?

Adrian softened his tone. "I promise I will deal with my father. You won't be held responsible. I'm going to stop by the mercantile and then I'll meet you at the stables."

The man's hands continued to wring, his eyes darting back and forth. But all Adrian could think about was how badly he needed to take a walk.

A walk to contemplate exactly what kind of man *he* wanted to be.

✦ · · · · ◉ · · · · ✦

"Ah, the orange chocolate, an excellent choice." The mercantile owner lifted the lid of a glass jar and withdrew a slab of chocolate the size of his hand. Edith would be delighted.

"That will be two silvers."

Damn. He'd given all the money to the trader for the cattle.

"Can you take credit for Caldwell Ranch?"

The shop owner gave him a flat look. "From Baron Caldwell? I'd never see my money again."

As always, his father's reputation was far reaching. But the shop-keeper must have read the disappointment on Adrian's face because his own suddenly softened.

"Is the chocolate for yourself, or for a lovely lady perhaps?" The man arched a silvered eyebrow.

"A lovely little sister who will be heartbroken if her brother does not bring her back any chocolate."

The mercantile owner nodded sagely. "I see." Then he smiled, flashing a golden tooth. "Tell me, Mr. Caldwell, does your sister look much like your mother?"

Adrian met the man's eyes, his curiosity piqued. "From what I remember of her, Edith is exactly the same."

The owner's smile widened. "I have many fond memories of Ada. She grew up here in town, you know. Prettiest thing to ever step foot in Saelum. Kindest too. It's no wonder your father snatched her up."

The way the man spoke made it sound as though his father had stolen her. He didn't like hearing his mother talked about as if she were a commodity. But then again, judging by the subtle gray flecking the mercantile owner's hair, he was the right age that perhaps he could have courted Ada himself. Maybe it was not his mother that had been snatched away, but the man's heart.

Adrian handed the chocolate back. "Maybe next time."

He turned and opened the door, the little bell ringing above his head. "Wait."

Adrian turned back, hope bubbling up like a spring inside his chest.

The owner paused for a moment, seeming to wage a war within himself. Finally, he sighed and opened the jar again. He wrapped a piece of chocolate in brown paper and held it out to Adrian. "For the daughter of Ada Caldwell. May she rest with the Saints."

Adrian took the small package, his throat tight. Maybe not everyone else in this world was a liar or a cheat.

"Thank you, sir. It will mean the world to her."

A gleam shone within the owner's eyes. "You have more of your mother in you than you do your father. Caldwell Ranch will be blessed someday when you are the new baron."

Something squirmed inside his stomach, and all Adrian could mutter was a quick thank-you before he ducked out the door.

CHAPTER

5

"*Saints above*, Cat. If you're going to run away, don't get caught at the border." Amos reached down and wrapped a calloused hand around her wrist. He hauled her up through the broken window, the chain rattling after her.

"Let's take care of that." Amos drew his infamous black revolver and took aim. With a crack, the chain snapped in two. "We'll have Pedro pick the lock on the cuffs when we get to the canyon. The rest of them are waiting for us there."

Cat noticed the stiff set of his jaw. She looked around, expecting to see the overwhelming numbers of the Wolves, but her gut sank.

There were only five other riders.

She'd bet her newfound freedom she knew exactly who disapproved of this plan to rescue her. *Little bastard*. "How in hell did you derail a train with only five men?"

Amos shrugged. "Lifted the tracks. Ain't that hard to do. Train derails itself after that."

Now that her head had stopped spinning, she could see there was only an engine and one other car in addition to hers. Dazed guards were beginning to stumble from the wreckage.

They climbed down the side of the overturned train car. A groan sounded from somewhere inside. Cat moved a little faster. "You could have killed me too, you know."

He waved a dismissive hand. "Nah. I knew you'd see what was comin' and protect yourself."

"You have far more faith in my Blessing gift than you should."

"You've got at least six of those nine lives left. I figured you'd rather not live all of them locked in a cage."

Cat let out a breath. "You figured right."

He gave her a smile as crooked as his teeth and offered a hand to help her down the last jump.

Her bare feet hit the scorching ground, and she yelped. The sand was as hot as the end of a branding iron. Amos headed to his horse and rifled through one of his saddlebags. He threw a pair of worn leather boots in her direction. "Got myself a new pair, so I figure you can have those. Gonna be too big, but better than blisterin' your feet out here."

Her throat tightened again as she slipped her feet into the soft, worn leather. She nodded her thanks but didn't trust herself to speak.

Her palomino mare, Almond, waited beside Amos. He hadn't sold her or given her to another rider. Cat swallowed hard and hoisted herself up. After weeks in that Casedian jailhouse, she almost cried, *almost*, at the comfort afforded by the familiar saddle. At the feel of the powerful beast beneath her. She leaned forward and rubbed the horse's neck, nuzzling into her mane to savor the familiar smell of horse she'd known all her life. Almond flared her nostrils and turned her ears forward. Cat smiled. "Good to see you too, girl."

"Where'd you disappear to, anyway?" asked a cool young man with a mop of dark hair hanging into his eyes.

Cat didn't know how to answer.

The corners of his mouth twitched, but Pedro Morales rarely showed any sign of emotion. He could rob a bank and act like it was the most boring thing he'd ever done in his life.

"Don't matter. She's back now. End of discussion." Amos settled himself onto his black horse, Tenebris, and clicked his tongue to get moving. Thunder rumbled somewhere in the distance. "Let's get movin' before another storm rolls in."

Pedro shrugged and turned his horse to follow. Cat mimicked them and nudged Almond into a gallop. The dry, charged wind whipped her hair back from her face. A familiar exhilarating energy rushed through her veins. She was tempted to throw her arms out to the sides and embrace the endless expanse of purpled sky above her. She was running again. She was *free*.

Soon the wreckage of the train disappeared against the hazy horizon. A distant set of hills grew larger the longer they rode. After several hours, the cut canyon of a small river valley finally came into view. A thin wisp of smoke curled into the air from the camp where the rest of the gang waited for them. The riders slowed their mounts. Another horse drew up beside her, the rider's skin as pale as the hair coating his head and face. A gleam of humor shone within his bright blue eyes.

"You look like you could use some meat on your bones. The food in that Casedian jail not as fine as the scraps they serve here in Saelum?"

"Leave her alone, Soap." Amos's voice floated back from the front.

"She knows I love her." Soap gave her a sappy smile.

Cat snapped her rope at the back of Soap's painted horse. It jumped and nickered in irritation.

"Saints, Cat. Retract the claws. I'm only teasing." Soap winked and Cat hissed at him for emphasis. But then she flashed him a grin to let him know he wasn't in *too* much trouble.

Johnny "Soap" Smith was as slippery as they came, especially in a pinch, but he was still like a brother to Cat. They always teased each other something awful.

"Seriously though," he said, his voice tightening. "Where'd you go? Nearly broke the old man's heart when you took off like that."

Soap must have missed her more than he was letting on. Cat rubbed at her temple with a free hand. "You know why I left."

"'Cause of Ricky? You can't take him serious, Cat. You know the rest of the Wolves would never follow a sniveling little coward like that. His personality is just big 'cause the rest of him is so small. He's gotta make up for it."

"Maybe." But she'd seen the jealousy lacing Ricky's eyes, like poison slipped into a whiskey. He seemed innocent enough—until you dropped dead with no warning.

Soap tossed her a canteen sloshing with water. "Well, you're home now. You know this is where you belong."

Cat didn't answer. She lifted the canteen to her lips. The cool water was soothing as salve on the parched dryness of her throat. The bitter taste of the laudanum still coated her tongue. This was *not* her real home, but it was as good a home as any. She would never set foot in Saint's Landing again. As it was, being half an hour by train outside of the town was as close as she'd come to it in almost ten years. It was still too close.

The camp materialized out of the shadows between the canyon walls. Three dozen horses were tied to the trees beside the river, picking at weeds and finding respite in the shallows of the slow-rushing water. The rest of the Wolves lounged around a small fire. They were a rowdy bunch of misfits and outlaws, united by Amos after the missions were shuttered, but Cat still felt a rush of affection for them. Well, *most* of them anyway.

Amos had been an Ordonian soldier stationed at a mission just outside Saint's Landing to protect the priests and lands owned by the clergy. Originally, Saelum had been a wild frontier of former criminals and poor migrants—all seeking somewhere to own land outside of the long-established circles of Ordonia. But slowly the land fell under the control of the cattle barons, growing wealthier and wealthier from the beef trade. What land hadn't been claimed by the barons had been taken by the missions for their holy work. They ministered to the local populations, seeking out the Blessed and working to help them realize their Saints-given purpose.

But ultimately, many of the barons grew restless, wanting to use the cursed magic of aurium without feeling shamed or condemned by the priests. Power struggles broke out between the priesthood and the landowners, and the Ordonian Emperor, fearing revolts from the loyal tax-paying barons, finally ordered the missions to keep to their churches. The cattle barons, just as wealthy as their gentrified superiors in the capital, pulled their connections with the governor and made a move on the mission lands. Of course, no one had the money to outbid them, so the peasants became workers, suffering under the will of the barons. All the soldiers that had been stationed to manage the missions were discharged, most with nowhere to go.

That had been thirty years ago.

Much to the chagrin of the barons, Amos had found a different use for his skills and training as a soldier. The Wolves spent most of their time stealing horses, cattle, and mercantile goods from the barons, selling them to rogue traders or across the border in Caseda, and making a healthy profit.

"So the cat came back to run with the Wolves after all." Ricky's tone danced with a mirth that didn't reach his watery eyes. He was shorter than all the men around him by a head, but they all angled themselves toward him anyway.

Amos ignored him. "Start packin' up, boys. I don't fancy stayin' the night this close to the city. We head north in an hour."

There was a general rumble of discontent. Ricky didn't move. Neither did the group of ten or so men sitting around by the fire. "Actually, *boss*, we was hoping to camp here by the river tonight if that's alright with you. There's a small town just west of here that—"

"It have a bank?" Amos cut in.

Ricky paused, a shadow crossing his pinched face. "A bank? No, but—"

"We been over this, Ricky. We don't rob the townsfolk. I'm fine hitting the banks that hold the barons' money, but we leave the peasants alone. They suffer enough as it is."

Resentment simmered in Ricky's dark eyes. He opened his mouth to argue, but Cat got there first. She fixed him with all the rage she'd built up since she was arrested.

"You heard the Wolf. We move north in an hour. Get your ass up and move, you little cockroach. *Now.*"

A hush swept through the camp. Ricky slowly got to his feet and stepped toward her.

"You wanna say that again, kitty Cat?" His voice was as quiet and deadly as a rattler about to strike.

Cat's hand twitched toward her belt before she realized she didn't *have* a belt, much less her guns. They were likely lost somewhere in the wreckage of the train car—if they hadn't been left back in Caseda entirely.

Soap jumped between them. "She's been through a lot, Ricky, give her a break. She just survived weeks in jail and a bloody train crash."

Ricky's lip curled.

Amos stepped in and threw a pile of clean clothes at her feet. "Have Pedro pick the locks on those irons and go wash up. You need to cool down."

"You're just gonna let her—" Ricky started.

"I don't let Cat do nothing. She does whatever the hell she wants. Same as the rest of you. This ain't a damn soldier battalion. You can leave whenever you want. You don't like it here, Ricky, then head on out." Amos threw his hand toward the canyon opening. "Go on, *get.*"

Ricky turned his back on both of them and settled back down near the fire, nursing his wounded pride.

"His bark is worse than his bite." Amos spat on the ground. "He knows he makes more coin running with us than he would on his own."

"He's a rotten one, Amos," Cat whispered. "No sense of honor whatsoever."

"Coming from the girl that killed three Casedian deputies before they finally got her locked down?" The old man arched an eyebrow at her.

"You know what I mean," she snapped back, whipping him with the shirt in her hand. "There are some lines you just don't cross."

Amos wrinkled his nose at her. "Go clean up, Cat. You smell like piss and blood."

Cat looked down at her filthy clothes and sniffed. "Yeah, you're right. I won't be long."

After Pedro picked the locks on her cuffs, looking bored as hell as he did so, she started down the dirt path that would take her a little farther down the river.

"Need any 'soap' to help you clean your more intimate parts?" Soap called after her.

Cat laughed as she sauntered away. "Soap, I'll shoot *your* most intimate parts clean off if you come anywhere near me while I'm bathing."

"Got it!" he yelled back with a mock salute.

The cold water of the river was heaven. Cat dipped her head beneath the surface one more time to savor the utter freedom of weightlessness. The inner curve of the river had very little current, and the sand gently sloped into a little beach guarded by bramble. She used handfuls of sand to scrub anyway any trace of that jail cell in Caseda.

When she was finished, she braided her wet hair back and put on the decently clean clothes Amos had given her. She recognized the leather pants and black buttoned shirt as her own. He had kept her belongings this entire time. Weeks after she'd left. He must not have given up hope that she would come back. Her eyes started to burn, and she blinked furiously until they cooled.

"Damn him," she mumbled to herself. Outlaws weren't supposed to *care* this much.

By the time she wandered back to the small fire, the dark clouds above made it feel like night had come early. But nothing was packed. All the men and their belongings remained scattered about the small canyon floor.

Cat curled her hands into fists and found Amos sitting by the fire. He was using the blade of his knife to eat beans out of a dented tin can.

"I thought we were leaving."

"In the mornin'." Amos shoveled another bladeful of beans into his mouth.

Cat pursed her lips. "You gave in to him."

"No, I decided it wasn't worth the fight. You gotta know when to pick your battles and when to leave them be. That boy is as proud as a damn parrot, but if you give him a treat instead of ruffling his feathers all the time, he's a bit easier to handle."

"I just don't like being so close to Saint's Landing. I want to get as far away from here as I can."

"You ever gonna tell me what you're runnin' from? Besides me this time?"

Guilt pooled in her stomach. She felt sick with it. "I'm sorry I ran, Amos. I thought I was protecting you."

Amos barked a laugh without any humor in it. "Protectin' me? From what? The parrot?" He nodded to where Ricky was telling some kind of filthy story. He made crude gestures with his hands. The group around him roared with laughter. By the way his chest puffed up, she could tell he was soaking in the attention. "Nah. He's harmless."

"You and Soap both keep saying that, but I heard him that night I left. He was saying they aren't all treated the same. That there's favoritism and it was time something be done about it."

"I'm fair. My men know that."

Did the old man have to be so stubborn? He was blind to what was happening right under his nose.

"I just think—"

"*I* think you need to stop running away from your problems, Cat. When I found you dying in the middle of the desert, not far from here, mind you, I knew you were running from something. Skinny little thing. Half-dead. You wouldn't have made it another day. Begged me not to take you home."

Cat winced at the memory.

"You ran from your problems then, and you ran a few weeks ago. Told yourself it was to protect me. I think you were scared. And your runnin' almost got you killed again. You keep trying to outrun the darkness behind ya, like night's closing in and you're dead set on chasing after the sun that's settin'. But the only way to catch the sun is to turn the other way. Face the night, run right through it. Catch the dawn on the other side."

They were both quiet for a long while. Cat didn't know what to say. Stop running? Face the darkness she always felt nipping at her heels? Even thinking about the home she'd run from made her chest tighten. She stared into the crackling flames of the fire, trying to calm her pounding heart.

They consumed the wood until all that was left were glowing embers. Nothing but ashes. Just as she'd watched the wooden beams of her once fine home succumb to greedy flames, her mother's screams echoing in her head . . . She slammed down the memories like an iron lid on a boiling pot.

"I won't run away from you again," she finally said. "I'll stay this time. I promise."

"Promises mean nothing. You show me your integrity by actually staying."

"Yes, sir." Cat saluted him.

Amos grunted, but the corner of his mouth lifted slightly. "We'll need to get you some new guns before the next raid. Can't run around as a cat with no claws, can ya?"

It happened so suddenly. A flash behind her eyes. A gun firing from somewhere behind them.

Cat didn't think twice; she shoved Amos to the ground just as the bullet knocked off his hat.

"Saints Almighty," he growled, rolling onto his stomach and pushing himself up. He shoved the hat back on his head and hunkered down beside her. "Stay down."

Cat immediately scanned the camp for Ricky, but the camp was already pandemonium. Shots rang out through the gathering darkness, their sounds echoing off the canyon walls and reverberating in her ears. Everywhere, members of the Wolves were scrambling for their guns or horses.

At the mouth of the canyon appeared a regiment of at least fifty soldiers. Each of them sat upon a fine white horse. The crisp blue arms of their uniforms came up, guns pointed.

"Fire," called a calm, clear voice.

The staggered pops of fifty guns went off, and smoke obscured the soldiers. Outlaws screamed and fell around her. The nearest body fell back, rigid as a board. Blood tinged with gold poured from a wound on his head.

Aurium bullets.

No . . .

The smoke cleared slightly. One of the soldiers nudged his horse forward to stand before the rest. A white bandage tinged with red was wrapped around his head, but it didn't hide his cold, handsome face.

Captain Freeman.

"Hold your fire!" he called to the men behind him, lifting a hand. He surveyed the damage. "You are surrounded. There's nowhere to run. Surrender and—"

But no one was listening. Already, the remaining Wolves were mounting their horses and scattering to the wind. Freeman should have known better. You couldn't bargain with criminals. When guns start going off, their only thought was to get themselves out of range.

Soap and Pedro and a few of the others were at least trying to return fire. Several soldiers fell from their horses in blurs of navy and gold.

"There's too many of 'em. Get out of here, Cat," Amos yelled, already loading bullets into his black revolver.

Every nerve in her body screamed at her to bolt, but she held his gaze with a determined fierceness. "No, I just told you. I'm done running—"

"I told you not to run, but I also told you to know when to pick your battles. This is one time you need to run."

"But this is my fault. He probably heard us say we were headed for the canyon—"

Amos roared in frustration. "Damn it, Cat, not everything is your fault. GO!" He wrenched her to her feet and shoved her toward a horse. *His* horse.

"I can't take your horse! How will you—"

He lifted his revolver and shot six perfect shots. Six soldiers fell to the earth, one after each pull of his trigger. Two more outlaws fell beside Soap and Pedro, who had now taken shelter within a copse of low trees as they fired back.

"Damn it, Cat. I was a soldier for twenty years. There's no winning this. If I have to tell you again . . ." He loaded more bullets into the barrel.

Cat flashed with another vision as the soldiers returned fire and charged toward them. She knocked Amos aside and saved him from another bullet.

"Knew I saved you for a reason." He gave her a crooked grin before forcibly throwing her onto the horse. "Stick to the river. They can't follow your tracks if you don't leave any. But get the hell out of there if the water starts risin'. You know what happens."

She reached down to him, tears threatening to break through. Memories of her parents' screams tore through the careful wall she always held them behind. The desperation she'd felt at not being able to save them. The guilt of knowing it had been her fault. She couldn't lose another parent. Not like this. Not after he'd just derailed a Saints-damned train for her. "Amos, please. Come with me."

"A true leader doesn't abandon his men when they need him most. I'll hold them off for as long as I can to give y'all a chance to escape." He placed a hand on the horse's flank. "Listen to me, Cat. Find a mission. Any mission. Tell the priest I sent you." He glanced over his shoulder. "And don't tell Ricky, but you always were my favorite." He winked.

A bullet blazed by them, leaving a golden trail. Amos slapped the horse's flank.

"Amos, no—" But the horse bucked. Cat grabbed the reins and steadied herself just before Tenebris took off at a gallop.

A fork of lightning flashed across the sky. She couldn't tell which *cracks* were coming from guns and which were coming from the clouds. Giant drops of water pelted her face until she was soaked through. Tears pricked behind her eyes, and she ordered them to stay back. If she let them fall, they'd drown her.

She'd run after all, after everything Amos had done to save her. And not just this time. The pressure built behind her eyes. Run, run, *run*. She almost turned around, but the thought of wasting Amos's sacrifice kept her moving forward.

She charged the horse into the river. Water flew around them as they crashed through the shallows. Shadows of other horses darted down the canyon. She couldn't stay down here with only one way out. The soldiers would hunt her down. Her throbbing eyes raked the side of the canyon, looking for goat trails or signs of a way up. Sure enough, a dirt path, probably used by the locals to reach the water, wound its way up through the shrubs.

She clicked her tongue and dug her heels into the horse's sides. For the third time in her life, she left everything she loved behind—and ran.

CHAPTER

7

His father was silent, but not in a way that made Adrian feel safe. No, this was the moment the rattlesnake stopped shaking its tail before it struck.

"Seven," William Caldwell finally repeated. His voice remained inexpressive, thoughtful even. He turned his pen over and over in his hand.

It didn't fool Adrian for a moment.

He lowered his gaze to his father's desk, a hole of shame burning into his stomach. "Yes, Father. You didn't give us enough coin for ten cows. I paid the fair price for—"

His father interrupted him with a sigh of exasperation. "Adrian, do you know how our family first came to Saelum?"

Adrian pinched his eyebrows together, confused at the direction the conversation had turned. "Yes, but—"

Mr. Caldwell began shuffling papers absently across his desk, his tone careful. Guarded. "My father—your grandfather—was a clever man. Though born to simple horse ranchers, he had a mind for business. Soon he found himself wealthier than he ever thought possible. But no matter the money he amassed, he was never accepted into the finer circles of Ordonia's capital. He had no chance of moving up in a world that kept him pressed under the yoke of his common birth. We had no name, you see. No lineage. Like breeding horses, the gentry of Ordonia did not like to mix their pedigrees with untamed mustangs."

He continued to move parchments around on his desk, raising his eyes to Adrian as if to make sure his son was paying close attention.

"Saelum Territory provided opportunities otherwise unavailable to people like . . . us. He took his skills west with a handful of others as clever and lowborn as he, and they established the largest beef market on the continent. They did not fit in the gilded, purebred world, so they created a world of their own. Where the sweat and blood of their hands could reap the rewards they deserved. Not because they were *born* to deserve it, but because they were willing to *work* for it. They were willing to do what was necessary to make their dreams a reality."

His father reached for a blank piece of parchment and dipped the delicate quill pen into a pot of ink. His fingers moved deftly across the parchment, writing words that Adrian could not see. "You see, this world is not fair. My father should have been recognized for the hardworking businessman that he was. Instead, he was shunned for being born to the wrong parents. For lacking a proper title to go along with his land. But that is just the way of things. When you understand this, Adrian, *truly* understand that the world does not care what is fair or right or just, you will stop trying so hard to make it so. You will realize that the only way to succeed in a world like this is to *take* what you want. Because the world surely will not give it to you just because you think you *deserve* it."

His father folded the parchment and handed it to him. "Deliver this to the ranch hands that accompanied you on your failed endeavor. I think it is important that it comes from you."

There it was. The deadly strike Adrian had been waiting for. His mouth went dry as he reached to take the parchment in his shaking hand. "What is it?"

"A notice of immediate termination. I sent them to do a job and they failed as much as you did. Their families will go hungry, and I want their suffering weighing on *your* conscience. Because you did not have the strength to do what was needed to succeed."

His father did not smile, did not seem to take pleasure in his cruelty.

It was simply as if he were a schoolmaster giving a failing student extra practice at his letters.

But Adrian shook with the restraint of holding his tongue. He did not agree with his father in the slightest. There were good people in this world. Honest people. Kind people. People who did the right thing simply because it was the right thing to do. The chocolate he'd gotten for Edith weighed heavy in his pocket. People like the shopkeeper.

People like his mother.

"And if I do not?" Adrian said stiffly, forcing his chin higher into the air.

"I will find someone to inherit this ranch who *will.*"

His threat hung as heavy in the air as the humidity before a spring storm. Adrian could see the thunderheads forming in his father's eyes. It was no idle threat.

Every swirling thought in Adrian's head screamed, *No, no, no!* But he swallowed hard and heard his mouth form the words, "Yes, Father."

By the time the heavy wooden doors to his father's study closed behind him, he was already forming a plan. Three ranch hands were losing their livelihoods because of him. No matter what his father said, they would not have hungry bellies because of his mistake.

Adrian sprinted to his own rooms and dug through a cedarwood box he kept beneath his bed.

"Aha!" His fingers closed around the soft leather bag. It jangled with the coins he had been collecting since he was a child. With a tug of the string, they poured out into his hand in a cascade of glittering gold. Plain gold, not aurium, but better than nothing. Imprints of the different faces of Ordonia's past emperors glowered up at him as if they already knew his plan to disobey his father's orders.

His conscience prickled with guilt, but he wasn't *technically* disobeying his father. He'd deliver the message he was ordered to; he'd just include a little parting gift with his deepest apologies. He hadn't known his actions would affect others besides himself in such a way. He was just trying to do what was right.

He absently fingered the golden chain around his neck. His hand dropped to the tiny golden dove, engraved with the name *Saint Veritas*—patron saint of truth and justice—that dangled on the end. He would find a way to bring justice to these poor men who had done nothing to deserve the hardship about to be forced on their families.

"*The world does not care what is fair or right or just.*"

Adrian tightened the cord around the small satchel. Perhaps the world did not care.

But he did.

* * * * * ⦿ * * * * *

The men appreciated the gift of gold, but Adrian swore the looks on their faces would rip his heart from his chest. They slumped out of the stables with hunched shoulders. His stomach twisted, but he reminded himself that he'd done what was right. He couldn't have cheated the trader like his father expected. He just couldn't.

The golden dove hung heavily around his neck.

He finally made it back to his rooms, a weight pressing on his shoulders, before collapsing onto the quilts of his bed. The door to his closet clicked and cracked open. Large doe-brown eyes peeked through the small opening.

Adrian sighed. "You can come out."

The door opened wider, and Edith emerged. Had she been hiding in his closet this whole time?

"You keep a box of treasures under your bed?" She climbed up beside him and squirmed under his arm.

He pulled her tight against him. She was a little breath of fresh air in his ever-suffocating world. "Don't pretend like you haven't found it under my bed before."

She shrugged and snuggled in tighter. "I did, but I didn't open it. I wanted to respect your privacy."

"Yes, and sneaking into my closet and hiding there does just that."

"I just wanted to be close to you," she said, her voice small. "I don't like it when you go away. I get so afraid you won't come back."

His heart swelled, and he squeezed his arm around her. "I'm here. I'm right here."

She sniffed and swiped at a tear that had started to fall down her cheek. Adrian was the only one who got to see Edith's softer side. To everyone else she appeared to be a minion of the Fallen One. But he knew the truth. Beneath her mischief hid a broken little heart that missed their mother just as much as he did.

"I have something to tell you," she whispered. "But I don't want to, because I know you won't give me my chocolate."

Adrian pinched the bridge of his nose with his free hand. He had a horrible feeling he knew what was coming. "Are you going to make me guess?"

"You probably already know."

He did. "Marta quit, didn't she?"

Edith looked up at him and gave a wicked little grin.

Adrian grabbed a pillow from behind him and whacked her with it. "You little fox. What am I going to do with you?"

Edith giggled and shoved the pillow away. "Give me chocolate to keep me sweet?"

Adrian groaned in frustration, but he reached into his pocket and handed it to her anyway.

Edith's squeal of delight at the paper-wrapped bar of chocolate eased a little of the ache inside his soul.

8

Tenebris was a fine horse, but hellish by nature. Usually he nipped at anyone that wasn't Amos. But at least he seemed to understand the danger they were in. He was being cooperative—for the time being, anyway.

His hooves stumbled on the narrow goat trail, almost tumbling them both into the canyon below. The rain pelted even harder, turning into a full downpour. Cat's hair flattened and stuck to the top of her head.

"Come on, boy. Steady. Steady," she said, rubbing his neck. He tossed his head, jerking at the reins and spraying her with water, but Cat held them tight. "We're almost up. Keep going."

A vision of a gunshot. Cat ducked her head as a bullet hit the canyon wall above her. *Saints Almighty.*

A group of three soldiers was following her up the goat trail, their own horses stumbling across the uneven terrain. Terror forked through her as hot and sudden as a bolt of lightning.

She urged Tenebris to go faster. The horse squealed as though he wanted to say, *I'm going as fast as I can, you weak little human!*

The rim of the canyon was just ahead, and by some Saint's mercy, the soldiers were still pretty far below. Tenebris stumbled again, and she ducked as another bullet whizzed past her shoulder with a trail of golden sparks. Finally, she and Tenebris cleared the lip and found themselves on solid ground.

A sea of sagebrush and chaparral spread out ahead, gently rolling in slopes of low hills. A dirt path cut its way through the brush like a pale, winding snake. The sky itself roiled in a violent purple backdrop. Cat pulled the reins and directed the horse toward the path. But he stepped sideways and shook his head. He seemed to have reached the end of his tether.

"*Come on!*" Cat snapped the reins again.

Tenebris whipped his head back to bite her, but she shoved his head away before his teeth could find her skin. He needed to know who was boss. "Don't you give me sass, Tenebris. I just saved us. Don't let them catch us now. *Get!*"

He whinnied in frustration, but he finally heeded her commands and sprinted down the path.

Cat had no idea where the path led, but she guessed it headed toward the nearby town that Ricky had mentioned. This was her best bet to find a mission. She still wasn't sure why Amos would tell her to run to one, but if there was anyone left in this world she trusted, it was the Wolf of the West.

The path twisted and turned through the broken desert. Cat began to shiver like a rattlesnake's tail. Her teeth chattered, and her soaked arms shook as she struggled to keep her grip on the reins. At times it was difficult to see more than twenty feet ahead. That would at least make it harder for the soldiers to follow.

Finally, Tenebris slowed and shook his head again.

"What—" she started to ask, but then she saw it.

Through the rain, distant gaslights glowed through windows. It was the town.

She glanced behind her. No sign of the soldiers, but that didn't mean they weren't still on her heels. She loosed a heavy sigh, and a soul-deep tiredness swept over her. The kind that almost made her want to give in and stop fighting. She was so sick of running. Always running from *something*. But she was too stubborn to stop. She had to be.

She nudged Tenebris toward the lights, her eyes sharp and searching the squat, drab structures for the symbol of the Saints. The buildings grew closer together as she neared the town center, a sad collection of wooden shacks and mudbrick storefronts stretching down the dirt road that cut through the center. The town was nestled between two low hills, sheltered slightly from the wrath of the passing storm. Gaslights glowed from within the saloon, and Cat wanted nothing more than to march through the swinging doors and drown her sorrows in ale. Or even something stronger.

Her gaze raked along the hills themselves. Finally, she spotted it. High on the hill above the small outpost sat a beautiful stone structure with a bell tower pointing like a finger toward the heavens. The circle of the Saints was engraved into the stones on the bell tower's face.

A mission. Hardly the largest or grandest she'd seen, but a mission nonetheless.

She directed Tenebris toward the hills. "Up a little higher, boy. Let's go."

With a snort and a stomp, Tenebris trudged up the dirt road. The bell tower grew larger and larger until Cat could see the individual crumbling stones. The copper bell was crusted green and hanging crooked off a wooden beam.

She eyed the building dubiously. Whatever priest was stationed here was doing a horrific job of keeping up the church. Behind the stone chapel sat a series of smaller stone structures, likely once used for housing the priests and priestesses in the days when it was a full-fledged mission. The courtyard separating them from the chapel was overgrown with sagebrush and weeds, the only occupant besides the crumbling statues of the twelve Saints a scampering lizard trying to escape the rain. Behind the church, however, stretched immaculately maintained rows of grapevines. They ran along the hill, standing in stark contrast to the obviously neglected buildings.

Cat did not have high hopes for what she'd find inside.

She dismounted Tenebris and led him to the carved wooden doors of the chapel. Her fist pounded several times against the symbol of the Saints, an elongated circle around a dove. Dust rained from the sides with each fistfall.

But no one came.

Cat ground her teeth. There had to be someone here. There was no way a vineyard that well maintained existed without someone to cultivate it. She yanked Tenebris's reins and pulled him around toward the back of the building. She was freezing and soaked and likely had a group of soldiers searching for her in the town below. They'd eventually make their way up here.

At the back of the chapel, a door was ajar. Cat could hear bustling and banging coming from within. So someone *was* here. The door creaked as she eased it open.

There was a panicked cry, a crash, and then a low murmur of colorful curses.

"Who's there?" the frantic, slightly high-pitched voice of a man called from behind a high wall of stacked wooden barrels.

"I'm a . . ." She couldn't exactly say *outlaw*. "Traveler. My horse and I got caught in the storm."

"Oh, thank the Saints," the voice mumbled so low Cat wasn't sure she was meant to hear.

From behind the wall of barrels materialized a squat little man dressed in a plain brown robe. A thick wooden circle of the Saints bounced against his chest as he moved. His arms and legs seemed relatively thin, but a large belly protruded beneath the rope secured around his waist. As he trotted into view, he ran a handkerchief across his perfectly smooth head and along the back of his sweaty neck. Cat's eyes dropped to the rich purple liquid drenching the bottom hem of his robe. The earthy scent tickled her nose. "Is that . . . wine?"

The priest's eyes went wide. He blinked several times before answering, "No. No, it isn't."

Cat cut him a look. Was he serious? Weren't the priests of the Saints supposed to always be truthful? And sober? "Yes, it is. I can smell it." She stepped closer to him. "On your robes and also your breath."

The priest attempted to stand up straighter, but she could see the intoxication shining in his watery green eyes. "I don't know what you are talking about."

"Sweet Saints. Of all the missions I could have run to . . ." Cat lifted a hand and rubbed her aching temple. She couldn't trust a drunk, dishonest priest. But where else could she go? Every muscle in her body ached, and the soldiers could arrive at any minute.

The priest leaned around her and narrowed his misted eyes at Tenebris. "Where did you get that horse, young lady?"

She snapped her gaze back to the priest, jolted with a sudden rush of energy. She stepped in front of the horse. "He was given to me," she said defensively.

"That is the horse of Amos Whitfield. I would recognize him anywhere."

It was Cat's turn to blink. "No, it isn't."

There was a pregnant pause between them. Each staring at the other.

Finally, the priest sighed. "Alright, my dear. I will be honest with you if you agree to be honest with me."

Cat tensed and readied herself to run anyway.

"I am Father Ignatius. I am the sole proprietor of this godforsaken mission on the outskirts of civilized society because my fellows in Ordonia see me as *unfit* to lead a more established institution."

Unfit? Cat cocked her head mockingly, her stance relaxing. "In other words, you've been banished to the wastelands of Saelum Territory?"

The priest twittered like an angry sparrow. "I wouldn't exactly say *banished*."

"For what exactly? The drinking? Or the bootlegging of wine you obviously sell out of the basement of your reputable 'institution'?" Cat raised an eyebrow.

Father Ignatius turned up his nose. "I sell very *reputable* wine, thank you. And since the barons have siphoned off all the funding in Saelum, I have to make a living somehow."

Cat snorted. This man was as depraved as she was.

"Now your turn, my dear, or shall I tell the soldiers I imagine are chasing you exactly where to find Amos Whitfield's horse and the mysterious young woman dressed in all black and running like she's escaped the realms of the Fallen Saint?" He arched an eyebrow right back.

Damn it. He knew exactly who she was.

She didn't confirm or deny his suspicions. "Are you going to hide me or not, Father?"

"Only if you can answer me one question first."

From the darkness of the night pressing in, the sounds of thundering hooves were coming up the hillside.

Cat hissed in frustration. The soldiers were closer than she thought. "Fine. Whatever you want, holy man."

"Is it true that Black Cat Whitfield is Blessed with the gift of foresight? That her gift is how she evades capture and can shoot a man before he even thinks to fire himself?"

When she had guns. "Isn't that what all the rumors say?" She glanced nervously over her shoulder. A horse whinnied somewhere in the distance.

"But what do *you* say?"

In her mind's eye, a vision flashed of a small group of five or so soldiers cresting the edge of the hill and heading straight for the mission. A warning. Which meant she had mere seconds until they appeared.

"Yes! Yes! It's true!" She met the priest's knowing gaze with desperation screaming from her own. "Please."

He clapped his hands together. "Then as a child of the Blessed, it is my holy responsibility to protect you. Go down deeper into the cellar, and keep that horse quiet!"

CHAPTER

9

Tenebris snorted impatiently, but he followed Cat into the twisting maze of wine casks. They came to a wooden ramp leading deeper into a basement. At first, Tenebris refused to go down, tossing his head and trying to bite her again. Cat was half tempted to release the beast into the wild, but she couldn't let him be seen by the soldiers.

Cat looked the horse straight into his eye and yanked him harder. Finally, that got him moving. His hooves clopped loudly down the ramp and then on the clay tiles of the basement floor, and Cat tied him to one of the support pillars. She crept further into the cellar, marveling at how many casks of wine Father Ignatius was aging down here. The cellar stretched the length of the chapel itself.

A booming knock sounded on the doors somewhere above her head. Cat froze.

She crouched down and held her breath, then quietly moved closer to listen to the voices trickling down through the aged floorboards.

"How may I help you this fine evening, gentlemen?"

"We are looking for an escaped outlaw. Dangerous and likely armed. A young woman. She looks like this." Cat assumed he was showing the priest her wanted poster. It was an awful rendering, in her opinion. She wasn't vain, but she did consider herself attractive. Small straight nose, oval-shaped face, with large hazel eyes from her mother, but the only accurate feature on the poster was the long chestnut-brown hair that was usually braided down her back. The authorities loved to translate her unpleasant reputation into her picture as well.

"I haven't seen anyone who looks like *that*," she heard Father Ignatius reply. Cat bit her lip to keep from laughing. At least the priest wasn't lying.

The soldier sighed in exasperation. "Have you seen a young woman this evening at all?"

"No, I haven't. I'm sorry to disappoint you. I will definitely alert the authorities should I see anything suspicious. But before you go, I'd be happy to supply you and your men with a little parting gift."

There was a rumble of appreciation, the clinking of several bottles hitting against one another, and finally the thudding boots retreated from the chapel.

Had an ordained priest of the Saints really just hidden a fugitive in his illegal wine cellar and bribed authorities off the property with bootleg alcohol?

Cat felt a rush of respect for her new friend.

Amos had known what he was doing in telling her to run to a mission. He'd known they would protect her as one of the Blessed. Her heart ached to think of the Wolf. She hoped he had escaped. Tears sprang up in the corners of her eyes, and she wiped them away with her dust-covered fingers. She almost never cried, but after so much loss, she felt as frayed as the edge of a raveled weaving. She prayed to whatever Saint would hear her that he was still alive somehow.

When she was sure it was safe, Cat slowly made her way back to Tenebris. She rubbed her face into his thick neck. To his credit, the horse didn't try to bite her. Instead, he stood perfectly still as she fought back the pressure building in her chest, stroking the matted strands of his mane. All she could do was relive over and over the moment Amos had thrown her on Tenebris's back.

You always were my favorite.

She hugged the horse even tighter.

"You know, horses can tell when we need comfort," Father Ignatius's voice said from the top of the ramp. He gave her a sad smile and motioned with a hand for them to come back up.

Cat sniffed and shoved the feelings down deep inside. She didn't want to deal with them right now, especially not when the loss went so much deeper than just Amos.

The priest took Tenebris's reins, leading the horse to the upper level. Then he reached out a hand and pulled Cat out of the stale darkness. His eyebrows scrunched together in concern. She expected him to spout some platitude or verse quoted from the holy scriptures of the Saints.

Instead, Father Ignatius searched her face and nodded sagely. "You need a drink."

Cat snorted. "Father, give me the strongest thing you've got."

✦ · · · · ✹ · · · · ✦

"You know, I am only condoning this because you are of age according to imperial law," Father Ignatius said, swirling the wine in his goblet.

They sat in the front row of the empty wooden pews, listening to the storm still raging outside. Cat's head felt heavy and warm from whatever alcohol Father Ignatius had poured into her etched metal goblet. She had been surprised to see him pull out the fancy golden chalices usually reserved for religious services, but she didn't question him. "If I weren't, I'd just lie and tell you I was anyway."

Father Ignatius shrugged. "Well, you clearly were not Blessed by Saint Veritas."

Cat lowered her goblet and smiled conspiratorially. "You are the strangest priest of the Blessed I've ever met."

Father Ignatius lounged back in the wooden pew. "Have you met many of us?"

Cat rolled her eyes and took another burning swig. "Yes."

"That surprises me."

Cat downed the rest of her drink and plunked her goblet down for a refill. "You'd be surprised by a lot of things about me."

Father Ignatius did not move to refill her cup. His eyes sparkled with mischief. "I know more than you might think."

Cat laughed darkly. "I doubt that."

Father Ignatius was silent for several moments, considering her. "I know that you are Black Cat Whitfield, Blessed by Saint Prudentia with the gift of foresight."

She saluted him with her cup. "I thought we'd established that already."

"We have. But you aren't a Wolf, are you?"

She tapped her cup on the pew, indicating she wanted more. But still, he did not move. "I guess not anymore," she conceded.

"You never really were, though. Amos is not your father."

He said it as a statement, not a question. An unsettled feeling stirred inside her stomach, and her skin felt suddenly too tight. She ignored him and tapped her cup again with insistence. What was his problem? She clearly wanted more, and the bottle was right there beside him. She wanted to drink enough to drown out the memories that wouldn't stop harassing her. Surely he understood that.

She reached for the bottle, and he lifted it out of her reach.

"Hey! What the—"

"Amos is not your father, is he?"

"Why do you care?" She made to snatch the bottle again, but now he stood and held it out of her reach. Anger roiled up inside her—she felt like a dog teased with a piece of dangled meat. She wanted to snap at him. She tried to stand, but the world tipped sideways.

"I care because I want to know who you really are."

"It doesn't matter who I really am." Cat swiped for the bottle and brushed it with her fingers, knocking it out of the priest's hand. It smashed onto the floor. Red liquid settled into the cracks of the stone tiles like blood freshly spilled from a cut.

Cat shrieked in frustration. Why was she even here? If he wasn't going to help her forget, she had no business staying. The soldiers were gone now. She could run far away from here and . . . and . . . well, she didn't know yet, but she knew she didn't want to be *here* a moment longer.

She tried to make for the door and stumbled into one of the pews. She clawed her way to the next pew, and then the next, using their sturdiness to keep her upright as she went. Her head swam with the wine. "If you aren't going to give me any more, then I'm leaving."

"I really wish you wouldn't, Catriona Macgregor."

Her birth name knocked the wind from her stomach as effectively as a punch to the gut.

She stopped and gasped for breath, her nails digging into the pew's weathered wood. She hadn't heard that name in nine years. Her real father's face swam behind her eyelids. Then her mother's.

"Catriona Macgregor is dead," she whispered.

Somewhere behind her, Father Ignatius's sandals scuffed against the stone. "That's what everyone thinks, isn't it? That the only daughter of Brian Macgregor died with them that night?"

"She did!" Cat turned suddenly and tried to swing a fist at the priest's face. How dare he talk about such things. He was an ignorant child poking at a sleeping beast.

But he dodged easily, and she lost her balance, falling to the floor. What little breath she had left rushed out of her in a *whoosh*. Her head throbbed. She coughed and pressed her burning cheek against the cool stone.

"How in the hell are you not as drunk as I am?" she grumbled.

Father Ignatius crouched down beside her. "I have been drinking to forget my troubles for many more years than you, my dear. It's my guess that this is one of the first times you've ever tried. I'm also sure you don't have any food in your stomach to temper the alcohol's effect."

Cat's stomach roiled in confirmation. Damn him. She turned her face fully into the stone floor, squashing her nose flat. "I hate you," she said, her voice muffled.

"I don't think it's me you hate, Miss Macgregor."

"Don't." Her voice was muffled by the stone. "Don't *ever* call me that."

"Why did you run? Why didn't you go back home?"

She pushed herself back up into a sitting position and faced Father Ignatius. She was sure her eyes raged with the pain she'd secretly harbored these last nine years. The shame had piled and built up like gunpowder in a storeroom, waiting for a spark to light. Her tongue burned with the words she'd never had the courage to speak out loud. But the fuse was now lit. Finally, they exploded out of her like a blast from a cannon.

"Because I killed them, okay? I killed my parents!"

CHAPTER

10

"You did not kill your parents." Father Ignatius shook his head in disbelief.

Cat shoved herself up from the floor of the chapel, but she swayed dangerously and plopped back down onto her backside. "I may not have pulled a trigger, but it's my fault they're dead."

Father Ignatius exposed his palms to her. "Help me understand."

"Why? Why do you even care?"

"Because you are Blessed." He spread his arms wide as if that explained everything.

Cat snorted. "And that matters because?"

He heaved a heavy sigh. "For centuries the job of the missions was to find the Blessed and help them achieve whatever holy task was given to them by the Saints. The Blessed receive many different gifts, each given by a specific Saint for a specific purpose. *You* have a purpose, Catriona. It is why you were given the gift of foresight when you were baptized as an infant."

Cat rolled her eyes and glanced up at the ceiling of the mission. Across the expanse of stucco were painted frescoes depicting the twelve Saints and the Great Mother. Each of the Saints had been human at one time. Anyone could pray to the Saints to petition the Great Mother on their behalf, and She granted the Saints, as her deputies, the ability to bestow blessings on humans and lead them in accordance with Her will. All except the Fallen One—the Saint whose name had been long forgotten. The Saint who betrayed his brothers and sisters by gifting the magic metal aurium to humankind. Now people had the power to raise their own wills over the will of the Saints, a way to find equality with the powers of the Blessed, no matter how twisted their intentions might be.

The only way to tap into aurium's magic was to offer prayers to the Fallen One. Another reason the faithful believed aurium to be cursed.

The faithful, like her real father.

"If I was given the gift of foresight for a reason, then I messed it up. The Saints made a mistake in choosing me for anything."

Father Ignatius's mouth pressed into a thin line. "That is not the way Blessing gifts work, my dear. People grew jealous of the Blessed because they viewed them as favored, but in reality, to be Blessed is a heavy burden. For the will of the Saints is not always clear, and sometimes what they want us to do turns out to be much more difficult than we expect."

Cat threw her herself back onto the floor with her arms over her eyes. Her gut lurched and she turned her head to the side just in time to empty her stomach beneath one of the pews. But because there was not much in it to begin with, she retched and threw up only the burning drink.

Father Ignatius rubbed her back in a comforting way. Her nose and throat felt as though a branding iron had been forced down them.

"Let me get you some water."

"Put some wine in it," Cat said feebly. Her head swam, and she closed her eyes.

Father Ignatius chuckled and padded back to her, the golden goblet now brimming with fresh cool water. Had he taken it straight from the holy fountain upon the dais? Oh well, water was water at this point. He helped her sit up and brought the goblet to her lips.

She coughed and choked, but took tiny sips until the nausea ebbed. Sticky sweat clung to her hairline and clammy skin.

"I want to know why you ran. You are the rightful heir to the Macgregor Ranch. You were identified as Blessed by Saint Prudentia in the mission of Saint's Landing when you were baptized as an infant. It's all in the church records. And as soon as the rumors began to swirl of an outlaw that used the gift of foresight to rob the ranches and evade capture, the priests began to speculate at our annual conclaves that it was you."

Cat rubbed her forehead. "You priests are a bunch of gossipy old hens."

The priest shrugged, not disagreeing with her.

"Anyway, I don't think you're the only ones who noticed," she said.

Father Ignatius waited for her to elaborate.

Fine. If he really wanted to know the truth, he would get all of it. Maybe telling someone would lift some of the burden off her shoulders. Perhaps he could even petition the Saints to stop punishing her.

"When I was a child, my father discovered a massive aurium lode on our lands. I'd never seen so much in my life. But he was very religious, so he wanted to leave it in the earth where the Fallen One had placed it to tempt us. He made my mother and me swear not to tell anyone."

If the priest was surprised to hear about this, he hid it well. His face remained calm and intent as he listened. She took a deep breath and continued. "I was friends with the son of the neighboring rancher. We played together nearly every day. I—I really liked him." The shame burned so hot that her face felt aflame with it. "I wanted to impress him . . . so one day . . . I . . . I . . . ." She had to get it out. She had to tell him, but she couldn't.

"You told the boy about the aurium on your land, didn't you?" Father Ignatius guessed.

Traitorous tears burned down her cheeks. Cat wiped them away and dropped her gaze to the floor, wishing more than anything that the Fallen One would open a chasm and swallow her into his realms once and for all. Shame burned a hole clear through her belly, almost making her want to retch again.

She nodded.

She had told that foolish boy. After her father made her swear never to tell another soul.

"What happened then?"

"He told his father. The next day, his father came to our home and offered to make a contract of betrothal. I was excited, because I was young and foolish and hoped we would marry someday, but my parents were not. They knew that his father had somehow discovered their secret and was trying to get to their land through me. My father said no and turned him away."

Father Ignatius closed his eyes as if in pain, as if he already knew what came next.

Cat tried to keep the memories back, to keep them from swallowing her whole. That night, her vision had flashed a warning—waking her from a deep sleep seconds before she heard her mother's screams. It was still dark, and the moon hung high like the wicked smile of the Fallen One. Shots fired. More screaming. More shots. Catriona had sprung from her bed and run to find her parents limp and bleeding inside the massive bedroom of their ranch estate. She'd rushed to them, throwing herself upon their bodies. Their blood had coated her hands as she screamed. Her throat ached at the memory. They had paid the ultimate price for her mistake.

Her father's golden ring, with a ruby set into the center of the Macgregor family crest, had gleamed like another drop of blood. She didn't know why, but a whisper inside her soul had told her to take it. She'd slipped the ring off his finger and pressed it to her lips. It had tasted of salt from his blood and her tears. That was when several men dressed in black had appeared from the shadows like demons escaped from the lowest realms of darkness.

"That night, men came. They killed my parents. One of them tried to grab me and told me not to be afraid, that he was just taking me to our neighbors' estate. That the rancher there was going to raise me from now on. Looking back, I think he was planning on keeping me as a ward until he could force me to marry his son. An easy, legal way to get his hands on my family's land."

"But you ran?"

Cat shook with the effort of holding herself together. "My vision flashed just before their hands reached toward me. I'd learned by that time that my visions always warned me of danger. So I knew I shouldn't go with them."

She'd run from the house, evading them easily. They hadn't known her home as well as she had. When she'd made it past the cattle pastures, she'd turned back once to watch the home of her childhood, everything her father had worked to build for her family, go up in smoke. Greedy flames claimed the estate house, spreading quickly in the dry heat of the summer night.

Her parents' deaths had been ruled an accident due to a fire from some untended lamp. The inferno covered all evidence of their true demise. The authorities never found *her* body, but Catriona Macgregor had disappeared, so everyone assumed she had died in the flames as well.

"It sounds like your gift protected you."

"No one protected me," she snapped. "The Saints watched silently as it happened. They were punishing me for my sin."

Father Ignatius's brow furrowed, and he was quiet for several heartbeats. She could tell by his face that he didn't agree.

"How did you end up with the Wolves?" he asked finally.

Cat flinched at the memory of stumbling into the sprawling desert that night. The brush pulling at her skirts, each branch like the fingers of her parents' murderers trying to grab her. She squeezed her father's ring in her hand, the last thing she had left of them. Her young friend's betrayal tasted as bitter on her tongue as her own shame for telling him. This had to be why her father had wanted to keep the aurium a secret . . . and she'd betrayed him. She'd killed her parents because she couldn't keep her promise. Because of a silly little girl's crush.

She remembered falling to her knees at the base of a small rock formation that jutted out of the earth like a swollen thumb. She'd driven her fingers into the hard ground, digging and digging until her fingernails bled. She'd placed her father's ring into the cool, dark soil and buried it. Burying his memory and legacy in the way she'd never be able to bury his body.

By the time she had stood, covered in dirt and the blood of her parents, she was no longer Catriona Macgregor. She'd buried her future, her dreams, her family legacy in the dirt with her father's ring.

"Amos found me some time after that, wandering the desert hills, half-dead with thirst. I was a ghost. I couldn't think or speak or find any desire to live anymore. He took me in and helped me put back the pieces into something that somewhat resembles a human." Cat pulled her knees up to her chest and hugged them. She felt as though her insides were spilling out onto the floor of the chapel, and she couldn't think of any better way to try to keep them in.

Father Ignatius blew out a breath. "And so Black Cat Whitfield was born."

Cat squeezed her knees tighter and did not answer. Her chest gave another painful throb.

A warm arm encircled her shoulders and squeezed. The kind gesture was her undoing. She turned her head into Father Ignatius's shoulder just as a wave of agony swept her out into the sea of grief. So much pain. So much regret. All because of her. Because of her foolishness. Her selfishness.

She wept—harder than she had in all her life.

Father Ignatius held her as she cried, never shushing her or telling her to stop. He must have known she needed this, to drain the infection in her soul as one would drain the infection from a festering wound.

To her surprise, the feeling ebbed as quickly as it had crested. Cat always thought that if she unleashed the agony inside her soul that it would drag her down into its depths forever. But the moment she released it, she could feel its power diminishing. The agony wasn't killing her after all. The wound was still there, but it throbbed a little less. A pressure had been released.

She sniffed and lifted her head from the priest's now-soaked shoulder.

"I'm sorry," she mumbled, wiping her nose.

"For what?" His voice was still kind. "For feeling? For grieving so much loss unfairly placed on you?"

"Fairly placed," she corrected.

At that, Father Ignatius frowned deeply. He cleared his throat. "Firstly, my dear Catriona, stop apologizing. You must not shoulder the guilt of other people's sins. We own our own shortcomings, and you have more than done so. Yes, you told that secret, but that hardly leaves you responsible for the horrible actions of others. Stop trying to pay penance for a mistake that is not your own."

Cat hiccuped.

The priest continued, "Aurium is cursed because it allows all people to exert their wills using the power of the Saints, for good or for evil. We are all responsible for our own actions. You were a child who made a mistake. Your parents died because of an evil man who took that mistake and used it for his own purpose. That is hardly something you can blame yourself for."

The priest's words sounded as pretty as spring blossoms after a harsh winter, but that didn't mean they were true. Cat took a deep breath, trying to let them sink deep into the soil of her soul. But all they did was bounce across like scattered grain, failing to take root. Perhaps—in time—they could grow into true acceptance. But then again, maybe not. Wishing something were true did not make it so.

The image of her parents' bodies burned behind her eyelids, and the seeds of hope shriveled in the light of harsh reality. If she hadn't told, if she hadn't made the choice she had . . . none of it would have ever happened.

Nothing mattered beyond that.

Father Ignatius leaned back and looked into her eyes. "I am afraid to ask because I have a feeling I already know the answer. But who lived in the neighboring ranch?"

Cat grimaced, hating the name almost as much as her own. She spat it out like its taste burned her tongue. "Caldwell. Baron William Caldwell."

CHAPTER

11

Father Ignatius mumbled a string of curses. The golden dove on the chapel's altar behind him glittered in the evening gloom.

Cat raised an eyebrow. "I'm surprised the Saints don't smite you for a tongue like that in their holy church."

"The Saints were human themselves once, I'm sure they understand." He waved a dismissive hand. "I'm just not sure what to do about all of this. What it all means."

"What is there to do?" Cat attempted to stand again but then promptly abandoned the effort. "What's done is done. Caldwell killed my family and tried to kidnap me to steal my family's land. It's pretty simple, if you ask me. I just need to make sure he never finds me. I've made it nine years so far. I don't care what happens beyond that."

Father Ignatius furrowed his brow in concentration. He didn't speak for several minutes, but when he did, it seemed like he was speaking more to himself. "Nine years. Of course. That's why he's making his move now. That makes sense."

One of Cat's eyebrows snapped up "What makes sense?"

The priest met her gaze with a flaming intensity. She leaned back as though he might burn her.

"Catriona, are you familiar with Ordonian laws of succession?"

She cut him a flat look. "Right, because I have *so* much respect for Ordonian law."

Father Ignatius ignored her. "When a landowner dies and no family member makes a claim, the local governor of the territory oversees the land for ten years. At the end of the ten-year period, if no blood relative has stepped forward, the imperial government repossesses it and determines how it will be used."

Bile rose in her throat at the thought of Macgregor Ranch being left to the hands of the Ordonian Empire. But then again, perhaps it was for the best. She would never set foot there again. She would never become a baroness herself. She had given up that dream the moment she told her family's secret.

"I know you've been in custody across the border in Caseda, but did news of Saelum Territory reach you there? What happened to Governor Pickett?"

Cat's memory flashed back to the paper in Captain Freeman's hands. GOVERNOR PICKETT OF SAELUM TERRITORY FOUND DEAD. EMPEROR LAWRENCE TO APPOINT SUCCESSOR.

"He's dead. So what?"

The burning in his eyes seemed to intensify as if he wanted her to understand something of vital importance. But Cat had no interest in politics. Any governor would order her arrested for her crimes against the barons, no matter who took Pickett's place.

"By all accounts, he was a healthy man. You don't think it's strange that he drops dead suddenly, and the barons will choose who they recommend for his replacement, just as your family's land and the aurium hidden within it are about to come under the governor's control?"

Cat blinked once. Twice. Three times. If the barons recommended a new governor and it ended up being William Caldwell, then . . .

Her hand flew to her mouth.

Father Ignatius nodded, obviously satisfied at her understanding. "The priesthood of the Blessed all agree that the governor's death was strange, though we could only whisper our suspicions. Now I have a possible reason. I fear that without being able to force you into marriage with his son, Caldwell is attempting to take your land before anyone else can get their hands on the aurium. If he is governor, he can grant the land to himself, or at least control what happens to it."

The idea that Caldwell would find a way to steal the Macgregor lands after everything, after spilling her parents' blood . . . her throat constricted at the thought. She didn't want anything to do with the land anymore, not when it was populated by all the ghosts of her past. She had always assumed the government would manage it. But for it to fall into *Caldwell's* hands? Her parents died to keep that land from him, and if he took it, it meant her parents died for nothing. Everything she'd lived through had been for nothing.

The gaping chasm of hopelessness that opened within her refused to even entertain the possibility. "You can't be sure that's his plan. It might just be a coincidence that this is happening now . . ." But even as she said the words she felt them ring hollow.

Father Ignatius grabbed her shoulder. "Tell me you don't believe it's true."

Cat bit her lip. She felt the truth of it down to her bones. "Even if I believed it, what could we possibly do?"

Father Ignatius's face split into a wicked grin. "Oh, I do believe there is something we could do."

"Kill him?"

"Saints, no, Catriona! I will not become an assassin!" He fanned himself with a chubby hand.

She shrugged. "You don't have to, I gladly volunteer for the position. I probably should have done it years ago any—"

Father Ignatius frowned. "I will not allow you to damn your soul any deeper than it already is. And besides, another murder will not help you clear your name. But if we can convince the other barons not to recommend Caldwell as their choice for governor, he will never get his hands on your family's land or the aurium within it."

"But how on earth could we do that?"

He tapped his chin thoughtfully. "We can find out how he plans to win their favor. Most of them despise him, so he must have some kind of plan in place to secure their votes. They will all be gathering in the next few weeks in Saint's Landing to discuss their recommendation to the emperor. Caldwell will try to use this as an opportunity to woo them, and we can sabotage his attempts."

But Cat still saw a gaping hole in this plan. "But how are we supposed to get close enough to find out his plans, let alone sabotage them?"

Father Ignatius began to pace back and forth before the altar, his sandaled feet rapping furiously against the stone. His forehead creased even deeper. "If we report his attempts to fix the vote to the empire, perhaps, but then we would need evidence . . ." He stopped and tapped his chin as if a sudden idea had struck him. "We need to get someone inside his house. Someone to get into his personal office. He's got to be bribing or blackmailing them somehow. We'd need evidence of what he's doing."

Cat—who had gone to take another sip of water—spat it back out. "Inside his house? There's no way. He's got dozens of servants and private soldiers working for him."

"Unless someone is needed there for other reasons."

Cat narrowed her eyes at him. "Where are you going with this, holy man? I'm not playing a woman of the street or anything like that."

Father Ignatius blanched, his cheeks turning pink. "No! Of course not! I would never ask you to do such a thing!"

"Then what are you thinking?"

The redness in his face seemed to calm. He took one more deep breath, as though cleansing himself from her suggestion. "Caldwell has a daughter, a younger daughter that is nearing ten years of age. She would have been born just after you left. The child is a bit . . . well . . . difficult. They have gone through many governesses over the years. If they do not need a new one now, I can promise you they will very soon."

"A governess?" Cat asked, fighting back a laugh. "What would I teach her? How to shoot and curse? How to rob a bank or steal a horse?"

"You were tutored yourself as a child. I'm sure you remember enough etiquette and protocol. You can read and write, can you not?"

Cat rubbed the back of her neck. "Yes, but it's been a while. And I'm not . . . great with children."

"How do you know?"

"I've never been around any."

The priest shrugged. "It's easy enough. I can help you brush up on your manners. And we can pretend you are a novice in training with the mission. That should allow you to travel back and forth to check in with me. It will also hide you in plain sight. Caldwell is hunting you, but he would never expect you to be hiding in his own home."

Cat hated the idea. It was horrible, the thought of having to see that man again. To see . . . to see . . . *Adrian*.

Saints. Even just thinking his name sent a sharp pain lancing through her. She couldn't do this. *Wouldn't* do this.

Father Ignatius must have seen the refusal forming on her tongue because he placed hands on either side of her face and held her firmly. "Catriona. This is a chance for you to avenge your parents. To save their land from the hands of their murderer. Surely that hardened heart of yours still cares about that."

It all sounded great in theory . . . but something nagged at the back of her mind. "What's in this for you, Father? Why do you care so much?"

Father Ignatius held her gaze. "For too long Caldwell has led the crusade against the missions. Men with guilty consciences do not like to be reminded of their sins. He has personally campaigned against us for decades, ensuring the empire stripped us of our lands and resources. I have no doubt that under his governorship, the missions will face even more opposition. We already struggle to carry out our calling to help the Blessed, but he would make it near impossible. *You* are my calling, Catriona. I will guide you on whatever path the Saints have placed before you. For you have a divine purpose, and I would have you realize it."

Cat wrinkled her nose. "How have you all survived this long? Surely your alcohol business can't support every mission in the territory."

"The Wolf of the West," he said simply. "Without his support, the missions of Saelum would have collapsed entirely."

Realization washed over her like a cresting wave. Amos. The money from the raids. Never robbing the townsfolk, only taking from the barons themselves. Her throat tightened again. She knew Amos was religious, but she hadn't known how far he was going to protect the missions. "He's been supporting you this whole time," she said softly. "He never stopped upholding his oath to protect you."

Father Ignatius nodded. "And in turn, the missions have used his money to take care of the poor and sick of Saelum. Despite what Caldwell and his peers might say, we do not care only for the Blessed, my dear. We were also called to be the hands of the Saints taking care of those who need it most."

Cat did not answer. She looked up at the frescoes painted on the ceiling, studying each of the Saints, their faces gazing lovingly down at her.

Is this truly the path you have for me? she asked them. *Is this what I am supposed to do with my gift?*

There was no answer, no voice speaking down from the heavens. She didn't really expect one. Silence as usual. She was left to figure this out on her own. She glanced at Father Ignatius. Well, maybe not entirely on her own.

"You really think you can get me into Caldwell's house as a governess?"

He nodded.

"And you really think that we can stop him from becoming governor and stealing my family's land?"

"That is my hope," he answered truthfully. "Then, if you wish, I will personally help you get across the border or buy passage on a ship to anywhere in the world you desire. I have connections in Rhetia if you wanted to go somewhere on the other side of the Dark Sea."

Protecting her family's land and having the priest's help to get the hell out of this Saints-forsaken wasteland once and for all? The thought was as tempting as the Fallen One's magic metal. "I don't care what happens to the land, but I don't want that man's hands anywhere near it. And if we can ruin him in the process, I wouldn't say no to that either."

Father Ignatius laughed and clapped his chubby hands together. "My dear, I would expect nothing less. Let's give him hell, shall we?"

"Let's give him hell," Cat agreed. "But first, I need a gun." She dimpled a cheek. "Maybe two."

CHAPTER

12

Several days had passed since Cat agreed to this foolish plan. Though her patience was wearing thin with the wine-loving priest and his incessant preparations and quizzes on social protocol, she had to admit that his eagerness warmed her heart at the same time. It was obvious that Father Iggy—as she now affectionately referred to him—relished having a purpose again. After meandering aimlessly through life as long as she had, Cat could relate. It felt good to have a goal, a point on the horizon to ride toward. Even if her memories of proper manners were a tad rusted.

"And what do we say when we need to excuse ourselves?"

"Excuse me. I need to take a piss?"

Father Iggy rubbed his temples and then waved for her to try again.

Cat groaned and cleared her throat. "Excuse me." Her voice came out unnaturally high. "I have an urgent personal matter to attend to." She twirled her hand and gave an exaggerated bow.

The corner of the priest's mouth ticked up. "Minus the unnecessary flourish, of course."

"Of course," Cat said, giving another flourished bow.

Father Iggy rolled his eyes but moved on.

The priest's enthusiasm reached its pinnacle the moment Father Ephraim arrived. That morning, a simple wagon rattled up, towed by a rather forlorn-looking mule. A large chest locked with an iron padlock rode in the back, while on the seat hunkered one of the oldest men Cat had ever seen.

The driver was as wizened as a walnut, and his head was just as bare. His dark brown skin was papery thin, like aged parchment that might catch fire if he got too close to a flame. The robes of the priesthood hung on his bony frame. With his unsteady, shaking hands, he attempted to unload the large chest, his spindly arms looking like they'd snap under the weight of it. Cat raced forward to help him.

"What the hell is in this thing?" She heaved the chest into the empty chapel, dropping it with a loud *thunk* onto a wooden table beside the door.

"You'll see soon enough, my dear." Father Iggy had located some old novice uniforms and was deciding which of them was the least moth-eaten and spotted with age. Several plain brown dresses lay across an empty pew. He lifted a headscarf and wiggled a finger through a hole as big as his nose before shaking his head and tossing it back into a wooden crate.

Father Ephraim finally hobbled in behind her, a knobby walking stick tapping against the stone floor. He fixed her with a reverent look, his misted eyes glistening with tears as though she were a lost Saint descended to walk among them. The back of her neck grew hot, and she resisted the urge to let loose a curse just to wipe the look off his face. She didn't want his adoration or expectations. She didn't deserve them.

"Cat, this is Father Ephraim, as I'm sure you have guessed."

"Miss Macgregor." The old man swept himself forward into a bow. "I am so grateful you have been found at last."

Cat took a step back. "Cat. I'm just Cat."

But Father Ephraim took her calloused hand within his own. "I cannot tell you how much joy it brings me to know the Macgregor Ranch will finally be restored."

Cat yanked her hand back, temper flaring. "I'm not restoring anything. I'm only here to bring down the bastard who stole everything from me in the first place. After that, I'm not sticking around to see what happens next."

Father Ephraim flinched. A stone of guilt settled heavily in her stomach. But it was *their* fault if they had unreasonable expectations. She had her plans to keep Caldwell's claws off her lands, and then after that, she was gone.

"Cat, try some of these dresses and see if any of them fit." Father Iggy snapped his fingers and pointed toward a confessional booth. "It isn't a formal dressing room, but it will have to do."

She could tell he was trying to cover for her behavior with Father Ephraim. She tightened her jaw and took the dress out of Father Iggy's grip a little more roughly than was necessary. "Yes, *Father*."

She opened the dilapidated wooden door of the confessional and wrinkled her nose at the stale scent of the dust settled into the velvet cushion of the seat. She closed the door behind her, the snap echoing through the chapel.

"She is not . . . what I expected," Father Ephraim whispered, oblivious to how easily his voice carried beneath the domed ceiling.

"She is an acquired taste, yes. But there is a heart beneath the prickly exterior, I assure you."

Cat's chest tightened. She ripped her shirt over her head and jammed her arms through the sleeves of the novice dress. The fabric scratched unpleasantly against her skin. Her scalp still itched from the fresh brown dye they'd used to cover the hints of red in her hair. Hopefully it was enough to mask her true identity.

"Do you really think this is wise, Ignatius? To send her into the den of the wolves? If Caldwell finds out who she is . . ."

"Then he must not find out."

"I will insist she take a vial of holy water with her just in case . . ."

Cat stepped out of the confessional, and though the hem of the skirt skimmed her ankles, she felt oddly exposed. She couldn't remember the last time she'd worn any kind of dress. The image of her mother's voluminous lace skirts danced within her memory. She used to dream of wearing dresses as beautiful as her mother's someday, that she would go to the gatherings and dance beneath the stars until her feet ached. She shoved the thought away. Such were the dreams of a foolish child unacquainted with the true ways of the world.

She lifted the heavy fabric of the skirt and let it fall back into place. "Are you sure I can't wear pants instead?"

Father Ephraim's face cracked into a smile. "My dear, without the skirts, how will you hide the weapons?"

Cat blanched. "Weapons?"

Father Ephraim shuffled over to the heavy trunk he'd brought with him. There was a brief rattle of a key in the lock, then the creaking of iron hinges. He eased it open and exposed the glorious contents within.

Cat's mouth fell open. Knives of every shape and size lined the lid and interior walls, waiting for her fingers to grasp them. And that didn't include the guns. *Oh, the guns.* She stepped forward with the gentle reverence of a mother approaching a sleeping baby.

"Is that a—"

"A Cody .44-caliber single-action revolver? Yes, I have several. I tend to find they are more balanced and ergonomic than the Daltons. Though with a thigh holster beneath your skirt, I imagine a Murietta pocket pistol would be more comfortable, if a somewhat less accurate shot." Father Ephraim reached into the chest and lifted a small polished silver gun out of its holster and into his shaking hands. Then, with the dexterity of a much younger man, he checked the barrel, spun it back into place, and twirled the gun on his thumb before jamming it back into its holster.

Cat blinked.

"You do not think we would send you into a den of wolves without the means to protect yourself? As Saint Comitas once said, we can be effective in our objectives without being damned fools."

Cat bit back a laugh. "I'm pretty sure no Saint ever said that."

Father Ephraim waved feebly. "I'm sure there's something like that in the holy texts somewhere. The point is, we can be ruthless and clever at the same time. Especially when times become desperate."

Perhaps Cat should have snuck into weekly mission services with Amos after all.

✦ · · · · ◉ · · · · ✦

It only took about a week before word came to the mission that the Caldwell household was—yet again—in need of a new governess.

"Why do they have such a hard time keeping someone?" Cat braced herself against the wooden side of Father Ephraim's cart as the uneven road tossed her back and forth like a mouse between the paws of a cat. The necklace Father Ephraim had given her, a tiny vial of holy water, engraved with the circle of the Saints, thumped unpleasantly against her chest with each pothole.

Father Iggy swiveled from his seat beside the driver to face her. "Ah. Well, the child . . . can be rather difficult."

"You said that before. What exactly does *difficult* mean?"

Father Ephraim snapped the reins, and the mule pulling the cart grunted impatiently. "I do not think the girl handled the death of her mother well. Ever since, she seems to have made it her personal mission to drive away anyone that could be seen as trying to take her place."

Cat's breath caught in her throat. She'd never paid attention to current events, let alone any coming out of Saint's Landing, but surely she should have heard news of that magnitude, even out in the wastelands. "Mrs. Caldwell *died*? When? How?"

Father Iggy's shoulders fell slightly. "It was an accident. On the road to Saint's Landing, her horse got spooked and threw her. The physicians believe she died instantly of a broken neck, so there was no pain." He circled a finger around his head as a blessing. Father Ephraim did the same.

Cat's breath finally escaped through her lips in a rush. *Ada Caldwell*. Adrian's mother. She'd been such a kind, loving woman. Her warm smile had always sparkled with a hint of mischief that Cat had appreciated. Memories of her laughter, the amused curve of her lip whenever Cat had shown up on their doorstep asking if Adrian was through with lessons and could play. The way she'd ruffle Adrian's thick mop of curly dark hair and shoo them out the door before Mr. Caldwell could pull Adrian back in for another lecture. The conspiratorial wink she would give them as she called out to her husband, swearing she had no idea "where that boy had gone."

What had Adrian done when—

No.

She would not think of Adrian or how he'd handled his mother's death. The thought of his name alone sent the edges of her heart throbbing. The memory of his betrayal. Her foolishness. Her selfishness. He, at least, had been spared the sounds of his mother's dying screams.

And now he had a sister—born just after Cat had left the Macgregor homestead. How strange to think she might have held the unruly child after she was born. The girl might have been her own sister someday. Another future burned to ashes by her mistake.

"Do you remember Mrs. Caldwell from your time as a child?" Father Ephraim asked her.

Cat kept her eyes on the dust swirling up behind the jolting wagon, but she could feel Father Iggy's gaze on the back of her head.

"Yes," she said. She did not elaborate.

The priests didn't press her for more.

"Another governess?" Adrian rubbed his temple. "Where did we find this one?"

Mr. Caldwell smoothed his thick mustache with his thumb and straightened his wide-brimmed hat in the gilded mirror. His long black coat billowed out behind him like a king's robe above his polished boots. His personal rooms were just as ostentatiously decorated. Heavy gilded oak furniture filled his office, as though he wanted to leave none in doubt of his power and influence. "Father Ephraim at the mission in Saint's Landing said he has a novice willing to take the position."

Adrian arched a brow. "I thought you despised anything to do with the church."

His father went silent.

Adrian nervously chewed the inside of his cheek. "I'm sorry, I just—"

"I do not despise the *Saints*, Adrian. I am no heretic. I merely despise the power-hungry priests who think themselves above the rest of us. They preach the evils of power and pride, while they seek to have us all bend the knee and kiss the robes at *their* feet." He grabbed his riding gloves and slapped them against his thigh. "I bow to no one but the Saints themselves."

"When Mother took us to church, they preached the dangers of putting our own will above the will of the Saints. I don't see anything wrong with—"

"And who interprets the supposed 'will of the Saints,' Adrian? The priests of the Blessed are only people. Humans are threatened by any power that challenges their own, simple as that. That is the only reason they preach the evils of using aurium. It was a gift from the Saints, not a curse, and the priesthood would have us all believe otherwise." He swept from the room and headed into the hall, his bootheels rapping impatiently on the tile. "I'm leaving. Don't expect me until late."

Adrian scrambled after him. "Wait! What am I supposed to do while you're gone?"

"I need you to oversee preparations for the summit gathering. Securing the favor of the other barons is essential to winning their votes for governor. They will be arriving over the next few weeks for negotiations before the summit next month. Emperor Lawrence will not come to Saelum to appoint the new governor until he has received our recommendation."

"He won't come before then?" Adrian nearly jogged to keep up with his father's long strides.

Mr. Caldwell clicked his tongue impatiently. "Do you ever listen, boy? The emperor doesn't care about Saelum. He will want to make his ruling and escape back to his precious capital as soon as possible. If it weren't for the law requiring him to appoint the new governor of a territory in person, he would not even bother getting our dust on his perfectly polished shoes."

Adrian winced at the harshness in his father's tone. "Sorry. I know."

Mr. Caldwell stopped abruptly. "I'm going to secure a shipment of horses because I obviously cannot trust you with such a task. Help the novice get comfortable and make sure Edith does not scare this one away." A shadow darkened his countenance. "If she does, I'll send her to the capital to join a convent herself. I will not let that child humiliate me and ruin our chances for the future."

Adrian almost swallowed his tongue. "To a convent? Father, that would destroy her. If you send her away—"

"Then make sure I don't have to." His father turned again and strode away without a backward glance. His words echoed painfully in Adrian's mind . . .

"Make sure Edith does not scare this one away or I'll send her to the capital to join a convent herself."

Adrian's heart began a frantic staccato in his chest. Hopefully this new novice was up to the challenge of taming his little sister.

* * * * * O * * * * *

"Please try not to look so feral," Adrian begged out of the corner of his mouth.

Edith narrowed her eyes at him and hissed like a cat.

Adrian sighed. This was going to be a long day.

They stood beside a line of servants waiting in the greeting hall of the ranch estate. Behind him, winding staircases led to the upper levels, oil paintings of his father and grandfather staring judgingly down at him from the wood-paneled walls. Vases of Ordonian roses lined the walls and tossed their delicate scent into the warm afternoon air.

At least Edith had put on a clean dress, even if it was hopelessly wrinkled. Adrian had tried to braid her hair, but little bits still stuck out from between the twin plaits like weeds growing between stones. It did not help tame her appearance. She'd sat still for the first five minutes of his pathetic attempt, but by the end of it, he'd felt as if he were trying to wrestle a rabbit into a carpetbag.

"Saints help us both," Adrian murmured. He was half tempted to reveal their father's threat to send her away. But he knew telling her would do nothing but fan the flames of her rebellion. What she needed was not only the firm hand of discipline his father favored but the loving comfort of a soul who would not abandon her. The grief of losing their mother felt too heavy for his own shoulders to bear—he could only imagine how heavy it felt upon Edith's. No, he could not break her heart further and let her know her own father viewed her as dispensable. He would protect her.

He would make sure this new governess stayed, no matter the cost.

A cloud of dust rose from the road outside the ranch estate, growing ever closer. Edith pulled at the high-buttoned neck of her dress and made a choking sound.

Adrian gently slapped her hand away. "Don't pull at it, you look fine. The dress is not going to suffocate you."

"Says you." She harrumphed and plopped onto the floor with her arms and legs crossed.

"Off the floor, Edith. You'll wrinkle your dress more than it already is." He reached down and tried to lift her by the arm. She went limp as a rag doll and fell back against the tile.

"I don't want tooooooo . . ." she whined, flopping out her arms and legs.

The servant standing beside the door lifted a white-gloved hand to his mouth and coughed to hide his snicker.

Adrian frowned. Through the window he could already see the two priests and the young novice dismounting from the simple wooden cart. They would be here any minute.

"Edith, *please*! Get off the floor!"

She began to chant in a singsong voice, "I'm a little starfish, stuck to the pier, come a little closer, let me sing into your ear . . ."

"*Edith!*"

There was a knock on the heavy wooden doors.

Adrian straightened and ground his teeth together. With a quick smoothing of his jacket and a tug at his own high collar, he nodded to the servant to let them in.

Edith let out a huff of frustration and clambered back to her feet just as the doors swung open. Adrian released his own breath.

One of the priests was unfamiliar to him, with a rounded belly and watery eyes, but he recognized the wizened, willowy frame of Father Ephraim. Adrian strode forward with an outstretched hand.

Father Ephraim gripped it firmly. "Adrian Caldwell. What a pleasure to see you again, my boy. You certainly have grown into a fine young man."

Adrian shifted his shoulders uncomfortably, allowing the compliment to slide off them. "Welcome to Caldwell Ranch, Father Ephraim. My father is away on business and apologizes for his absence."

"No worries at all. I know Mr. Caldwell is a *very* busy man, and surely with the upcoming summit, there is much for him to take care of."

"Indeed." Adrian leaned around for a better look at the novice hiding timidly behind the second priest. Her reluctance even to meet his eye did not bode well for his confidence.

The portly priest stepped forward instead. Adrian's gut flickered with intuition. There was an almost protective air to the way he shielded the novice from view. "Mr. Caldwell, I am Father Ignatius from the mission in Polvo. It is a pleasure to make your acquaintance."

"Yours as well." Adrian bowed respectfully. He had honestly never heard of a town called Polvo, nor did he have any idea where it was. It couldn't be a very important mission to the church. "Father Ephraim informs us you have a novice willing to take the position of governess to my lovely little sister?"

Edith made a disbelieving sound in the back of her throat. Adrian's smile became fixed as he reached behind her and flicked the back of her shoulder in warning. Edith harrumphed and crossed her arms again.

"May I present Miss"—Father Ignatius's eyes darted quickly to the side—"Rose. A novice of mine serving at the mission in Polvo these last six years."

Finally, the priest stepped aside to reveal the girl behind him. She looked young, perhaps close to his own age, with an attractive oval-shaped face and large hazel eyes. Something about the cleverness within them tickled the back of his memory, as if he'd seen her somewhere before but could not place it. Her hair was hidden beneath a brown bonnet that matched her simple brown dress. A length of rope was tied tightly around her middle, accentuating the feminine curve of her hips. The back of Adrian's neck grew warm. He couldn't shake the feeling that he knew her somehow, or at least that she reminded him of someone . . .

The novice—Rose—stuck one of those hips out and cleared her throat. Adrian's eyes rushed immediately back to her face, which was now shadowed with distaste. He noticed a smattering of freckles across the bridge of her nose. But her jaw clenched suddenly tight, and her eyes narrowed in warning.

"Sorry, um, it is lovely to meet you, Miss Rose," Adrian said, the back of his neck positively aflame.

She gave a quick, sharp nod but did not speak. Neither did her tensed jaw relax. Adrian got the distinct impression that the novice did not like him. At all.

His cheeks warmed with embarrassment. He shouldn't have let his gaze linger on her like that. But he knew better than to let the ghost of a memory steal his manners away from him. Of course he'd offend her when his sister's future depended on them both making a good first impression.

At least Rose was not as timid as he had initially assumed. "We are so grateful you are here. I'd like to introduce you to"—he gritted his teeth and nudged Edith forward—"my sister, Edith Caldwell."

Edith and Rose stared at one another, both with arms crossed and eyes narrowed. The tension in the entrance hall grew thick, as though each person gathered around them was holding their breath to see what would happen.

"You don't look like a Rose," Edith finally said, tilting her chin up in challenge.

Adrian sucked in a breath.

But to his surprise, Rose tilted her chin right back. "Perhaps you should file a complaint with my father."

Edith blinked. Once. Twice. Rose did not flinch.

Then the most incredible thing Adrian could have ever imagined happened.

Edith lifted her silk-and-lace skirt and curtsied, the perfect picture of elegance and refinement. "It's a pleasure to make your acquaintance, Miss Rose. Welcome to Caldwell Ranch."

Adrian's jaw wasn't the only one to drop open, but he also didn't miss the roguish glint in Edith's eyes.

CHAPTER

14

Cat's heart beat so hard she thought it was trying to escape the prison of her rib cage. Perhaps with her arms crossed across her chest, she could keep it contained. Of all the places in the world she thought she'd end up after running away, the estate house at Caldwell Ranch was the last one she expected. In fact, it was the last place she ever wanted to be again.

"I can show you to your room," Adrian offered, gesturing with a gloved hand to the polished wooden staircase.

Cat glanced at Father Iggy, who gave her a nod of encouragement. "We are heading back to the mission," the priest said, "but remember that we will see you at Sunday services. And you can always write if there is anything you wish to consult us on." He lowered his chin as if to say, *Good luck.*

She swallowed the knot that had formed in her throat and followed Adrian up the stairs. Her small carpetbag bounced against her thigh with each step.

Cat had expected to feel a range of emotions when she walked across this threshold after so many years, but she hadn't expected sheer panic. Darkness clung to the edges of her vision as if she were about to lose consciousness. Sweat moistened the palms of her shaking hands, and her legs twitched with the desire to run.

Stop it, she chastised herself. *They don't know who you are. You are tougher than this.*

She told herself that was the only reason. That she was afraid of being caught. Not that she was back in the home of her parents' murderer.

But the house looked exactly as she remembered from ten years ago. As if no time had passed at all. As if so much tragedy and change had not turned her into an entirely different person. A twisting wrought-iron gate had ushered them onto the homestead, a dirt path edged with manicured hedgerows leading up to the sweeping ranch estate itself. The house was the same cold white stone with columned, wraparound porches on both levels. It was stunning to behold, even if the inside of the home festered with corruption and greed, not unlike a saloon dancer hiding rotten teeth behind her pretty painted lips.

The moment the carved wooden doors opened, Cat had been overwhelmed not only with the scent of Ordonian roses, but also a flood of memories. She could still see the younger versions of herself and Adrian sprinting up this very staircase, or hiding in the expansive gardens while palm trees swayed lazily overhead. They would chase birds through the trellises lining the estate's courtyard, or try to catch fish in the splashing tile fountain. Mr. Caldwell would grumble and complain that they were disturbing his "peace," while Adrian's mother slipped them extra sweets from the kitchens with a finger pressed against her lips.

And then there had been Adrian himself.

The sight of him felt like taking the butt of a rifle to her chest. The roundness of his face had sharpened, defining the angular slant of his jawline, though the same messy dark hair curled out from beneath his perfectly perched black silk hat. A clean white collar and black tie hugged his neck, and a golden watch chain dangled from a pocket of his embroidered silk vest. He'd donned a black morning coat in honor of welcoming her, but his rigid posture gave him an eerily sophisticated air that reminded her of his father.

The thought soured her already unsettled stomach. Had he become as heartless and corrupt as his father too?

He led her down a wood-paneled hallway, more oil paintings of various family members following their progression with unseeing eyes.

"I hope this room will be comfortable for you," he said. He opened the door, and Cat stepped inside, taking in the cream-colored rosette wallpaper and the polished oak furniture likely brought in from the capital itself. She hadn't slept in a room this nice since . . . She snapped that thought shut before it could continue any further.

"Thank you," Cat said with a tight smile. She waited for him to close the door and give her some privacy to collect her thoughts, but he stepped into the room instead.

Her spine went rigid. "Oh, I was really hoping to get settled on my own . . ." she started to say.

But Adrian marched straight past her to the four-poster bed and threw back the quilts. Then he suddenly pounced onto her bed, his gloved hands cupped as though trapping something between them. Thoroughly confused, Cat took a step forward to see what on the Mother's great green earth he was doing.

Adrian straightened, his hands still firmly clasped together. A muffled croaking sound came from beneath his fingers.

"Sorry about that. Edith put a frog in the bed of the last governess when she arrived, and I wanted to make sure you did not have the same . . . ah . . . experience."

Cat's eyes went wide. "She put a frog in my bed?"

"Just a little one this time. Nothing like the toad we found before." He walked to the doorway with a nervous chuckle. A servant was already waiting with an empty tin pot, as if this were an everyday occurrence. Adrian dropped the warty little creature in with a sigh and then wiped his gloved hands on his trousers.

"One more little check before I leave you to get settled, if you don't mind?"

Cat blinked. "I . . . um . . . no, go right ahead."

Adrian stooped low to check under the bed, shifted through the linens inside the wardrobe, and inspected the chamber pot. All seemed to pass his inspection until he stopped beside the vase of dried roses sitting innocently on the dresser. His nose wrinkled as he leaned toward it.

"Oh, Edith, surely not," he mumbled to himself.

Cat's throat tightened. "What is it?"

Adrian sighed and lifted the bouquet out from the vase. He peered inside and immediately recoiled, gagging. "Let me . . ." He coughed, his eyes watering slightly. "Get you a new vase sent up straight away."

Cat narrowed her eyes. "Why? What's inside it?"

"Nothing to worry about." He hid the porcelain vase behind his back, a much too exaggerated smile fixed across his face.

He edged his way toward the door, keeping his back facing away from her. "We would be delighted if you could join us for dinner tonight. Mrs. Rothschild makes the most delicious steaks this side of the Leonis River." He tipped his hat toward her with his free hand and closed the door behind him with a snap. A faint scent of urine wafted past Cat's nose in the wake of his exit.

Had the child . . . Saints Almighty. What had she gotten herself into?

＊ · · · · ◉ · · · · ＊

Cat had no desire to sit in a fancy room and twiddle her thumbs waiting for dinner to start. The sooner she got the information on how Caldwell planned to rig the vote and gave it to the priests, the sooner she could stop him from becoming governor and get out of this Saints-forsaken house. Propping a foot up on the wooden vanity stool in front of the mirror, she checked the knife strapped to her thigh. She doubted she'd need it, especially with Mr. Caldwell out of the house, but it was better to be safe than sorry.

Her carpetbag containing two extra novice dresses and bonnets also concealed the small Murietta pistol Father Ephraim—bless him—insisted she take with her in case of an emergency. She hid it deep within the linens of the wardrobe, away from any prying eyes. Nothing would raise questions faster than a supposedly peaceful young novice with a pistol stashed inside her room.

With the door cracked open, she checked the hall. It was mercifully empty. She slipped out onto the landing, the wooden floorboards beneath a plush rug creaking under her laced boots. At least if anyone caught her snooping around the house, she was new enough that she could make up the excuse of getting lost. In an estate this size, that wouldn't be a difficult task.

But Cat was not lost. After the number of times she'd seen his thick mustache poking out from the door to shush her when she played as a child, she knew exactly where William Caldwell's office was.

The double wooden doors were situated at the end of the first floor's main hallway. After making her way down the stairs and giving a placid smile to a passing maid, she turned right and feigned fascination with the various portraits hanging on the walls. When she was sure no one was looking, she turned the handle to Caldwell's office and slipped inside.

She immediately bit back the curse that bubbled up to the surface of her tongue. Mr. Caldwell was not sitting at his desk . . .

But Adrian was.

The quill pen froze in his hand as he looked up to see who had disturbed him. His eyebrows pulled together as he considered her.

"Miss Rose? Can I help you?"

Saints! Cat dropped her chin, her cheeks aflame. She wasn't used to being surprised. Why hadn't her gift warned her of the danger waiting behind the door? "I . . . I'm so sorry, sir, I must have gotten lost on the way to the . . . um . . . library. This house is so big and I just don't know my way—"

Adrian smacked a hand on his forehead. "Of course. I'm so sorry. That is my fault entirely. I should have given you a tour myself. I forget that not everyone is accustomed to living in a house this size. I've just been a little distracted with everything going on." He offered her a sheepish grin.

She took several steps back, scurrying away from him like a cornered hare. "No, no, I'm sorry for getting lost. I'm a remarkably quick learner, I'll just—"

"Nonsense." Adrian was already rising to his feet, shuffling whatever papers had been on his father's desk into a drawer and turning a small key. "It is my responsibility to make you feel welcome, and so far I feel I've done a shameful job of it."

Panic fluttered like moth wings inside Cat's chest. She didn't want to be around him any more than was absolutely necessary, and the failure of her Blessing gift to give her fair warning had thrown off her emotional balance. "No, really. It's fine." Her tone came out sharper than she intended.

Something inside his eyes softened. "I'm sorry if I did anything to offend you in the hall when you first arrived. I know I let my gaze wander far too long than is polite, but please let me explain."

Cat didn't want to hear any explanation he had to offer, her focus on getting away from him as quickly as possible, but he seemed determined she heard it before she escaped.

"It's just . . . something about you seemed familiar and I was struggling to place it. It was foolish of me, but it caught me off guard. I assure you there was no inappropriate—" He stepped toward her.

Cat's mouth went as dry as sand. She fumbled for the door behind her. "No—really—" Her heart beat a frantic rhythm behind her eardrums.

But Adrian stopped in front of her, his hands outstretched and pleading.

"Please do not place any poor judgment on my sister because of me or my behavior. You have no idea how important it is to us that you stay."

Cat's hand froze on the doorknob. She cocked her head slightly to the side, momentarily distracted. There was something he wasn't telling her. Something that had him clearly concerned about whether she left. Her instincts prodded her to ask, "Why is it so important for me to stay?"

Adrian lowered his outstretched hands and balled them into fists at his sides. He seemed to be chewing at the inside of his cheek.

"If . . ." He cleared his throat and continued, "If Edith scares away another governess, my father is going to send her to a convent."

Ah. His concern was for his sister. He was afraid for her to be sent away. Though from what she'd seen, the girl might benefit from such an arrangement. "Would that be such a bad thing? It sounds like she could use some structure."

Adrian winced as though she'd slapped him. "I can't do that to her . . . not after . . . she's been through enough loss. *We've* been through enough. I am the only thing she has left in this world, and I'll be damned if I let her down too. She needs to know she's loved, not have more rules shoved down her throat by people who don't care about her."

Cat considered this. Did Edith need him, or was it the other way around? He seemed just as reluctant to lose her. Cat's hand relaxed slightly on the doorknob. "Does Edith know? That she's going to a convent if I quit?"

Adrian ran his fingers through his hair. "No. I haven't had the heart to tell her. And to be honest, I'm afraid the thought that our father cares so little for her might aggravate her behavior even more. He *does* care about us, he just has . . . different ways of approaching problems than I do." His eyes suddenly snapped up as if realizing something.

Cat bit back a derisive laugh. William Caldwell certainly had some different approaches to problems. It was curious that Adrian didn't seem to agree. Perhaps her initial assessment comparing him to his father had been a hasty one. But perhaps not.

She arched a brow. "And why do you hold such different opinions than your father, Mr. Caldwell?"

Adrian's gaze did not meet hers. "Because it's what my mother would have done."

It was not an answer she had expected. The shadow of a deep and terrible grief flickered within his eyes, but it was gone as quickly as it had appeared. Adrian suddenly straightened, pulling at the lapels of his coat. "Anyway, I was going to give you a quick tour of the house." He gestured toward the door. "And perhaps afterward, if you are amenable, we can discuss exactly how much I have to bribe you with to get you to stay." He gave her a teasing wink, but it did not mask the bitter aftertaste of his previous desperation. He was still asking her to stay, even when his sister was putting frogs in her bed and piss in her flower vase. The Saints knew what other tricks the girl had up her frilly lace sleeves.

Cat didn't know how to tell him that she had no intention of staying. Not here, not anywhere. She'd get what information she needed from this house, turn it over to Father Iggy and the Ordonian authorities to keep his father's bloody hands off her family land, and be done with the entire Caldwell family once and for all.

With one last regretful look back at the desk, she followed him out into the hall. He chattered away about how the house had been built by his grandfather, how the Saelum barons migrated here from the heart of the Ordonian Empire to build a better life away from the nepotism and favoritism shown in the capital, what he hoped to do to grow the family name someday. She pretended to listen, but her attention was somewhere else entirely.

She told herself the tightness in her chest meant nothing. Sure, their mother had died, but so had hers. They weren't the only ones who had faced tragedy. Ada Caldwell's playful smile swam behind her eyelids, and guilt pooled in the pit of Cat's stomach. She fought back against it by asking herself whether Adrian's heart had ached at all after he'd told his father about the aurium on her land. If he'd cried at all when *her* parents died. The thought stomped whatever fledgling pity she had for him beneath the boot of harsh reality.

Sometimes life was just harsh, and there was nothing anyone could do about it. The sooner Edith learned that lesson, the better off she'd be anyway.

CHAPTER

15

Adrian wondered if telling Rose about his father's edict had been the best idea. Would it put too much pressure on her? Would she be more likely to leave? He glanced over at her solemn face and rigid jaw as he led her past the main dining room. She already looked as on edge as a sinner in a Sunday service. There had to be something he could do to make her feel more comfortable, more at home.

"So where are you from?" he asked conversationally.

She shrugged a noncommittal shoulder, her attention fixed on a landscape painting of cows grazing on the plains. "Polvo."

"I can't say I am familiar with the township, is it far from here? Under which baron's jurisdiction?" If it was close to Saint's Landing, it had to be on either Baron Fraser's or Baroness Carson's land. Possibly Macgregor's, which would mean it was under the governor's control for now.

Her jaw tightened again. "It's just a ramshackle little spot. Nothing of consequence." She lifted a finger and ran it absently across the bottom of the portrait's gilded frame.

"Oh. Does your family live there too?"

"No. My family's dead." Her hand flopped back to her side as she turned her face away from him.

Adrian swallowed hard. "Oh. I'm so sorry. Yes, that would make sense that you are a ward of the church."

Rose refused to meet his eyes. "So, do you have a stable around here or . . . ?"

"Yes, of course. Some of the finest mounts you'll find in southern Saelum." Grateful for the sudden change of subject, he lifted a hand to show her the way.

This was going abominably. If he didn't rectify the situation quickly, he'd be lucky if she lasted out the week.

The stables were constructed of the same white stone as the house itself, with a beautiful arched overhang and a view of the rolling foothills that spread out behind the Caldwell homestead. Their lands extended for miles across those foothills, where the cattle grazed free range until it was time to wrangle them for market. There were several townships and smaller homesteads scattered across Caldwell lands, all leased, the residents hired through the generosity of his family. Adrian thought briefly of the ranch hands that he'd been forced to let go. He prayed to the Saints they'd been able to find work under another baron.

The corner of Rose's mouth twitched upward at the sight of the stables. Hope fluttered inside his chest.

"Are you fond of horses?" he asked her, opening the door as the musty smell of hay washed over them.

Her eyes seemed to brighten. "Yes, I am."

They walked down the row of stalls, pausing to scratch at the occasional nose or neck. The novice clearly had a way with the beasts, but they also seemed to have a way with her. The further down the stalls they went, with each greeting returned by a horse's flapping ears or nicker, the tension in her shoulders seemed to ease, as if she were finally somewhere she knew she belonged. Adrian watched her closely, his heart racing a little at the sight of joy flickering to life on her face.

Toward the end of the row of stalls, Rose froze in front of the stall holding a beautiful palomino. The horse's golden coat stood in deep contrast to the dark wood paneling behind it. Rose whirled to face him.

"Is this one yours?" Her nostrils flared almost as large as the horse's.

Taken aback by her sudden change, Adrian rubbed the back of his neck, appraising the horse. It wasn't one he recognized. "No, I think this is one that Captain Freeman's regiment brought back to the house a few days ago. They raided an outlaw camp and captured some of the horses left behind. Considering the horses were stolen in the first place, he wanted to see if any of them were ours."

Rose chewed nervously on her bottom lip. Something about what he'd said was upsetting.

Adrian rushed to reassure her. "Don't worry. The outlaws wouldn't dare come here looking for them. Whoever survived the attack would have been arrested or shot on sight. A few managed to escape, but we'll hunt them down soon enough. Captain Freeman is ruthless and incredibly efficient."

Rose lifted a hand to her chest and rested it across her heart. "Oh. I'm . . . I'm glad to hear it." She walked over to a painted mare next, another one of the horses brought back by the captain. With shaking hands, she gently rubbed the side of the horse's face, briefly touching her forehead to its nose. Then she straightened and cleared her throat. "Let's tour the gardens next, shall we?"

He could tell something about the captured horses unnerved her. Perhaps she had a sensitive heart and hurt for the previous owners who'd lost them. She might even have lost a horse herself to thieves at one time.

"I'll make sure these horses are returned to where they came from." Adrian tried again to assure her.

He expected her to look grateful, but instead, Rose just sniffed and nodded before scurrying out the door.

Well, he'd somehow mucked that up too.

✦ • • • • ◉ • • • • ✦

Edith's grin was far too large for Adrian's comfort. She settled herself at the dinner table with exaggerated elegance, including a delicate little flourish of her lace napkin before placing it across her lap with exceptional care.

Adrian arched an eyebrow at her.

Edith continued to smile as sweetly as an angel of the Saints. "It is so good to see you, dear brother. I am looking forward to our evening meal together."

Adrian snorted. "What did you do, Edith?"

Edith blinked, her smile never slipping. "I don't know what you mean, dear brother."

"Firstly, *dear sister*, I don't think you've ever called me 'dear brother,' so that's your first tell. Secondly, I have never seen you looking so polite at a dinner with a new governess. You are clearly up to something."

Edith pouted and feigned great insult. "Would you really think so poorly of your dear little sister?"

Adrian reached over and flicked the tip of her nose. "Absolutely. Unless you've been suddenly and miraculously Blessed by Saint Pietas with the gift of obedience, which I highly doubt."

Edith stuck out her tongue but retracted it the moment Rose appeared in the doorway.

Adrian jumped to his feet, rattling the porcelain dinnerware sitting on the lace tablecloth. Edith hid a snicker.

Rose's cheeks pinked slightly, but she bowed her head in greeting before taking her seat across from Edith.

The little girl cleared her throat. "I'm so glad you could join us for dinner, Miss Rose."

Rose's eyes narrowed as if she didn't trust Edith either. "Thank you," she said tentatively, reaching for her napkin.

But she withdrew her hand immediately, eyes widening as though a sudden thought had seized her. Her gaze darted to Edith but then slowly returned to her napkin. Her shoulders rose and fell with a deep breath before she lifted it up.

Adrian's hands shoved against the table, almost toppling himself over the back of his chair. Rose, however, remained calm at the sight of the large sandy-colored desert tarantula squatting on the lace tablecloth next to her dinner fork. The furry critters roamed the foothills and were completely harmless aside from their tendency to spook the horses—and Adrian himself, if he was entirely honest.

"How did you get in here, little buddy?" Rose said, nudging the tip of her finger against its bulbous abdomen. Adrian fought back the desire to gag. The tarantula tentatively stepped into her open hand before she looked directly at Edith and gave her the biggest, brightest smile. "If you'll both excuse me just a minute, I'll take this little guy outside."

Edith blinked at Rose, her mouth slack with surprise.

The novice disappeared back into the hall, her hands clasped around her catch. A few moments later, the sound of the heavy front doors booming shut echoed through the house.

"Edith . . ." Adrian started to say through gritted teeth. He turned to face her, face aflame.

But Mrs. Rothschild chose that exact moment to appear, carrying platters to place on the table. Roasted potatoes and carrots sizzled in melted butter, while freshly cut rounds of steak steamed invitingly upon a bed of greens. The scent of the food nearly overwhelmed his senses as his stomach gave an irritated growl.

"Oh, look, dinner's arrived. How splendid!" Edith clapped her hands together and then reached for a freshly baked roll.

Adrian slapped her hand away from the basket. "We are waiting for Rose to get back first."

Edith made an exaggerated sigh of frustration and crossed her arms across her chest. "Ugh! *Fine!*"

"A tarantula, Edith? Under her napkin?"

"What?" Edith spat, her attitude deteriorating with each passing second. "It's not like they're poisonous or anything. And she didn't seem to mind at all."

Adrian's temper simmered dangerously close to the surface. "Do you *want* to be sent away?"

Something fractured behind her eyes, and her puffed-up posture deflated. "Away? What do you mean by that?"

Adrian plopped his elbow on the table and covered his eyes with his hand. "Nothing. I'm sorry. It's nothing."

By some Saint's blessed mercy, Rose returned just then to the dining room. He was sure the tension hovering over the table was as heavy as pipe smoke hanging over a saloon. Rose's chair scraped against the wooden floor as she scooted herself into place.

"Well, I'm sure the tarantula will be happy in his new home," she said conversationally, reaching for a roll from the basket.

Adrian cleared his throat. "Shouldn't we say a blessing over the food before we begin?"

Rose's hand snapped back to her side, her cheeks aflame. "Oh, um, yes. Of course. Would you like to do the honors, Mr. Caldwell?"

He'd never seen a novice forget to give a blessing over a meal before. But then again, her nerves were likely still on edge from her first day. The spider surely didn't help on that front either.

"I don't mind at all," he said, fingering the golden dove that rested just above his heart. With a quick prayer of thanks, dinner commenced, both Edith and Rose tense and silent as they ate their meals.

CHAPTER
16

Cat waited all evening to hear the squeal of terror coming from down the hall. As she studied her reflection in the vanity's polished silver mirror, a satisfied smile curled at the corner of her lips. If the child wanted to play games, Cat would show her exactly what kind of rules she played by. She ran the hairbrush through the gentle waves of her unplaited hair several more times as she waited. It was much darker than she was used to, thanks to the hair dye Father Iggy had procured, but if she looked closely, she thought she could still make out the slightest hints of red in the flickering candlelight, like a tiny glimpse of who she really was beneath the novice robes.

There was a sudden shriek followed by the slam of a door. Then a pitter-patter of tiny feet in the hall and a frantic knock at her own door. Cat laid her hairbrush down with a gentle clatter upon the vanity's tabletop, then took her sweet time to adjust a shawl around the shoulders of her nightshirt. She padded to the door in her bare feet and arranged her face into a welcoming smile.

She turned the handle of the door and feigned surprise. "Oh, Edith. What a pleasure to see you so late. Can I help you with something?"

The little girl stood before her, hands on her skinny hips and radiating rage befitting an irritated bull.

"You put the tarantula *under my pillow.*"

Cat's smile stretched even wider. "Well, I figured since you are the one who removed him from his home in the first place, you wouldn't mind sharing your room." She blinked innocently several times for emphasis.

Edith's mouth gaped as she floundered for a response. "I . . . I . . . will tell my father what you did!"

Cat picked at her thumbnail with casual indifference. "Go right ahead, my dear. I will happily explain to him where the lovely creature came from in the first place."

Edith twittered like an angry sparrow. "You—you can't . . . You wouldn't *dare!*"

Cat bent at the waist to lower her face to Edith's level. "I have faced dangers far worse than your father. I am not afraid of him in the slightest. Nor am I afraid of you."

The little girl made a sound of disgust and lifted her finger in a rude gesture. Cat's hand immediately shot out to cover it.

"Don't you ever do that to me, do you understand?"

Edith whined, trying to pull her hand away. "Ow, stop it, you're hurting me."

"What you did hurt me. And I don't care how angry or how sad you are, we do not hurt other people intentionally. Do you understand me?"

Tears shone in the little girl's eyes as she looked up at Cat's stone-cold expression.

"Do you understand?" Cat repeated.

A single tear trailed down Edith's cheek before she nodded. "Yes. I won't do that again," she said quietly, her lower lip quivering.

Cat released her hand and straightened. "Good. I am looking forward to our first lessons in the morning. I expect you to meet me in the library immediately after breakfast."

Edith slowly backed away from the door, looking at Cat as if she were a ghost. She nodded, her eyes wide and confused, and scampered back down the hall to her room.

Satisfied, Cat went back to her vanity table to patiently wait for the rest of the house to quiet. Servants moved about the various levels, extinguishing lamps, polishing frames, and dusting surfaces. She made a mental note to get a book from the library just to keep her busy in the hours after everyone else went to bed. Because unlike everyone else, Cat had no plans to sleep.

She waited an additional hour after the last sound of cleaning had gone silent, just to be safe, before snuffing out the candle on her bedside table. With the moon as high and bright as it was this evening, the halls should be sufficiently lit for her to sneak down to Caldwell's office. She stuck as close to the walls as she could, minimizing creaks in the floor. The house was eerie in its stillness, as if more than ghosts wandered these halls in the hours of darkness. But ghosts and demons had been her companions for the last nine years, and it would take more than that to scare her away from her sole purpose for returning.

The door to Baron Caldwell's office was locked this time, but Cat had learned to pick locks long ago. She slipped the pins from her hair and gently wiggled them into the keyhole. She tried not to think about Pedro Morales, who had been the one to teach her. He and Soap were likely rotting away on the bloodied canyon floor or in jail cells in Saint's Landing. Seeing Soap's painted mare in Caldwell's stables had nearly snapped her self-control. He was gone because of her. Always because of her.

She shook the thoughts away and focused on feeling for the tiny click that told her the pins had done the trick. When she felt it, a surge of pride rushed through her, warming her chest all the way down her arms to her fingertips. This was it, what she came here to do. The first step toward avenging her parents' deaths and making sure Caldwell's greedy hands stayed far away from her family's land and the aurium hidden within it.

The door swung open, revealing an expansive wooden desk illuminated by the moonlight pouring in from high windows framed in red velvet curtains. Father Iggy had said she needed to find out what Caldwell's plans were to secure the votes of the other barons. With his reputation, there was no way in hell that he could secure their favor on his own merit. No, there was something shady and underhanded going on, and she would make sure she discovered exactly what it was. Then they could expose him and ruin his chances of ever becoming governor.

Cat gently closed the door behind her. She strode straight to the desk and got to work picking the locks on the drawers themselves. It took her several minutes, but Pedro's skills were legendary, and though she was nowhere near as gifted, she'd been a diligent student. The first drawer's lock clicked, and she wrenched it open. Sure enough, piles of papers greeted her from within its cedar depths. Lifting them onto the desktop, she began riffling through them. Wanted posters sporting various faces from Amos to Ricky to herself stared up at her. She bit back a laugh at the image of Soap looking as though he was blowing a kiss at the sketch artist. Lifting her own poster, she noticed several jotted notes along its edges—dates and locations, supposed sightings, and theories about where she could be. The bottom right corner had "Captured in Caseda, June 7th. Freeman dispatched" scrawled in blotched ink.

She'd suspected from the beginning that Freeman had been hired by Caldwell. Who else would be willing to pay such a high sum to bring her back? He'd either want to make sure he killed her himself so that she couldn't show up and disrupt his plans to claim her family land, or he'd somehow force her to marry Adrian just so that he could exercise his family's control over it instead. That had been his original intent anyway. To raise her as his ward and force their marriage without her parents alive to object. Too bad he'd had no idea who he was dealing with.

There had been a time when marrying Adrian had been her heart's desire, as a young infatuated child who dreamed of marrying her best friend. But now the thought brought a bitter taste to her tongue. Adrian had betrayed her as much as his father had. If he hadn't told his father about the aurium, none of them would be in this mess in the first place.

Except you are the one who told him first, a nasty little voice seemed to whisper into her ear.

Exactly. And it was exactly why it was her responsibility to right this wrong and make sure the cursed aurium on Macgregor land stayed exactly where it was. A wrong that, should her plan with Father Iggy work, was entirely possible to right without her ever having to acknowledge her identity to anyone.

She dropped the poster back onto the desk and continued her search through the various business receipts for cattle shipments, purchases of wine from vineyards across the territory, bills for blacksmithing or merchant ships. All typical forms of paperwork one would expect to find in a landowner's desk. Nothing particularly exciting.

There were the plans for the summit itself, of course: a copy of the invitation to the Caldwell homestead for a gala to kick off the summit's festivities. Order forms for food and decorations, extra help and lodging accommodations for the visiting barons. He had a copy of a campaign flyer advertising himself as a candidate for governor, listing all of his accomplishments as a landowner and defender of the law. There was even a ridiculous sketch of him sitting upon his horse in a regal uniform, chin and mustache tilted toward the sky as if he were the emperor of Ordonia himself. Cat bit back a laugh. Surely the other landowners would think this as ridiculous as she did. Would they honestly in their right minds ever vote for him?

No, no, they would not. Not with his reputation for corruption and cheating. There had to be more to it. Which was exactly what she was trying to find out. Caldwell was no fool; he would not put everything to chance and trust the votes of the other barons, not with Macgregor Ranch at stake. There had to be evidence of blackmail or bribes here somewhere. But so far, nothing seemed to be suspicious.

Cat huffed in frustration and kept digging. There had to be *something*. Only two weeks were left until the vote, and she had to discover his plans before then.

Her attention caught on a map outlining the border boundaries for all of Saelum Territory. Cat traced her fingers along the snaking lines, following the edges of each of the twenty-six land grants purchased by the barons from the Ordonian government. She could still see the erased lines of the lands that had once belonged to the missions, now blurred and incorporated into baronial boundaries as if they'd never existed at all. As if the barons had always owned every square inch of land in Saelum Territory. She supposed Ordonia didn't mind; the barons probably paid better taxes to the empire than the missions ever did. Business and cattle trade were much more profitable than charity or religious work, after all.

Cat snorted and turned the map over, hoping to find some scribbled notes like those she'd found across her wanted poster. Suddenly she froze. The map of the territory had been retraced across the back of the parchment, the outside of it darkened with thicker ink as though separating it from the rest of Ordonia. Above the top, instead of a heading showing it to be Saelum Territory, a handwritten label read, A UNITED CALDWELL. *Caldwell.* As if it were the title of an independent nation like Caseda.

Holy Saints. Was she reading this right? Caldwell wanted to unite the other barons and break away from Ordonia entirely? He couldn't be that big of a fool, could he? The empire would never allow it. Her mind floated back to the stories Amos had told her around the fire, of other territories that had tried to break away and failed. The military might and wealth of Ordonia were almost unmatched. Only Caseda had been successful in their attempt for freedom because they'd had the backing of a foreign nation that funded their rebellion . . . and Ordonia hadn't cared to fight too hard to hold on to a poor territory of potato farmers. It wasn't as if they provided the revenue the cattle barons did. The Ordonian Empire would not be inclined to lose Saelum.

Cat breathed out heavily through her nose, her head swimming with what she'd just seen. She had to tell Father Iggy right away. William Caldwell wasn't just planning on becoming governor to steal her land, he was planning a Saints-damned revolution against the empire.

17

Cat leaned back on her heels, stunned into silence. This was . . . so much bigger than she ever could have imagined. She shuffled through the last few sheaves of paper in the bottom of the drawer, looking for any hint at *how* he planned to make all of this happen. But the rest of the papers were more receipts for some winery outside of Saint's Landing and another political flyer. She grit her teeth. He could not have a plan this big without some serious means to achieve it. How was he planning to do this? *How?*

She had just undone the lock on the second drawer of the desk when a shadow passed over the crack beneath the door, momentarily blocking the moonlight reflecting in the hall. Her vision flashed a warning of the office door opening. Cat bit back a swear and shoved the pins back into her hair. The thudding of booted footsteps came next, along with the muffled sounds of men talking in low voices. Whoever was outside was blocking her only exit out of the office. Cat's gaze darted around the bookshelves and useless spindly armchairs before falling on the long velvet curtains. They were her only chance. She whipped behind one and yanked it around herself, making sure her toes did not stick out beneath the bottom. Her heart threw itself against her rib cage just as the door opened.

"I've told that boy a million times not to leave my office unlocked,"

growled a voice that sent shivers of fear down Cat's spine. She couldn't
see him, but she could imagine the thick black mustache twitching and
Baron Caldwell's dark, cold eyes. Her fists clenched, fingernails biting
into the palms of her hands. This was the closest she'd been to the murderous bastard in almost ten years.

"He's just a child, what do you expect?" sneered another voice she
recognized all too well. She could picture Captain Freeman's harshly
handsome face. Her fingernails dug harder into her palms.

"He's not that much younger than you." Caldwell chuckled. His
desk chair scraped against the wood floor and one of the spindly armchairs creaked beneath a body's weight.

"Age does not trump experience, Mr. Caldwell," Freeman said. "And
unfortunately, Adrian does not have much experience outside the ranch
itself."

Caldwell sighed heavily. "I know. That boy is still more concerned
with his far-fetched ideals than anything else. I'm not trusting him with
anything beyond helping with the welcome gathering and keeping that
sister of his out of my hair until the election is finished. Though he might
prove useful in other ways too."

There was a faint tapping sound as if someone was impatiently tapping their boot against the floor. "Are you still hoping to bring her in
alive then?"

A snort. "No. She's clearly too wild to muzzle into marriage. It
would have been the easier option, to just have them marry and do the
whole thing legally, but her actions suggest she won't be amenable, no
matter the threat. I think elimination is our only option now, and I've
got other options for Adrian that can prove just as useful."

Cat fought the urge to snicker. At least he was finally giving up hope
on that stupid idea. Forcing her to marry Adrian against her will would
be about as effective as wrestling a bobcat into a potato sack. All that
was going to happen was a lot of hissing and bloodshed.

"So the 'dead' reward will have to suffice for me, after all."

"That's if you can even find her. You and your men have failed me
so far on that front."

Cat couldn't see it, but she imagined Freeman's long, thin nose wrinkling in disgust. "She managed to escape the carnage in the canyon, but we haven't been successful in locating where she went from there. She was tracked to the hills outside a small township, and with the perimeter we've established around Saint's Landing itself, she has to be hiding somewhere close by. We thought we had her cornered on a farm not too far from here, but it turns out it was just some terrified farmer's daughter. We paid him well for the misunderstanding and buried the evidence out in the desert. The coyotes should take care of the rest."

There was a grunt of approval. "Keep searching. I can't have her ruining things. Without that aurium, we can't move forward. She needs to be disposed of. If she were to walk into that courthouse and declare herself, any Ordonian judge would immediately grant—"

Freeman scoffed. "She'd have no proof. And her criminal record is a mile long."

Cat couldn't help but agree. No judge would just forgive her crimes that easily.

"She's got the Blessing gift, you fool. The priests know exactly who she is and they'd vouch for her without a moment's hesitation. You know how they favor their precious Blessed. No, if she is alive, she'll claim the land before I can."

"Then why hasn't she? Surely she would have done so by now if that was her intent."

These idiot men had no idea. It was exactly what she'd told Father Iggy back at the mission. There was no way on the Mother's great green earth she would ever consider claiming her birthright. She wanted no reminders of the pain and suffering she'd inflicted upon her family, of the blood practically dripping from her own hands. It would be living with the ghosts of her betrayed father and mother for the rest of her life.

There was a low growl. "I don't know why, but she's been biding her time. I bet you half the aurium on that Saints-forsaken dirt of hers that she'll do whatever she can to stop me from taking it."

"How are you so sure?"

"I have my reasons, Freeman. Just trust me on that."

Well, he was damn right about that. That was the whole reason she was here in his office in the middle of the Saints-forsaken night trying to stop him from becoming governor.

The armchair creaked again. "Well, she's on her own now. We won't stop hunting until I can bring you her head on a silver platter."

"I'm going to hold you to that, Freeman. If you want any chance at a leadership position in the coming era, do not let me down."

"Of course. In the meantime, I've secured a blacksmith named Rogers who thinks he can provide what you are looking for. It should arrive within a fortnight. And Thompson has agreed to your terms as well. It will be ready before the summit."

Cat's ears perked up. *What* would be ready before the summit? Who was Thompson? Why did they need a blacksmith?

"Excellent. Tell Rogers I want a demonstration before I pay him. I'm not taking any chances." A chair scraped again as Caldwell must have stood. "And do feel free to join us for dinner tomorrow evening if you're still in the area."

"Of course, sir." There was a rattle of military medals. "I'll take care of everything."

Another grunt, this time of dismissal. The sound of Freeman's boots disappeared into the hall, and Cat slipped a hand over her mouth to hide her breathing in the sudden silence. *Please go to bed*, she prayed in her head. *Please leave the office too.*

But Caldwell didn't leave. There was the sound of drawers opening and a cork being popped off a bottle of fresh ink. The scratching of a quill pen filled the silence as sweat began to bead on Cat's forehead, trickling down the side of her face and into the neck of her nightgown. Her back ached as she fought to hold as still as possible. The dusty smell of the curtains filled her nose and throat. She fought back a sneeze. Minutes lurched by in unending agony. Finally, after what felt like hours, Caldwell finally stood up from his desk and headed back into the hall. He closed and locked the door behind him. She waited until his footsteps creaked up the stairs before she collapsed, pushing aside the curtains. She fell hard onto her hands and knees, sucking breath into her throbbing lungs. That had been so close. *Too close.* She didn't even want to think about what would have happened if Caldwell had caught her in his office, if Freeman had seen her face and recognized exactly who she was. She dry-heaved at the thought.

A glance out the window showed a faint pink haze already growing brighter behind the foothills. Damn it, it was already almost morning. The servants would be awake soon. And she had to start her first lesson with the heathen child just after breakfast. Cat softly unlatched the office door and locked it behind herself, relying on her gift far more than she ought to give her any forewarning of coming danger. But she managed to make it back to her room without incident. Her eyelids felt as heavy as sandbags and her back ached something awful. She felt like she had barely collapsed onto the straw mattress when a maid bustled into the room with a loaf of bread, a small pat of butter, and a cup of hot black coffee.

Cat nearly screeched at the woman to go away, but such behavior could be construed as unbecoming of a novice of the church. She settled for a seething glare at the maid's back as she ripped open the curtains to bathe the room in fresh morning light. Cat fought back the desire to hiss as the brightness overwhelmed her senses.

"Good mornin', miss. Breakfast is ready for you on the dresser." The maid gave a quick little curtsy before scurrying out to the rest of her morning duties.

Cat groaned and shuffled over to the breakfast tray. She unceremoniously ripped a chunk of bread from the loaf with her teeth and chewed. The coffee was strong, which was good; she'd need the extra kick to make it through the morning. Her eyes were red and puffy from exhaustion, but there wasn't much she could do about that now. She braided her hair and piled it into a mass on top of her head, pinning it into place before she covered the entire thing with her novice bonnet. It was as good as it was going to get.

Edith was already waiting for her at one of the library tables by the time she finally stumbled into the library. Tutoring the child was going to be a complete waste of her time, especially when she could be searching for more evidence of how Caldwell was planning his take-over of the territory.

"You look like hell," Edith remarked coldly, eyeing Cat up and down.

"Don't say hell, it's not polite," Cat corrected, plopping down at the table beside her. A throbbing pain had started behind her eyes.

"You just did," Edith smirked.

"I am not a lady, I can say whatever the hell I want."

"That's strong language for a novice."

Cat shrugged a shoulder. "I'm not like other novices."

Edith's eyebrows raised as she turned away. "Clearly."

Cat propped her elbow up on the table and waved her hand in the general direction of the books. "So how does this work? What do you want to learn about first?"

Edith made a noise of disgust. "Aren't *you* supposed to be the one who decides that, Miss Rose?"

Saints. That was her job, wasn't it? Her eyes were already feeling so heavy. Her head felt as though it had been stuffed with cotton. There was no way sitting in this warm library and watching the child read text-books all day was going to help her stay awake. She needed some fresh air. "Well, I say we are heading outside."

Edith blinked. "Outside? Why?"

"Because truth be told, I don't want to be stuck inside on a beau-tiful day like today. Grab a book and let's take the lessons outside for the morning."

Something like a smile pulled at the corners of the girl's mouth. "Really? You're serious?"

Cat nodded as a large yawn overcame her. She stretched and got to her feet. "We can start with science, that's an interesting one. Pick a science book and let's head outside."

Edith hesitated, watching Cat closely as if she were waiting to be told that she was only joking.

But Cat motioned once more toward the stack of books. She didn't care which one the child picked, she just needed to look like she was learning something. "Pick one."

Edith stifled a giggle. "Um . . . okay!" She skipped into the stacks and started pulling books at random, studying their covers, and then shoving them back into place. Finally, she found one that interested her. She skipped back, her twin braids bouncing atop her shoulders, the book clutched against her chest.

"You get a good one?" Cat asked.

"Yes, I think so," Edith said breathlessly. "The cover is a pretty one."

"That's all that matters to the barons anyway," Cat mumbled to herself, leading the way toward the courtyard.

The sun grew warmer as the morning wore on, beating down upon the hedges and trees that lined the tiled courtyard. Above the fountain, several jewel-green hummingbirds swooped toward the lapping water. There wasn't much of a breeze, but at least the air was fresh and the scent of the desert flowers heavenly. Cat tilted her face toward the sun to let its light warm her cheeks while Edith read aloud.

"'When a tributary meets the larger river, they converge to carry the water to the ocean itself . . .' Wait, so all water flows downhill until it reaches the ocean?" Her gaze popped up from the book's pages.

"Yup, it does," Cat answered, not opening her eyes.

"Why doesn't it go somewhere else?"

"That's the way water flows. The path that's carved out for it. It doesn't really have a choice."

"What about the rain that soaks into the sand out in the desert? It doesn't always flow downhill to a river. Where does that water go?"

Cat thought for a moment. "That water usually goes underground and gets trapped down there. That's why we can get water from wells. You dig down deep enough, you find the water eventually."

Edith bobbed like a duckling on the surface of a pond. "It doesn't always sink down, though. That's why we get flash floods during the monsoon season, right? How come that water doesn't just sink down?"

Saints, the child liked to ask questions, but this was at least better than fishing frogs out of her bedsheets. "Well, the ground in the desert is really hard. So during the spring rainstorms, there's too much water all at once. Some of it does sink down, but the rest of it will run downhill until it finds a river."

"What do you do if you're in its way when that happens?" Edith asked, leaning forward in anticipation.

"You get the hell out of the way," Cat said with a snort.

Edith giggled. "Have you ever seen a flash flood? The ranch hands are terrified of them."

Cat winced. The ranch hands were right. There was nothing more terrifying than being caught in a canyon with a wall of water coming at you. The Wolves had lost nearly an entire herd of stolen cattle that summer when they tried to sell them across the border in Caseda. And a man or two along with them. "Sure have."

"What did you do?"

"Climbed to higher ground. The waters can come on pretty quick. A stream might look innocent, but the second the storm starts, you get outta there. Climb a tree if you can, find a crevice in the rock wall, whatever it takes to get you out of the rush of water. If you get caught in it, keep your feet up and pointed downstream so you don't get them wedged and dragged under."

"Can't you just swim?"

"Nope. Six inches of water moving fast enough is all it takes to knock you off your feet. You just keep your head above the water and hope you can grab onto something."

Edith's eyes went wide with wonder before diving back to her book. She surfaced a few more times, asking questions left and right about the shapes of rivers and why some curved but others were straight, why some had rocks while others just sand, where the fish liked to hide. Cat hated to admit it, but something about the little girl's curiosity was beginning to tug at her heartstrings.

"Tell you what," Cat finally said. "Let's go down to the river and take a look, shall we?"

Edith snapped the book shut, already bouncing on her knees. "Really?"

"Sure, we can be explorers and find the answers for ourselves."

The little girl squealed with excitement and threw her arms around Cat's middle for the briefest of moments before pulling back, looking shocked with herself. She dropped her gaze to her shuffling shoes and fiddled with the end of one of her braids. "Um, let me just get my boots and I'll meet you back here."

Cat stared after her as she rushed back inside the house, her own eyes wide with surprise.

18

Edith skipped ahead along the wide dirt path toward the river. The late-morning sun rose high over their heads, beating down on the back of Cat's neck with increasing intensity. She adjusted the novice bonnet to try to cover some of the delicate skin. Thick purple clouds swirled against the distant horizon, too far away to offer any immediate relief. Cicadas buzzed from the twisting brambles and shrubs that squatted beside the path. The day was going to be a scorcher.

"Don't forget to watch for rattlers," Edith called over her shoulder, continuing to skip joyfully as though such creatures were mere figments of her imagination.

Cat had taken this same path down to the river countless times as a child. It wasn't a large river by the end of the dry season, just a flat winding stream a few yards across and a few inches deep. Its bed was covered in large stones sticking up just enough to be good for jumping. It poured out of a crooked canyon in the nearby hills, spilling out onto the plain and serving as the border between Caldwell and Macgregor lands. Her throat tightened at the thought. This was going to be the closest she'd been since . . .

"Almost there!" Edith said, her bouncing frame disappearing behind a curve ahead. Cat froze, knowing that the curve would let her see the land itself for the first time in almost ten years. But it didn't matter. Once she stopped Caldwell, she'd never have to set eyes on the cursed dirt ever again. She steeled her spine, took a breath, and followed.

The familiar rushing of the water across the rocks welcomed her back. The water was even lower than normal for this time of year, but with the desert monsoon season just beginning, that would soon change. Scraggly brambles and rugged chaparral lined the banks on either side. It looked no different from the last time she'd played here, just as the land on the other side had not changed. At least she couldn't see her family's estate—or what remained of it—from this vantage point. Thank the Saints. That thought alone gave her the courage to keep going.

She let Edith take the lead, picking their way along the riverbank toward the hills. Cat pointed out features of the river, explaining how to tell which parts were deepest, and some of the creatures that lived along the river's edge. A white heron took flight at their approach, a small fish clasped in its razor-thin beak. Edith seemed particularly excited about a fat frog, chasing it into the shallows and catching it easily between her hands.

"Well, that explains the frog in my sheets." Cat grinned, crossing her arms across her chest.

A twinkle glinted in Edith's eye. "I'm surprised you didn't mention it before."

"Well, your brother caught it before I had the chance to discover it for myself. He also replaced the flower vase."

Edith let out an exasperated sigh, finally letting the frog go and then splashing her way back to the shoreline. "He always ruins my fun."

"That's what brothers do."

"Do you have any brothers?"

Cat's thoughts drifted to Pedro and Soap, their names sending a prickle of pain along the edges of her mind. The closest things to brothers she'd ever had. "I used to."

"What happened to them?" Edith's tone took on a sudden note of panic. A pang of pity twinged inside Cat's chest. Clearly the idea of losing her brother worried Edith.

"I haven't heard from them in a while, but I'm sure they are fine. They just . . . left to do other things." She forced herself to smile, appeasing the child's fears.

"Oh." A noticeable weight seemed to lift off Edith's shoulders. "That's good."

Cat hadn't realized how deep the girl's fears ran. Adrian really did mean the world to her. Cat didn't want to think about what would happen when she quit. Would Caldwell really send Edith away to a convent? Would Edith's heart survive being separated from her brother? Hopefully their father would be arrested by the Ordonian authorities before he could do any such thing.

Cat watched the little girl play, kicking water into the air and laughing as though all her worries had taken flight with the flock of sparrows she'd startled from the bushes. She had no idea what her father was planning, what Cat was planning. In Edith's mind, she was playing in the river with her governess while her loving brother waited to welcome her home. Something about her joy, her freedom, her—well, maybe not *innocence*—but certainly her childlike understanding of the world built a pressure inside Cat's chest. Tears stung the corners of her eyes, and she blinked them back.

Was this what she'd been like as a little girl? Blissfully ignorant of the evils that swirled around her like hungry buzzards, circling, waiting for their moment to strike? Cat shoved the thought down.

She cleared her throat. "Have you ever caught tadpoles? It's fun to watch them grow into full-grown frogs." Cat lifted a small glass jar she'd pilfered from the kitchens while Edith had gone to change. "An excellent way to study the life cycle of frogs. For science, of course."

✦ · · · · ◉ · · · · ✦

After several hours of tadpole hunting, they stood on the riverbank soaked to the waist and caked in a fine layer of mud. Their jar was full to the brim with river water and a few wiggling tadpoles of acceptable quality.

Edith tapped the jar with her finger. "I didn't know frogs started out like little fish."

"They eventually grow legs and can come out of the water. We will have to find them a bigger home as they grow, but you'll get to see them change for yourself."

"I love the river." Edith sighed with contentment, hugging the jar to her chest.

Cat blinked up at the sun, which was just beginning to tip into late afternoon. The buzzing of the cicadas seemed to grow louder as the heat of the day intensified. "I used to dream about running away and living at the river when I was little. I had it all planned out, I'd live in one of the little caves in a canyon, hunt fish, and drink fresh water from the spring." She tickled a finger into Edith's side.

Edith giggled. "That sounds wonderful. But I'd want to bring Adrian with me. He could be my servant and pick berries or something."

"I'm sure he'd love that," Cat smirked.

"He'd have to work to earn his keep, or I'd throw him right out into the desert."

"You're a harsh master."

Edith shrugged. "The desert is a harsh wilderness. If Adrian can't handle it, then he'll get the boot."

Cat laughed, one of the first true laughs she'd experienced since her time in Caseda. It felt refreshing in a way, like warming her hands over a fire after wandering through a cold, dark night. Edith laughed too. Perhaps Adrian had been right—there was a sweet little heart beneath her sour exterior after all.

They made their way back toward the house, Edith peppering Cat with more questions about frogs and the life cycles of various animals. Cat assured her they would write all of her questions down and hunt for the answers together in the library for tomorrow's lessons. Edith seemed delighted.

They were so busy chattering as they entered the courtyard, they didn't notice Baron Caldwell standing in front of the fountain until his voice cracked across the open space like a whip.

"*Edith!*"

Both girls froze, the jar of tadpoles almost slipping out of Edith's now trembling grip. Cat's heart skipped a beat. She wasn't hiding behind a curtain this time. She could see the harsh lines of his face, the thick brush of his mustache, the air of superiority hanging about him like an expensive cologne. She willed herself to move, but her muscles remained as frozen as a hare's caught in the gaze of a stalking predator.

His black traveling coat billowed out behind him as he strode toward them from the direction of the stables, sparks dancing inside his dark eyes. "What on the Mother's great green earth have you been *doing*? You are covered in mud. "

Edith's lip shook, and she took a small step back, clutching the jar tight against her chest as if it were a talisman that could protect her from her father's disapproval. "I'm sorry, Father. I—we were—we just—"

Her father grabbed a handful of her sleeve and then withdrew it in disgust, wiping the dried flakes of mud off his perfectly white gloves. "When I come home, I should not have to worry about the inappropriate state of my daughter. What if I had guests with me? Where have you been?" He made no effort to acknowledge Cat's presence, treating her as though she were nothing more than another one of the potted palms lining the courtyard.

"The river," Edith said, sounding as small as a mouse.

"The river," he repeated flatly. "Again."

"We were . . ." She lifted the jar to show him and swallowed hard. "Studying tadpoles for my lessons."

She flinched as he ripped the jar from her grasp. "Tadpoles?" he scoffed. "Is this how a proper Ordonian lady behaves? Stomping through mud and the Saints know what else to catch wild animals?" He lifted the jar and regarded the tadpoles as if they were loathsome insects.

"We were studying them, Father. I wanted to see how they would—"

"*Studying* tadpoles? What use is that to a baroness? To a lady of the court? You should be studying languages, etiquette, something befitting the future wife of a landowner."

Tears pooled in the corners of Edith's eyes. She reached toward the jar. "Father, please, I just want to—"

Cat felt the urge to step in, to say something in Edith's defense. But the thought of Caldwell turning that gaze onto her, of really studying her face in detail, kept her tongue tightly behind her teeth.

Her father snorted once more in disgust. "No. I will not allow *my* daughter to behave like . . . like some kind of . . ." He couldn't even finish. His nostrils flaring, he tossed the jar to the side, sending the glass shattering to pieces and the tadpoles flailing against the sun-heated courtyard tiles. Cat's heart lurched, but her fear kept her rooted in place.

"No!" Edith screamed. She dove for the ground, her desperate fingers reaching for the tiny suffocating creatures.

But Caldwell caught her by the arm and wrenched her back up. "Don't you dare crawl on the ground like a servant. You stand straight and tall and proud. Like a Caldwell." His tone was low but dangerous.

"No!" Edith screamed again, trying to wrench herself out of his grip. "They'll *die*! Let me go!"

The restraint in Caldwell's temper seemed to snap. "How dare you disrespect me," he said, lifting his hand into the air.

Edith's pupils contracted in fear. And finally, Cat could take it no longer.

"Stop!" Cat stepped forward. "It was my fault!"

Caldwell turned slowly to look at her with the same disgusted regard he had given the tadpoles. "Excuse me? Who the hell are you?"

Cat cleared her throat and steeled her spine. "I'm Rose. The new governess. From the mission."

Caldwell straightened and appraised her, his nose wrinkled ever so slightly above his thick black mustache. "From the mission?" It clearly was not a positive recommendation.

Cat exposed her palms to him, her pulse pounding a panicked beat inside her ears. "It was my idea to go to the river and catch the tadpoles. I'm so sorry. Please do not place any blame on the girl. I take full responsibility."

The sound of bootheels running and then skidding to a stop filled

Cat's ears. When she turned, Adrian had materialized beside them. Instead of the fine suit he'd worn to greet her yesterday, he wore simple work slacks and a plain white buttoned shirt. Perspiration dampened beneath his arms, and he smelled strongly of hay. He tipped his hat back out of his face and discreetly ushered Edith away from Caldwell and behind him instead. She clung to his legs, eyeing their father with a mixture of terror and hatred.

"What's going on?" Adrian asked casually. "I was coming in for a drink and heard screaming."

"The new governess thought it appropriate to take Edith to the river to catch *tadpoles*." He sounded almost amused, as if he wanted Adrian to share in the outrageousness of such an idea.

Adrian blinked at Cat, his brows pulling together in confusion.

"We were studying science," Edith mumbled from behind her brother's legs.

The baron's face reddened again, but before he could say anything else, Cat cut in instead. "This was entirely my fault. I'm sorry, I wasn't aware of the preferred subjects. Now that I know, I assure you we will focus on topics appropriate for a young lady."

Caldwell leveled a threatening gaze toward his son and lifted a finger, shaking it a mere inch from Adrian's nose. "Make sure this is taken care of. I refuse to let Edith embarrass me any more than she already has. I have more pressing matters to attend to."

With the swish of his dusty traveling cloak, he stormed toward the house, leaving Cat's heart still thundering in her chest.

CHAPTER
19

Adrian released his breath in a huff. His father could have done so much more damage, but his haste to get back to the house had spared them from far greater upset. Edith threw herself on the ground the moment their father was out of sight, scrambling to save the suffocating tadpoles. He and Rose bent down to help her. Together, the three of them saved the creatures and found them a new home in the fountain. The tadpoles' exhausted little bodies wiggled back to life as they floated above the painted tiles. It wasn't the river, but it was good enough.

"That way you can still watch them grow into frogs," Rose said, placing a hand on the little girl's shoulder. "And when they are big enough to start croaking, we'll sneak them back to the river."

Edith leaned into the governess's touch. Adrian's chest tightened at the sight of Rose offering comfort to Edith, of Edith willingly accepting comfort from anyone other than him. What had passed between them since dinner last night? How had Rose gotten through to her? He hadn't dared to dream such a thing would ever be possible after their mother died.

Edith wiped her nose and nodded. "I'm going to head upstairs and get cleaned up."

"That's probably for the best." Adrian glanced toward the house.

"Father is having some guests join us for dinner tonight, so his standards will be higher than usual."

Edith grimaced before she scampered off to her rooms. Adrian watched her leave, the tightness in his chest squeezing a bit harder.

"Who will be joining us?" Rose asked tentatively, still standing beside him.

"I believe it's the captain and a few of his men. We have preparations to make before the guests start arriving for the summit. It should be a pleasant evening, though. Mrs. Rothschild always outdoes herself when the captain dines with us."

"Pleasant indeed." Rose looked as though she'd swallowed something bitter. "And is this a dinner I must attend? Surely it would be better if—"

"Nonsense. My father will expect you there to keep Edith in line. And I would love to have your company there as well."

"If you insist." Cat gave him a tight smile and turned to leave.

"Wait," Adrian called before he could stop himself. "I—uh—wanted to thank you. For what you did for Edith."

"What do you mean?"

"Standing up and protecting her from my father like that. I—" He rubbed the back of his warm neck. "I could tell it meant a lot to her. And it meant a lot to me."

Rose's cheeks pinked. "Well, he was being an ass," she mumbled.

"Excuse me?"

"I mean . . ." The pink in her cheeks deepened. "It *was* my fault. I couldn't let her take the blame. It was my idea to go to the river. A bad idea, obviously."

He could have sworn she'd said . . . oh well. Maybe he had misheard her. "It wasn't a bad idea at all. My father just disagrees about what is appropriate to teach a young lady. He pretends like he doesn't, but he cares very deeply about what our peers in the capital think. She did seem to be having fun though. I've never seen her like that with another governess."

Rose crossed her arms. "Because all the rest sound like they were dead boring. I don't blame Edith for scaring them off."

Adrian stared at her.

"Anyway"—she waved a dismissive hand—"I'll make sure we cover more appropriate and useless topics tomorrow. Perhaps you could provide me with some kind of list? How to properly twirl one's skirts and which fork to use at dinner perhaps?"

He bit back a laugh. "Perhaps. Though I'm sure my father believes the ladies of Saelum make better use of learning to manage a homestead, things like math and financials, writing eloquent letters, horse riding . . ."

Rose's head snapped up, a glimmer of excitement shining across her countenance. "Horse riding?"

But Adrian sucked in a breath. He hated to stifle her excitement. "That's probably one area you won't have much luck, I'm afraid."

Her face fell. "Why? I'm very capable with horses. I'm sure I can teach her one of the only useful things she needs to learn."

He wanted to eat his words. She must have thought he didn't think she was capable. "No, no. It's not that. It's just—Edith is afraid of them. I haven't been able to get her on a horse for two years."

Rose scoffed. "That's unacceptable. Everyone needs to know how to ride a horse, especially the daughter of a cattle rancher."

"I agree. But if I may offer you my suggestion, I would avoid the stables with Edith. I don't imagine it would end well for either of you."

But he could already see the idea sparking back to life and solidifying into a plan within Rose's hazel eyes.

"Perhaps you need not coddle her. Give her a chance to face her fears?" she said with an arched brow.

The novice was clearly as stubborn as his sister. He lifted his hands in defeat, smiling a little despite himself. Rose had convinced Edith to like her more than the others so far. Maybe she was more capable than he imagined. She certainly kept taking him by surprise. "Fine, you are welcome to try, but don't say I didn't warn you."

"We shall see, then, Mr. Caldwell. I don't recommend underestimating me." Rose turned up her nose at the challenge, a smile flashing across her face.

Adrian fixated on the gentle curve of her lips, her smile illuminating her features like a ray of sunlight breaking through a cloud bank. He lost his memory for words for a moment.

She must have noticed because just as quickly as it appeared, the smile was gone, hidden back beneath the clouds. Her gaze returned to the ground. Saints Almighty. He'd messed things up again.

"Speaking of horses," she said more to her feet than to him. "May I use one this Sunday?"

Adrian swallowed. Hard. "Um, yes. That shouldn't be a problem. May I ask what for?"

"To ride into Saint's Landing for Sunday services at the mission. I promised Father Iggy I would check in with him from time to time. He told me he'd be at the mission in Saint's Landing until after the election."

Ah. Of course she'd want to attend church services and visit with the priest who had raised her. "Nonsense. The roads are much too dangerous for a young woman to travel alone. I can take you in the coach."

Rose did not look up. "No, I really don't mind—"

But Adrian clapped his hands together. "It's already decided. I won't allow you to travel alone, and we haven't been to services ourselves in several months. I think it would be good for Edith to get back into the habit."

"Thank you, sir." She curtsied briefly, though still seeming more put out than grateful. "Now if you'll excuse me, since you are insisting I attend, I should probably clean up for dinner too."

Adrian blew out his breath again as he watched her go, needing a cold drink of water now more than ever. He felt like a fool for clearly upsetting her again. He couldn't place his finger on what it was, but something about Rose unsettled his stomach. It was not an unpleasant feeling, more of an anxious flutter that made him want to follow her and find out exactly what about her intrigued him. He felt as though he knew her already somehow, a familiarity in spirit that comforted him as much as it excited him. His father would never approve of any attentions toward a governess, much less an orphaned ward of the church. Not to mention, the girl was a novice. But then again, she'd taken no vows yet. Perhaps she had no mind to join the church permanently . . .

He shook his head to clear his thoughts. Why on earth was he considering what Rose's plans for the future were? He had no business wondering such things. It must just be his relief at her choosing to stay, her seeming to form a connection to Edith. She clearly disliked him on some level. Perhaps his attraction toward her was nothing more than his desire to prove her misjudgments about him incorrect.

Yes, yes, that had to be it. He did not like anyone to misjudge his character. It was his greatest frustration in life, for others to assume him like his father, not to see him as an individual with his own heart and mind and soul. This mysterious draw toward Rose was simply his own desire to prove the quality of his character to her. Nothing more.

Nothing more at all.

✦ · · · · ◉ · · · · ✦

Adrian carefully washed away any trace of dirt beneath his fingernails and selected one of his best dinner jackets. Captain Freeman dined at the house often enough, but his father's expectations for excellence never wavered, even in familiar company. Adrian had just finished putting on his gloves when a servant's knock sounded at the door.

"Your father asked to see you before dinner, sir." The servant bowed his head.

"Thank you, Joseph. In his office, I assume?"

"Yes, sir."

Adrian checked his appearance one last time in the mirror before deeming himself acceptable enough for his father's scrutiny.

Baron Caldwell was waiting for him, already seated behind his desk like a king upon his wooden throne. Adrian entered his domain with tentative caution.

"Adrian." His father nodded a quick greeting. His eyes briefly assessed Adrian's attire for acceptability, which must have been met because he continued, "We have an important matter to discuss before the summit next week."

Adrian swallowed. "Alright."

"Sit." His father motioned to the empty chair facing him. Adrian obeyed, his nerves stretching tighter, waiting for the moment they would snap. His father never invited him to *sit*.

The older man folded his gloved hands across the surface of the desk and regarded Adrian with a peculiar look—something close to pity. An unpleasant taste rose in Adrian's throat.

"I know you are young, but with the political instability likely to take place in the wake of the governor's death, we need to secure the favor and support of the other barons."

Adrian furrowed his brow. Hadn't he told his father his thoughts on the political climate only last week?

"I'm sure you are aware of my intentions to run as his replacement, of the importance of impressing our guests once they arrive."

"Yes, I know the barons vote on the recommendation they will make to the emperor—"

"My standing," his father continued as if Adrian had not spoken, "*our* standing amongst the barons would be greatly improved through an alliance with one of the more powerful families of Ordonia."

"Father, we are already one of the most influential—"

"Yes, we are. But power and influence can always grow, and we need it now, more than ever. Especially when influence does not always translate into *favor*. For that, I will need your cooperation."

Adrian rubbed his chin, unsure how he had anything to do with this. "For the vote?"

A muscle twitched with impatience in his father's forehead. "Yes, for the vote," he said tightly.

"Alright, but what does that have to do with me?"

"We need *alliances*," his father repeated as if it were obvious. He reached down and slid a piece of paper across the desk. Adrian glanced down, quickly scanning the five or so names of young women neatly written in his father's hand. He knew the names, of course: all daughters of prominent barons and baronesses across the territory.

All daughters of marriageable age.

The realization slammed into Adrian like a kick from a horse. He opened his mouth to object, but his father lifted a hand and cut him off before he could.

"I already said I know you are young. We do not need to rush any plans for a wedding, but I do believe it is time you showed some interest in the marriage market. Ask some ladies to dance at the summit gathering we are hosting, allow me to spread word of your search for a future baroness. The desire of the other families to make a prudent match for their daughters might provide some excellent leverage that I—we—can use to our advantage."

Adrian's jaw snapped shut. His father wanted to use him as leverage with the other barons? He shouldn't be surprised; nothing would stand in the way of his father's ambitions. But Adrian had no desire to begin any kind of search for a wife. He had assumed he still had several more years at least. He knew it had been ages, but the thought of marrying someone, anyone who wasn't—

As if he could read Adrian's thoughts, his father's tone softened uncharacteristically. "You must accept the fact that she is gone, Adrian."

Adrian's eyes snapped up, his heartstrings thrumming. "What do you mean?"

His father sighed. "I will not pretend I haven't noticed. You have shown little interest in any young lady since you've come of age. I was courting ladies left and right when I was nineteen. I know you had visions for your future, but Catriona Macgregor is dead. The sooner you accept that fact and move on, the better it will be for you."

A lump formed in Adrian's throat. For some reason, Rose's brief flash of a smile flitted through his thoughts.

"I wouldn't say I've had *no* interest . . ."

His father exposed his gloved palms. "Adrian, please. I wanted you to marry her too. I did everything in my power to arrange it. I would still arrange it now if it were a possibility. To unite the Caldwell lands with the Macgregors' would have been an excellent arrangement for us all. I also know how much you cared for the girl—as much of a handful as she was," he added with a roll of his eyes. "You two were inseparable. And your mother desired it as well."

A burning sensation began behind Adrian's eyes at the mention of his mother, but he stuffed the feeling down. He didn't want to show any weakness in front of his father. Even if his father had been paying closer attention than he'd realized.

It wasn't that he *pined* after Catriona. Saints, they'd only been children. But he'd always imagined, in the way that children do, that someday he would marry his best friend. After she died, he'd just lost interest in letting himself get that close to someone again.

He thought about the geode sitting on the dressing table in his room—a rough, unappealing outer layer of stone that hid beautiful purple amethyst crystals within its depths. He remembered the day he and Catriona had found it in the desert, how she'd cracked it open and squealed with joy that they'd found such a beautiful treasure. How she had insisted he be the one to keep it. "*Remember that things aren't always what they seem to be,*" she'd said. "*You look like your dad on the outside, but you're something much better on the inside.*"

He'd looked at that rock on his dresser every morning for the last ten years as he put his mother's necklace of Saint Veritas around his neck, letting them both remind him that he wasn't the same as his father. That he could be something better.

Finally, he looked his father square in the eye. "I *know* she's gone. I just haven't thought about anyone in that way because I've had other things to worry about."

His father stood with a triumphant smile, pushing his chair back from his desk. "Well, it is time you worry about more adult concerns, for your own future." He thrust the list of names toward Adrian again. "At least make an effort."

Adrian stared down at the list, wanting to read each of their names aloud, but all of them tasted bitter on his tongue. None of them would ever replace Catriona. But for once, his father was right. She *was* gone. She had been for almost ten years. He had avoided this issue for long enough.

Again Rose's face danced along the edge of his thoughts. A governess. An orphan. A novice. He didn't need to imagine his father's response were he to give any of his precious leverageable attention to anyone outside the gilded circle of the barons.

He took up the list and folded it before placing it in his pocket.

His father smiled, the whiteness of his teeth standing in stark contrast to the dark hair lining his upper lip. "Thank you, Adrian. It's much easier for you to cooperate than for me to make the final decision for you."

Adrian turned to leave the office. The list weighed as heavy as a boulder in his pocket.

20

Cat tried not to panic that Captain Freeman was coming to dinner. There was no reason for him to suspect her. But if anyone were to disrupt her plan to stop Baron Caldwell, it would be that young, arrogant bastard.

She considered skipping dinner altogether, feigning illness or hiding in her room. But she also knew that would draw more attention. Besides, there was a chance she could hear some important conversations. Conversations that could involve their plans to secure the governorship. She had to be there; there was no other option.

It would be dangerous to let Freeman see her face close-up, but at least on the train, she'd been filthy and bruised after weeks in that jail cell. Her face had been coated in a layer of dirt, her hair had been matted and far redder than it was now. And he wouldn't be *expecting* to see her here, which would work in her favor, but she'd need to take some extra precautions just in case. After hiding her hair securely beneath her bonnet and adding extra powder to her nose to disguise her freckles, she finally descended the steps to dinner. Her vision flashed a warning just before she entered the room.

She knew being in such close contact with Captain Freeman was a risk, but it was a risk she had to take. The captain and a few of his men were already sitting, deep in conversation with Baron Caldwell at the head of the table. An empty seat waited for her between Adrian and Edith, mercifully at the other end from the captain. When she stepped inside, the men immediately rose to their feet in greeting. She could feel Freeman's dark gaze focus on her, and she kept her own firmly focused on the floor, the perfect appearance of humility and supplication.

"Gentlemen, my daughter's new governess, Miss Rose from . . . some mission in Polvo," Baron Caldwell supplied quickly with a brief flick of his hand. Cat lifted her gaze to curtsy. The soldiers all nodded in greeting before returning to their seats, obviously as dismissive of her presence as the baron. Freeman, however, eyed her much longer than the others, fixing her with a scrutiny that sent shivers down the length of her spine. She met his gaze only briefly, enough to watch the corner of his mouth curl up into a cruel semblance of a smile, just as she'd seen in her vision. But then he turned his attention back to the baron and took his seat as well. Cat tried to steady her shaking hands.

Adrian leaned over to her the moment she sat down. "You look lovely this evening, Miss Rose. I'm so glad you could join us."

She offered him a small smile but did not speak. She wasn't sure she trusted using her voice in front of Freeman just yet.

Edith tugged on Cat's simple brown sleeve. "What are we doing tomorrow?" she whispered conspiratorially.

"Something fun," Cat whispered back. "Don't worry, we'll find a way to make your dad happy that doesn't involve both of us wanting to poke our eyes out."

Edith dimpled. From the corner of her eye, Cat noticed Adrian smiling and shaking his head.

"I still don't think it's a good idea, Miss Rose," he said.

"How unfortunate. I happen to think it's a splendid idea."

"Oooo, do you know what she has planned for tomorrow?" Edith whispered around Cat to her brother.

"I do, but I believe it is a secret and I don't want to spoil the surprise." Adrian lifted a fist to his mouth to hide a snicker.

Cat's stomach soured unpleasantly. "I think that is a wise decision, Mr. Caldwell. Knowing when to keep important secrets is an admirable virtue, after all." A steel edge had slipped into her tone—and Adrian seemed to catch it.

His face turned more serious as he considered her. "I couldn't agree more, Miss Rose."

She offered him another tight smile and turned to watch the servants bring in the first course. She could still feel Adrian's gaze upon her, so she turned to address Edith instead.

But Edith was looking between Adrian and Cat with a look almost like concern. "Are you mad at my brother?" Edith asked in a small voice. "Has he done something wrong?"

The little girl was clearly astute and sensitive to the goings-on around her. Cat made a mental note to be more careful. "Absolutely not. Everything is fine."

Edith didn't look so sure; she continued to glance between them. Cat reached over and placed a hand over Edith's. "I am just nervous in present company is all. I promise it has nothing to do with your brother."

"Nervous in present company? I am sorry to hear that, Miss . . . Rose was it?"

Cat knew the voice before she even looked down the table to see who had spoken. A fist seemed to tighten around her throat.

She swallowed hard. "I just mean to say that I have not been around many soldiers, and it is my first meal with the baron himself. I hope to make a good impression."

"Oh, I'm sure you will make a fine impression. You certainly are off to a wonderful start from what I hear," Freeman said, his lip curling again. "Where did they say you are from again?"

"The mission in Polvo," Cat said, the tightness in her throat intensifying.

"I wasn't aware the priest in Polvo had any wards under his care." Freeman took a casual sip of wine from his glass. He was baiting her. She didn't need her vision to warn her that her next words must be carefully chosen.

"I've been at the mission in Saint's Landing the last few years, but I still consider Polvo my home. I was very close to the priest there as a child."

"Hmmm." Freeman took another sip of blood-red wine.

"How are you liking the vintage for tonight, Freeman? I favor the Davenport more myself, but a nice bottle from the vineyards of Casterleigh complements the beef, I think," the baron interrupted. He must have decided that too much conversation had been wasted on a lowly governess because he immediately reengaged Freeman in some discussion about the local wineries.

The first course, a warm potato soup with tiny sprigs of rosemary, was placed before her, and she couldn't help but notice Freeman watching her out of the corner of his eye. She bowed her head and prayed over the meal, making sure she did not make the same mistake she'd made with Adrian the night before. The captain seemed appeased, though he still threw glances at her throughout the rest of the meal.

She also tried to watch Edith's table manners, making sure that her elbows were not on the table and that she was using the right utensils. That some part of her brain still remembered these foolish customs amazed her. She thought the instructions from her own governess had disappeared somewhere beneath Amos's lessons of shooting and stealing cattle. They were rusty to be sure, but still more present than she imagined they would be. Father Iggy's refreshers over the past week must have helped too. She tried not to giggle at the memory. Father Iggy was surprisingly refined for an exiled, bootlegging priest.

"What has you grinning?" Adrian asked.

"Just thinking of proving you wrong about Edith tomorrow," she said sweetly.

A sparkle of mischief shone in his eye. "Shall we make a bet on that, Miss Rose?"

She placed a hand over her heart and feigned great insult. "I am a novice, Mr. Caldwell. I do not participate in such things as gambling."

He gave her a flat look.

Cat blinked.

"Fine, I'll take that wager," she said, rolling her eyes. "But if I win, Edith gets to decide your punishment."

Adrian's eyes went wide with mock horror. "I don't know, that's a very steep bet. I shall only agree if my prize for winning is that she does the same for you."

"I like this wager," Edith said, popping a roll into her mouth. "Oh, the fun I will have . . ." Her expression became wistful and dreamy.

"Adrian, are you listening?" the baron snapped from down the table.

Adrian's head whipped around so fast that Cat swore she heard his neck crack. "Um, no, I'm sorry, Father. I was speaking with—"

"I was telling Captain Freeman about your decision."

"My decision?"

His father's eyes narrowed. "Your decision for the *future*?"

"Oh. Um. Yes." Adrian quickly wiped his mouth with his napkin and returned it to his lap. "Just that my father has asked me to consider courting one of the daughters of the other barons. To strengthen our alliances with some of the more powerful families."

Edith squeaked in surprise, but Cat placed her hand over the little girl's again to remind her to hold her tongue. Adrian himself seemed suddenly uneasy, almost as if he was avoiding making eye contact with Cat. "Not that I have anyone selected or am in any rush to hasten the process," he added.

"A pity the girl from the Macgregor homestead disappeared," Captain Freeman said, twirling a noodle around his fork. "What an excellent alliance that would have been. Two of the largest ranches in southern Saelum united." His gaze again flitted to Cat.

Cat swallowed hard, the pounding in her ears nearly drowning out Adrian's response.

"Well, she didn't *disappear*. She died in the fire with her family." Adrian seemed suddenly very preoccupied with his napkin. "She's no longer an option."

"Such a pity," Freeman repeated, sliding the twirled noodle off his fork with his teeth.

"You mentioned to my father you had a shipment coming into one of the storehouses this evening. Are you in need of any assistance bringing it in?" Adrian said, clearly wanting to change the subject.

Cat's attention sharpened. A shipment coming in? Of what? Could it be from the blacksmith Freeman had mentioned in Caldwell's office last night?

Freeman waved a hand. "No, no. My men can handle it just fine. You have much more important things to manage, I'm sure."

Baron Caldwell grunted his agreement. "Freeman's right, Adrian. We will retire to the study after dinner and discuss our plans for this next week."

Adrian nodded, seeming somewhat deflated. "Yes, Father."

Cat, however, felt a rush of excitement. It looked like she wouldn't be getting much sleep again tonight either. Taking the risk to come to dinner had paid off indeed.

✦ · · · · ◉ · · · · ✦

Cat waited for the house to settle for the night before sneaking down to the laundry and finding a clean pair of slacks and a shirt. They were probably Adrian's, but there was no way she was sneaking out to one of the ranch storehouses through the brush in the middle of the night in a long novice dress. The slacks were much too big for her, but with a leather belt around her waist and her Murietta pistol shoved into the waistband, they would stay up well enough. Her short novice boots looked a bit odd with her unorthodox attire—she would have much preferred her own taller ones—but she was not going for fashionable.

She was going for revenge.

With the house finally quiet and the servants gone to bed, Cat sneaked out the back. She had vague memories of the storehouses being out past the stables, so she stuck to the shadows and made her way toward them. The moon was not quite full, but large enough to cast a silver glow across the sparse shrubs. She wove between them like a wraith, keeping her back bent and her tread light. The heat of the night hung heavy and imposing—lighter than the oppressive dry heat of the day, but only just.

Finally, several hundred yards past the stables, three looming shadows broke the smooth outline of the distant foothills. They had to be the storehouses.

While two of the side buildings remained dark and lifeless, in the center the flicker of gas lamps shone inside one of the upper-story windows. A horse whinnied. A man's voice called out something Cat couldn't quite hear. But clearly she'd found where Freeman was overseeing the incoming "shipment."

With a thrill of victory sending her pulse fluttering, Cat stalked forward.

"Alright, Caldwell," she whispered to herself, eyeing the ladder that rested casually against the side of the storehouse as though it were waiting for her. "What the hell are you hiding?"

CHAPTER

21

The ladder appeared much taller from the top than it had from the solid safety of the ground, but Cat had had no choice but to climb it if she wanted to spy on the contents of Caldwell's mysterious midnight shipment. She gripped the rough, splintered wood of the windowsill with every ounce of her strength, the wooden ladder wobbling precariously beneath her. Damn, murderous cattle baron. This had better be worth literally risking her neck.

Cat kept her head low as she peered inside, the scent of dust and mildewed wood filling her nose. The storehouse was large, with an open space in the center and crates and barrels piled high along the walls. A small group of soldiers was gathered around a simple wooden cart—a cart holding what appeared to be several plain sacks of flour.

Flour? Surely the baron's mysterious shipment was not baking supplies for the upcoming gathering. Cat blew a strand of stray hair out of her face and lifted her head a little higher to get a better look. The sacks were not stamped with images of wheat, but *horseshoes*. These sacks had come from a blacksmith. What on earth did a blacksmith make that was transported as a powder? Gunpowder? No, that wasn't right. Usually such a flammable and fragile substance was shipped in barrels or powder kegs. And certainly not stored in sacks in a crowded storehouse where a single spark could destroy everything around it.

"Get them unloaded quickly. And by the Saints, be *careful*!" Freeman ordered his inferiors, his back to where Cat was hiding.

Two of the soldiers jumped into the cart and began tossing the sacks to two more on the ground.

"Sir, is this the package you were talking about?" Another came around from the other side of the cart carrying a small parcel wrapped in simple brown paper. "Rogers said to get it to you directly."

Freeman took the package gently into his gloved hands. "Excellent. The baron will be pleased. I'll take this up to the house myself. Finish unloading and make sure they get packed into the crates before dawn. We need to get them shipped out first thing in the morning."

"Yes sir."

Cat watched them unload the sacks and pile them up beside wooden crates. It was too far away to make out any address or name stamped onto the crates, but she had a funny feeling that if she inspected them, she'd find the name Thompson somewhere on the wooden boards.

There weren't many of the mysterious sacks of powder, only about a dozen. Just as two soldiers were lifting one of the last sacks into a crate, the corner of the sackcloth snagged. She did not hear the small rip, but she watched with fascination as a glimmering gold powder dribbled out and onto the floor.

It was gold dust . . . or even possibly powdered aurium?

"You idiot! You're spilling it," one soldier complained. "Seriously, Edgar, you should just spare us all from your clumsiness and shoot yourself now."

Cat was not used to being taken by surprise. When you were Blessed by Saint Prudentia, patron saint of wisdom and forethought, threats against you were always flashed inside your mind a moment before they happened. It did not, however, warn her of danger to others.

She bit back a scream as Edgar, the young soldier who'd ripped the bag, pulled a gun from the holster around his hip and placed the barrel against the side of his head. His companion's eyes went wide, his hand lifting as if to stop him before . . .

BANG.

Cat squeezed her eyes shut as the bullet tore through Edgar's temple. The *thump* of his body hitting the floor echoed through the stunned silence of the storehouse. One of the other soldiers yelled. There was a flurry of activity, and when Cat looked back, his body was obscured from view by the legs of the other soldiers.

"I warned you all to be careful," Freeman said, sounding rather bored and detached. "Bury him out in the desert and get back to work."

Cat's pulse thundered in her veins. She wanted to take her pistol out of her waistband and lodge a bullet in *Freeman's* head, but she knew that would draw unwanted attention. Plus, it wouldn't help her discover Caldwell's intentions for the aurium powder.

The ladder beneath her wobbled precariously. *Damn it!* She'd shifted her weight out of shock when the gun had gone off. She gripped the window ledge for dear life just as the ladder cracked and then toppled out of sight. Cat clung to the peeling windowsill, her fingers screaming in protest. The bushes and brambles covering the ground had muffled some of the rickety ladder's impact, but apparently not enough.

"Did you hear something?" Freeman snapped suddenly. Cat prayed he couldn't see the tips of her reddened fingers peeking over the window ledge from where he was standing. "Check the perimeter. Bring anyone you find straight to me."

Cat's throat tightened in terror. If she pulled herself up, Freeman would see her for sure. She glanced down to where her feet dangled several yards above the ground. A drop from this height would not end well either.

But better to break an ankle than face Freeman alone. She grit her teeth and let go.

The impact rattled her bones. She tried to bend her knees to absorb some of the shock, but it wasn't quite enough. A jolt of pain rocketed up both her legs as she toppled sideways into the brush and landed hard on the ladder. Bramble thorns dug into the skin of her exposed forearms. Her left ankle in particular gave a nasty throb as she scrambled on her hands and knees, trying to get as far away from the storehouse as she could.

When the sounds of boots running reached her ears, she froze, not wanting to draw attention to her location. Her chest rose and fell in rapid breaths as she lowered herself on her stomach beneath a creosote bush. The strong scent of its leaves surrounded her as she strained to hear their voices over the pounding of her heart.

"Looks like a ladder."

"I saw that thing up against the barn earlier. Think someone could have been on it?"

Cat heard the sound of a boot kicking the rickety wood. "Nah. This thing don't look strong enough to hold a man. Probably just a coyote or something sniffing around."

There was a grumble of general consent from the other soldiers before they began to shuffle back to the storehouse entrance.

Cat let out a breath. That'd been too close. She eased herself out from beneath the bush and gingerly tested some weight on her ankle. It didn't seem broken, but it would swell up something nasty by the morning. She'd be limping for a day or two at least.

But that seemed to be the least of her worries.

"*Saints*," she hissed, inspecting the cuts running up and down her arms. Tiny bits of crushed purple flowers clung to her skin, and a rash was already beginning to turn red and itch. Of all the luck on the Mother's great green earth—she must have fallen into a bush of scorpion weed. A string of curses that would have made Father Iggy blush escaped her mouth. If she didn't treat it soon, she'd be even more miserable than she was now.

Stumbling back toward the house was a considerably clumsier experience than her excursion out, but her gift remained blessedly silent, meaning there was no danger to her. At least not yet. Freeman and his men were likely still occupied with their shipment of aurium powder.

Aurium powder? What in the name of the Fallen Saint could they be doing with aurium powder? The cursed metal only worked for as long as it touched the skin. As soon as its magic was spent, it would dissolve into dust. The more aurium you had, the longer the magic's effect. So why powder? Powder wouldn't last more than several minutes at the most before disintegrating. What would the purpose of only several minutes of magic be? What could Caldwell possibly be doing with it?

And perhaps more troubling, the powder appeared to be cursed with the corrupted power of Saint Pietas. Aurium tainted by the Saint's power affected its victims with forced obedience—as Edgar had found out when he touched it and his companion flippantly told him to shoot himself. That one brief contact had been enough to end his life. With that kind of power, a few minutes could change everything.

Cat dragged her nails across the skin of her arms, nearly shrieking in pain. The rash was beginning to blister and itch like nothing she'd ever experienced. It drove all else from her mind. She could worry about the aurium powder in the morning. She needed some kind of remedy now. And fast.

She tried to force her brain to focus. What had Amos taught her about scorpion weed? She knew what it looked like, how to identify the uniquely shaped purple flowers. That the plant caused severe rashes because of tiny stinging hairs along its stem. But she couldn't for the life of her remember what to do if you actually stumbled into some. Amos had just taught her to avoid it like the creature of its namesake. And she'd always obeyed.

The kitchens. Surely there had to be something in the kitchens that could help. She had no idea what, but if she had to slather herself in everything she could find until the burning itching stopped, she'd do it.

The house was dark and quiet by the time she threw herself through the servant's entrance. She tried to keep herself from scratching, but it took nearly every inch of her willpower. The servants would all be asleep this time of night, thank the Saints, but she remembered where the kitchen was from the number of times she and Adrian had nicked sweets from the cabinets. As she turned the last corner, she noticed a flicker of candlelight reflecting off the polished wood floor of the hallway.

She stopped, listening intently to the clank of a milk bottle against a glass. Someone was getting a late-night drink. She glanced back at the empty hall. She could go back to her room . . . but another attack of itching seared her arms and she knew it was not really an option. She needed to get into the kitchen and find a remedy. *Now.*

Maybe whoever was in there could even help. Perhaps milk could ease some of the itching? Her gift was still not flashing any warnings, so whoever was there was not a threat.

Cat took a deep breath and stepped through the doorway.

But as soon as she saw who it was, she cursed her damn gift straight to the depths of hell. How had it not warned her? Surely this would be considered a *threat*?

"Miss Rose?"

Adrian sat at the scrubbed wooden table in the middle of the kitchen, his eyebrow raised as he stared at her, the glass of milk in his hand frozen halfway between the table and his mouth.

CHAPTER

22

Adrian blinked. The last person he expected to walk through the kitchen door was Rose. He blinked again, thinking he'd clear his vision. But no, it was definitely Rose—wearing a pair of his pants and one of his shirts? An odd squirming sensation wriggled through his gut at the sight of her wearing his clothes, her hair disheveled and falling out of a loosely held braid. He cleared his throat.

"Can I help you with something?" he asked her.

Her wide eyes suggested she was just as surprised to see him as he was to see her.

"Uh . . . no. No, I'm fine." She backed toward the door, her arms twisting behind her back. He hated that she seemed so skittish around him. He didn't know why, but he really wanted to see her at ease . . . heck, to even see a glimpse of her smile again.

"I've got some fresh milk if you'd like to join me. I'm sure there's a fascinating story behind why you're wearing my clothes. I'd love to hear it."

Her hazel eyes went—if possible—even wider. She glanced down at herself as if she'd forgotten what she was wearing.

"Damn it," she hissed. Then she fidgeted even more, shifting uneasily from one foot to the other.

Adrian couldn't help it. He laughed. "You've got one of the filthiest tongues I've ever heard on a novice."

She continued to fidget. Adrian wondered if she needed a visit to the outhouse.

"Um, if you need—" he started to say, but before he could finish, she wrenched her arms out from behind her back and let out a whimper of pain. She ran her nails across the red, blistered skin of her forearms, unable to stop herself from scratching.

Adrian sucked in a breath and jumped to his feet. "Saints! What did you do to yourself?"

He strode toward her, yanking her arms apart. "Stop scratching. You'll make it worse."

Rose yanked her arm back defiantly. "I didn't *do* this to myself. I fell in some scorpion weed."

Adrian hissed. "How did you fall in scorpion weed in the middle of the night? I'm fairly certain there isn't any around the house."

Rose glared at him. "Can we worry about that later? I need to find something to put on it before I peel my damned skin off."

Adrian narrowed his eyes, but he was sure they'd have time to talk about it momentarily. He nodded in understanding, remembering the excruciating rash that could be brought on by exposure to scorpion weed. He also remembered exactly what one of the ranch hands had done to relieve it when he'd accidentally encountered it.

"Sit down," he ordered her, jabbing a finger at the bench beside the table.

Rose settled herself onto the bench, sweeping her messy braid over her shoulder and tilting her chin proudly toward the rafters in the ceiling. She obviously didn't like to be told what to do, but she was also desperate enough for relief that she obeyed.

The corner of Adrian's mouth twitched. "This isn't the most pleasant of treatments, but it is quick and effective." He reached for one of the clay jars lining the herb shelf along the wall.

Rose lowered her chin and bounced in place. She sat on her hands to keep herself from scratching. "If it's quick and effective, I don't care how unpleasant it is."

"Well, don't say I didn't warn you." Adrian lifted a stem of woolly plantain from the jar and tipped it toward her as if in salute. The ranch hands always knew the best remedies for ailments on the range, and this was no exception. He popped the stem in his mouth and started to chew. Its bitter, herbal flavor exploded across his tongue. Once it had been chewed into a sufficiently wet wad, he pulled it out of his mouth and held it up.

Rose eyed the wad of chewed plant dubiously. "What are you going to do with that?" She scooted back on the bench.

"I'm going to put it on your arms like a poultice."

Rose's mouth hung open as she stared at him.

"Do you want the itching to stop or not?" He lifted a brow in question, teasingly waving the wad in front of her.

"You're sure it will work?" she asked.

"Yes, I'm sure."

"How sure?"

"Very sure."

"How are you so sure?"

He sighed and fought the urge to laugh. "Because I fell in some myself a few years back and the ranch hand did it for me. It helps, I promise. Trust me."

The words *trust me* hung between them like a dare.

Finally, she bit her lip, closed her eyes, and shoved her arm toward him. She might be stubborn, but at least she wasn't unreasonable.

Adrian took her hand, his skin tingling where it touched hers. He glanced at her face, still scrunched as she closed her eyes and waited for him to administer the treatment. Candlelight flickered across the planes of her cheekbones, across the tiny spray of freckles that coated the bridge of her nose. She really was beautiful when she wasn't hiding beneath her novice bonnet. And it drove him crazy that something about her seemed so familiar. He wished more than anything he could figure out why. Maybe he'd seen her at the mission before? Or somewhere in town?

He gave his head a little shake, reminding himself to focus as he patted the small poultice into place over one of her larger scrapes. The tension in her face began to relax as the herb took effect. She opened her eyes and sighed in relief.

"It's working," she said, her voice tinged with hope. He was still holding her outstretched hand as their eyes met, and the gratitude and joy shining in her gaze nearly knocked the breath from his lungs.

"Can we do more?" She pulled her hand back.

He felt a tingle of disappointment. "We'll need quite a bit more, so you can help me chew the stems if you want." He reached for the jar and offered it to her. "It's not as sweet as the candy the cook used to hide in here."

Rose laughed and took a stem. They both chewed in silence for several minutes, laying poultice upon poultice until her forearms were coated in a second herbal skin.

"I look like some kind of monster." She laughed, turning her arms this way and that to admire their handiwork.

Adrian smirked at her. "At least you are a monster that is no longer scratching itself to death."

"I'm serious, though. Thank you, Adrian. I would have been a horrible mess without you."

That wriggling sensation in his stomach started again. "You're welcome."

"Well," she said, rising to her feet and feigning a sinuous stretch that reminded him of a cat. "I better go rest after all that excitement—"

"Nice try," Adrian said, patting the bench beside him. "You're not going anywhere until you tell me what happened."

Rose's hands settled on her hips. "I don't have to tell you anything."

"I am technically your boss, so actually you do."

Rose scoffed. "You're not my boss. Your father is."

Adrian opened his mouth to argue, but Rose cut across him. "What are *you* doing up so late anyway?"

"*I* was getting a glass of milk because I couldn't sleep."

"Why couldn't you sleep?"

She was trying to redirect the conversation—a tactic he recognized from Edith. It would have been effective if he didn't already have so much experience with it. But then again, if he could get her talking, maybe she would stay.

"I was just thinking about my future," he said. It was true; he'd been worrying about his father's edict to begin searching for a future baroness. He just didn't feel ready for such a major step forward.

Rose snorted. "The future? I find the past a far greater distraction. At least the future you can change."

"A future that is unknown? A future dictated to you by others?"

"You're worried about finding a bride," she guessed.

Adrian shrugged, the back of his neck warm.

She sat down on the bench beside him. *Aha. It's working.*

"Why does finding a bride worry you? That should be a joyous occasion, shouldn't it?"

"Not if I don't want to find a bride."

"So find a groom," she said sagely.

Adrian laughed. "That's not the problem either."

"Then what is?"

Adrian shifted uncomfortably in his seat. "I don't know, I just never saw myself marrying."

"Never?" Rose raised an eyebrow.

"Well, no, not never. Just not since—" He couldn't finish. She wouldn't understand.

Rose dropped her gaze to the table. "You wanted to marry the girl who died. The one Captain Freeman mentioned at dinner."

Adrian winced at the memory of Catriona. It felt odd to sit here and discuss her with Rose. "I guess I always thought we'd end up married. I mean, we were best friends. Don't all kids think that of their best friends? Before they have any idea what marriage and all that means."

"You miss her," Rose guessed again, still not meeting his eyes.

"I do. But it's been such a long time."

Rose traced her finger along a crack in the table. "What happened to her?"

"Her family was robbed and then murdered. The house was burned to the ground with everyone in it."

Rose flinched. Not that he blamed her. It was awful. He still didn't like to think about it.

"Surely you'd have moved on by now, though. Enough to find someone else."

"Do you ever move on from something as traumatic as losing your best friend in such a way?" The grief had haunted him for years, the shock of realizing the truth of mortality so young. Then his mother had died suddenly as well. "I just haven't been good at getting close to people since. Like, what if I get close to them and something happens to them too? I don't know." He gave her a sad smile. "Anyone other than Edith, that is. I feel pretty protective of her, so much so that I probably let her get away with more than I should."

Rose did not answer, but nodded as if she understood. The conversation had turned so sad and dark, Adrian decided to steer it back to where he wanted it to go in the first place.

"So why *are* you wearing my clothes?"

She sighed in exasperation and threw her hands up in frustration. "Fine! Because I hate the novice dress. It's uncomfortable."

Adrian snorted. "And you were outside falling into a scorpion weed bush in the middle of the night because . . . ?"

Rose groaned and put her hand over her eyes. "I couldn't sleep either. I wanted to go outside and visit the horses."

"Did you get lost?"

She let out a huff. "Obviously."

He supposed it made sense. He'd seen how the horses had been a source of comfort to her. She had been uneasy at dinner with all the soldiers and his father, and now she was embarrassed that she'd gotten lost. Adjusting to being Edith's governess couldn't have been an easy task either, even for someone as clever and stubborn as she was.

He reached out and placed his hand over the one she'd left on the table. "I'm sorry this has been such a difficult transition for you. Is there anything I can do to make things a little easier?" He kept his tone soft and reassuring.

Rose lowered her other hand away from her eyes, staring at where his hand covered hers. It felt so cold and small beneath his fingers. Then she lifted her gaze until it locked with his.

The tension between them intensified. It wasn't unpleasant. It was like a magnetic force, something powerful pulling him toward her. He knew he shouldn't, that she would likely just push him away, but he wanted more than anything to just lean in, to see what would happen if . . .

She leaned toward him too, her eyes almost pleading in the flickering candlelight. And his resistance snapped.

He started to close the distance between them.

She jumped up as if she'd been stung by a wasp. "I'm sorry," she said suddenly, her voice breaking.

And then she bolted from the kitchen quicker than he'd ever seen someone run in his life.

CHAPTER
23

Damn it. Damn it. *Damn it.*

What the hell was she thinking, almost kissing Adrian like that?

She hadn't been thinking. Clearly. What if he'd found that Murietta pistol hidden in the back of her waistband? He was smart enough—he wouldn't buy the excuse she'd been going to visit the stable again. He hadn't seemed *entirely* convinced she was just trying to see the horses, but thankfully, he hadn't pressed it.

She had a job to do. A mission to complete. She couldn't let him distract her from it or put it in jeopardy. After all, he'd put her in this position by telling his father all those years ago. She had to stop his father from becoming governor. She had to avenge her parents and honor their sacrifice.

No, she definitely had no business kissing him. Or feeling anything toward him at all.

But then why did she?

Cat threw herself on her bed facedown, her thoughts a messy swirl of questions and unsatisfactory answers. She burrowed into her pillows as if she could muffle them, but it didn't help in the slightest.

He'd just been so sweet . . . so attentive. Not only taking care of her wounds after her brush with scorpion weed but also being concerned about her adjusting. He'd looked at her as if he *saw* her, the real her, the one hiding beneath so many facades and masks. Of course, he couldn't *really* see her . . . he had no idea who she really was.

But then to hear him talk about their past together, to hear how much he missed the Catriona she used to be. How much her supposed "death" had affected him.

Maybe it was just that small part of herself that was still the little girl he'd known, the one who had wanted to marry him too. The one that missed him. She'd have to keep that part under strict supervision. It had no place in this world of cursed gold, murderous barons, and lost futures.

It had no place in her revenge.

Caldwell's original plan had been to see them married to gain access to her land, and she wasn't about to hand it to him so easily. Even if the government was willing to overlook her crimes of the past decade. Like she'd told Father Iggy, taking her place as Baroness Macgregor wasn't a real option anymore. Her record was a mile long and as black as her nickname.

Cat flipped onto her back and stared at the strip of moonlight streaked across the ceiling. Tomorrow she would find a way to get Edith to ride a horse, and then on Sunday she would go to Saint's Landing and tell Father Iggy everything she'd discovered so far: That Caldwell was planning on becoming governor not just to take over her land but to use its aurium to fund a revolution against the empire. That he was working with a blacksmith who had created powdered aurium cursed with the power of obedience, as well as something in that small package that was meant to serve as a demonstration of some kind. And finally, that someone named Thompson, whose name kept cropping up, was a key part of Caldwell's plan.

If she could manage to get back into his office one more time before Sunday, she would. The welcome gathering to kick off the summit was Monday night, and that gave her barely a week before the vote itself took place. She had to figure out how Caldwell was planning to rig the vote before then so she and Iggy could find a way to stop him. Clearly the powder was going to play a role somehow . . .

That definitely left no time for kissing boys from her past—even if the memory of that near kiss turned her insides into a warm puddle. He had certainly grown up to be different than she'd expected . . . No. Adrian was off limits for more reasons than she could count. She could not, *would* not, let it happen again.

But that didn't mean she couldn't still crush him in their little bet tomorrow. Edith was far braver than he gave her credit for, and Cat was confident she'd have her on a horse in no time.

✦ · · · · ✹ · · · · ✦

"No. No. Absolutely not."

Edith dug in her heels with impressive strength at the stable entrance. It was like pulling on the lead rope of a stubborn mule that refused to go a step further.

"It will be fun, I promise." Cat pulled on the little girl's arm, trying to make her budge.

Edith, however, pulled her hand free and crossed her arms across her little chest. She glared with a rage that almost made Cat take a step back in surprise.

"It will *not* be fun," the little girl said, the deadness in her voice cold enough to chill the blood of the Fallen One himself.

Cat reached out for her hand again, but Edith just braced herself against the doorframe.

"No! You can't make me!"

Cat huffed and mopped the sweat off her forehead beneath her novice bonnet. This was going to be a lot harder than she'd thought.

"Having much luck yet?" came the last voice on this earth Cat wanted to hear right now. Adrian strode toward them dressed in his work clothes for the day. Cat tried not to notice the snug way the plain white shirt he wore clung to the lean muscles of his chest. She rolled her eyes and looked away from where he stood just outside the stable entrance.

"It's going fine. We are about to head inside and select a horse."

Adrian's gaze raked lazily over Edith still braced in the doorway and

Cat leaning against the wall, her face dripping in sweat. "It looks like it's going fine."

"It is, thank you," Cat snapped at him. "I'm sure you have work to get to with your cows."

"Steers," Adrian corrected.

Cat let out a groan. These Caldwells were going to be the death of her.

"You see, we are castrating some of the young bulls today." He smiled as if he knew he was being deliberately annoying. "So it's steers, not cows, I'm working with today."

"I'd like to castrate . . ." Cat started to mumble before Edith looked up and raised an eyebrow at her. "The . . . young bulls with you. You know, uh, just to see how it's done?" she finished rather lamely.

Edith and Adrian both stared at her with amused faces.

"Your bulls are waiting for you," she said, smiling sweetly at Adrian. "I'll let you know when I've won our bet."

Adrian laughed and wished her luck once more before sauntering off.

Cat turned back to Edith, her hands clasped together in pleading. "Please don't make me lose to your brother. If he loses, remember, he has to do whatever punishment you decide. You can't tell me that wouldn't be fun."

Edith's face grew thoughtful, if somewhat mischievous, before she slowly started to lower her arms from the door frame.

"Fine. But you have to promise we'll be safe."

Cat noticed the fear tainting the little girl's features and realized the problem. Their mother had been killed by being thrown from a horse.

"Are you afraid the horse will throw you like it did your mom?"

Tears filled Edith's big brown eyes, and her chin wobbled slightly as she gave a sharp little nod.

"Ah. I see." Cat knelt down until she was at eye level with her. "I promise we will not go on the horses at all today if you don't want to. All we are going to do is make friends with them and get to know them a little bit, okay?"

Edith tilted her head to the side. "You're not going to force me to ride one?"

"Not if you aren't ready. I promise."

Edith pondered for a moment.

Cat held out a hand to her. "Trust me?"

Edith surveyed her face as if searching for something. She must have seen what she was looking for because she finally put her hand in Cat's and let her lead the way into the stables.

Cat wasn't as familiar with the Caldwell horses as she was with her own, so she took Edith straight to the stall that housed her palomino, Almond.

Edith jerked back. "Aren't these the horses that were taken from the outlaws?"

"Yes, but I can read horses really well. I can tell this one is a sweetheart and would love to meet you."

Edith stepped forward tentatively.

"Horses can sense how you're feeling, so if you are scared and nervous, you will make the horse scared and nervous too," Cat told her, reaching to rub Almond's nose.

"The horse is scared too?" Edith took another step forward.

"Only if you are scared. Try just patting her neck, right here. Introduce yourself and tell her a little bit about you."

Edith swallowed hard and lifted her fingers toward Almond's neck. She pulled them back once or twice, before briefly brushing them across Almond's smooth golden coat.

"It's so soft," Edith whispered. With a little more bravery, she reached forward and stroked the horse's neck a few more times. "And her eyes are brown just like mine."

"She likes you," Cat said, smiling at Edith's progress.

"Really?"

"She does, see how her ears are pointed forward like that? Tell her a little about yourself. Horses are the best listeners."

Edith giggled nervously. "Um, okay. Hi, horse, my name is Edith Caldwell. I live here, up in the big house, with my dad and my brother." She looked back at Cat and grinned. "And with my governess, Rose. I wasn't very nice to her at first, but she's pretty good now, I think. I hope she stays."

Cat's heart twisted at the little girl's words. She swallowed hard and cleared her throat. "Do you want to brush her?"

Edith looked nervous again.

"It's easy, here, I'll show you. You can just brush her neck like you were doing with your fingers."

The little girl eventually conceded, and before too long, both she and Cat were inside the stall with Almond. Cat showed her the proper way to brush, how to clean out and check Almond's hooves, and all the while Edith kept chattering away as if the horse were her new best friend in all the world.

After another hour, when Edith was finally feeling more comfortable, Cat decided to try a little experiment.

"I'm going to get a few apples from the bucket outside to feed her. Do you want to keep talking to Almond while I'm gone?"

"Okay!" Edith chirped.

"I'll be right back," Cat said.

She slipped out into the main walkway of the stables and strained her ears to hear over the rustling and nickering of the other horses.

Sure enough, it wasn't long before she heard Edith telling Almond all about her mother, talking about how much she missed her and how hard it had been since she was gone. Cat's heart swelled.

She remembered Amos doing the same thing for her when she was young, when she'd first been found by the Wolves and had been drowning in grief and guilt even more than she was now. Her secret had felt like a weight pressing on her chest, threatening to crush her alive. Despite Amos's questions, she'd refused to talk about where she'd come from or why she was running away. Amos had told her that horses were the best listeners and, finally realizing Cat wouldn't tell him anything, told her to take one of the horses outside of camp and tell it everything.

"*Whatever it is that's eating up your insides, kid, you need to talk to someone about it or else it's going to kill you,*" he had said.

She'd been only ten at the time and had thought it the stupidest thing she'd ever heard. But she did as she was told, and after the first five minutes, she found herself spilling her deepest, darkest secrets to the beast.

After several hours of venting everything rotten inside of her, she'd come back to camp feeling lighter. Nowhere close to healed, but at least as though she could breathe again. Ever since, whenever life was bothering her, Cat would talk to her horse as if it were a priest in a confessional.

It seemed Edith felt the same.

Her chest gave a painful throb at the memory, at the thought of Amos saving her one last time in the canyon. A few tears for him escaped before she forced back the burning behind her eyes. When she came back with the apples after purposely taking as long as she could, Edith was sniffling and wiping tears of her own from her cheeks. Cat came up behind her and gave her shoulders a squeeze.

"Do you want to try feeding her an apple?"

Edith nodded, wiping away the last of her tears and putting her brave face back on. Cat showed her how to hold the apple pieces flat in her hand so that the horse wouldn't bite her fingers by accident. Edith squealed when Almond's lips tickled against her hand and lifted the apple off with ease.

Edith beamed at Cat, pride shining from every pore of her face.

Cat braced herself for the next step of their training. "Alright, Edith. You've done amazing so far. Are you ready to try and ride her?"

Edith blanched. "Ride her? I—I don't think I'm ready." Her little chest rose and fell in terrified little breaths.

"That's okay," Cat said in a hurry, not wanting to send the little girl into a panic. "But if you wanted to, I thought maybe we could do it together. I'd sit up there with you. Just to make sure you get to punish your brother, of course."

Edith's quickened breathing eased somewhat. "Together? Will that still count?"

Cat gave her a wicked smile. "Our bet was that I couldn't get you on a horse. We never said you had to be on the horse *alone*."

Edith's mouth curled into a wicked grin to match Cat's. "Okay. Let's do it!"

24

"I still don't think it counts," Adrian protested the next day.

"Oh, it absolutely counts. And now Edith gets to decide your punishment." Rose grinned at him from the bench seat on the other side of the coach. Adrian placed a hand against the velvet-lined wall to steady himself as they bounced along the uneven dirt road. He much preferred horseback, but the coach was the only way to get Edith to Saint's Landing. Something that apparently—thanks to Rose—might soon change.

He still couldn't get over the shock he'd felt when he came back up the hill from the pastures and saw *Edith* trotting around the paddock. Rose had miraculously managed to get her on the horse by joining her in the saddle, one arm secured around his sister's waist while the other directed the reins. The governess's bonnet had fallen off at some point, and the two of them laughed as they completed several laps around the fenced enclosure. Sunlight illuminated hints of red in Rose's brown hair and flushed her cheeks, but nothing lightened her countenance as effectively as her carefree smile. She nearly stole the breath from his lungs. A strange pressure had built behind his eyes as he watched them together. He never thought he'd see Edith ride a horse again.

"You said I couldn't get her on a horse, and I got her on a horse," Rose said matter-of-factly.

"I was absolutely on the horse!" Edith chimed in.

Adrian sighed. He knew he was hopelessly outnumbered by these two stubborn women. But if he was honest with himself, he secretly loved it. He hoped to be outnumbered on many more issues concerning Rose and his little sister.

Rose was now back in her shapeless brown novice dress, a drastic difference from the cinched waist of his pants and shirt that she'd borrowed that night. It was as if two different versions of her existed—the skittish, standoffish novice who was about as accessible as an iron safe, and the bright, lively wildflower that seemed to peek out from between the weeds if he was lucky enough to catch a glimpse.

That night. Sweet Mother of the Saints, he wished he could go back to that night . . . to what had *almost* happened between them and ensure that it actually did . . . He shifted his position and tried very hard not to think about such things.

How was he supposed to focus on finding a wife at tomorrow night's gathering when all he kept thinking about was how he wanted to snatch that ridiculous bonnet off Rose's head and watch her beautiful red-brown hair tumble down her back? To see her face joyously alight as it had been when she was on the horse with his sister?

Perhaps it was a good day to go to church after all.

The journey into town would take about two hours, and he had been looking forward to the time they'd spend locked up together in his father's coach. But ideally, his little sister wouldn't be bobbing like a cork in a pond between them. If they were lucky, she'd fall asleep at some point like she usually did on long coach trips.

"Are you looking forward to returning to the mission?" Adrian asked.

Rose's hands twisted in her lap. "I suppose so. I'm just really looking forward to seeing Father Iggy—I mean, Ignatius."

"I'm glad Edith and I could accompany you. This would have been a lonely trip to take on your own."

"And dangerous," Edith said. "Father says that bandits like to wait along the road and rob whoever passes through to Saint's Landing."

"There will be no bandits," Rose assured her. "And if there are, I'd scare them off anyway."

"And how would you do that?" Adrian asked, tilting his head in question.

"Oh, I can be very terrifying when necessary, Mr. Caldwell."

Adrian chuckled. "I believe it. And now I know better than to bet against you."

"Hmm, I still need to think of your punishment." Edith tapped her cheek, assessing him with that shrewd little gaze of hers.

"Take your time," Rose whispered to her. "Make him squirm as he waits to know what horror awaits him."

Adrian lifted a hand to his chest. "Really, Miss Rose. You would encourage her to be so cruel to her own brother?"

"Most definitely," she responded without a moment's hesitation.

"Most definitely," Edith repeated like a little magpie.

"Fine, but I'm not buying *either* of you any chocolate while we are in town," he said with a triumphant smile. His proclamation was met with much protest, even though they all knew he'd give in to them anyway.

✦ • • • • ◉ • • • • ✦

The side streets of Saint's Landing were busy for a Sunday morning, but perhaps Adrian shouldn't have been surprised. Most of Saelum's barons were staying in town for the coming summit. Their families and security entourages would be here as well. While the docks would be even busier with incoming shipments, their little party would be staying on the high street this time, attending services at the mission and perhaps visiting a shop or two before making the trip back to Caldwell Ranch.

Adrian smoothed the high white collar of his Sunday clothes. It had been months since he'd last dressed so fancy, and if he were honest, he missed it. While most young men hated dressing up, Adrian had always been one of the strange few who enjoyed it. It made him feel more grown up, more sophisticated. He chanced a glance at Rose, wondering briefly how she'd look in a fine lace gown, her hair pulled up into an elegant style befitting the upper classes. He sighed.

He'd bet all the aurium in Ordonia she'd be breathtaking. Especially if she let that guard of hers down.

The high street was just as busy as the side streets, the dusty air packed with stagecoaches and horses. Upstanding townsfolk bustled between shops, while the less-than-savory types already stumbled toward the saloons. At the end of the high street sat the capitol building and courthouse, a beautifully carved red sandstone structure with a sweeping staircase leading up to its expansive face. Behind the sharply slanted roof of the front building rose an elegant clock tower topped with carved parapets.

Flanking the courthouse on one side was Fort Astor, the bleak gray prison and headquarters for the Ordonian soldiers stationed in Saelum Territory. On the other side was the glittering marble dome of the Saint's Landing mission. Twelve Corinthian columns guarded the entrance, one for each of the twelve Saints they represented.

Rose's mouth fell open as she took in the scene.

"Busier than usual for this time of year, isn't it?" Adrian leaned forward to poke his head out the window with her.

Rose just nodded.

A line of coaches already crowded the mission entrance, and people dressed in their Sunday best strolled arm in arm between the pillars.

"I think Joseph's going to drop us off a little closer to the fort to avoid traffic. You girls don't mind a bit of a walk before the service, do you?"

Edith bounced with excitement, and Rose responded with a smirk. Adrian exited the coach first, arranged his hat, and offered a hand to help Rose down. She stared at it briefly before gritting her teeth and taking it. He could feel the warmth of her hand through the fabric of his glove as he steadied her balance on the steps.

Soldiers in navy-and-gold uniforms swarmed the entrance to the fort like bees around a hive, clogging the street as effectively as the churchgoers in front of the mission. Perhaps getting out here wasn't a wise choice after all. Adrian glanced around, looking for a clear path for them to take.

"Stick close to me so we don't get separated," Adrian barked over his shoulder, taking Edith's hand as he led them forward through the pressing bodies around them. The smell of dust mingled with perfumes and colognes and wafts of booze drifted over the crowd.

"Mr. Caldwell. What a surprise to see you in town," called a familiar voice.

The crowd eased around Captain Freeman, who had materialized beside them in a perfectly crisp uniform. His sharp chin was tilted high into the air as usual, his dark eyes ever alert and watchful.

"Ah, Freeman. A pleasure to see you as well." Adrian tipped his hat in greeting.

The captain's gaze raked over Rose for the briefest of moments. "Where are you headed this morning? Perhaps I might accompany you on your errands."

"We are headed to services at the mission, actually. You are more than welcome to join us."

Freeman's jawline went—if possible—even more rigid. "I'm afraid not, Mr. Caldwell. Do enjoy your time with the *Saints*. I am sure I will see you at the summit gathering tomorrow night." He turned to leave just as quickly as he'd appeared.

Rose glared after the captain's retreating back.

"Does Captain Freeman not attend church?" Edith asked, following the direction of Rose's bitter stare.

"I don't think he's particularly religious," Adrian conceded.

"Why not?"

He smiled at his sister's incessant curiosity. "Because not everyone worships the Saints, Edith. Some think they show too much favoritism to their chosen ones, and question their benevolence. Others doubt their existence entirely. Though how you could with the evidence of aurium and the Blessing gifts—"

"Which one is Captain Freeman?" Edith asked.

Rose cleared her throat. "Probably one who is jealous of those Blessed by the Saints but too full of himself to admit it."

Adrian shot her a glare of warning. Rose just shrugged. She clearly harbored a distaste for the captain after dinner that evening. He wasn't the biggest fan of Freeman either—the man *was* as proud and arrogant as the peerage in the Ordonian capital—but he was still under the employ of Adrian's father and deserved to be treated with respect.

"Mother always said we cannot question the will of the Saints. That they have their reasons for Blessing some and not others," Edith said.

Adrian patted the back of her Sunday bonnet. "They certainly do."

"Which gift would you want if you could be Blessed by the Saints, Miss Rose?" Edith pulled Rose closer so that she could hold both of their hands at once, walking between her and Adrian like a child between her parents.

"I wouldn't want to be Blessed." Rose kept her eyes on the mission ahead.

"Why not?" Edith asked. "Saints, I think I'd want to be Blessed by Saint Honestas . . . ooo, no, Salubritas!"

"Salubritas? You'd want the ability to turn invisible?" Adrian arched a brow at his little sister.

"Imagine all the fun I could have. And no one would *ever* be able to find my hiding places!"

Adrian chuckled. "Well, I forbid you from petitioning Saint Salubritas for any Blessing gifts. The Mother only knows what I'd do with you if he granted it."

"Why wouldn't you want to be Blessed, Rose?" Edith asked again.

They'd finally passed the courthouse, the clock tower behind it booming the hour from its massive bells. Ten chimes for ten o'clock. They'd be right on time for the service if they could find seats.

Rose worried her bottom lip between her teeth. "Being Blessed is a major responsibility. The Saints only grant their gifts when they have a mission to be carried out. It's as much a burden as it is a Blessing."

"Have you ever met anyone who is Blessed?"

"Yes," Rose said. But she did not elaborate. Adrian imagined that being raised in the church exposed her to many a member of the Blessed. He'd only ever met one . . . and hadn't met any since her untimely death. Sometimes not even the Blessed got the chance to realize their given purposes. He shoved the thoughts of Catriona Macgregor back into the deep recesses of his memory.

Edith opened her mouth to ask another question, but Adrian could tell Rose didn't want to talk about it. Perhaps the member of the Blessed she was thinking of hadn't been able to realize their calling either. So instead, he pulled a silver coin from his pocket and tossed it to his sister. "Don't forget your offering for this morning."

Edith caught the coin, that ever-present glimmer of mischief in her eyes. "I think I know *exactly* which Saint's fountain I'm offering it to."

"I think we all do," Adrian said, rolling his eyes as they made their way up the marble steps of the mission of Saint's Landing.

25

Cat hadn't been inside the Saint's Landing mission since she was Edith's age. A million memories flooded over her as she walked among the towering marble columns, each carved with an elegant likeness of one of the twelve Saints. Inside the mission courtyard, smaller versions graced the tops of the offering fountains, where coins and prayers could petition for a particular Saint's favor.

Though the crowds had thinned as the churchgoers took their seats in the main cathedral, there were still a few stragglers milling about the courtyard to offer last-minute petitions to the Saints. Waist-high hedgerows and Ordonian rosebushes wound through the courtyard, separating out twelve distinct prayer gardens. Bougainvillea climbed up the surrounding trellises, throwing their scent and color into the holy stillness.

Of course, Edith dragged them right to the fountain of Saint Salubritas, patron saint of wholesomeness and cleanliness. Cat couldn't remember what great deed the man had done while human to earn his designation as Saint Salubritas, but she was sure he was a Saint that wanted nothing to do with her. Despite her appearance as a novice of the mission, Cat was about as *unwholesome* as it was possible to be. Then again, Edith wasn't exactly the epitome of purity either.

Maybe petitioning for his favor could do the girl some good.

The gravel of the path crunched beneath their feet as they turned past the last hedge, exposing Salubritas's carved marble fountain. The statue's face tipped toward the heavens, serene and peaceful as the sunlight illuminated the glittering stone. Water splashed joyfully into the basin at his robed feet, where dozens of silver and gold coins winked like metallic fish upon the tile.

Edith squeezed her eyes shut, her lips moving in a quick, silent prayer before she flipped the coin into the fountain. It splashed through the water's surface, sinking to the bottom to join the other offerings.

"Any Saint you'd like to petition for favor?" Adrian leaned in and whispered in Cat's ear.

Cat's gaze immediately flicked to the fountain topped with Saint Prudentia, patron saint of wisdom and forethought. The Saint responsible for her own Blessing gift.

"Here." Adrian pressed a silver coin into her palm. "I'm going to make an offering myself before we go in. Take however much time you need."

She watched him and Edith make their way to the fountain of Saint Veritas, patron of truth and justice. A snort almost escaped her lips. Of course *Veritas* would be Adrian's favorite Saint. Although, if he were suddenly Blessed with the gift of telling truth from lies, she would be in a lot more trouble than she already was. Luckily, Blessing gifts were usually bestowed upon infants at their baptisms. To receive one as an adult was almost as rare as finding an untouched lode of aurium.

She stared down at the silver coin in her hand, her feet carrying her to the base of the fountain of Saint Prudentia. The statue's face was sharp and clever, stone eyes so intense it felt as if they could actually see. Her sweeping marble robes fell almost to the fountain's waterline.

Why did you choose me? Cat wanted to scream at her. *You're supposed to be so wise, so clever. Surely you foresaw what a foolish choice it was to bless me with anything.*

The only sound that answered was the gentle splashing of water.

I don't even know what to ask for. I guess if it was anything, it would be for you to take your Blessing back. Give it to someone who can actually do some good with it, who can accomplish whatever it is you thought you wanted me to do.

She tossed the coin into the water, watching it slowly sink to the bottom, its silver surface reflecting daylight back up at her. She released an exhausted sigh.

"She chose you for a reason, you know," a deep, wheezy voice said from somewhere beside her.

Cat jumped. Father Ephraim had come to join her, the deep brown of his bald head shining brighter than the silver coin in the morning sun. He leaned heavily on his walking stick, staring down into the water where her offering had settled. Though he seemed fragile and aged, Cat hadn't forgotten the agility with which he'd handled the pistols in that trunk of his.

"She chose you for a reason," he repeated, lifting one of his wizened hands to gesture at the form of Saint Prudentia.

"I guess even the Saint of wisdom can make a mistake, can't she? They were human once, after all."

Father Ephraim chuckled. "Yes, they were human once. Which I think is sometimes what allows them to understand us even better than we understand ourselves. They've walked in our shoes, so to speak."

"I doubt she has any idea what it's like to walk in my shoes."

The old priest considered her as if he could see something no one else could. "Someday, my dear, you will have to stop running and embrace the destiny the Saints have chosen for you. A destiny that will involve facing the truth of who you *really* are. It's the only way you will find the peace you seek."

Peace? Cat almost laughed. Father Ephraim sounded just like Amos. "*The only way to catch the sun is to turn the other way. Face the night, run right through it. Catch the dawn on the other side.*" But they didn't know what burdens she carried. They didn't understand how dark that night behind her really was.

There was no option for peace. Or to claim her real identity. She'd be arrested the moment anyone realized that Catriona Macgregor was now Black Cat Whitfield, outlaw and adopted daughter of the infamous

Amos Whitfield. She wouldn't become a baroness and—despite what the priesthood clearly hoped—wouldn't have the power or influence to save anything. The only thing she would find was a short drop and a sudden stop at the end of a hangman's noose for her many crimes. She didn't feel like arguing, so she changed the subject instead. "Where's Father Iggy?"

"He is inside, anxiously pacing and waiting for you to share what information you've gathered on Baron Caldwell's plans."

Adrian and Edith began crunching their way across the gravel path toward them.

Father Ephraim winked before turning to greet Adrian and Edith. "Ah, Mr. Caldwell. It is such a pleasure to see you and Miss Edith back at Sunday services. It's been a while, has it not?"

"Too long." Adrian offered a nod in greeting. "It feels good to be back."

"And how have the arrangements with Miss . . . Rose worked out for you?"

"Very well," Edith blurted out. "We like her very much."

Father Ephraim's eyes went wide. "Really? I am . . . delighted to hear that." He glanced over at Cat and lifted a quizzical brow, a dozen questions swirling in his dark eyes.

Cat plastered a smile across her face. "We should really get into the service, I think it's starting." As if to emphasize her point, the teeth-rattling tone of the organ's first notes shook the dust from the domed ceiling.

"Of course, of course. May the Saints grant you *all* clarity and guidance for the path ahead."

Cat could feel the intensity of his gaze follow the back of her head all the way into the main cathedral.

✦ · · · · ◉ · · · · ✦

The service lasted about two hours. It took every ounce of Cat's patience not to run up to the dais, shake the priest who was delivering the sermon, and demand that he *get on with it.* Saints above. His voice was as dry as a creek bed in the heat of summer, and he spoke about as slowly as a tortoise trying to cross it. He rambled about the importance of honoring the will of the Saints, of the dangers of taking fate into our own hands, through our own choices or through use of aurium.

"To use the corrupted power of the Saints," the man droned, "is to think ourselves better than the Saints. To think that we can better decide our fate than they can. It is an abomination, a curse in the face of the Creator Mother who chose the Saints just as they, in turn, choose us . . ."

Cat groaned internally. Even the Mother herself would be bored sitting here listening. There had to be a better way to pass the time. She leaned over to where Adrian sat rigid and attentive beside her. He was such a ninny sometimes. He always had been. Obsessed with following the rules and order of things. Even when they were children, she'd always had to push him to be more interesting, more adventurous. Though in the end, his dedication to telling the truth and doing the "right" thing had damned them both anyway.

"How much longer do you think he can go?" she whispered.

Adrian gave her an impatient look.

"Seriously. I doubt the man's vocal cords can last much longer."

The corners of Adrian's mouth twitched.

The priest took a shuddering breath, giving Cat the brief hope that he was finished, before continuing on. "The Fallen Saint, who shall remain nameless, always desired greatness. To be recognized above his brothers and sisters. When we use the power of aurium, we are committing the same sin, the desire to take power and influence that was never ours to begin with . . ."

The only time Cat sat up straight was when the priest beckoned to the family of a baby brought to be baptized. They shuffled to the front of the cathedral, lining up next to the baptismal font.

Perhaps this child would receive a Blessing gift. Cat's parents had told her many times of the day she received hers. When the priest dipped the chalice into holy water and sprinkled it on Cat's forehead, the droplets had flashed silvery blue. At the same time, Saint Prudentia's statue took on a glow of its own. The congregation had gasped and then begun to whisper. Even the priest had seemed impressed.

But today, the moment passed. No flash of magic when the priest intoned the baby's name, no Saint glowed to life. Cat slumped back into the pew. Once again she wondered, *Why me?*

The last half hour passed in a droning blur of words. "Would it be a sin to fall asleep during the service, you think?" Cat nodded her head to the row in front of them, where an older man in a top hat tipped his head precariously as though fending off a fainting fit. "If so, somebody better warn that one's wife . . ."

"Rose," Adrian hissed, though he was clearly fighting to contain his smile. "You are being disrespectful."

"This sermon is disrespectful to the alertness and wakefulness of the entire congregation."

Adrian snorted, but hastily lifted a gloved hand and turned it into a cough.

Edith, who sat on Adrian's other side, stopped swinging her legs and looked over at them with a curious quirk of her eyebrow.

"Your brother is fine," Cat assured her. "He just choked on a little dust is all."

"When is the service going to be over?" Edith whined, careful to keep her voice low. "I'm *bored*."

"You are both awful," Adrian scolded. "The man is almost done. Pray to Saint Severitas for some self-control if you need to."

Edith crossed her arms and harrumphed at the exact moment Cat did the same, which almost sent Adrian into another laughing-masked-as-holy-coughing fit.

To all of their relief, the organ *finally* began playing again, announcing the time to move into the next part of the service.

"For true believers of the Saints, this is a time to receive a Cleansing. If you fear you have been touched by the influence of the Fallen One, either in thought or deed, or through exposure to the cursed substance known as aurium, to be cleansed with holy water blessed by the Mother herself will absolve you and protect you . . ."

There was a great rustling as hundreds of churchgoers rose to their feet and filtered into the aisles to form a queue. At the head of the dais, a line of priests waited to welcome them, each holding a golden chalice presumably filled to the brim with water from the Mother's fountain. Cat thought back to the small vial of holy water Father Ephraim had given her when he and Father Iggy were preparing her. *Keep this with you*, he'd said at the time. *You never know when you might need an antidote to aurium's effects.* Preferring more proactive approaches to defensive ones, she had left it in her bag, choosing to protect herself with a knife hidden beneath her skirts. But maybe she should start keeping it with her. Especially after seeing what had happened in the storehouse. Aurium was somehow involved in Caldwell's plans, she just didn't know how it was going to be used . . .

At the end of the line of priests stood Father Iggy. He impatiently dipped his thumb into the chalice and brushed it across the foreheads of the line of churchgoers in front of him, mumbling the blessing prayers so quickly that the priestess beside him kept giving him wide-eyed admonishments as though she wanted to scold him for not doing it properly. But he seemed unconcerned, his anxious, watery eyes darting over the crowd searching for something.

Or someone.

Cat sighed, knowing what she was going to have to do. She rose to her feet, Adrian and Edith standing to let her through.

"Oooo, can I do the Cleansing too?" Edith whispered to her brother as Cat shimmied past them toward the aisle.

"That depends. Have you committed any sins this week in need of Cleansing?" Adrian asked.

They stared at each other for a moment. The dimple in Edith's cheek deepened ever so slightly.

Adrian blinked. "Yeah, alright, let's go too."

While Adrian and Edith joined the queue in the center, she inched her way over to the end, where Father Iggy's line was dwindling much faster than those beside him. The priest finally caught sight of her—and nearly dropped his golden chalice in surprise.

If his doled-out blessings had been rushed before, it was nothing compared to how quickly he moved now, hardly glancing at the recipients of his prayers and rushed swipes across their foreheads. Several times he seemed to forget to dip his thumb entirely. The priestess beside him cleared her throat suggestively.

But finally, it was Cat's turn. She stepped forward, kneeling down on the small velvet pillow that rested at Father Iggy's feet. He leaned down, whispering not a blessing, but a quick question.

"Have you found anything?"

Cat glanced up as he dipped his thumb and ran the cool water in an arc across her forehead. "Yes," she mumbled, barely moving her lips.

The priestess beside Father Iggy still hovered like a hawk, her shrewd gaze now focusing on Cat. She didn't dare say more here.

Father Iggy leaned forward under the guise of placing a hand of blessing upon her head and whispered, "The last confessional, the one furthest from the dais, would be an excellent place to *share what is on your heart* after the service."

Cat nodded in understanding before returning to her seat in the pews.

She certainly had some things on her heart to share with the priest, things that would hopefully lead to William Caldwell rotting away in a prison cell for the rest of his days.

26

The wooden door of the confessional closed behind Cat with a snap. Tiny motes of dust floated in beams of light from the latticed windows.

"Catriona? Catriona? Is that you?" came Father Iggy's panicked voice.

"Settle your horses, Father, it's me. And don't call me Catriona. It's Cat. Or Rose now, I guess."

"Ah, Catriona," he breathed a sigh of relief.

Cat rolled her eyes.

She could hear the bench beneath him creak as he leaned forward. "What have you found out, my dear? Do you know how Caldwell is planning to secure the vote?"

Cat rubbed her eyes, which were beginning to burn and water from the dust. "Um. Not quite."

Father Iggy sputtered in surprise, "Not quite? Catriona, the vote is *this Thursday*! We are nearly out of time!"

"I know. I know. Listen, I have learned *some* things at least."

"Well, spill it, my dear!"

"Is that how you usually handle confessionals? 'Well, spill it'?"

She heard him sigh through the lattice. She couldn't help it, she smirked.

"Catriona . . ."

"Stop calling me Catriona and maybe I'll be a little more cooperative."

"You are aware we are on the same side, are you not? I am trying to help you stop a selfish murderer from stealing *your* land and becoming governor—"

"Yes, yes, I know." She didn't need a lecture. "He's not just planning on becoming governor, though. Based on the maps I saw in his office, he plans to use the aurium to fund a Saints-damned revolution against the empire."

"Language, Catriona, we are in the holy mission."

"*Language?* I tell you he's planning a revolution and the first thing you say is—"

Father Iggy made an impatient sound. "It's called shock, my dear. Please give me a moment to take this in."

Cat huffed herself into silence for a few moments. She could hear Father Iggy trying to collect his breath.

"Alright," he finally said. "I will pass this information to the other priests at our meeting this evening." He seemed to be trying to sound calm and collected, but Cat caught the hint of panic beneath his words. "And as for the planned vote itself?"

Cat chewed her lower lip. "I couldn't find any evidence of blackmail or bribery, not in his office at least. But there is a blacksmith named Rogers that made . . . *something* for him. He talked with Freeman about a demonstration of some kind before the vote and then he had a shipment brought in of what looked to be aurium powder."

"Aurium *powder*?"

"That was my thought too. Powder won't give you more than a minute or two of magic at most, won't it?"

"And you didn't find out what the powder was cursed to do?"

Cat scratched absently at the fading remains of her scorpion weed rash. "I received a pretty graphic demonstration. One of the soldiers touched it and then shot himself in the head. I'm guessing it's cursed with obedience."

"Holy Saints." She heard his robes swish as he must have made the blessing symbol of a circle around his head. "Well, this is a lot more than we knew before. So he's planning to use powdered aurium to influence the vote somehow . . ." Father Iggy mused. "But how? And more importantly, how can we stop him?"

"Caldwell is hosting the welcome gathering at his house tomorrow evening. I'm sure he and Freeman will be distracted enough for me to get into his office one more time. I tried again last night, but the man never seems to sleep. He's in there all hours of the night."

"Won't you be occupied with your charge during the event? We need answers, yes, but you also need to be careful, Catriona. If you are caught or suspected . . ."

"I'm sure I can slip away for a moment. Maybe I can convince Adrian to . . ." She let her words fade away as she weighed possible options to keep Edith distracted.

"How are things going with young Mr. Caldwell?" There was an odd tone to the priest's voice, like he was trying to be a little *too* casual about the question.

Cat felt her spine straighten. "Fine. Why?"

"Oh, nothing, nothing. The other priests and I were just wondering how the two of you were getting along after being reunited after so many years. Many here remember you both as children, you know."

"You all have a bet going on or something?"

Father Iggy didn't answer.

Cat's jaw went slack in surprise. "You do, don't you? What are you all betting on? Whether I'll kill him or kiss him?"

There was another pregnant pause.

"Well, Catriona, downtime between services can get very boring, and as you know I don't have my vineyard here to occupy my time—"

"So you're running a priestly gambling hall out of the mission now too?"

"Oh for Saints' sake, don't be so *dramatic*. It's a harmless little wager between myself and a few of the older—"

"What did you bet on?"

Again, she was met with silence.

"Father Iggy . . . what did you bet?"

"We really need to focus on the mission at hand, my dear. We need to discover what the baron is planning to do with that aurium and *how* he's going to use it to rig the vote."

She narrowed her eyes at the lattice, sure that the priest's face would be burning as red as a branding iron if she could see it properly. "Fine. There's also someone named Thompson involved, but I haven't been able to figure out how or who that is."

"Thompson?" Father Iggy repeated. "Hmmmmm. I wonder . . ."

"Does that name mean anything to you?"

"Actually, it might. I have something I need to look into to be sure, but—"

There was a sudden rapping at the door of the confessional.

"Brother Ignatius? Are you in there?" squawked a matronly voice.

Father Iggy's next words came out in a hurried rush. "Find out whatever else you can tomorrow night and send it to me with a rider. We only have a few more days. I will do the same for you if my suspicions about Thompson are—"

"Ignatius!" demanded the priestess's voice again. "We need to discuss some items of *importance*, if you don't mind."

Father Iggy whispered a choice curse.

"Language, Father. We are in the holy mission after all," Cat said, grinning despite herself.

"You are lucky you are such a delight to work with," he hissed, but she could hear the teasing in his voice.

"You know you care about me!" she whispered after him, fighting back the temptation to laugh and earning her own scolding from the priestess waiting for Father Iggy outside.

"We *all* do, Catriona. If only you realized how much."

＊ ・ ・ ・ ・ ◉ ・ ・ ・ ・ ＊

"It felt good to be back at Sunday services," Adrian mused as the coach headed back to Caldwell Ranch. The sun was starting to tip into late afternoon, bringing with it a dry wind that whipped across the low rolling hills and chaparral and forcing them to close the coach's windows.

Edith was already digging into a paper sack of chocolate that Adrian had purchased for her at the general store. Little chocolate smears coated the corners of her lips. To Cat's surprise, Adrian had slipped a small brown package into her own hands as they'd stepped out of the shop. When she opened it, she'd found a large slab of orange-sweetened chocolate. It had always been her favorite as a child, a treat her father would bring back from Saint's Landing whenever he'd traveled into the capital for business. She'd fought back the thick feeling that threatened to close her throat and mumbled a quick thank-you without meeting his eyes.

Kill him or kiss him? Which side *had* Father Iggy bet on?

It didn't really matter. Neither side was going to win because if all went according to plan, by this time next week she'd be on a ship across the Dark Sea. Or a train across the border into Caseda. Her heart twisted as she looked over at Edith nestled into Adrian's side, licking the remnants of her treat off her fingers. She'd be torn up when Cat finally decided to leave. Hopefully her father would be locked up and unable to send her away from Adrian at least.

Because as much as she didn't want to admit it, she was starting to care for the girl. She told herself this was the best gift she could give Edith moving forward: saving her from her corrupt father. And—she glanced up at Adrian—well, at least he hadn't given in to his father's moral bankruptcy. He'd managed to hold on to his principles and kindness. Still, that didn't mean she forgave him for telling her secret all those years ago.

Cat snapped off a corner of her own chocolate piece and slipped it into her mouth. Its tangy sweetness exploded across her tongue, nearly bringing tears to her eyes. She hadn't tasted real Ordonian orange chocolate like this in years. She glanced up again, and this time, Adrian was watching her.

"What?" she asked.

"Nothing. I was just wondering how you liked the chocolate."

Cat swallowed. "It's, um . . . really good. You didn't have to buy any for me, though."

"I know." He smiled.

"So why did you?"

"Well, you've done quite a lot for Edith in such a remarkably short time. It was the least I could do."

Cat shrugged. "That's my job as governess, isn't it?"

"It's okay to admit how much you really like us, Rose. I don't know what your home was like before you became a ward, but you always have a home here if you need one."

Cat nearly dropped the bag of chocolate. How was she supposed to stay angry at him, to keep pushing herself away from him when he kept doing things like . . . like . . . this! Buying her chocolate, tending her wounds, offering her a home? It would be a hell of a lot easier if he'd just turned into a miniature version of his father after all.

Kill him or kiss him?

Perhaps none of them would get to find out—because at that moment a vision flashed before Cat's eyes. The sound of a bullet cracking through the desert sky before smashing into the side of their coach.

She didn't hesitate, she jumped forward and shoved both Edith and Adrian to the floor.

CHAPTER

27

A gunshot rang through the air, and splinters of wood arced above Adrian's head. Edith screamed. He was taken aback by Rose's sudden movement, at first thinking she was hugging him for giving her the chocolate, but then the next second he and Edith were both shoved to the floor of the coach, Rose's body pressing them down.

The coach swerved precariously, nearly tipping itself sideways as it careened off the main road. Edith screamed again. Adrian threw an arm around her and pulled her tight against his chest, bracing her against the impact as the wheels caught in a rut and jerked them to a violent stop. Rose slid sideways off them, hitting the back wall with a hollow thud and a cry of pain.

Dust poured in through the broken windows—along with the neighing of horses trying to disentangle themselves from the twisted remains of their harness. Edith's cries mixed with those of the horses.

Adrian's hands fluttered across her tearstained cheeks. "Are you okay?"

She nodded but buried herself into his arms with a sob. He tried to twist around to see Rose.

"Rose?"

"I'm okay," she groaned, stretching her back from where it had hit the front wall of the carriage. A shallow cut above her eye oozed blood into her eyebrow. She wiped it away with the sleeve of her novice dress, only for the blood to pool once more.

Keeping one arm around Edith, Adrian pushed himself into a sitting position and pulled a handkerchief from his coat pocket. He thrust it toward Rose's head, pressing it against the wound as she winced. Other than that, she seemed to be okay.

"Joseph!" Adrian yelled. He couldn't imagine their coachman had managed to keep his seat after an impact like that. "Joseph, are you okay?"

There was no answer.

"Wh-what happened?" Edith asked.

Adrian's eyes focused on the bullet hole staring into the coach like the eye of a Peeping Tom. "Someone shot at us."

Rose reached for the door, but Adrian grabbed her wrist. "Stop. Don't go out there."

She immediately withdrew her hand as if the handle had burned her.

Sure enough, the sound of thundering hooves grew louder. Someone was approaching.

"Stay here," Adrian ordered them both. He reached into his waistband and withdrew a small Crockett pistol. It held only a single shot, a gentleman's gun typically kept for ceremonial purposes only, but it was better than nothing. Rose's eyes went wide at the sight of the tiny pistol.

"Adrian, don't be a fool—" Rose started to say.

"Stay with her." He jammed a finger toward Edith.

"You can't seriously be thinking of facing whoever is out there with only—" But she bit her tongue at the look on his face. She slid onto the floor next to the shaking child, wrapping her arms around her. Edith turned her face into Rose's chest. The sight of them huddled together flared the flame of protectiveness that burned inside his chest. He didn't care what it took, he would keep both of them safe. At the expense of his own life if necessary.

The thundering hooves finally came to a halt just outside. A man's voice cackled, "Ooooo, looks like we got a *fancy* one here . . ."

Adrian's pulse pounded behind his ears, and his hand shook around the tiny handle of the Crockett. He tightened his grip and threw the door open, pistol raised.

"Stop right where you are!" he ordered. "I'm armed!"

There was a moment of silence as he took in the scene. The coach was angled sideways, one wheel cracked and sunk into a shallow ditch along the side of the main road. The horses still struggled in their restraints, and several yards away, the weakly stirring form of Joseph lay sprawled across the scorching sand with a bloody wound across his head.

As for the new arrivals, there were only two riders. One had skin so pale it was a miracle it wasn't already blistering in the Ordonian sun. White-blond hair coated his unshaven face and poked out from beneath the brim of his wide hat. His clothes were filthy and coated in so many stains it was hard to see what color they'd originally been. The other was his opposite in every sense, deeply tanned skin and a perfectly clean face, wearing a neatly tied bandanna around his neck and polished boots. His dark hair was swept to the side across his sharp eyes. ·

"Well shit, kid. We're in a pickle then," the blond one said, cocking back the hammer of his Dalton six-shooter. "'Cause we're armed too."

The other outlaw sighed and looked down at his nails as though Adrian was of no particular interest to him. Adrian's neck prickled at the insult of being called "kid." These ruffians were hardly older than he was.

The blond narrowed his eyes at Adrian's outstretched arm and then let loose a belly laugh. "Pedro! Look at that! Is that a gun or a toy? Damn! Where'd you find a little thing like that?"

"It's a pocket Crockett, Soap. A gentleman's dress gun," Pedro explained as though it were obvious. He continued to stare at his nails as though bored.

"Oh, a *gentleman's* gun. So we have a gentleman on our hands, do we? A baron's son perhaps?" The man called Soap dismounted and stalked closer. His spurs rattled with each step. "A baron who might be willing to pay a pretty copper or two to keep his son's neck from being snapped?"

Edith's whimper came from the wreckage. Adrian took a step back instinctively.

"Don't make too much of a mess. I just cleaned my boots," Pedro said, sounding exasperated.

Adrian's breath was coming in shallow, panicked gasps. He glanced back to where Rose and Edith were hidden. He only had one bullet. If he shot Soap now, would Pedro shoot him and go after the girls? Did he try to find a way to draw them both away from the scene? His thoughts felt as slow as a fly trapped in molasses as he tried to find a solution . . .

"Soap!" Rose's voice suddenly screamed from the coach. The door slammed open again and the novice clambered through the opening, stumbling on the hem of her dress.

Soap turned the gun toward Rose, nearly making Adrian jump to put himself between them. But before he got the chance, Rose ripped the novice bonnet off her head and let her red-brown braid tumble down her back. Her eyes sparked with a fury Adrian had never seen before.

Soap's eyes went wide, actually taking several steps back as though she were a predator closing in on him. Adrian's jaw went slack as Rose marched right up to Soap and ripped the gun out of his trembling, still-raised hand. She emptied the six bullets onto the ground.

"What the *hell* are you doing here?" Rose screamed at him, throwing his now empty pistol on the ground.

Adrian blinked. Soap blinked. Pedro . . . well, he continued to stare at his nails as though a novice of the church hadn't just materialized out of a wrecked carriage and assaulted his partner in crime.

Soap's mouth opened and closed like a gaping fish. "I—I—" he stuttered.

Even Edith peeked out of the coach door to see what was going on.

Then, to Adrian's horror, Rose let out a sound halfway between a laugh and a sob and threw her arms around the outlaw's neck. "I thought you were *dead*," she cried.

Soap pushed her back, staring at her face as though not quite believing what he was seeing. "Is that really you?" Then he laughed and pulled her back into a bone-crushing hug. "I thought *you* were dead."

Rose leaned in and whispered something in his ear, which made him laugh even harder and hug her tighter.

Pedro finally dropped his hand back onto his saddle horn and made an impatient sound. "Well, clearly we are all still alive. I'm glad we've established that."

"Wait." Adrian pointed between Soap and Rose, suddenly furious. "I don't understand—"

"Adrian," Rose wiped a tear from her eye. "These are my . . . brothers. My stupid, foolish, idiotic brothers."

"Brothers," Adrian repeated flatly. Again he took in Soap's white-blond hair and Pedro's inky black. There was no way they were all related.

"Adopted," Pedro said simply, correctly guessing the direction of Adrian's thoughts. As though that explained anything.

Rose sniffed and wiped a hand across her nose. "We grew up together at the mission before these two ran off and became outlaws. *Right, boys?*"

Soap nodded vigorously. "Yup. At the mission. That's where we grew up, alright."

Pedro shrugged.

"Edith, you can come out. It's alright," Rose called toward the coach.

"It is *not* alright!" Adrian burst out. His father's coach was ruined, Joseph was bleeding on the ground after having been thrown the Saints only knew how badly, one of the horses had managed to get free and was nothing more than a distant puff of dust against the horizon. And these two had *shot a gun* at his little sister. "They were planning to hold me for ransom!"

Rose lifted her hands placatingly in the air. "I'm so sorry, Adrian. I'm sure they had no idea who was in the coach."

"But they knew someone was in there! They had every intention of robbing if not killing us!"

"Nah, wouldn't have actually killed you, mate." Soap slapped a hand on Adrian's shoulder, but Adrian pulled it away.

"And what if that bullet had gone too far astray?"

Pedro actually laughed. "A bullet from a Dalton go astray? Does this boy know anything about pistols?"

Adrian's chest puffed up. "Of course I do, but when it's your *little sister* sitting inside—" Edith's head still peeked out of the coach's interior, but she hadn't moved to join them yet.

"Check the bullet hole," Soap said, angling his hat and pointing to the body of the coach. "It's too high to have hit anyone. It was just meant to scare ya into stopping. Your driver's fault he panicked and drove the thing off the road."

"You need a driver that doesn't spook so easy," Pedro added.

"*You shot at him!*"

"Okay." Rose stepped between them, lifting her arms. "Clearly these two were idiots. I'm not surprised, they always were." She glared at them, and they both dropped their chins like scolded puppies. "But they have no intention of robbing anyone right now, do they? In fact, they intend to *help* us repair the wheel, track down the horse that ran away, and offer their most sincere apologies before they go."

Soap and Pedro grumbled their agreement and got to work hoisting the coach out of the small ditch. Adrian attended to Joseph, who—although shaken and banged up—seemed to be okay. The cut across his head looked much scarier than it actually was.

Edith scurried out of the coach and into Rose's arms as Pedro and Soap unloaded repair supplies from a trunk underneath the carriage.

Adrian sidled up next to the governess, his mind abuzz with questions. "If they were wards with you at the mission, how did they end up as thieving outlaws?" He crossed his arms across his chest as he watched them.

Rose pursed her lips briefly. "Not everyone is born as fortunate as the child of a baron."

Something about her tone piqued his curiosity. "What do you mean?"

Rose sighed. "Pedro's parents died of the plague when he was only six. He survived by stealing, but by the time he made it to the mission, he'd been given the *T* brand for 'thief' on his wrist by the Ordonian authorities. Do you have any idea how hard it is to secure work with a brand like that?"

Adrian shifted uncomfortably on his feet. He knew for a fact that his father would never hire a ranch hand with a brand, even if he'd been branded as a child. "*A wildcat doesn't change its spots*," his father would say.

"What about Soap?" He glanced over to where Soap laughed as he wiped sweat out of his eyes before digging into the repair kit.

"He was an Ordonian soldier for a few months before he was dishonorably discharged. He has the *D* brand on his wrist. And again, I'm sure you're aware how difficult that makes it to find honest work."

"What did he do to deserve a *D* brand?" Ds were reserved for deserters, as far as he knew.

Rose's lips pursed again. "He fell in love with one of his commander's daughters and asked to marry her. Her father didn't approve, so he had him kicked out."

"He can't be kicked out of the army for that, that's not a legal reason. There has to have been something else."

Rose laughed bitterly. "You think they care what's actually legal? The moment that brand touched his skin, his future was over. Any chance he had with the girl burned as quickly as his own skin. That's all his commander cared about."

Adrian blanched, staring again at the two young men. With brands like those, they'd never have a hope of finding jobs that paid well enough to support themselves. "So they turned to their only option to survive," he concluded.

Rose nodded, hugging Edith a little tighter to her side. "Again, not everyone is born the child of a baron."

"That's so sad," Edith said.

"That's just life, sometimes. It's sad and it isn't fair, but we do the best we can with what we're given." Rose let her gaze meet Adrian's and held it there. "And instead of judging or making assumptions, we can have a little bit of compassion in understanding that not everything is as simple, as good or bad as we think it is."

Adrian took her words like a blow to the gut. They knocked the very wind from his lungs.

But as he pondered them, he realized that she was right. How tightly had he always held to the teachings of Saint Veritas? That truth and justice were black and white, easily discernible as right and wrong. But then he looked down at Edith. By all accounts, *she* should be a black-and-white issue. To some observers, her behavior warranted the business end of a cane and a one-way ticket to a convent, but Adrian knew different because he saw deeper than that. He saw the little girl crying out of her pain, the little girl desperate for love and attention—and managing those emotions, not correctly, but the only way she knew how. Not that it excused her inappropriate behavior . . . but it made the difference in viewing her as a fellow human being deserving of grace or not.

Saint Clementia taught the value of gentleness and mercy, and maybe there was a reason Saint Veritas was not the only Saint that mattered. There was a place for truth and justice, yes, but there was also a place for mercy. The cattle barons were the major employers in the territory, the ones responsible for almost the entire economy of Saelum. If they were unwilling to work with young men such as these, who, through no fault of their own, had found themselves dealt such unfair hands to play . . . was that true justice? He thought of the ranch hands his father had let go because of *his* mistake, their families and livelihoods affected for no better reason than the baron's desire to teach his son a lesson.

Pedro rolled up his shirtsleeves and lined up their tools in a perfect row across the dirt. The scarred *T* stood out against the rich brown skin of his forearm. Had he really been given such a permanent wound as a *child*?

Perhaps Adrian could even understand their anger toward the barons.

Adrian drew a deep breath. Then, he rolled up his sleeves, strode purposely over to Soap and Pedro, and bent down to help them with the wagon wheel. At first, they looked at him as if he'd grown a second head, but after they saw his determination to work beside them, they fell into an easy pattern. Adrian wasn't a weak gentleman's son, after all. He'd grown up on horses and out in the fields working alongside the ranch hands.

He could feel Rose's gaze hot on the back of his neck and tried to ignore the feeling it brought up in his stomach. Finally, after a few more hours of working on the broken wheel and hunting down the runaway horse, the coach was finally in shape enough to reach the ranch before dark.

Joseph was still lightheaded and nauseous from his fall, but Soap offered to drive them back.

"It's alright, I can manage the coach," Adrian said.

"I insist," Soap said, giving an elegant, exaggerated bow toward Edith. "It's the least we can do after ruining your fine afternoon."

Edith giggled, and Rose looked at Adrian with an expectant expression.

Adrian glanced up at the stars blinking awake in the fading daylight. The wind sweeping across the chaparral was beginning to cool. They really did need to get home. He took a deep breath and said, "Fine. I would be honored to compensate you for your time as well."

Soap's eyebrows nearly disappeared beneath the brim of his hat. "We'd sure appreciate that, kid."

Adrian clenched his jaw briefly. "It's Adrian, actually. Adrian Caldwell. And I do believe we are in need of some new ranch hands if you two are looking for some honest work. I'm sure my father would be happy to hire the two young men who 'saved us' when we were stranded on the side of the road with a broken wheel."

Soap whooped with excitement, whipping his hat off his head and beating it against his thigh. Pedro almost smiled.

But it was the smile of gratitude that lit up Rose's face, as radiant as a fresh sunrise, that had one finally pulling at the corners of Adrian's lips too.

CHAPTER

28

They still had another hour's ride back to the Caldwell homestead, and after such an eventful afternoon, Edith quickly fell asleep with her head in Cat's lap. Joseph rode next to Adrian, eyes shut and snoring gently.

Cat looked down at Edith's peaceful face, cheeks round and soft, slightly pinked and chapped from the wind earlier. She reached out and gently brushed away a tendril of dark hair that had escaped from her pigtail braids. A strange emotion seemed to tighten inside her chest, but Cat didn't quite know what it was.

"She's gotten so attached to you," Adrian said, his face half hidden in the growing dark. She swore she could see the brightness of his eyes sparkle through the shadows.

"I know," Cat said. She wasn't entirely sure that was a good thing.

"You sound like you're worried about that."

"It . . . can be risky to get too attached to people sometimes. You never know when they might leave you. Or betray you." Her throat tightened. "Sometimes even those who were once our dearest friends betray us."

She couldn't meet Adrian's eyes.

He was silent for several heartbeats.

"What happened to you?" he finally asked. "How did you end up a ward of the church?"

"I told you, my parents died."

"How did they die?"

"It doesn't matter!" Cat snapped so suddenly that Edith roused. Cat's hand absently rubbed her back until the girl settled again.

She still couldn't bring herself to look at Adrian's face.

"I'm sorry," he finally said, his voice low and soft. "For whatever happened to them."

I'm sorry. Cat nearly snorted in disgust. He thought he was apologizing in general, apologizing for the pain she felt because of their deaths. But he had no idea—*no idea*—that he owed her an apology for playing a role in their deaths, for telling his father about the aurium on her family's land all those years ago. Red-hot anger boiled behind her ears and left a metallic tang on her tongue.

But Adrian leaned forward from where he sat directly across from her, their knees inches apart in the coach, and placed a hand over hers— just like he had that night in the kitchen. It doused her anger like a bucket of water tossed over flaming coals.

"I know what it feels like to lose a parent. It is not a pain I wish on anyone in the world. I can't even imagine losing two," he said.

Her heart squirmed painfully. She wanted to be angry at him, to scream at him for having been such a foolish, trusting child, for ruining her life with his one stupid choice, but even as the accusations bubbled to the forefront of her consciousness, she knew in her heart that it wasn't really Adrian she was angry with.

It was herself.

Because it wasn't Adrian who had been a foolish child all those years ago. *She* had been. She'd been so infatuated with him, so hopeful that her secret would impress him, that she'd broken the promise she'd made to her father. She'd promised she'd never tell their family secret, and yet she had. That one choice, one stupid, stupid mistake. It had been the pebble that set off the rockslide that buried her—and her family right along with her.

Adrian always struggled with being compared to his father; she'd known that about him even then. He had hated whenever people told him he looked like his father or that he was a "chip off the old block." It was why that geode had meant so much to him when they'd found it as kids. He'd been so fascinated by it, and she'd told him to keep it, to let it remind him that something's outsides didn't always reflect its insides.

Adrian looked like a Caldwell, but he was different from his father. He cared so much about doing the *right* thing, about always telling the truth. Maybe that was to show himself just how different from his father he wanted to be. The number of times she'd had to talk him out of confessing their numerous misdeeds, convincing him one way or another that the right thing was *not* to get themselves in trouble. She bit back a tragic laugh at the thought.

Of course he wouldn't have wanted to keep a secret from his father. Of course he'd have wanted to tell the truth. She should have known that about him. It was who he was, who he clearly still was—good, honest, kind.

She was the rotten seed. She always had been. Sneaking into places she didn't belong, stealing sweets from the kitchens, getting mouthy with her governess and refusing to practice her lessons, using her gift to keep herself out of even more trouble.

Telling secrets she'd sworn never to tell.

Even now, Adrian was trying to take care of his little sister and show kindness to an orphaned novice, and she was the one with a red ledger and a wanted poster, lying to him and Edith about who she really was and what she was doing.

Why the hell would the Saints ever have Blessed her with anything?

She glanced down at Edith's peaceful, sleeping form, the soft rise and fall of her little chest. She was going to break this little girl's heart when she got what she needed from their father and disappeared. She'd do as much damage to Baron Caldwell as possible, getting him thrown into Fort Astor's prison if she could. What would happen to Adrian and Edith then? She was going to destroy their family just as thoroughly as Caldwell had destroyed hers.

But what was the alternative? To let Caldwell win? To let him rig the election and steal the aurium from her family's land and fund a revolution against the empire? She couldn't let that happen either.

A tear slid down her cheek as her mind swirled in a twister of thoughts, leaving more emotional destruction in their wake. A warm, gloved hand reached up and brushed the tear away.

"I'm sorry," Cat finally said, her voice thick with everything she wanted to tell Adrian but knew she never could.

"For what? For feeling pain from your past? For making such an impression on my sister? For teaching me to have some compassion where I didn't have any before?"

Cat gave a watery chuckle. "For more than you could ever know."

✦ · · · · ✪ · · · · · ✦

If Cat thought Baron Caldwell had been uptight and controlling before, it was nothing compared to the following morning.

He'd been furious with Adrian for returning so late the day before, seeming to miss the tiny detail that they'd been *stranded* on the side of the road with a broken wheel. They'd all left out the details of Soap and Pedro scaring the living daylights out of the driver, and Joseph had felt bad enough that he'd driven off the road that he didn't want to contradict the story and risk Caldwell firing him either. At least Caldwell had agreed to hire the two young men that had "stopped to help them."

Somehow, however, the ordeal was still Adrian's fault, for not being more prepared, for not taking care of things faster. Cat had listened to him lecture and humiliate Adrian for the better part of an hour before she'd finally decided to go up to bed.

She hadn't had a chance to ask Soap or Pedro if they knew what had happened to Amos. Both were sent to the bunkhouse as soon as Caldwell looked them over.

She knew that Caldwell would likely spend the entire night in his study again, but it didn't stop her from checking several times throughout the night just to be sure. But every time she'd tiptoed down that first-floor hallway, light poured out from beneath the closed office door along with the occasional grunt, scratch of a quill, or clink of a bottle.

Damn him, did the man *ever* sleep? She was going to have to sneak in there during the gathering itself, the only time he'd probably be too busy to hide away in his office.

The servants were in a state from the moment Cat opened her eyes that morning. The cheerful maid, who usually bustled in to throw open her drapes and leave a tray with coffee and bread upon her dresser, threw open the door without a drop of decorum, making Cat yelp and almost reach for her knife. The maid plopped the tray unceremoniously on Cat's side table, rushed to throw open the curtains, and then bustled out without even a "good morning."

Cat knew from the harried expression on her face that today was going to be an interesting day.

And it was. The house was scrubbed from top to bottom until every picture frame gleamed and the wooden floors and paneled walls reflected the fresh flowers placed strategically upon every surface imaginable. The formal dining hall was a flurry of activity, and the dance floor and table settings were laid out with the utmost care. Even the gardeners prowled between the hedgerows and bushes with clippers, looking for any leaf that dared to step out of line and threaten the image of manicured perfection.

Adrian flitted between everything like a bee obsessed with visiting every flower. It was a job that typically would have fallen to the baroness of the house, but with Mrs. Caldwell gone, the responsibility had fallen to Adrian. His father, of course, would be busy handling more *important* matters.

Captain Freeman was already there, strolling lazily throughout the setup and giving strategic instructions to the soldiers who would be overseeing security of the event. With every baron in Saelum Territory in one location, Caldwell was sparing no expense when it came to safety. Or anything else, it appeared, given the heavy aroma of roasting steaks and corn muffins, savory herbs, and sweet cake frosting wafting from the kitchens. This was his chance to show off and impress the peers who would be voting to recommend the next governor in only three short days.

Which left Cat with the major task of keeping Edith out of her father's line of sight and thereby avoiding his temper. They spent the morning in the library going through some Saints-awful etiquette rules that Edith was likely going to need that evening. By lunchtime they were both ready to pluck out their eyeballs and begin playing marbles with them, so Cat took Edith out to the stables to visit with Almond. They brushed her coat, fed her apples, and even took her for several turns around the paddock. Edith still wasn't ready to ride on her own, but she was getting more comfortable. A few more weeks and—

Cat slammed the thought down. She wouldn't be here in a few weeks.

"Are you alright, Rose? You seem sad about something." Edith tensed in the saddle in front of her.

Damn the girl's perceptiveness.

"It's nothing. I'm just thinking about what I'm going to do tonight while you are having a splendid time at the gathering."

Edith turned around, and her mouth popped open. "You aren't coming with me?"

"I didn't think I was, does your father want me there?" Cat pulled the reins to slow Almond to a stop. She dismounted and then helped Edith down from the horse's back.

Edith's eyes began to swim with tears. "I don't want to go without you! Adrian said you could come if you wanted to."

"It's okay," Cat said quickly, sensing the girl was about to have a panic attack. "I will be there if you need me."

Edith sniffled, wiping a hand under her nose. "I can't remember all those stupid rules. I'd rather hide in the kitchens and just steal bites of cake."

"Well, frankly I'd rather do that too," Cat said with a smile, pulling Almond's lead rope to take her back to the stables. "But your father probably wouldn't approve of such unladylike behavior."

"That's why I need you there." Her eyes swam with pleading.

Cat thought about how *she* needed to get into Caldwell's office, but there had to be a way to be there for Edith too. She would just have to be creative.

"I will be there," Cat said again. "There's just one little problem."

"What that?" Edith asked.

Cat playfully bumped into her. "Whatever shall I wear?"

To her surprise, Edith dimpled. "Actually, Adrian already took care of that for you, just in case you decided to come. It should be in your room already."

Cat stopped and regarded Edith with a look of exasperation. "What do you mean, 'Adrian already took care of that'?"

Edith squealed like an overexcited piglet and began sprinting toward the house. "You'll see!" she called over her shoulder.

Unease swirled through Cat's stomach. What had Adrian done now?

"Edith," Adrian said, assessing his little sister in the mirror. "I still can't believe how grown-up you look."

Edith made a gagging sound and pulled at the lace and frills hugging all the way up to her throat.

"Just lovely," he said, rolling his eyes.

She glared at him, her hands inching up toward the elegant braided updo the maid had managed to inflict upon her. He gently grabbed her fingers and lowered them away from the maid's hard work.

"Don't touch it, you'll ruin it."

Edith growled. "Where's Rose? She promised me she would come."

"I'm sure she'll meet you as soon as she's ready herself. Father's instructions are for you to stay with her the entire evening."

"I can't wait to see the dress you picked out for her."

Adrian pulled at his own high collar and cravat. He was already exceptionally warm in the black formal coat, but his father insisted upon dressing like the peerage in the capital for tonight's event. "I didn't *pick out* a dress for her, I just had one of Mother's altered to fit her."

"The white one with the red roses?" Edith sighed. "That was always my favorite."

Adrian cleared his throat. "Yes, the one with the roses."

"I bet she'll look *beautiful.*"

Adrian secretly agreed, but he wasn't about to say as much in front of his little sister.

A hard, fast knock sounded behind him. Adrian turned, surprised to see his father standing framed in Edith's doorway. The man was the picture of elegance. His dark mustache had been groomed smooth and shaped into fancy little curls on the ends. Atop his head sat a stylish silk top hat, and his evening coat was perfectly pressed, with gleaming golden buttons. His boots shone like black beetle shells, and a golden watch chain dangled from a pocket of his embroidered silk vest.

"Oh, Father, I'm so sorry, is there something I missed? I can—"

"No, you're fine, Adrian. I'm actually here for Edith."

"She's ready, and the governess will be with her at all times tonight—"

But the baron cut him off. "I'm not here for any of that. I'm actually here to give Edith a gift before her first social event."

Adrian blinked. Beside him, Edith's spine went rigid.

"A—a gift?" Adrian asked.

"Yes, a gift. You think I don't recognize what an occasion this is for her? This is her first introduction into finer society. Why do you think I work so hard, Adrian? It's to secure a better place for—" But the baron took a deep breath and stopped himself before the lecture began in earnest. "Regardless. I want my children to appear just as impressive as their father this evening. We will show the rest of Saelum Territory, and all of Ordonia, exactly what it means to be a Caldwell."

He withdrew a small brown paper package from beneath his jacket and held it gently between his gloved hands.

Edith sucked in a breath of surprise. "What is it?" she whispered, reaching for the package but stopping herself at the stern look in her father's eye.

Baron Caldwell peeled back the simple brown paper and revealed a small white box. He opened it, and sitting upon a blue velvet cushion was a beautiful golden necklace. It was an intricate chain woven of delicate links, and at the end dangled a golden Ordonian rose pendant the size of Adrian's thumbnail.

Edith gasped, her lace-gloved hands covering her mouth. "Father, it's . . . *gorgeous*." Her voice sounded hushed, as though this was a holy moment.

Adrian smiled. Perhaps it was.

"Face the mirror and I'll put it on you," their father instructed.

He took the chain and looped it around Edith's neck. "You will not embarrass me tonight, Edith. You will obey me and show the other barons what a finely behaved and well-mannered child you really are. You will stay with your governess and you will make your family proud."

Edith's face, which moments before had been alight with excitement, went almost blank as if all traces of her feisty personality had been erased like chalk from a schoolmaster's chalkboard. "My family proud," she repeated. She glanced down at her hands. "Yes, Father. I will not embarrass you tonight."

Adrian's heart ached at the sight.

His father stepped back and clapped his hands together. "Well, that is that. I do believe it is time for us to head downstairs and welcome our guests. Adrian, make sure her governess is there to supervise her, please. I want your attention focused on the young ladies we discussed, not on what your sister is doing."

Adrian nodded, his stomach suddenly fluttering with nerves. "Yes, Father." He noted how flat and subdued his own voice sounded.

While Edith followed the baron out of the room and down to the entrance hall, Adrian stopped by Rose's door and let his gloved knuckles fall against its surface.

"Rose, are you ready to go downstairs? The guests should be arriving any minute and my father wants you on Edith duty as soon as possible."

There was a jumbled sound of rushed movement from within, followed by a low curse.

Adrian smiled despite himself. She really did have the filthiest mouth he'd ever heard from a novice.

"Is everything okay?" he asked again.

"Shit! Shit, shit, shit . . ." was the only response.

"Rose?" Adrian pushed the door open, seriously worried that something was wrong.

But nothing seemed to be wrong, aside from the fact that Rose was standing in front of her tall, plain mirror with the back of her dress completely open, exposing her corset. Her fingers slipped across the buttons as she struggled to do the thing back up.

Adrian nearly swallowed his tongue. "I'm—oh Saints—I'm so sorry, I had no idea you were still indecent—I thought—"

But to his surprise, Rose just growled, "Oh, stop being such a gentleman and get in here and help me."

Adrian's neck flushed so hot he worried it was going to burn through his starched collar. He stepped inside and glanced back toward the door as though waiting for someone to save him from such an improper situation.

"I—don't understand. Didn't the maid—wasn't she supposed to—"

Rose let out a huff of frustration. "Yes, she did help me, but then I undid it to . . . uh . . . fix something . . . and now I can't get it done back up. I need you to do it."

Adrian took a step backward. "I can see if I can go find a maid—"

Rose gestured impatiently for him to come closer. "They've already all gone and lined up downstairs. Which is where we are supposed to be and you *know* your dad will not be happy if we're late."

Adrian swallowed. Hard. She was right. If they were late, his father would be furious. Especially if he missed greeting any of the arriving daughters his father had instructed him to court.

"I—uh—alright. Fine." He finally stepped forward, trying not to blush at the creamy skin of her exposed back and the crisscrossing ribbons of her corset. He had the sudden desire to rip them open instead of covering them beneath the silk and lace of the dress . . . a desire he immediately shoved down so deep within himself he swore he'd never again let it see the light of day.

He let his gaze wander briefly over the curls of her red-brown hair, arranged into a beautiful cascade that tumbled down across her right shoulder. He swallowed again. Edith was right, she *was* beautiful, especially in his mother's evening gown. The cream-colored silk and lace flowed out into a full skirt like a wedding cake, coated with embroidered red Ordonian roses at regular intervals. The neckline dipped down her chest into a V, while the lace sleeves clung to her upper arms, exposing the delicate skin of her throat and shoulders.

Adrian couldn't help but think how beautiful a string of Dark Sea pearls would look across her slender neck.

"Adrian. Help me," she repeated, pointing at her back. "I'm not going down there with my corset hanging out like this."

Adrian shook his head to collect his thoughts and immediately reached out to start redoing the tiny silk buttons. There was no way her fingers were ever going to reach these on their own.

"Thank the Saints you came when you did," Rose said, leaning forward and bracing herself on the dressing table to give him better access to the buttons on her lower back. "I was seriously in trouble."

Adrian's heart thrummed a frantic rhythm beneath his breastbone as he tried to focus his attention and not let his hands fumble. He could feel the heat of her skin, and he wanted nothing more than to let one of his fingers trace the pattern of the freckles on her back like a constellation of stars.

But he was a gentleman, and as beautiful and exposed as she might be at this moment, he would not touch her in such an intimate way without her permission.

Finally, *finally*, he finished the last of the buttons and stepped back, as breathless as if he'd just run up one of the foothills.

Rose smoothed out the gathers on her skirt and turned this way and that to check her reflection in the mirror. "There. That's much more appropriate for the gathering."

"You look incredible." The words slipped out of Adrian's mouth before he could stop himself.

Rose lifted a lace fan off the dressing table and flourished it dramatically before batting it in front of her face with a laugh. "Why thank you, can you tell I have so much experience dressing like this?"

"You look as if you were born to dress like this."

Rose lowered the fan, a shattered look filling her eyes so fast it nearly knocked the breath from his lungs.

Damn it, he'd offended her. Again. What was wrong with his tongue that it was now apparently operating of its own accord without any consideration for what was appropriate?

"Saints, I'm so sorry. I didn't mean it like—"

"No, it's alright. We just—probably need to get downstairs." She swept past him toward the hallway, as though she couldn't get away from him fast enough.

Which was probably for the best. He needed to clear his head if he was going to be paying attention to anyone other than her tonight.

CHAPTER

30

Cat hurried down the stairs and skidded to a halt right beside Edith. She expected Edith to greet her with a smirk or at least *some* kind of snarky greeting, but instead, the girl barely glanced up, her hands kept neatly folded in front of her, her posture rigid and proper.

It struck Cat as odd, but then again, Edith was standing next to her father, so perhaps the pressure of the evening was getting to her. Cat mimicked Edith's erect stance, and Baron Caldwell cast an approving glance over the pair of them. Adrian appeared on the baron's other side, his face slightly pink and flustered, but looking handsome and put-together in his evening attire.

One of the servants gestured with a white-gloved hand to an older gentleman and his wife who had just walked through the front doors into the entrance hall ahead of their two teenage daughters. "Baron and Baroness Hernandez, and their daughters, Evangeline and Francesca Hernandez."

Baron Caldwell greeted the Hernandez family warmly, asking mundane questions about their journey to the capital and how their cattle were faring. Cat tried to remember which part of Saelum Territory the Hernandezes were from. She was fairly certain it was a large section of land in the southeast.

There were twenty or so Saelum cattle barons in total, some owning great swaths of land that covered hundreds of square miles, while others were less prominent but still landowners in the eyes of the empire. Tax-paying citizens who kept the beef trade alive and thriving across all of Ordonia. The only real difference between them and their peers in the older, more established regions of Ordonia was in the age of their titles and the prestige of their names. The barons of Saelum were "new money" according to the peerage, self-made but wild mustangs that tried to keep up with the purebred stallions.

Cat's grandfather had been one of them: the first Baron Macgregor, founder of her own family's homestead, one of the largest in southern Saelum. He'd traveled into the wilds of the untamed western territory when he was only eighteen to stake out a claim upon his own plot of land and ultimately helped build Saelum's prosperous cattle trade. He'd been the stubborn third son of an earl, with no inheritance or real prospects of his own. The Macgregors had more name prestige than some of the other families from more humble beginnings, but her grandfather had started with just as little as the rest of them. And he'd built it into just as much.

What would he think of her now? Of what she'd done with her family's legacy? She shook her head to focus on what was happening in front of her.

Adrian was greeting the two Hernandez daughters, striking up easy conversation with them as if he did this sort of thing all the time. His smile was dazzling, which left a strange hollow sensation inside her chest. She didn't like to see him give that smile to someone else, but she quickly reminded herself how foolish a thought that was. She looked at Evangeline Hernandez, statuesque with long dark hair that hung down her back like an ebony waterfall. Her full lips smiled warmly at Cat, and Cat felt her gaze drop. Perhaps in another life, they would have been equals, friends even, but not anymore. Evangeline could greet her with kindness, but their circles no longer overlapped. Now Cat was a lowly governess overseeing and teaching a real member of their class, but no longer a member herself.

And not that she *wanted* to be. Frilly lace collars and voluminous skirts, polite conversation and parties? Hell, Cat knew herself better than that. She'd hated those things as a child anyway, preferring to explore the river barefoot and ride her horse with her father. She remembered Edith hopping through the mud chasing after tadpoles, and a smile tugged at her lips . . . at least until she glanced down to where Edith dipped into a perfect curtsy to Baroness Hernandez, her upper lip as stiff as her father's.

The child was not acting like herself at all. Had the baron said something to frighten her? Cat's intuition prickled with unease.

The guests continued to arrive, one gloriously fancy coach after another. Soon the courtyard and ballroom were filled with laughter and the tinkling of crystal glasses. A string quartet played a lively tune that lent a jovial feel to the overall atmosphere. The gas lamps reflected off the polished surfaces of the paneled walls, and flaming candelabras lined the glowing courtyard.

As much as Cat hated to admit it, Caldwell had done an excellent job. After greeting the guests, he circulated around the space, socializing and schmoozing in that way that politicians always did. Edith followed him around like a tiny duckling waiting for her moment to be introduced, after which she stood silently beside him, a prop in his charade of having perfect control and influence over his "well-behaved" children.

Edith following Caldwell around meant that Cat did as well. Many of the barons and baronesses introduced themselves to her, under the impression that because of her dress, she was somehow one of them, until Caldwell made sure to emphasize her title of *governess*. Then they gave nods of understanding before turning to engage far more important figures in conversation. Cat wasn't surprised in the slightest; a novice turned governess wasn't of particular interest when they had *real* matters to discuss. Such as Baroness Higgins getting married for a third time, or Baron Archer losing an entire head of cattle in a bet to Baron Sanchez, or the rumored aurium rush along the Sequine River in northern Saelum. And, of course, the whispered conversations about the upcoming vote, of which barons or baronesses stood the greatest chance of securing the vote of their peers.

All in all, Cat was horrifically bored. They passed a dessert table laid out with tiny chocolate and orange cakes and fruit-filled tarts with cream. Her mouth watered. She remembered her parents hosting parties like this when she was young. She'd had to stay upstairs with her own governess, but she'd sneak down to try to steal cakes or sweets from the tables anyway. That was the only interesting part to a seven- or eight-year-old. Caldwell and Edith passed right by the cakes on their way to greet the next guest, and Cat grunted in disappointment.

But after another mind-numbing thirty minutes of pleasantries, Edith's continued "perfect" behavior did not waver. Cat's concern deepened.

She finally tapped the child on the shoulder. "Edith, do you want to get a treat with me? Those chocolate cakes are singing our names."

Edith turned, her face impassive. "No, thank you. I am not permitted to have sweets until after the main meal." Her tone was as flat as her expression.

But that was when Cat noticed it. A golden sheen shone across Edith's dark eyes, barely reflecting in the glow of the gaslights. Cat's heart stuttered.

Saints! Was she cursed? Who would do such a thing to a *child*?

Her glare narrowed toward Baron Caldwell, who gave an exaggerated laugh and slapped one of the other barons on the shoulder.

"Edith, why don't we go to the ladies' room to freshen up?"

Edith blinked, gold barely glittering behind her lashes. "No, thank you, Miss Rose. I'm fine."

Cat's pulse pounded behind her ears. She had to do something. She glanced up to where Adrian was waltzing with Evangeline Hernandez. The dance floor had been set up in the center of the ballroom, and dozens of couples swirled around it, the ladies in their lace dresses like blooming desert flowers. She hated to interrupt him, especially when they seemed to be having a lovely time together . . . well, no. That was total crap. Seeing him dance with someone else felt like a sad fiddle twanging her heartstrings. She didn't have a problem interrupting them at all.

"Excuse me just a moment," she said to Edith before making her way to the dance floor. She marched right up to Adrian and Evangeline, giving a polite curtsy to Evangeline before widening her eyes meaningfully at Adrian.

"I am so sorry to interrupt, but may I have a quick word with Mr. Caldwell?"

"Rose? Is everything alright?" he asked, dropping his hands from Evangeline's waist as though he was embarrassed.

"Of course. I was just a little concerned about Edith not feeling well and was wondering if you might be able to assist me?"

Evangeline glanced between them, her smile still warm and kind. "I have little sisters as well. I understand if you need to go."

Cat supposed she should be grateful. Evangeline seemed really pleasant, but for some reason she just felt annoyed. Adrian bent down to kiss Evangeline's hand and thanked her for the dance, promising to find her again, which didn't help Cat's annoyed feeling at all. She shoved it down—there were more important things to worry about.

She grabbed Adrian's hand and dragged him toward the edge of the ballroom.

"Rose, what's—"

Cat finally stopped and spun around to face him. "Edith is cursed."

Adrian's mouth gaped open. "Cursed? What do you mean?"

"Cursed! She's under the influence of the corrupted power of a Saint. She's been exposed to aurium somehow but—" She hadn't realized how frantic she'd become until Adrian gripped her by the shoulders and squeezed.

"Breathe, Rose. It's okay. Slow down."

"Adrian, she's *cursed*! She's just a little girl!" Tears built inexplicably behind her eyes. Why was this affecting her so deeply? Something about seeing that free, mischievous spirit, not so unlike her own, reined in and broken like an abused horse, totally powerless, forced against her will . . .

Cat took a deep breath and tried to steady herself.

"Hey," Adrian said, rubbing her arms reassuringly. "It's okay. I'm sure she's fine. There's no way she could have been exposed to . . ."

But Cat grabbed his hand again and dragged him—rather forcefully—toward where his father was entertaining a large group with a joke about ranch hands. Edith stood silently on the outskirts, the perfect picture of compliance and obedience.

"Tell me that's normal," Cat demanded as they got to the little girl's side.

Edith made no acknowledgment that her brother or governess had just arrived. She continued to stare toward her father with a serene expression.

Adrian's brow furrowed. "Edith? Are you alright?"

Edith slowly turned to face him, her face spreading into a vapid smile that nearly turned Cat's stomach. There was something almost *evil* about it.

"Why, yes, brother. Thank you for your polite inquiry. I am quite well."

Adrian blinked before turning to Cat with a horrified expression.

Cat chewed her thumbnail. "Her eyes, Adrian, look at her eyes. There's a gold sheen of some kind behind them."

Adrian bent down and studied the girl's face, staring into her eyes the way a physician might assess for a head injury.

Edith continued the vapid, eerie smile.

Adrian must have seen the same thing as Cat because he straightened suddenly. He met her gaze with a look of concern mirroring her own.

"Edith, I need you to go upstairs with Miss Rose," he said to her. Then he turned to Cat. "I will tell my father she isn't feeling well and meet you in her room." He peeled off his gloves and handed them to her. "If you find any aurium, make sure you don't touch it with your bare skin."

Cat nodded, steering Edith toward the staircase by her shoulders.

"I'm really feeling fine. My father wants me to stay with him, I must *obey* him . . ." Edith started to ramble, but the word *obey* stuck out like a prickle in a flower patch. With a shock, Cat remembered the bloody scene in the Caldwell storehouse, where that unsuspecting young soldier had shot himself after touching powdered aurium.

Saint Pietas. Patron saint of dutifulness and obedience.

Those Blessed with his gift were granted the ability to influence others, to win them over to their cause. A dangerous gift, but granted only to those hand-chosen by the Saint to do his will.

But the *corrupted* power of his gift? Aurium cursed with the power of Saint Pietas mind-controlled the victim, forcing them into perfect obedience against their will. A power even more dangerous in the hands of those who could use it for whatever purpose they chose . . .

Edith resisted, but apparently part of her directive involved not drawing attention or causing a scene, so Cat managed to rush her up the stairs without any incident. As soon as they got into her bedroom, Edith turned and faced the door with her arms slack at her side like a servant waiting for orders.

Cat immediately checked her hands and wrists, looking for signs of aurium. Then she noticed the golden chain winking from around Edith's neck. She slipped on Adrian's gloves and delicately lifted the chain. Sure enough, the gold was beginning to tarnish, slowly turning to dust as the magic was spent. This much aurium was meant to last several hours before dissolving entirely.

The door behind her slammed open against the wall as Adrian rushed in. "Did you find it?" he asked, his voice tense.

Cat nodded somberly, lifting the tarnishing chain a little higher. "It's the necklace. I think it's cursed with the power of Saint Pietas."

"Pietas?" Adrian repeated. "Patron saint of . . ."

"Obedience," Cat finished for him, reaching back and undoing the clasp.

The necklace slipped off Edith's neck and slithered to the floor like a coiled golden snake. Brownish-green stains dotted the chain's length and wilted the petals of the small golden rose that dangled from the end.

The moment the necklace left her skin, Edith's demeanor shifted. Her shoulders dropped, her posture relaxed, and life and spirit rushed back into her brown eyes—along with an abundance of tears. She launched herself into Cat's arms, letting sobs shake her small body.

"Is it gone?" she cried. Her fingers clawed at Cat's neck as though she couldn't hug her tightly enough. "Am I me again?"

Tears built up behind Cat's eyes too as she squeezed her back. Her throat went tight. "It's gone. It's gone," she repeated over and over, rubbing Edith's back. "You're okay."

Adrian carefully picked up the necklace with his handkerchief and examined it with a deep frown.

"Where did you get the necklace?" Cat asked Edith, gently pulling back and wiping a tear from the child's cheek. "Did someone at the party give it to you?"

But it was Adrian who answered, his voice cracking with emotion. "No. It was our father."

31

Edith was hysterical—and understandably so. Cat held her until she hiccuped herself into silence, shuddering with each little inhale of breath. When she finally calmed down, Cat helped her into her nightdress and into bed.

Adrian, who had hovered nearby to help with anything, remained thoughtful and silent, but a subtle anger seemed to radiate from him like heat from simmering coals. When Edith was finally tucked beneath her quilt, Cat stepped back so that he could bend over and kiss Edith's forehead.

"I will talk to our father about this, I promise."

Edith sniffed, her voice growing in panic as she realized she would have to go to sleep. "But what if it happens again? How do I protect myself? What if I have nightmares?"

Cat's heart twisted at Edith's fear. Having your will taken forcefully from you, being in your body but not truly in control of it—Cat shivered at the thought. Edith was obviously going to have a hard time falling asleep, as worked up as she was. Cat wished she could take her fears away, protect her, hurt anyone that tried to take the little girl's freedom from her ever again. But then she had a sudden idea.

Her thoughts went back to Amos, who'd been a father to her in so many ways it made her chest ache just to think about him. That first year he'd taken her in had been so difficult, it had taken a long time to realize how much Amos had done to help her, to put her somewhat back together again. For an outlaw, he'd really had a heart of pure gold.

She remembered she'd been afraid of Caldwell's men finding her, shrieking from nightmares of men dressed in black with reaching hands. The other men complained about Cat waking them up at all hours of the night, but Amos had taken her over to the fire and asked what her nightmares were about.

Cat had told him very little, just that bad men were trying to take her away. Amos nodded thoughtfully and then reached into his saddlebag and pulled out a small pocketknife. Cat remembered being too afraid to take it at first, but he showed her how to hold it properly and some basics of how to use it if someone tried to come near her.

"I can't take away the threats, Cat. But I can show you how to protect yourself from them. That's how you face your fear: you empower yourself, don't give in to it," he'd said.

That was when her training had begun in earnest, first with a knife, and then eventually with her guns. She would never be a helpless kitten again. She would forever be a wild cat with claws, able to defend herself.

"Actually, Edith, there is something you can use to protect yourself. Hang on, I'll be right back." Cat tapped the girl on her nose before bustling back to her room.

She rifled through her carpetbag until she found the simple silver chain Father Ephraim had given to her. A small crystal vial the size of half her thumb dangled from the chain's end, sloshing with a small amount of blessed holy water. She'd intended to start wearing the necklace herself, but Edith needed it more than she did right now.

She slipped back into Edith's room, and Adrian arched an inquisitive eyebrow.

"The best way to face your fear is to empower yourself," Cat said matter-of-factly, lifting the chain and letting the vial of holy water swing back and forth like a pendulum. "Maybe you can't stop them if someone tries to use aurium against you, but you can protect yourself if they try.

Holy water blessed by the Mother negates the power of aurium, and I happen to have some of it right here."

Edith sat straight up in bed, her reddened eyes twinkling with hope. "Really? It protects you from aurium?"

Cat nodded. "If someone tries to use it on you, just open this little bottle and put it on your skin and you'll be safe. You don't ever have to let someone take your will from you again."

Edith released a deep breath of relief as Cat secured the silver chain around her neck. "There. This necklace is a much better one anyway."

Edith gave a watery chuckle and wiped a hand across her nose. "Thank you, Rose." She leaned forward and hugged her one more time.

Cat held her tight, a strange sensation building in her throat. A voice whispered inside her head. *You're going to just leave her? Get your revenge on her father and then leave her alone, another orphan with no parents?* Cat shoved it away. She couldn't think about that right now.

She looked up at Adrian, who was staring at her with an odd pained expression, as though what he was seeing almost broke his heart.

He finally cleared his throat, his eyes briefly glistening with something suspiciously like tears. "I need to get back down to the gathering, Edith. Are you and Rose okay to stay here?"

"No!" Edith said suddenly, pulling herself out of Cat's arms.

Cat laughed. "No? You *want* to go back down there?"

Edith snorted in disgust. "Of course not. But I had a plan for tonight."

It was Cat's turn to arch an eyebrow. "A plan? What kind of plan, you little fox?"

Edith's mischievous dimple reappeared in her cheek. "I finally decided Adrian's punishment for losing the bet against you."

"Oh?" Adrian asked, now smiling as well. "And what horror do you have in store for me?"

"You have to dance," Edith chirped.

"Edith, I've been dancing all night." Adrian feigned exasperation.

"No. That's not what I mean. You have to dance *with Miss Rose*." Edith's dimple deepened. "Twice."

"Twice?" Adrian was already shaking his head.

"I know more than two dances is considered inappropriate, so only two dances," Edith argued quickly. "You promised you would do whatever I chose for punishment, and that is my choice!"

"Edith." Cat started shaking her head too. "Wouldn't you rather me stay up here with you?"

"You can come back up after! And bring me a piece of cake, of course!"

Cat laughed. "Of course."

The little girl crossed her arms and turned her nose into the air. "You both promised, and I will not be satisfied until you have fulfilled that promise. Or are you telling me you both lied to an innocent child?" Her eyes went as wide and imploring as a puppy's.

Cat threw a pillow at her. "Innocent child, my boots. Like I said, you are a little *fox*."

Edith giggled and settled herself back into bed with her hands folded neatly across her stomach. "I will patiently wait here for you to report back on the dances and bring my cake. One with chocolate and orange." She waved her hand in a shooing motion. "Go on."

Adrian met Cat's gaze with an amused expression before offering her his hand. "Well, Miss Rose, are we going to deny such a sweet, *innocent* child her request?"

Cat sighed, her stomach squirming uncomfortably. She swallowed—hard—before putting her hand in Adrian's and letting him help her to her feet. "I guess we don't have a choice."

"One with chocolate and orange!" Edith reminded them with her wicked little smile before the door closed between them.

The moment they were alone in the hall, Cat pulled her hand back from Adrian's. A panicky, fluttering feeling was building inside her, and her palms were growing moist.

"Rose? Are you alright?" Adrian asked.

"I—um—" She glanced toward the staircase, the music from the ballroom drifting up like the haunting call of a siren from a distant beach. "I don't know how—to, um—"

Her rebellious cheeks flamed with her embarrassment. She fiddled absently with one of the embroidered roses on her skirt.

"Ah," Adrian said. "You don't know how to dance, do you?"

Her cheeks burned even hotter. She couldn't meet his eyes. As the daughter of a baron, it was something she would have learned as she got older, but she had never got the chance. And Amos didn't exactly prioritize teaching her dancing over lessons with a horse and guns.

Cat shook her head.

Adrian was quiet for a moment. "Hmmm, we cannot break our promise to Edith, as she clearly pointed out. And I will not force you onto a dance floor if you are uncomfortable. What if we took a leaf out of your tricky little playbook and found a way to fulfill her requirement in a different way?"

Cat looked up, her curiosity piqued. "What do you mean?"

"Well, you said you'd get her on a horse and left out that you'd be on the horse *with* her, and that still counted as a win. I suggest we make a similar arrangement." He sounded so formal in his suggestion, but his eyes sparkled with a mischief not unlike his little sister's.

"I knew there was some rebel in you after all," Cat said, crossing her arms. "What do you have in mind?"

"Well, we said we would dance two dances. But we never specified *where*."

Cat grinned. "Clever. I like the way you think, Caldwell."

Adrian offered her a hand, and this time, Cat didn't hesitate to take it.

✦ • • • • ✹ • • • • ✦

Adrian led Cat to the courtyard outside the ballroom. The fountain where they'd hidden the tadpoles splashed joyfully, and the light of candles and gas lamps mixed with the natural light of the almost full moon hanging in the purple velvet sky above them. All around, flowers climbed the trellises, and perfectly trimmed hedges and rosebushes grew from the planters lining the tile paths. A heavy scent of Ordonian roses tickled Cat's nose in the warm evening air.

The music of the hired band could still be heard through the open windows of the ballroom, and with the nobility of Saelum crammed inside the elegant space, Adrian and Cat had the courtyard relatively to themselves. Still, she couldn't help but notice he chose a stretch of tile hidden behind a strategically placed hedge, keeping them out of sight of the open windows themselves.

Adrian pulled her close, putting one hand on her waist and lifting the other into the air. Cat's heart nearly leaped into her throat. She had no Saints-damned idea what she was doing.

"You sure your father and Miss Hernandez won't mind you dancing with a *governess* alone in the courtyard?" Cat teased, trying to distract herself.

"I really couldn't care what my father thinks at this particular moment," Adrian said. His smile was light and playful, but there was a razor's edge to his tone. She didn't miss that he failed to mention Miss Hernandez.

"I don't know what I'm doing," she blurted out suddenly, as Adrian started to move them in time with the music.

The corner of his mouth ticked up. "Don't worry, I've got you. Just follow my lead."

Cat chewed on her lower lip and anxiously watched the movements of their feet, certain she was going to tread on his toes like a clumsy pony.

Adrian laughed, reaching forward and tilting her chin up. "Stop watching our feet. Just relax."

"Easy for you to say. The first time one of your toes feels the heel of my boot we'll see how *relaxed* you are," Cat grumbled.

"I've danced with Edith. Trust me. My toes can handle it."

Sure enough, despite how hard she tried, the heel of her boot did indeed find his toes. But to her surprise, he didn't even flinch.

"Steel-toed boots," he said sagely. "You didn't think I would dare attend a gathering where I'd be forced to dance without them?"

Cat actually laughed, letting her shoulders relax a little. Adrian suddenly twirled her out and away from him. Cat squeaked in surprise before he whirled her back, her hands slamming into his chest as she gripped him for dear life.

"*Shit!* Warn me next time you're going to do something like that!" she scolded him.

Adrian threw his head back and laughed too. "You and that mouth."

"What's wrong with my mouth?" Cat pouted.

"Nothing, actually. I think it's quite perfect."

They were still so close, the heat of his chest seeping into her hands. Had they stopped dancing? Cat didn't notice. All she saw as she looked up into his eyes was something deep and endless that she wanted desperately to explore. His head dipped toward hers but hesitated, a million questions lingering in his eyes.

Cat focused on his slightly parted lips, thinking how soft and warm they looked, wondering just for a moment how they'd feel against hers. Maybe it was the music, or the heavy scent of the roses, or this stupid dress that let her believe for just a second that nothing had changed. That they were just Catriona and Adrian, friends from the time they could walk, partners in crime stealing sweets from the kitchens, treasure prospectors searching for gold out in the desert, or frog hunters terrorizing the river.

Was this where they would have ended up had her father never found the aurium on his land? Had she never told her family's secret? Would they be dancing together at a gathering like this one? Would he take her out into the garden like this not to hide their dance, but to perhaps propose?

Was there really any harm in letting that fantasy play out for just a moment? A stolen moment before reality dragged her back with cruel, grasping fingers like those of her would-have-been captors?

Cat took a breath and then closed the distance between them.

Their lips met, so briefly, so softly at first that Cat wondered if it had happened at all.

But then his lips were back against hers, this time with more urgency, more passion, more need. She met his need with her own, surprised by the intensity of it. She drank him in like she'd been parched of water for days, like someone starving who'd finally tasted the sweetness of fresh fruit.

She made a small sound in the back of her throat, and her fingers were in his hair, pulling him closer. He reached his own hands forward to spread across her lower back, to pull her in.

There was nothing else outside of Adrian. There never really had been. She'd been a fool to try to deny it.

He broke the kiss and found her throat next, tracing his mouth down the length of her neck. If they weren't in a public courtyard separated from every baron in the territory by only a flimsy wall of leaves, she might have thrown him down on the gravel and had her way with him right then and there.

His gloved hand traced the open skin above her gown, dipping down toward the plunging neckline. She threw her head back and closed her eyes, relishing the feel of his silk glove against her flesh, silently begging for his hand to dip even lower, while his other teased the gap where her skirts met the bodice of her dress . . .

He withdrew from her suddenly with a yelp of pain.

Cat's eyes flew open to find him cradling his hand. A small stain of red was spreading across the tip of one of his gloved fingers.

"Um, Rose . . . why is there a *knife* in your dress?"

Cat gasped, her hands flying to her mouth. She'd hidden it there for when she tried to sneak back into Caldwell's office during the party. It was the reason she'd undone her dress after the maid had buttoned her up. Of course she couldn't tell Adrian the real reason, but she could come up with one close enough to the truth.

"Oh my Saints! Adrian, I'm so sorry! I forgot I put that there. With so many strange men coming tonight, I just wanted to protect myself in case—" Shame flooded through her as she buried her face in her hands.

But Adrian was already laughing, pulling her back into his chest as he tried to persuade her to free her face from her hands. "You don't have to apologize to me for wanting to protect yourself."

"Well, I told Edith to empower yourself against your fears, and I always take my own advice."

Adrian chuckled. "I just hope I'm not one of the strange men you needed to protect yourself from?"

Cat lifted her face from her hands, her mouth open in horror. "No, no! Mother above, you have no idea how long I've wanted to—" But she stopped herself. Of course he had no idea. They were supposed to have known each other only a few weeks, not years.

Adrian smiled, tucking a strand of hair behind her ear. "I think I've wanted to do this for a while too. I don't know why, but it feels like we've known each other so much longer, doesn't it?"

Cat's laugh sounded slightly hysterical, but he didn't seem to notice as he pulled her in for another kiss.

CHAPTER

32

Adrian knew he should be spending his evening courting the refined daughters of the barons, but he couldn't pull himself away from Rose. Something about her just felt . . . *right*. He wished he could understand why it seemed as if their souls already knew each other somehow.

He'd felt it that first moment he saw her in the foyer, that strange familiarity that tickled at his memory. Whatever the reason, he knew he wanted to be right here—in this garden—with her and no one else.

Even if she did hide sharp objects in the bodice of her gown.

He'd have to change his gloves before he went back into the party, which was fine. He wasn't in that much of a hurry anyway, not when Rose was melting into his arms as though it was where she'd always belonged. And if he had his way, perhaps it was somewhere she *could* belong.

Watching her with Edith, the way the two of them had formed such a strong attachment in such a short amount of time, he knew that Rose was in their lives for good now. He might as well try to find a way to make it official. His father would be furious, of course, would certainly never approve, but Adrian would find a way. He didn't know how or when, but he would find a way.

He was half considering taking her up to his room for a little more privacy when a servant cleared his throat pointedly as he passed, breaking them out of the isolated little world they'd enveloped themselves in. Rose giggled and stuffed her hand in her mouth to stop.

"I really should be going." Rose tried to step back, but Adrian refused to let her hand go.

"What if I preferred you stay here?"

Her smile was so genuine, so radiant, he nearly had to catch his breath.

"Believe me, I'd rather stay too, but we both know Edith will want her cake and I'm sure she won't stay put in her room for long if we make her wait."

A laugh escaped him. Of course she was correct. "Edith is so lucky to have you. I don't know what we'd both do without you anymore."

Rose's eyes hardened suddenly with pain at his words, so Adrian lifted a hand to her cheek and caressed it with his thumb. "Don't worry, we don't have to."

"Your father might have something to say about that."

"I'm rather beyond caring what he thinks at this very moment."

"For now. You've always cared so much about what he thinks."

Adrian furrowed his brow. "What do you mean?"

Rose stepped back, suddenly flustered. "Um, I mean, from what I've seen the last two weeks. You really seem to care a lot about what he thinks and how he does things."

He reached for her, to pull her back in. "Actually, I've worked really hard to be different from him. I'm learning that what I'd have to be to make him proud is not who I want to be at all."

Tears were suddenly streaming down her cheeks. What was going on? Why was she suddenly getting so upset? Perhaps she was afraid of his father and how he'd likely respond to the revelation that they were spotted in a passionate embrace in the garden.

"You won't get in trouble for this, I will make sure of it. I won't let my father—"

"You can't promise that. You can't really promise me anything."

"I'm not like my father. When I make a promise, I don't break my word. I may look like my father, but I'm nothing like him."

She looked up at him then, tears still clinging to her thick lashes. "I know. You look like him on the outside, but you're something so much better on the inside."

Adrian blinked as her words washed over him. Suddenly in his mind, he didn't see Rose, but the freckled nose and auburn hair of a young Catriona Macgregor. They were crouched down on the floor of the desert, inspecting the trove of rock treasures they'd collected. "*You look like him on the outside, but you're something so much better on the inside.*" Those were the exact words she'd said to him when she'd given him that geode. The geode still sitting on his dresser reminding him every morning that he didn't have to be like his father.

He shook his head. Was it just him, or were Rose's eyes *exactly* the same shade of hazel Catriona's had been? How had he not noticed before?

This time, it was his turn to step back as he looked at her. In fact, there was an awful lot about Rose that seemed so familiar . . .

Because it *was* familiar. The realization hit him like a blow to the stomach as that unknown quantity about her that had always tickled his memory came suddenly screaming to the forefront of his consciousness.

Rose probably couldn't tell what had happened, only that something had changed between them. She turned to head back inside and leave him alone out here in the garden, her shoulders slack and defeated.

Adrian didn't know what he was thinking, but there was one way to know for sure, one that Rose would never be able to explain away.

It was stupid. So stupid. If he was wrong . . . but no. He had a horrible feeling he wasn't wrong.

He retrieved a small rock from the garden path and chucked it as hard as he could at the back of her head.

Rose didn't even hesitate. Without having any way of seeing behind her or of knowing what he'd done, she moved to dodge the rock so that it sailed right past her.

She whirled suddenly to face him, her hands on her hips and her face blazing with rage.

She'd sensed the coming danger and avoided it. With her Blessing gift from Saint Prudentia.

Everything snapped into place. It made so much sense, as if he'd been underwater and his head had finally broken through the surface. How she'd been acting since she arrived, certain phrases she'd used, actions she'd taken. Seeming so evasive and uncomfortable, not behaving like a real novice, being places she wasn't supposed to be, hiding a knife in her dress. Even pushing him and Edith to the ground before Soap's gun had ever gone off on the road . . . it all made sense.

Her hands clenched into fists as she glared at him in disbelief. "You threw a rock at my head! Is that what you do anytime a girl rejects you? Chuck projectiles at her like a ten-year-old throwing a tantrum?"

"You *lied* to me," he said, his voice low and dangerous.

She marched right back up to him, jamming her finger into his chest. "I didn't lie to you about anything. I made you no promises, how dare you—"

"Didn't you lie to me? About everything, *Catriona*?"

Her mouth fell open, the guilty truth written across every plane of her face.

"I—what—I don't—I don't know who you're talking about—" She stumbled back, tripping over the hem of her dress.

Adrian stalked forward. "Yes, you do. You know *exactly* who I'm talking about. Your name isn't Rose at all. You're not a novice. You're not a real governess. You're Catriona Macgregor, heiress of Baron Macgregor! I can't believe I didn't see it before."

"You're—delusional. Catriona Macgregor died ten years ago, you said so yourself. In a fire." She waved a hand in front of her face before turning to walk away from him again.

But Adrian wasn't buying it for a second. Now that he saw her, he really *saw* her. It was impossible not to. She was different of course—taller, older, her face thinner and not as freckled—but it was so obviously her.

"Don't make me test your gift again, I know it's you," he said, his voice cracking.

She tensed but didn't turn around to face him.

"Where did you go?" he asked, his voice thick with emotion. "You let me think you were dead. Do you have any idea what that did to me, Catriona? What that did to my *mother*?"

Rose—no, Catriona—was shaking, trying to contain whatever it was that was threatening to burst out of her. Because something was clearly boiling just beneath her surface. Adrian wanted to push her, to find out exactly what that something was, because he had to know. He needed some kind of explanation—

"You let us *all* think you were dead. Why? Why would you just abandon everything? Didn't you *care*?"

She let out a shriek like an irritated bobcat. "Do you have *any* idea what happened? Who really killed my parents, you arrogant, self-righteous ass?"

Adrian blanched. "What do you mean?"

"It was *your* father! Your father killed my parents and tried to *kidnap* me to raise me as his ward and force me to marry *you*!"

No. That wasn't right at all. There was no way on the Mother's great green earth that could be true.

"That's not possible. My father wanted us to get married, just like your parents wanted too. There's no way he'd kill them over something so—"

Catriona gave a hysterical laugh halfway to another shriek. "Don't you remember that glorious little secret I told you, Adrian? The secret I told you never to tell another soul and you did anyway?"

Adrian wracked his memory, trying to think back to those last few times he'd seen her. The aurium. She'd told him that her father had found a massive lode of aurium on their land. She'd told him not to tell anyone, but he'd told his . . .

"My father wouldn't have killed them." His father was corrupt, greedy, and selfish, yes, but a murderer? To kill your own neighbors for the sake of cursed gold? That required another level of evil his father just couldn't be. He refused to believe it.

He used cursed gold on his own daughter, a nasty voice whispered in his head. *Isn't he capable of something so cruel for the sake of advancing his own name?* Adrian shoved the thoughts deep into the back of his mind for now.

"Oh, he wouldn't have? You don't think he would have been desperate and angry after my father rejected his offer of betrothing us? Of denying him a chance at greatness? He killed them, Adrian. I *saw* your father's men kill them and then they tried to take me—to take me *here!*" She was breathing so heavily, her chest rising and falling. "So of course I ran. I ran because I knew I couldn't let them catch me. And I never came back because I knew it was my fault they died. My fault for being stupid enough to tell *you!*"

How long had these thoughts been simmering inside her? Waiting for her chance to finally release them? She shoved past him then, the unleashed anger and frustration finally breaking through. Adrian grabbed her hand to try to stop her, but she wrenched it out of his grasp.

"Don't!" she screamed. "Don't touch me!"

"Is there a problem out here, miss?" One of the sons of a lesser baron had materialized in an open window frame, glancing uneasily between her and Adrian.

Adrian tried to shoo him away with a pleading look, but the baron's son narrowed his eyes as if he didn't trust Adrian. Damn his father's wretched reputation straight to hell. Did everyone have to think him just as untrustworthy?

"Catriona, please," Adrian called, chasing after her.

"Don't call me that!" she yelled back.

Finally, he caught up to her. "I will not call you anything but your true name," he said.

"My name is Cat now. 'Black Cat' Whitfield, if you want to be more specific." She was nearly to the other side of the courtyard now. He could still see the baron's son watching them suspiciously through the window.

But for the second time that evening, Adrian felt as though a horse had kicked him in the head.

Black Cat Whitfield? Her wanted poster swam behind his eyes. The infamous daughter of outlaw gang leader Amos Whitfield, Wolf of the West?

"No, no, you can't be."

She finally stopped and faced him again. "Can't I be, Adrian?

I've made a new life for myself, one as far away from you and this Saints-forsaken family as I can manage."

Her words hit him like an arrow to the heart. But she'd come back, she'd built a relationship with him, with *Edith*. "What about Edith? Why did you come back then?"

"Because your greedy, backstabbing father is trying to rig the vote for governor. Once he's governor, he can grant himself my land and all the aurium on it to fund his little revolution against the empire. I don't give a rat's ass about the empire or who becomes governor, but you better believe I'm going to do everything in my power to stop him from getting his bloodstained hands on my family's land after what he did. I came back to expose him for what he really is."

Adrian's head was swimming. "I don't understand."

"Oh, has he not told you? Ask him what all the aurium powder he brought in last week is for. What those maps in his office are. Who the hell Thompson is and how he plans to manipulate all the barons into voting for him."

"Thompson?" Adrian's brow wrinkled. His thoughts felt so slow, trying to keep up with all the information she was throwing at him. Each new piece hit him like a rock over the head. How could he have missed so much going on in his own home?

She opened her mouth to say something else but didn't get the chance. At that moment, the music in the ballroom ceased, and everyone broke into rapturous applause.

"Ladies and gentlemen of Saelum," came his father's voice. Of course, at the worst possible time imaginable. He and Catriona both froze in place. "As you all know, I am officially announcing my intentions to become governor. It is my hope to secure each and every one of your votes for the recommendation to Emperor Lawrence at our meeting later this week."

There was more applause. Catriona looked as if she wanted to rip the dagger out of her dress and chuck it through the open window. Adrian himself still felt numb with disbelief and overwhelmed with everything he'd learned in the last few minutes. His thoughts were as confused as a fly trapped in a whiskey barrel. All he could do at this moment was try to steady himself and listen to his father's speech as he droned on from the ballroom.

"But I do not merely wish to *tell* you my intentions to improve Saelum Territory as governor, I wish to *prove* them to you. For years, the barons have been harassed by the outlaw gang known as the Wolves, but I single-handedly managed to subdue them and capture their leader, sending them scattering to the wind."

More applause. Catriona's lip began to curl. Adrian suddenly wondered if Soap and Pedro had been among those "scattered to the wind."

His father's voice boomed with authority as he finished his triumphant announcement. "As a show of my intention to restore law and order to the territory, I invite you all to be my guests in front of the courthouse tomorrow afternoon to witness the execution of Amos Whitfield, the Wolf of the West himself!"

Adrian thought his heart couldn't handle anymore, but the look of horror on Catriona's—no, *Cat's*—face reminded him just how much pain and fear there was still left to feel.

CHAPTER

33

The name echoed inside Cat's mind. *Amos Whitfield. The Wolf of the West.* Her first thought was gratitude that he was still alive. But the relief was swamped by a cold, creeping feeling of terror. Amos may be alive now, but according to Adrian's father, he wouldn't be for long. He was scheduled to be executed. Tomorrow afternoon. In Saint's Landing. In front of the courthouse and every baron in Saelum.

Panic sent her gasping for breath. She leaned a hand against the wall, the other pressed against her heart. She had to do *something.* Anything.

Adrian was beside her in an instant. "What can I do?" His concern and tenderness chafed against her nerves.

"Nothing," she breathed. "You've already cost me one father. I guess I shouldn't be surprised you'd cost me another."

Adrian stiffened. "What does that mean?"

Cat stared daggers at him. "Amos Whitfield. The Wolf of the West—that man is the only reason I'm alive. He saved me all those years ago and raised me like his own daughter. He was—*is*—the father that yours took away from me. He's also the reason the missions have survived as long as they have after the barons tried to defund them."

Adrian's eyes were wide. She could tell this was all too much for him to process at once. But she didn't have the patience to deal with his naivete right now.

"The missions? Amos has been funding the *missions?*"

Cat made a frustrated sound in the back of her throat. "Yes. To you, he's a criminal, but to me and the priesthood of the Blessed, he's a savior. Every penny he stole from the barons that he didn't use to pay his men, he donated back to the missions."

Adrian swallowed hard. "And now my father is going to execute him."

"Yes, and with him likely any chance that the missions of Saelum will survive much longer. Or the territory itself, I guess, if your father becomes governor. I didn't get the chance to figure out exactly how he's planning to rig the vote on Thursday, but I've got more important things to worry about now." Cat moved to go around him, a rough plan already forming in her head.

Yes, she still needed to discover Baron Caldwell's plans for the vote and get that information to the priests, but that was still three days away. The issue of Amos being executed was a little more . . . urgent. She needed to find Soap and Pedro. They would likely be in the stables tending to the horses and coaches of the gathering's guests—maybe not the best assignment for former outlaws, but hopefully their fingers hadn't been too sticky. Or the barons had been smart enough not to leave anything of value in their coaches.

She left the courtyard, fully expecting Adrian to head back into the gathering. So she was surprised to find him beside her, keeping pace with her hurried steps.

"Where are you going?" he asked.

"Why do you care?"

"Because if even half of what you said is true, then we can't let Amos be executed tomorrow. And I—" He cleared his throat. "I can't make up for my own role in the death of your parents, Cat. But I can make sure you don't lose another father."

A fist seemed to close around her heart and squeeze, but she didn't know what to make of it. She was touched, but the emotion was laced with a burning aftertaste of anger. If they had any hope of getting into Fort Astor before tomorrow afternoon, perhaps Adrian's help would not be unwelcome.

✦ · · · · ◉ · · · · ✦

"Amos is alive?" Soap repeated, jumping to his feet. "We have t' do somethin', we can't let them hang him!"

Pedro nodded his agreement, his usually inexpressive mouth pressed into a thin line of concern.

Cat had caught them rifling through one of the coaches drawn up outside the stables, but she didn't really care. They'd feigned innocence the moment they saw Adrian accompanying her, but Cat nipped that whole charade in the bud. They didn't have time to waste.

"He knows who I really am now, so we can drop the act."

Pedro narrowed his eyes at Adrian. "Then he knows who *we* really are?"

"Yes, and *he* can speak for himself. He wants to help you save Amos." Adrian's tone was sharp as a blade.

Soap opened his mouth to make what Cat assumed would be some kind of smart-ass comment, but she silenced him with a look. "I don't care what you're about to say. Adrian might be useful, so leave it alone, Soap." She took Soap's reproachful glare as a sign of his cooperation, so she continued. "Listen. We need to figure out some kind of plan. We have to get in and out of a stone fort protected by hundreds of Ordonian soldiers in a very short window of time."

A hint of a smile pulled at Soap's lips. "Oh, I have an idea of how we can get out. It's the gettin'-in part that's the trick. They won't let anyone into the fort before an execution like this, especially not to see a high-risk prisoner like Amos. They usually won't even let family in to say goodbye."

"Is there any way for us to sneak in? Like a back door or secret entrance or . . . ?" Cat asked.

Soap snorted. "Sneak in? To Fort Astor? You have seen the place, haven't ya, Cat?"

Soap had been stationed at the fort during his brief stint as a soldier. If anyone knew the building and its workings, it was him.

"Well, what about stealing guard uniforms or something?" Cat threw out.

But Soap was already rolling his eyes. "You think the Ordonian Empire just leaves official uniforms lying around? This ain't a dime novel we're talking about here, Cat. This is the fiercely proud Ordonian military. And their schedules are so regimented, if we tried to disrupt a rotation to knock someone out to steal their uniform, believe me, they'll notice—"

"Well, you come up with a damn idea then. Since all you're doing is shootin' holes in mine," Cat snapped at him. Her heart was racing. Every second they wasted was a second they could be using. "They'll be giving him his last rites before we can even think of something!"

Adrian gasped suddenly, pulling all their attention to him. "His last rites," he said.

Cat waved an impatient hand, waiting for him to elaborate. "What about them?"

Adrian blinked, his eyes darting briefly between their impatient faces. "They don't allow family members in before a high-risk execution, but don't they allow the priesthood to give him his last rites? A final blessing to reconcile his soul to the Saints before he passes?"

Soap's brow furrowed as he strained his memory. "Actually, I think you're right. It's part of Ordonian law that every prisoner has the right to speak with a priest."

Cat felt a flutter of excitement. "So what if I went in as a priestess of the Blessed under the guise of giving him a final blessing? Pedro's taught me enough about picking locks, if I can get a minute or so with the right tool . . ."

"I think it could actually work," Soap agreed.

Pedro shrugged, which Cat assumed was his agreement.

Adrian, however, crossed his arms across his chest. "I don't like it," he complained.

"I don't really care what you like or don't like at the moment." Cat narrowed her eyes at him.

"You are just as wanted as Amos, Cat. If you got caught, you'd end up hanging next to him tomorrow afternoon."

"That's a risk I'm willing to take."

"Well, it's not one I'm willing to take. I care about you too much. And so does Edith."

Soap cleared his throat suggestively. Cat resisted the urge to reach over and punch him in the gut.

"I'll go with you," Adrian finally said.

"With me? Why?"

"Yes, with you. I can dress up as a curate and we can go in together. That way if anything happens, maybe I can use what little influence I have as the son of a baron to protect you."

"I don't need your protection." Cat's fingers twitched toward the knife still hidden in the bodice of her dress.

"Maybe not my physical protection, but you certainly could use my political protection if things go sideways."

He had a point. Which just made her even angrier. But even she couldn't deny the wisdom of using Adrian's political clout to keep her out of a hangman's noose if she needed it. She wouldn't do any good to anyone dead.

"Fine," she agreed through gritted teeth. "Adrian and I will sneak in as members of the mission, he can pretend to give the blessing while I pick the lock, and then Pedro and Soap can do whatever they're planning to do to help us get out?"

Adrian's expression darkened as he turned toward Soap. "What *are* you planning? I refuse to participate in anything that involves killing innocent soldiers—"

"Don't you worry your pretty little baron brain about it. It's something I've wanted to do for a long, long time." Soap's expression turned wistful. He grinned at Pedro, who actually grinned back.

Adrian—rightly so—looked even *more* worried. But he pursed his lips and didn't argue.

"Then what are we waiting for?" Cat demanded.

Pedro let his gaze wander up and down the length of her. "Probably you. Unless you plan on wearing that dress to Saint's Landing? Can't imagine it would be too easy to ride in a thing like that."

Cat looked down and swore violently.

Soap let out a low whistle and then chuckled. "Saints, Adrian. How'd you ever buy Cat was a novice of the church?"

34

All thoughts of the party fled from Adrian's mind like a tumbleweed caught in an afternoon thunderstorm. His father was going to kill him for leaving during such an important event, but then again, he'd probably kill him for the reason he was leaving anyway. Executing Amos was supposed to garner favor with the other barons, and here Adrian was making plans to help the wanted outlaw *escape*. He didn't want to think about the consequences of a decision like this; he just knew Cat would do anything to save her adoptive father—and that Adrian would do anything to save *her*.

They agreed to meet in the stables in fifteen minutes, just enough time for him and Cat to change out of their party clothes. It also gave him time to grab his book of common prayers, a knife, and some extra gold coins—all of which would be useful if he was going to pretend to be a curate and sneak off to Saint's Landing in the middle of the night.

Adrian threw open the door to his room and rushed to his dresser. He quickly changed into his darkest riding clothes, with an odd sensation that it was more than his attire he was darkening with this choice. Digging through the top drawer, he pulled out a small knife and tucked it into his boot. Then he found his book of prayer.

It was a battered little thing, worn leather with faded letters stamped in gold. Just the kind a junior priest of the Blessed might carry to give a doomed prisoner their last rites. It had once belonged to his grandfather, a family heirloom that now would be used to potentially destroy his family's legacy. How ironic.

His gaze caught on the geode sitting on the dresser top, the geode Catriona had given him.

"You look like him on the outside, but you're something so much better on the inside."

Hopefully he'd get the chance to prove that to her tonight.

"What are you doing?" came a small voice from his closet.

Adrian cursed and dropped the book of prayer on the dresser top with a thump.

"Saints, Edith." Adrian pressed a hand against the frantic thrashing of his heart. "Aren't you supposed to be in bed?"

Her large brown eyes materialized in a crack in the closet door. "You were supposed to bring me a piece of cake, remember?"

Adrian ran an impatient hand through his hair. "Yes, I'm sorry, Edith. We got a bit distracted . . ."

"Where's Rose?" She opened the door and stepped out into his room, clothed in only her simple white nightshirt. Her twin dark braids hung limply against her back as she nervously rocked on her feet. She searched the space as if expecting her governess to make an appearance at any moment. Adrian's chest gave another painful throb.

"She's um . . . she's downstairs. Edith, I'm sorry, but I don't really have time to—"

"Why do you have a knife?"

"Excuse me?"

"A knife. I'm not blind. I saw you put one in your boot. And you're dressed like you're going somewhere."

Adrian almost cursed again but was saved by a knock at the door.

"Adrian, are you ready? We need to go now if we are going to make it there before sunrise." Cat's voice was harsh and harried.

"Where are you going?" Edith squeaked. "You're not riding to Saint's Landing at night, are you?"

This time it was Cat's turn to curse. She pushed open the door to the hallway and stepped in too. Unlike the elegant young woman who had accompanied him downstairs earlier this evening, this new young woman had changed almost as dramatically as her clothing. The dress had been replaced with tight, dark fighting slacks and a black buttoned shirt to match. Worn leather riding boots rose to her knees, and a Murietta pistol hung from a holster at her hip. Her hair was no longer done up in curls, but hanging down her back in a simple braid. Even her face had hardened, her hazel eyes crystallizing into freshly mined gemstones. She looked every inch the outlaw she truly was.

Edith's eyes went wide, darting to the gun at Cat's hip. She took a small step back. "Rose? What are you *wearing*?"

Cat's eyes softened, and Adrian swore he saw silver dotting their corners. "Edith, sweetheart, I need you to go back to bed, alright? And not ask any questions."

Edith gave her a flat look as if to say, *Seriously? You expect me not to ask questions?*

"I promise I will explain later. But there is something really important your brother and I need to take care of. Can you trust me that I wouldn't lie to you?"

Adrian snorted.

Cat cut him a dark, warning look.

Edith just glanced back and forth between them, the fear and panic evident on her small features. Their mother had died during a night ride into Saint's Landing. She'd been on the way to help a friend who was giving birth, but he knew that's where Edith's mind would go. His mother had left at night to ride to Saint's Landing and never came back.

"Edith, I promise everything will be okay. I just need to handle something with . . . *Miss Rose.*" He felt awful, but Soap and Pedro would already be waiting for them and they still had to sneak down and out through the servant entrances without being seen. "Can you be a big girl and help us?"

Edith worried her lip between her teeth, her eyes swimming with tears, but she eventually nodded.

Cat gave her a swift hug and kiss on the cheek before gently pushing her out into the hall and closing the door behind her. They waited for her little feet to retreat down the hall.

"You had to say something in front of her?" Adrian finally hissed.

"How was I supposed to know she was in here with you? We were supposed to run up and change really quick, not take our sweet time."

"I was grabbing my prayer book. If you want this ruse to work, we have to make it convincing, or else it isn't even worth the trip to Saint's Landing. You'll end up hanging right alongside him, Cat. *And I won't let that happen.*"

There was a creak in the hallway outside. Cat and Adrian both froze, listening, but after a minute, there were no other sounds. Still, they shouldn't be talking about these things in the house, not where servants and nosy little sisters lurked behind every closed door.

"No one is hanging tomorrow. Not me, and not Amos," Cat finally said with such conviction that Adrian was tempted to believe her.

But he also had a horrified feeling in his stomach that something was going to go wrong. That even though they promised Edith everything was going to be okay—it wasn't a promise they could realistically keep.

✦ · · · · ✺ · · · · ✦

The ride into town took several hours, and none of them talked as they spurred their horses to their limits. By the time the sun was beginning to stretch its rays beyond the line of the horizon, they passed the first houses on the outer edges of Saint's Landing.

"We head to the mission first to get some robes for Cat and Adrian. I'm sure the priests will help us if we are trying to save Amos," Soap said, slowing his horse to a trot. Dust from the road coated the pale features of his face, making his blue eyes stand out even brighter.

"Will we put them at risk by involving them, though?" Cat asked.

Adrian couldn't help but wonder the same thing. If they did succeed in saving Amos, would the mission be held accountable for their role?

"Cat already has her novice dress, and we can just steal some robes for Adrian off the clotheslines at the priest bunkhouse," Pedro suggested.

"I'd rather protect Father Iggy. Allow him plausible deniability." Cat directed her horse up next to Adrian's.

Adrian's stomach tightened as he looked over at her, drinking in her face for the first time since they'd left the ranch. This was the most comfortable he'd seen her since she arrived at Caldwell Ranch, as if she were finally back where she belonged. He shifted uncomfortably in his saddle.

This wasn't where she belonged. But she didn't seem to know that yet.

They tied their horses behind a brothel and found a small storehouse filled with barrels of booze. Soap figured the occupants of the building would be sufficiently occupied or intoxicated for at least several more hours, so they hopefully wouldn't be bothered.

"How did you know the storehouse was here, Soap?" Cat asked him with a quirked eyebrow.

"A man has needs, Cat. And the owners have need of gold." He shrugged.

"As long as you didn't promise to marry every single one of them." She laughed and punched his arm again, and he swatted at her backside in response.

"You know I'm saving myself to marry you, Kitty Cat."

Cat stuck out her tongue and danced out of his reach.

Adrian's cheeks flamed at the casualness of their relationship, but as much as they teased one another, there didn't seem to be any romantic undertones to their banter. They truly seemed to care about each other as friends, nothing more. That knowledge did at least settle some of the unease that swirled in his stomach.

Adrian didn't ask how, but Pedro disappeared and returned half an hour later with some lock-picking supplies and a set of priest's robes. While he and Cat went over strategies for picking the kind of lock she was likely to find on Amos's cell, Adrian changed into the plain brown garments.

His hair wasn't shaved around the edges like a modern priest of the Blessed, but he could keep the hood up like the more traditional priests preferred to do. He felt odd to be standing behind a brothel dressed as a priest with a knife in his boot and a book of prayers tucked beneath his arm. It was as if the two versions of himself—the side determined to do whatever it took to keep Cat safe and the side that hated the idea of breaking any rules of any kind—had gone to war and clashed on his very person.

"Do you think he'll pass for a curate?" Cat asked when he emerged from the alley outhouse wearing his robes. Her eyes raked him up and down in assessment.

"Well, just as well as you passed for a novice, sweetheart." Soap crossed his arms and leaned casually against the wall of the storehouse.

"So we are in trouble then?" Adrian said.

Pedro smirked, and Adrian felt a spark of pride at his own joke.

"Hang on." Cat reached up and pulled at his hood, the warmth of her hands mere inches from his cheek. Adrian's back went rigid with tension. "There, that covers your hair better."

"Thanks," Adrian muttered.

Soap finally clapped his hands together. "Alright, lady and gentlemen, are we ready to break into one of the most secure forts in the empire and give 'em hell?"

Adrian swallowed. "Um, yes?"

"Let's give 'em hell." Cat grinned. "And save the Wolf of the West as we do it."

CHAPTER

35

Cat's hands would not stop shaking. She tried to hold them still as she gave the guard her best attempt at an innocent smile.

"You're from the mission?" the guard repeated. His sharp eyes raked up and down her novice dress, catching briefly on the small bag that hung at her hip.

"Yes," Adrian repeated. "We are here to give the prisoner scheduled for execution his last rites. The records do say we are coming today, don't they?"

The guard checked the leather-bound book in his hand. "It does, but you aren't scheduled to arrive for another three hours."

Cat's stomach clenched, but she kept her smile fixed. "This particular prisoner has a lot of sins that must be cleansed. We wanted to make sure there was adequate time to prepare his soul for the afterlife. Unless you'd prefer to damn him to the realms of the Fallen Saint?"

The guard blinked, tightening his grip on his rifle. "No, no, of course not."

"There must have been a miscommunication with Father Ephraim. I guess we can go all the way back and just come back later," Adrian said to Cat, feigning great frustration.

"I guess if his soul festers forever in eternal torture simply because we did not have enough time, the Mother will know who to blame." Cat rolled her eyes suggestively. "Saints forbid we don't follow the schedule *exactly* . . ."

A muscle tightened in the guard's jawline. "Fine. Let me clear it with my supervisors first."

His polished boots tapped away down the hallway, and Cat released her held breath.

"Do you think it will work?" she whispered to Adrian.

"Hopefully," he whispered back, hugging his book of prayer tighter against his chest.

The guard returned a moment later.

"You've been cleared. You will have the privacy required for the ritual, but the bars to his cell will remain closed for the duration of the visit. I will also need to search your bag."

Cat nodded, opening the bag for him to look inside. He leaned over to see the small loaf of bread and canteen of holy water. He lifted a hand to inspect the bread, and Cat squeaked in protest.

"Please, sir. The bread has been sanctified and we do not wish to corrupt it before the prisoner can partake in the Cleansing." It was a good enough reason. And the small loaf actually contained the hidden tools she would be using to pick the lock.

The guard grunted. "Fine. You may proceed."

"Thank you, sir. Saints bless." Adrian gave a little bow, and the guard gave them instructions, then stepped aside for them to pass.

Fort Astor was just as imposing on the inside as it was from the outside. The floor was a highly polished dark wood that swam with the lights of the regularly spaced gas lamps, rippling like dark rivers of the underworld. The stone walls reminded Cat forcefully of her own time in prison, and her throat began to close up at the memory. The main courtyard of the fort had been swarming with soldiers like a hive of wasps dressed in navy-and-gold uniforms, all rushing around in preparation for Amos's coming execution, which would take place later that day outside the courthouse.

Pedro and Soap, dressed in their own priestly robes, were waiting for them in the fort's stables. Soap's plan for escape was dependent on their signal. Somewhere above their heads, the clock tower of the court-house next door boomed the eighth hour, each toll rattling her nerves as she realized they only had a few hours until Amos would meet his end if they failed.

The hallway led to a small rickety staircase that descended into the bowels of the fort itself. Of course, they couldn't risk allowing their most prized prisoners to have even a window. A guard waited for them at the foot of the stairs to direct them to the right cell.

"My partner and I will be standing at the end of the hall if there are any issues. I don't anticipate the prisoner will cause any, though. He seems to be the religious type, so he shouldn't be a threat to you. He's at the end on the right-hand side."

"Thank you," Cat mumbled. She squeezed the strap of her side bag to keep her hands steady.

The guards turned their backs, taking their original positions as she and Adrian made their way down the line of cells. Many were empty. The prisoners contained within the others were too beat down and tired to pay them any mind. She scanned their weary, fearful eyes, their ragged, dirty clothing, the dire state of their condition. Her heart twisted at the freshness of the wounds some of them sported, wondering if the guards were not as upstanding as they appeared to be. The conditions here were just as bad as hers in Caseda had been—inhumane and degrading. Her heart throbbed at the thought that Amos had been trapped here for weeks, at what she might say to him after all this time.

Finally, they reached the last cell.

Amos sat crumpled in the corner beside a filthy wooden bucket that overflowed with human excrement. Fresh bloodstains coated his clothes and a bandage around his head. His face—aged but handsome—was bruised and swollen beneath his salt-and-pepper goatee. His teeth had never been what anyone would consider healthy, but the gaps were more pronounced now, as if he'd lost several more than he had before. His cheeks and ribs seemed sunken with both injury and starvation. Cat had to grasp the bars of his cell to steady herself at the sight. And the smell.

"*Amos*," she half sobbed. "What have they done to you?"

Amos turned his head, eyes swimming with confusion. "Cat? 'S that you?"

"It's me, Amos. I'm here. I've come for you," she whispered, reaching a hand through the bars.

"Why?" he croaked. He didn't move, just blinked at her from the corner.

Her gut burned with guilt. Why had it taken so long? She was furious with herself. "I'm so sorry I didn't come sooner. I thought you were dead. I came the second I heard you were here." Tears swam in her eyes, blurring her vision of him.

"No . . ." he rasped, "you were free. You should have left me here."

"I would *never* leave you here, Amos. You saved me, taught me everything I know. Hell, you derailed a Saints-damned train for me. You think I'd just let them hang you?"

"Always prisoner to your past, aren't you, Cat?" He laughed weakly before coughing and spitting blood onto the floor. "Can't just leave it where it is."

"You aren't my past. You are my present, and you will damn well be in my future. We are here to help."

A door closed somewhere outside the line of cells, and they all froze, listening. There was a thudding of several pairs of boots, but when Cat glanced at the distant backs of the guards, they didn't seem to have moved. It must have been somewhere above their heads.

"We?" Amos turned his gaze to Adrian. "Soap? Pedro?"

"This is Adrian. I will explain later. But first, we need to get you out." She reached into her bag and dug the small lock-picking tools out of the loaf of bread. Adrian positioned himself in front of her, blocking her partially from view as he opened the book of prayers and began to read in earnest. His deep voice reverberated throughout the long hallway, bouncing off stone and iron as words of hope and life filled the space that had before been filled with only death and despair. Even the other prisoners stirred as Adrian's prayers washed over them.

Cat, however, quickly put the skills Pedro had taught her to work.

Outside of a few anxious glances toward the guards' backs, she made quick work of the iron padlock, easing it open and laying the heavy thing gently on the floor.

"Can you walk?" she whispered to Amos.

He grunted but pushed himself into a sitting position. "Haven't tried to in a few days, but I'm sure once the adrenaline of you busting me outta here kicks in, I'll be able to do plenty."

Cat nervously chewed at her lip. She hadn't counted on Amos being so sick and injured. Would she still be able to get him to the stables in this state? They didn't really have a choice. Adrian looked down at her—still reciting from his book of prayers—and gave her a reassuring nod as if to say *ready when you are.* They'd discussed this next part in great detail, but it was time to see if Adrian could actually follow through.

"Okay, here's what I need you to do . . ." She then explained their idea to the Wolf in a hurried whisper.

Amos nodded, already shifting his weight onto his feet. "You got it, Black Cat."

She took a deep, steadying breath, waiting for her gift to warn her if her next move was not a good idea. But it remained silent. So she handed him the sharp lock-picking tool, and with a quick snap of her wrist, she threw open Amos's cell door. "*Now!*"

Amos lunged. She screamed. The guards at the end had heard the commotion and were already rushing toward them. Amos was slower than he should be, but he didn't hesitate to wrap an arm around Cat's neck, the sharp lockpick pressed against her throat.

"Don't move! Or I'll open the novice's neck!" Amos growled. He pressed the pick harder against her flesh for emphasis.

Cat let out a terrified whimper, her eyes imploring the guards for help.

"Do something!" Adrian said, sounding panicked. "Don't let him hurt her!"

"How did he get out?" One of the guards lowered his bayonet toward Amos and Cat.

Amos dragged Cat back, but as he did so, she could feel the shaking in his hands, the strain he was exerting to keep them both standing upright.

"Hurry!" she squealed, directing her desperate gaze at Adrian and hoping he understood her double meaning.

"Drop the novice now, or we will shoot," yelled one of the guards.

Amos just chuckled. "I'm dying today anyway. You think that's going to stop me?"

While the two guards were distracted, Adrian inched himself behind them both. With a quick blow to the back of the knees, one of the guards found himself suddenly sprawled on the ground, his rifle skidding away and out of his grasp. Adrian grabbed it and knocked the guard unconscious. Adrenaline pounded in Cat's ears, sending her pulse racing. His fellow lost his own concentration, turning to see what had happened. Cat pounced, forcing him to the ground and wrestling his own rifle from his grasp. A foot into his stomach. A well-placed fist to his jaw.

It took only a few seconds, but Adrian and Cat managed to get both guns and leave both guards knocked out on the floor.

"Well, that went relatively well," Adrian said, puffing out his chest with pride.

"Don't get cocky, Caldwell," Cat hissed. "We still need to get the hell out of here." She turned toward Amos, who was leaning heavily against the stone wall and drawing pained breaths. "Stay behind us until we get into the courtyard. Soap and Pedro will meet us there with the horses."

Amos grit his teeth and nodded. "I'm also not gonna ask why you have a Caldwell with you."

"Probably a good idea, old man," Cat gave him a teasing wink.

"Watch who you're calling old, little girl." He winked right back.

Cat's stomach clenched with an odd combination of affection and fear. She missed him and was so happy to see him alive, but there was still the matter of them escaping and making sure he stayed that way. She wanted to wrap her arms around his neck and never let go, but she knew he'd push off such open displays, even if he did it with a glint of tears in his eyes. He liked to pretend he was tough, but Amos was as soft as an armadillo's underbelly when you got beneath his shell.

The kind of outlaw that gives you the boots off his feet, or the horse out from underneath him so you can escape while he stays behind.

Damn him.

"Just keep yourself out of the line of fire," Cat begged him. "No heroic crap to save me."

Amos grunted but didn't agree to her terms. And Cat didn't miss it.

Adrian poked his head out into the hall and then pulled it back in. "The hallway is clear, no one is on their way down here yet."

"That's odd. Don't you think they'd have more guards down here?" Cat asked him.

Adrian shrugged. "You saw the state of Amos and some of the others. They aren't really up for doing much, are they? Maybe they don't think the extra security is necessary?"

"Hmmm." It still didn't sit easy with her gut. But there was only one way out, so they took the stairs anyway, rifles leading the way. Adrian would never actually use his, but that didn't mean that Cat wouldn't— to protect the ones she loved, of course.

The sound of running boots and distant shouting reached their ears, so Cat shoved Amos into a side room of some kind, while she and Adrian hid their guns behind them and pretended to be frightened, peaceful victims escaping the "murderous, escaped outlaw." The group of soldiers ran past, following the direction of their shaking, pointing fingers.

"Best evacuate the premises, miss," one of them told her.

She pretended to clutch at her chest in terror. "Absolutely, we are headed toward the stables now."

When the soldiers rounded the corner and out of sight, she pulled Amos from his hiding spot, and they sprinted for the door the soldier had pointed out to them.

Adrian led the way, Cat stopping to support Amos as he stumbled sideways. A disturbing cough wracked his frail frame. Adrian reached the door first, his hand already reaching for the handle to open it.

"Okay, when the door opens, we're going to—" she started to tell Amos, but the words suddenly stuck in her throat as a vision flashed before her eyes. The breath rushed out of her lungs.

"Adrian! Wait! Stop—"

But it was too late. Ordonian daylight blinded her eyes as the door to the courtyard flew open.

And when it cleared, just as her vision had predicted, a line of soldiers waited for them, rifles raised and ready as though this had been their plan for days. And standing behind them, twin looks of triumph upon their faces, were Captain Freeman and Baron William Caldwell.

CHAPTER

36

There was no way what she was seeing was real, but her visions had never been wrong before. And this was not just a vision. Baron Caldwell and Captain Freeman stood right in front of them. A faint buzzing filled her ears, along with the clicks of a dozen or so rifles being cocked. Her heart thudded painfully as she fought to keep Amos upright.

"Well done, Adrian," Baron Caldwell said, his face splitting into a wicked grin. "Just as we planned. Thank you again for alerting me to the situation."

No. She *definitely* hadn't heard correctly.

The buzzing in her ears intensified. She supposed she should feel furious, but instead she just felt numb disbelief. She couldn't reconcile everything Adrian had said and done the last twenty-four hours with what was happening now. She needed answers. Confirmation that what his father said was not true.

Cat's gaze immediately shot to Adrian's face. His mouth hung open in surprise, a look of outrage contorting his features.

But was it outrage at the absurdity of what his father had said? Or outrage that his father had betrayed the truth?

Adrian never got the chance to explain because soldiers were already dragging him away back inside the building.

"Cat! No! Wait! There's been some kind of mistake. CAT!!" he screamed.

But what was the mistake? That she'd been a fool to trust him? Adrian had done exactly what he did when they were children. How could she really have expected anything different? She'd told him a great secret. He'd tattled out of some sick, perverse sense of doing the "right" thing.

And just like before, it was about to cost her everything.

The numbness in her soul began to tingle like an ember, an ember that was slowly fanning into a flame of righteous rage.

"So he told you?" she said calmly, directing her attention back to Baron Caldwell.

"I must admit I was surprised. We've been looking for you for a long time, Catriona. To think you've been right under my nose." He was smiling, but it was a tight, restrained smile. She could tell it killed him that she'd been so close all along.

"I'm still not going to marry him. Especially not now."

"No, I figured that would be the case for a while now. That would have made things easier for everyone, yourself included, but you've always been a wild little thing. Getting Adrian into trouble for one thing or another."

Cat smirked. "Funny. Your wife always seemed to cherish that about me."

"Ada did have a soft spot for you. I'm glad she didn't have to live to see what you've become. Some angels fall too far past redemption, unfortunately."

"We both know I was never really an angel to begin with." Her chest felt hollowed out with the truth of those words.

Caldwell snorted. "Certainly not."

Captain Freeman, who stood silently watching from behind Caldwell's shoulder, subtly moved his hand to the holster at his hip. His handsome features seemed serene, but the tight line of his jaw betrayed his tension. He wanted this over with. Perhaps he was embarrassed at his own failure to find her.

"Nice to see you again, Captain. How's your head?"

His white-gloved hand instinctively touched the newly healed skin of the gash along his forehead, but he didn't answer. A vision flashed behind Cat's eyes . . . a vision of an explosion that sent a jolt of excitement through every muscle of her body.

"Cat, we gonna get this over with or not?" Amos finally grumbled. His legs shook from where he struggled to keep upright.

"You're right, I'm so sorry, Amos. You must be exhausted, in your state." She blinked sweetly at Captain Freeman. "You mind if we sit down for just a moment?"

"What—" Freeman started to ask, his hand tightening on his gun. But it was too late.

Cat and Amos dropped to the ground and ducked, covering their heads with their hands just as an explosion ripped through the wall of the stables behind them.

Chaos reigned.

Soap and Pedro had timed the explosion perfectly. First, they had methodically loosened the gates of every horse stall in the stable. Then, a well-placed bag of gunpowder, a lit fuse—just enough to blow open the gates and spook the animals. The screams of men and horses followed the bang as every beast in the stables stampeded into the courtyard.

The air became thick with dust as terrified horses galloped left and right, searching for a way out. Some soldiers ran for cover, while others tried to wrangle the escaped animals. But there were dozens of them, all bucking, kicking, and panicking, tons of muscle and sharp hooves.

Cat rolled, dragging Amos with her before hooves could find them. She had no idea where Caldwell and Freeman had gone, and she didn't care. All she cared about was the sight of Soap helping her and Amos to their feet and onto the backs of their own calmed mounts. Amos couldn't ride on his own, so Soap helped him onto the back of Cat's horse. The Wolf wrapped his arms around Cat's waist and held on for dear life. More shouts through the clouds of dust. Shots rang out. Amos jerked suddenly against her, but he kept holding on. They had to get out of here—and fast.

Pedro waited for them at the main gate, throwing it open as the stampede escaped the courtyard and headed into the main street of Saint's Landing. Soap was ready with a third horse he held by the reins, directing it smoothly toward Pedro as they ran by. Pedro didn't even hesitate. With the fluid grace of a dancer, he swung himself into the saddle and joined them in their escape.

Cat's body was rigid with adrenaline as they passed through Fort Astor's thick wall, running with the stampeding horses into the throngs of people diving out of their way. Everyone would expect them to head out of town immediately, which would result in a massive chase through the desert they likely had no hope of winning. Once the Ordonian forces gathered their wits, there would be an almighty reckoning.

No, they could not outrun them—but they could hide.

"The mission!" Cat screamed at Soap's and Pedro's backs, hoping they heard her. "Go to the mission!"

They turned their horses to the left and began to force their way through the panicked crowd. Thank the Saints they'd heard her.

People were already taking cover in the mission, hiding behind its massive columns and running toward the entrance. When they got close enough to the main steps, the crowd was so thick that the horses became more of a hindrance than a help. Soap and Pedro abandoned their mounts and helped Cat ease Amos off the back of hers. They lowered him onto the stairs as bodies parted around them to give them space.

The Wolf wobbled dangerously, his eyes glassed over with pain. A faint hint of red bubbled at the corner of his mouth.

"Amos, are you—" Cat looked down and screamed.

Blood blossomed across his chest like a spring rose, staining his already filthy shirt even darker red. He kept a hand pressed against the wound, but it was clear. He'd been hit by a bullet during their escape.

"No," Cat sobbed, pressing her own hand against the wound in his chest as though she could force the lifeblood back into his body. "No! No, no, *no!*"

Soap looked down and swore violently, slipping his arm behind Amos's shoulders as the outlaw finally slumped onto the marble stairs.

Pedro's normally passive face was pinched with worry, tears shining in his eyes. "We can't stay here," he said sharply. "We have to get him inside."

Soap and Cat lifted Amos back up and began to drag him toward the cathedral's front doors. Blood spatters trailed behind him, glistening crimson against the cold white marble. Several women in church dresses watched them pass, delicate hands pressed against their open mouths. Cat wanted to scream at them to help, but really, what could they do? Especially if their identities became known. For now, people probably assumed they were common citizens wounded in the horse stampede.

"Father Iggy! Father Ephraim! Help!" Cat screamed as they entered the mission's atrium. Her cries echoed off the domed ceiling as the paintings of the twelve Saints watched their slow progress. A group of priests and priestesses rushed forward, Father Ephraim among them. She launched herself into Father Ephraim's arms, clutching at the front of his robes. "He's been shot! Help him, please!"

Father Ephraim squeezed her hands in a reassuring sort of way before gently, but firmly, pushing her to the side to inspect Amos's injuries.

"You know where to take him," he instructed a curate. "Catriona, you will probably want to stay with him."

She wanted to ask why, but one look at Father Ephraim's face told her all she needed to know.

Amos wasn't going to make it.

Someone's hand settled on her shoulder, but Cat shook it off, grabbing Amos's hand and refusing to let it go, even as they brought a stretcher and lifted him onto it. They carried him to a small room with three simple metal beds and a line of candles. There were no medical supplies, and no one was rushing to tend to him. Instead, Father Ephraim stood over him with a simple book in his hand, whispering prayers and making odd hand motions.

"Cat . . ." Amos whispered, his glassy eyes distant and unfocused.

"I'm here, Amos. I'm right here," she whimpered, pulling his bloodied knuckles to her lips and kissing them.

"You saved me," he said quietly.

"No. I didn't. I failed. Amos, I'm so sorry—"

"No," he coughed, bringing even more blood to his lips. "You *saved* me." His eyes began to flutter. "Now you have to save yourself."

Father Ephraim laid a hand on Amos's forehead, his whispered prayers growing more intense.

"What do you mean?"

"Stop chasing the sun, Cat. Face the night . . . face it . . ." He took a deep, shuddering breath.

And then his breaths were no more.

"Amos?" Cat whispered, her heart shattering into a thousand tiny fragments. A burning pressure built behind her eyes. "Amos? Please! No no no no . . ."

Father Ephraim reached down and closed Amos's eyelids with gentle care. "I'm sorry, Catriona. He's gone. He is at peace with the Saints."

Cat made a strangled sound in the back of her throat. At peace? How could he be at peace after what had just happened? How could the Saints have abandoned such a faithful servant of theirs to a fate like his? Beaten and broken in a jail cell? For what? Wanting to support their holy missions?

"You did save him," another voice said behind her.

Cat recognized it as Father Iggy, but she didn't turn around to face him.

"No. I didn't." Her tone was flat, expressionless as she rose to her feet. Before her lay the broken, bleeding body of the second father in her life. Again, her hands were covered in blood. Again, it was entirely her fault for trusting Adrian.

Pressure was building inside her chest. It filled her up, burning its way from deep inside her to the very tips of her fingers. It was going to explode out of her.

"Come away, my dear. We will make sure his body is buried in a place of honor in the mission's graveyard." Father Iggy reached for her hand.

Cat jerked it out of his grasp. "Did your little bet include Adrian betraying me?"

Father Iggy blinked at her. "*What?*"

"He told his father we were coming to save Amos."

"No, that can't be possible—"

"Well it is!" she screamed, throwing her arms into the air. "And now Amos is dead! Because of *me*!"

"Catriona, he was scheduled to die anyway, you made sure he died on *his* terms—"

"No! Don't!" Her chest began to rise and fall with the intensity of holding back the pressure still building inside her.

Father Iggy exposed his palms. "Catriona, please. Let's go sit down and get a drink, have some rest. I figured out who Thompson—"

"I don't care anymore," she interrupted. "I'm done. I'm done with all of this."

"Catriona, wait, please."

"No! I'm done! Do you hear me? I don't care what damned Saint chose me! They made a mistake! They never should have chosen me for anything! All I do is get people I care about killed!"

"That is not true." Father Ephraim whispered.

The pressure burst out of her in burning desperation. It filled her eyes and fractured her vision with tears. "*Yes it is!*" she screeched, gesturing wildly toward Amos's body.

Father Iggy took a step toward her. "Catriona . . ."

But Cat took a step back. She couldn't do this anymore. Pretend to be someone she wasn't. Try to reconcile any of the mistakes from her past. She needed to get out, to get as far away from Saelum Territory as it was possible to get.

"I'm sorry, Fathers. I tried. It just wasn't enough."

And she sprinted from the room that hung heavy with death and broken promises before either of the priests could stop her.

CHAPTER

37

Adrian slammed himself against the locked door one more time for good measure. They'd thrown him into what he assumed was Captain Freeman's office, but he would be damned if they managed to keep him here.

He'd heard the explosion, the chaos that ensued in the courtyard. He knew Soap and Pedro had set off their plan for escape without him. Which meant all he could do was pray that the others managed to get away safely. If he had to take the fall for them, then so be it. He would shoulder that responsibility on his own. He'd made his choice. He would live with the consequences.

But his choice had certainly *not* been to tell his father about their plan. Adrian hadn't told his father anything. He had kept his word to Cat, but that look of shattered betrayal in her eyes . . . he would never unsee that expression on her face for as long as he lived.

And not to be able to fix it, not to be able to set the record straight and call his father's lie for what it was before he was dragged away . . .

He threw himself against the door once more, crying out at the pain in his already severely bruised shoulder.

She had to know the truth. Even if she didn't care for him the way he cared for her, he couldn't let her think that he'd betrayed her like that again.

The door's handle rattled, and Adrian jumped back, preparing himself to spring at whoever came through. He tensed the muscles in his legs but released his stance the moment the barrel of Captain Freeman's gun fixed him squarely between the eyes. The young captain was covered in dust from head to toe, with a wild, frantic look in his dark eyes.

"Saints, Freeman. Lower your weapon. You don't need to shoot my son's head off," Baron Caldwell barked. He was busy brushing dirt off his traveling cloak. The dust had settled into the hairs of his mustache, giving the impression he'd aged a decade overnight.

Freeman lowered the gun but narrowed his eyes at Adrian as if he didn't trust him. The wild look in his eyes did at least ease slightly.

Adrian rounded on his father. "How did you find out? I didn't tell you anything!"

Caldwell whipped back his hand and connected it with Adrian's cheek, sending him flying into the wall.

"I know you didn't. But you should have. How could you betray your own family like this?"

Adrian's eyes danced with stars as he pushed himself upright. His cheek throbbed. "You really want to talk about betrayal? After what you did to Cat's family?"

The baron snorted. "Oh, I'm sure she had plenty of stories of what I've supposedly done, all designed to twist you around and make you doubt everything you've ever known. You're really going to trust a little snake like that? One who has been murdering and robbing since the time she ran away?"

Captain Freeman laughed, while the baron surveyed Adrian with disbelief. Adrian snapped his jaw shut. He felt like an embarrassed child who was throwing a tantrum while the adults looked on with amusement. Of course he believed her. But now, a tingle of fear and doubt crept in. Could she have been lying to him to manipulate him? He didn't want to think that was possible. The Catriona he'd known wouldn't do that to him. But was she even the same Catriona? He didn't know if he could honestly say yes to that either.

Adrian decided to steer the conversation into safer pastures. "How did you find out what we were planning?"

"Edith," his father answered simply. "She understands the importance of family. When she overheard what you were planning, she came right to me and told me everything."

His heart twisted. Edith had told their father. He felt the sharp stab of betrayal deep beneath his breastbone. "And so you just let us walk ourselves into a trap?"

"Stop acting like a petulant child. I let Catriona condemn herself through her own actions, and I'll dismiss any charges against you when I become governor." He waved a dismissive hand.

Adrian felt sick. "What happened in the courtyard? Is the execution still scheduled for this afternoon?"

Freeman ground his teeth together. "No, your little friends managed to get away. But we've got the city surrounded and there is no way they will escape this time. And trust me"—the corner of his mouth turned up—"when we do, it will be a *double* execution."

＊ · · · · ◉ · · · · ＊

As the vote wasn't scheduled to take place for two more days, Adrian and his father headed back to the ranch to wait for news and host some guests for dinner. His father wanted to repair some of the damage to his image that had occurred with the escape. Freeman remained in Saint's Landing, overseeing the search for the fugitive outlaws.

Adrian walked into his room and closed the door, plopping himself on his bed. He waited for sleep to drag him off somewhere he didn't have to think about the aching in his chest.

There was a creak inside his closet.

His face burned with a sudden rush of anger. "I know you're in there," he growled.

The closet door slowly creaked open, and sure enough, Edith's big brown eyes peered out.

"Where's Rose?" she asked tremulously.

"Her name isn't Rose. Which I'm guessing you already know by now too. It's Cat. And she's gone now, thanks to you."

Edith made a squeaking sound in the back of her throat.

"Is that what you wanted? To get her in trouble? Because you succeeded, Edith. And now we will both never see her again."

"No! That's not what I wanted at all! He was supposed to stop you from leaving!" Her voice cracked.

"I told you we needed to go! I told you we would come back," he yelled, knowing that he shouldn't be taking out his anger and frustration on her, but he couldn't stop himself.

"But *she* didn't come back! Mother promised she'd come back too and she never did!" Edith sobbed. "I didn't want to lose you and Rose the same way I lost her!"

"CAT!" Adrian bellowed. "Her name is Cat, Edith! And now they will catch her and hang her. All because you couldn't keep your mouth shut!"

Edith wailed like a wounded animal, and before Adrian could stop her, she threw open the closet door, sending it banging against the wall so hard the mirror above his dresser rattled. She sprinted from the room, her twin braids bouncing on her back. He knew he should go after her, take back the horrible things he had said, but he couldn't make himself move. Hopelessness swirled around him like a heavy rain cloud. He'd find Edith later and apologize.

It *was* her fault for telling their father, but she'd had no idea what telling him would do. She didn't understand the repercussions of her decision, and her motivation had clearly been out of fear and love. She had said goodbye to their mother on that final night and had never seen her again. He knew that left a wound in the heart that never truly healed. Edith had just wanted to stop them from leaving because she cared about them so much and didn't want to lose them.

But anger burned a hole through his chest. He was too upset to do anything about that right now. He needed to calm down first. Get his head back on his shoulders.

He spent most of the afternoon staring at the cracks in his ceiling, watching the shadows elongate as day tipped into evening. At some point he'd gotten up and fetched the geode off his dresser. He absently played with it, tossing it from one hand to the other.

Finally, there was a knock at the door. "Sir, your father is requesting your presence at dinner."

"I'm not hungry," Adrian said, still not moving from his spot on the bed. He tossed the geode back and forth a few more times between his fingers, savoring the scratchy bite of its surface against his skin.

"He said it wasn't a request," the servant's voice answered back. "Some of the visiting barons will be joining you, and your father wants you there to make an impression."

"Of course," Adrian muttered to himself. Fine, he would go down to dinner, but he wouldn't make himself presentable or be pleasant about it. He was still wearing the same clothes they'd come home in, ones his father had made him change into after discarding the stolen priest robes. They were wrinkled and covered in dirt from the coach ride, but Adrian just didn't care anymore.

He dragged himself downstairs to where his father and the guests, Baron Hernandez, his wife, and their two eldest daughters, were already waiting at the table. His father—dressed to the nines in a fresh dinner coat and polished leather boots—scowled as he took in Adrian's bedraggled look.

"You'll have to forgive my son's appearance, Hernandez. We had a long journey home from the capital this morning and he isn't feeling his best."

"It is understandable," Baron Hernandez replied. He ran a finger across his thick mustache. "If he isn't feeling well, he doesn't need to—"

"Of course he doesn't *need* to," chuckled his father. "But Adrian would love to be here to enjoy the company of your lovely girls, isn't that right, Adrian?"

Adrian grunted and looked around the table. "Where's Edith?"

"*Right, Adrian?*" his father repeated.

Adrian shook his head. "Yes, I'm happy to be here. But where is Edith?"

"I don't know. She wasn't with you?" his father asked, sounding impatient.

"No, she ran out of my room a few hours ago and I haven't seen her since."

His father frowned and motioned for one of the servants to come over. "Where is Miss Edith?" he asked.

The servant shook her head. "I'm sorry, sir. No one has seen her all afternoon."

His father scoffed. "She's probably just hiding somewhere. She'll turn up eventually like she always does." He promptly turned his attention to the steaks swimming in gravy that had just arrived at their place settings.

But Adrian didn't touch his fork. His intuition prickled with unease. "Father, she was really upset earlier. I think we should send someone to look for her."

"Fine, fine. Joseph, have the servants start searching the house. I want her to be able to greet our guests properly anyway."

Baron and Baroness Hernandez glanced uneasily at each other, as though embarrassed. Adrian couldn't blame them. Most people upon hearing that their daughter was missing cared to find her for the sake of finding her, not just so that she could greet their dinner guests.

They made it through dinner, Adrian continually glancing at the doorway waiting for Edith to materialize and join them.

But she never did.

Nor did any of the servants arrive with news of her whereabouts. The dinner conversation had—of course—turned to the possibility of Adrian marrying their daughter, Evangeline, but still there was no sign of Edith. After cigars and brandies in the parlor, night was beginning to settle, and Adrian began to feel a flutter of panic. Edith never stayed missing this long.

"I'm going to help the servants look for her," he announced, rising up from the parlor's love seat where he'd been seated next to Evangeline.

"Do you want some help?" Evangeline offered, following him to his feet. "I have little sisters at home too, and I know how these things can go." She seemed genuinely concerned. Adrian was touched by her compassion.

He swallowed. "Um, sure. We can start in her room."

Together they made their way upstairs to Edith's room, where they began searching her usual hiding places. She was not beneath her bed, in her wardrobe, or behind any of the curtains. Adrian was inspecting behind her bookcase when Evangeline called him over.

"Adrian, look what I found in her vanity." She held out a scrap of paper with a hastily scribbled note.

I'm sorry I ruined everything. You'll never have to worry about me again, I promise.

"Oh my Saints," Adrian said. His knees gave out as he collapsed onto Edith's empty bed.

"What does that mean? Did something happen?" Evangeline sat down beside him, her gloved hand over her open mouth.

Adrian's stomach swirled with nausea. He should have gone after her. He shouldn't have said those horrible, horrible things. Now it was too late, and the desert was an incredibly dangerous place to be out alone at night. Especially for a nine-year-old girl. They had to find her immediately.

Adrian dropped his head into his hands. How much more damage could he do to the ones he loved? "She's gone. She ran away. And it's entirely my fault."

CHAPTER

38

The whiskey at this particular bar was strong, which was more than fine by Cat. She wanted the strongest stuff they had if she was going to numb the memories and emotions that kept snapping at her heels like hungry hounds. If she couldn't outrun them, at least she could do her damnedest to ignore them.

"Another," she barked at the barmaid, slamming her cloudy glass down on the polished bar top.

"You gotta pay if you want any more, sweetheart. It's a two-drink limit on tab."

"Fine." She threw a silver coin at the buxom redhead. "Just fill it as high as it'll go."

The woman's wild eyebrows rose to her hairline, but she slid the coin into her cleavage and took the empty glass.

Cat didn't have much money left after buying her ship ticket. The Saints were probably going to damn her to the depths of hell for stealing coins out of the fountain of Saint Prudentia on her way out of the mission, but Cat figured half her problems were Saint Prudentia's fault anyway. She never should have chosen her to be one of the Blessed. Just like Cat never should have trusted Adrian to help her break Amos out of prison.

Amos. His name sent a fresh throb of pain lancing through her chest. Where was that damn barmaid with her drink? The ship was scheduled to depart in an hour, which meant she had one hour to waste getting as good and drunk as she could. She didn't really care that—based on the distant booming of the courthouse clock tower—it was only ten in the morning.

While she waited, she carefully listened in on the conversations of the drunkards around her, making sure no one recognized or suspected her. With the brim pulled low and her hair tucked up into her hat, she hoped she was inconspicuous enough to make it out of Saint's Landing without being recognized. It had been almost a full twenty-four hours since she'd escaped, and since then, she'd bribed the captain of the small merchant ship to take her on as his "niece." The authorities were looking for a group of escaped fugitives, not a lone young woman. As long as no one questioned it, she'd finally be on her way, chasing the setting sun out across the Dark Sea and leaving the growing shadows of Saelum Territory behind her once and for all.

The general rumblings of the other patrons didn't interest her— mostly complaints about cattle prices and overtaxation by the barons for land rentals. But one name caught her ear.

"I heard Caldwell is offering a pretty hefty reward."

"Don't blame him. I'd give every penny I owned if it were my daughter."

Cat leaned in closer. Caldwell's daughter? A reward?

"Such a sad situation. I hope they find her before it's too late. Kids that go missing in the desert aren't usually alive when they're finally found."

Her grip on the edge of the bar tightened just as the barmaid returned with her filled drink. "Have you heard anything about Baron Caldwell's daughter?" she asked, trying to sound casual.

"Caldwell? Oh, yes, I heard about that. Poor little thing."

Panic dug its claws into Cat's heart. "What happened? Is she okay?"

The barmaid shrugged. "Don't know. She's missing. Rumor has it she ran away. The baron is offering an outrageous sum of gold for anyone who finds her and brings her home. He's got almost every able body in town scouring the desert for her."

Cat tapped her hands anxiously against the bar's surface. Edith was missing. She'd run away. She had no idea why or what would have prompted the little girl to make such a decision. Hopefully someone would find her soon. Guilt squirmed in her gut . . . was it her fault Edith had run away?

"And no one's had any luck?"

The barmaid put down the glass she'd been polishing and grabbed another. "Not that I've heard. Though they better hurry, the spring monsoons are starting and you can tell the storms are already building out that way."

A memory flooded back to Cat of their playdate at the river, when they'd spent hours together catching tadpoles for their science lesson. Something she had told Edith about herself as a little girl . . .

I used to dream about running away and living at the river . . . I had it all planned out, I'd live in one of the little caves in a canyon, hunt fish, and drink fresh water from the spring . . .

Cat would bet every ounce of aurium on her family's land that Edith had run to the canyon. There were enough crevices and hidey-holes that she was sure no one would find her if Edith didn't want to be found.

But Edith also wouldn't be able to see how quickly those waters would rise during a thunderstorm, when the river could swell and flow like a cut throat. As if to emphasize the danger in her thoughts, a deep peal of thunder rattled the glasses behind the bar.

The barmaid shuddered. "I hope they find the poor little thing soon."

Cat grunted in agreement and threw back the glass in one gulp. The whiskey burned her throat and made her eyes water. At least, she told herself it was the whiskey.

"Thanks," she said, slapping another coin onto the counter in thanks and pushing back from the bar. She needed to get to the ship; the captain had already told her he wouldn't wait if she wasn't there when they left. She stepped outside. A rush of warm wind off the desert rushed past and nearly took her hat with it. The air was heavy and charged, oppressive with monsoon humidity.

Cat glanced behind her, where dark thunderheads rose high into the sky above the distant hills. The hills Caldwell Ranch backed up to. She turned without thinking toward the horse stables.

But then she murmured a swear she was sure would make Adrian chastise her. She walked several steps and then turned back toward the harbor. She could get on the ship, pretend none of the past few weeks had happened—pretend *all* of her life had never happened—and start anew. Start fresh. But even thinking that way left her chest feeling hollow and empty.

Could she really? Could she ever run fast enough, far enough, to truly forget?

The sky churned with dark clouds, and another blast of wind rattled the window shutters of the shops and homes, throwing up a mini dust devil in the middle of the side street. Most of the townsfolk were staying inside. Like creatures of the desert, they knew when it was time to take cover from the looming storm. It was why the captain wanted to get out of the harbor and into open water as soon as possible.

A beam of sunlight broke momentarily through the clouds, lighting up the street around her. She could almost hear Amos's voice. "*Stop chasing the setting sun . . .*"

She turned and looked at the dark clouds one more time.

"*Face the night . . .*"

"Saints Almighty." What the hell was she thinking?

She pictured Edith's smile, the mischievous glint in her eyes when she was being playful, the sweet innocence of her sleeping face in Cat's lap in the coach, the tearful way she'd hugged Cat on more than one occasion. Her look of fear and anguish after being controlled by that damned necklace. The relief when Cat had comforted her and given her the necklace of holy water instead.

And Cat knew in the depths of her heart what she was going to do.

She couldn't leave Edith. She couldn't. Not when she was probably the only person alive who knew where to find her. Yes, she could run, but if Edith had shown her anything, it was that some things were more important than her own pain.

She took a deep breath, her mind made up—and sprinted toward the stables.

* • • • ◉ • • • •

Fat raindrops pelted Cat's face as she spurred the rented horse to its limits. It took her several hours to reach the canyon, and by the time she made it, she and the desert around her were soaked through. The raindrops transitioned to a torrential downpour, and the river where they had caught the tadpoles had already swollen to three times the size it had been. The water rushed over its former banks with the level still rising.

That's when she heard it.

A girl's scream.

Cat immediately jumped from the horse. She flung its reins over a nearby juniper bush and ran to the canyon's steep ledge. Her eyes skimmed the interior, from the sloping rock walls to the rushing mud-colored torrent that had replaced the gentle river. Her vision was blurred by the unforgiving rain, but finally, a splotch of bright blue caught her attention. Down below, half-submerged in the turbulent brown water and clutching the tangled remains of a dead tree, was Edith.

The girl screamed again, her tiny hands bloodied as they clutched at the twisted limbs.

"Edith!" Cat yelled, throwing herself over the canyon's edge and slipping hazardously down toward the water. Her boots sank into the sand and mud as she slid down as close as she dared to the water's edge.

"Rose?" Edith cried. "Rose! Help me!"

Cat's throat constricted with panic as she assessed the situation. She couldn't get much closer without getting dragged in, but Edith couldn't hold on much longer. The water was a powerful force as it cascaded past, and Edith was trapped on the opposite bank. She had no way of getting to the other side to reach her.

"I'm here, Edith! I'm here!" She tried to reassure the girl, but in reality, she had no idea what to do. Her brain swirled as chaotically as the eddies in the river itself, aimlessly spinning and rushing on without any clear destination in mind. What could she do? *What could she do?*

"Rose! Help—" Edith cried again. The snap of a branch echoed like the crack of a breaking bone, and Edith's head disappeared beneath the torrent.

The chaos in her mind went suddenly clear. There was only one thing to do.

She dove in after her.

CHAPTER
39

The water was warmer than she'd expected, but far more powerful as well. The currents instantly jerked her forward like a doll out of the hands of two feuding siblings. Her head went under, and muddy water cascaded down her throat. She kicked with every ounce of her strength, finally forcing her head to break through the surface. Fresh air filled her lungs for a brief moment before the water dragged her back under again. This was the stupidest thing she could have ever done. She'd told Edith the dangers of floodwaters. She knew them well herself after the gang had lost a member to them three springs ago.

And yet . . . the moment Edith had been swept away, Cat hadn't hesitated. All her thoughts had been about reaching her.

She kicked again and finally managed to break through to the surface and stay there. She swung her legs around to the front, keeping her feet out in front of her as she fought with her arms to stay afloat. Her eyes scanned the choppy water for Edith's blue dress or dark hair.

"*Eeedith!*" she called, choking as water tried to fill in the new space made available by her open mouth.

"Rose!" A voice answered not too far ahead.

Oh Mother, please help me reach her. Please. Take me instead. Just spare her—Cat threw her frantic prayers toward the heavens.

Her vision flashed. A thick log was about to smash into the back of her head. A warning, but also an opportunity if she could use it. Cat twisted around and threw her arms over the sodden trunk, hoisting her torso partially up and out of the water.

And for the second time, a hint of bright blue caught her eye. Edith was fighting to stay afloat against the current not even three yards away.

Cat ripped her empty gun belt off from around her waist and tossed the holster end out in her direction. "Edith! Grab my belt!"

Edith's head swiveled toward her, her panicked eyes going wide. She flailed through the water, trying desperately to make her way to where Cat's belt stretched toward her.

"Swim! You can do it, Edith! I know you can!"

The girl sobbed as she clawed at the water with her bloodied hands, her face red and splotchy and covered in mud and tears. But she swam, and swam, fighting against the waves slapping her in the face, against the currents pulling her skirts. Cat wanted to cry out with pride at the strength of the girl's spirit. Edith had fight in her, and that fight was the reason she hadn't been dragged under yet.

Finally, after what felt like an eternity of watching her struggle, of being helpless to do anything more, Cat saw Edith's fingers take a death grip on the belt's empty holster. As soon as she was sure of her grip, Cat pulled her in.

Cat helped Edith get her arms over the log and held her in place with her own body. The dead tree sloshed this way and that, but Cat held on firmly, her own hands growing bloody as she gripped the straggly branches. After a short time of riding the rapids and currents, the canyon began to curve. Along the outside of the bend was a flat stretch of sand still untouched by the swollen river.

"Can you help me kick toward shore?" Cat yelled, tilting her head toward the river bank.

Edith gave an exhausted nod. The poor thing was shaking like a leaf in a harsh wind, but bless her, she was still fighting. Edith's little feet kicked out with what energy she had left.

Pride bloomed in Cat's chest, and the muscles of her legs screamed in protest as she pushed them past their limit, trying to move the log in the right direction. The current must have worked in their favor—or perhaps it was with the divine help of the Mother, Cat didn't care to question how—but the crescent of sand loomed closer and closer. Finally, the raging river washed them close enough that Cat thought they could swim ashore.

"When I say let go, let go and swim with everything you have left in you," she instructed.

Edith gave another exhausted nod.

"NOW!"

She shoved Edith's body toward the sand, but in doing so, she lost her own grip. The water gained the upper hand and dragged her under. Her boots slipped along the bottom, across the smooth river stones that refused to give her any traction. She tried to push herself off the bottom—and that was when the heel of her boot wedged itself between two rocks.

Cat knew she was in trouble. This was the most dangerous part about getting trapped in a flood—getting stuck and held under. Her breath escaped in her panic. She yanked as hard as she could, but the boot would not budge. She couldn't even reach her arm down as the current pulled at her with relentless ferocity. She was going to drown here, in this rain-swollen river she'd grown up playing in as a child. Her lungs burned and ached at the lack of oxygen. The warm, muddy water was filling her mouth. Blackness pressed in around her from all sides. Perhaps she shouldn't have offered her own life in trade for Edith's after all. She should have asked for them *both* to survive . . .

Edith had fought so hard, and Cat would too. She wouldn't let this river defeat her. Not now, not when she was so close. With one last yank, her foot came free from the trapped boot. Leaving it behind, she shot to the surface. Cool, clean air rushed back into her lungs as she coughed and vomited up the water she'd swallowed. Heavy drops of rain still pelted her in the face, but she welcomed them like tears of gratitude from the heavens.

She'd been spared. Somehow, her foot had come free.

She fought the rest of the way to the shore, where Edith lay sprawled and gasping like a caught fish. Cat dug her fingers into the sand and dragged herself alongside Edith. Flipping onto her back, she let the rain wash away the mud and sand that clung to every inch of her clothes and skin.

But then Edith threw herself across Cat's stomach, nearly knocking what little wind she had left out of her lungs. Cat groaned and curled in on herself. Coughing some more, she placed a reassuring arm across Edith's back.

The little girl sobbed and clutched at her, repeating "I'm sorry" over and over and over again.

Cat shushed her reassuringly, finally sitting up and wrapping her arms around her properly.

"Edith, you have nothing to be sorry for. You're safe. I'm here. I'm here."

"Noooo! You don't understand! This is my fault! It's all my fault!"

"Sweetheart, you ran away. You had no idea a storm was coming and that you were going to get caught in a flood. That's not your fault—"

"No! It's all my fault! You have to forgive me, Rose. I'm so sorry!"

Cat laughed a little exasperatedly. "It's really not—"

But then Edith pulled back, tears falling thick and fast down her puffy cheeks. "No, you don't understand. I told my father about you and Adrian going to Saint's Landing. Adrian got so mad at me! He told me that you were going to die and that it was all my fault for telling! I'm so sorry!"

Cat stiffened. *Edith* had been the one to tell her father? "Wait . . . I thought Adrian told your father."

"No! It was me! It was me! I was so scared. I'm so sorry!"

A million thoughts collided in Cat's brain at once. Adrian hadn't told his father. Edith had. That meant that Adrian hadn't betrayed her at all. She knew and understood exactly why Edith had told, and she also knew that Edith had had no idea of the repercussions of her decision to tell her father.

Cat wrapped her arms around Edith even tighter. "Listen to me, Edith. This is *not* your fault."

"Yes, it is! If I hadn't told him, none of this would have happened!"

"Maybe that's true. But you didn't understand what was going on. You can't hold yourself responsible for what your father does and does not do. What *anyone* else does, really. We can only do what we think is best in any given moment. We don't make choices for others. We can't take that responsibility on . . . on ourselves . . ." Her voice faded as she realized that she wasn't just talking to Edith.

She was talking to herself.

She looked down at Edith, tearstained and terrified, pleading for forgiveness . . . and for the briefest moment, she didn't see Edith in her arms. She saw the nine-year-old version of herself, just as broken, just as scared and confused.

Feeling just as guilty for the actions of someone else.

Should she have told Adrian about the aurium on her parents' land? No. Should Adrian have told his father after telling Cat he wouldn't? No. Should Edith have told her father about them going to Saint's Landing? No. But those were small mistakes, children behaving like children, as children are expected to do. They had no control over what Adrian's father had done with those mistakes. That responsibility lay solely on his shoulders then just as much as it did now.

Cat hugged Edith tighter, comforting her in the same way she was finally comforting the little girl inside of herself. "I forgive you. Not because any of this is your fault, though. You only did what you thought was best in that moment, Edith. You were trying to protect us, and for that I am thankful. I am so sorry that your father took what you intended for innocence and turned it into something bad. But that is *not* your fault, and I will not let you apologize for his actions, do you understand?"

Edith cried, burying her face in Cat's soaked shirt. Cat continued to rub her back, letting her release the emotions as she knew she needed to. In fact, the longer Edith cried, the strangest thing began to happen. Cat felt a burning behind her own eyes. Then, tears began to fall down her cheeks too. Slowly at first, one by one sneaking out as though they weren't sure they had permission to do so. But soon Cat was crying in earnest along with Edith. Allowing the last ten years of pain and guilt to seep out of her as the desert rain that poured from the dark clouds overhead cleansed them both of their sins.

She didn't know how long they sat there together, holding onto each other as they cried. But when the rain stopped and a beam of sunlight broke through the clouds, Cat almost swore she heard Amos's voice whisper.

"Catch the sunrise on the other side . . ."

Cat smiled to herself. Yes, she had finally faced the night. It had hurt—oh Saints, the pain of allowing that poison in her soul to finally reach the surface had been painful—but now that it had found its way out, there was a surprising clarity to the world around her. It was as if a numb limb had suddenly tingled back to life, the painful pins-and-needles sensation giving way to full feeling again.

"What do we do now, Rose?" Edith pulled back and looked at her, expectation shining in her eyes.

"Well, first things first. I think I'd like to introduce myself to you properly." Cat smiled and tapped Edith on the nose.

Edith's eyebrows scrunched together. "What do you mean?"

"My name isn't Rose." A strange sensation wriggled inside her stomach as she contemplated her next words carefully. It was something almost like excitement. She held out her hand as if it were the first time they'd ever met. "My name is Catriona Macgregor, and I am the rightful baroness of the Macgregor Ranch."

CHAPTER

40

"Where are we going?" Edith asked.

The little girl rode in front of her in the saddle as the seemingly endless expanse of chaparral stretched out before them. It had taken them several hours to make their way up the side of the canyon and back to where Cat had tied her horse, the river having washed them several miles away from where they'd started.

"There is something I want to show you," Cat grinned.

"But there's nothing out here but rocks and sagebrush."

"Ah, there's actually a special treasure out here we have to find."

"If you say so." Edith snuggled back against Cat's chest, and Cat sensed she'd go anywhere as long as they were together.

Although Cat knew exactly what they were looking for, finding it was taking a hell of a lot longer than she had anticipated. Finally, after hours of searching, and more clouds rolling in to bring the next late-afternoon thunderstorm, a familiar rock formation jutted out of the earth ahead of them like a swollen thumb. It had been almost a decade since she'd last seen it, but its outline was forever burned into her memory. The formation in whose shadow she had buried her father's ruby ring.

The sun began to tip into a gorgeous sunset just as they reached the base of the formation, staining the thunderheads a deep gold and red that matched the ring itself. The sky seemed to celebrate the fact that she had returned for it.

She guided the horse to where she remembered burying it and dropped to her hands and knees to start digging. Edith helped, and finally, the ring materialized in the freshly dug hole.

"It looks just like one my dad has," Edith said, staring wide-eyed at the ruby ring.

Cat lifted it out of the hole and began to wipe the dirt off it with the corner of her already filthy shirt. "Every landowner is granted a ring by the emperor as a symbol of his or her status. The dukes and duchesses of Ordonia, the oldest and wealthiest of families, are awarded diamond rings. Then earls, who receive sapphire rings, then the barons, who receive rubies, and so on down until you get to the plain gold bands of the territory judges. The landowners of each territory function as the emperor's representatives, electing the local governments on his behalf. That's why the barons will vote on who becomes the next governor of Saelum. They are acting on the emperor's behalf so that all he has to do is come and bless the appointment."

"That's why all the barons are here now, to vote for governor? That's tomorrow, isn't it?"

Cat frowned. "Yes, and unfortunately, I think your dad is somehow planning to use aurium powder to rig the vote and make sure he is elected."

Edith gasped, her hands flying to her mouth. "But how? There's so many barons, and you'd have to get all of them to vote at the same time without anyone noticing aurium."

"I wish I knew. That's what I was trying to find out when I came to your house as governess."

Edith's cheek dimpled. "You mean you didn't come just to enjoy the pleasantness of my disposition?"

"Well, that was just an added bonus." Cat winked while Edith broke into a fit of giggles.

She looked down at the ring in her palm. It was a thick, heavy thing, engraved with her family's crest and set with the ruby of a baron in the center. To Cat, it still looked like a drop of blood. It wouldn't fit her dainty fingers, so she'd settle for looping it through a necklace chain when they got back into town.

Because that was where they were headed next. She had a rough plan forming in her head, and that plan did *not* involve taking Edith back to Caldwell Ranch.

No, for this next phase, she needed to head back to Father Iggy and the mission in Saint's Landing. She couldn't stop Baron Caldwell as Black Cat Whitfield, but perhaps she did have a chance to stop him as Baroness Catriona Macgregor.

✦ · · · · ◉ · · · · ✦

"I've sent word to the Caldwell homestead that Miss Edith has been found safe and is being housed here at the mission for the evening." Father Iggy grinned as he placed another blanket at the foot of Cat's bed. "I imagine Baron Caldwell plans to pick her up on his way home from the vote tomorrow."

"If the vote takes place," Cat conceded.

The novices who used this room had been shooed to another dormitory so that Edith and Cat would have a place to sleep for the night.

"Have you given much thought to what you will do after tomorrow?" Father Iggy asked. The springs of the metal bed creaked beneath his weight as he sat down on the edge.

"That all depends on how tomorrow goes. Are you sure the priesthood is prepared to take the risk I'm asking them to?"

Father Iggy scoffed. "My dear. We are priests of the Blessed. We did not choose to enter this line of work because it was safe and comfortable."

"Or profitable?" Cat quirked an eyebrow.

He tossed a pillow at her. "You better get some rest, you little heathen."

A giggle came from the lump on the neighboring bed that was supposed to be Edith's sleeping form.

"*Both* of you little heathens," Father Iggy sighed.

Edith's lump giggled again.

"Yes, *Father*." Cat didn't bother to hide her smile.

Father Iggy returned it with an affectionate one of his own before slipping out the door.

"Don't gamble too much tonight!" Cat called after him.

"Heathen!" he called back.

She chuckled to herself before her eyes drifted to the dress that hung on the simple wood-framed mirror in the corner. Perhaps she was crazy for thinking this plan could work, but she couldn't think of any other option. Fathers Iggy and Ephraim had agreed it was the best way, although they might have agreed to anything in the excitement of her return.

She tossed and turned for several hours, but instead of finding the sleep she needed, the anxious pounding of her heart kept her wide awake. Finally, she slipped out of bed and padded out into the hall.

The novice and curate dormitories were as silent as a grave at such a late hour—which gave her an idea. Making her way down the stairs and into the courtyard, she found the section of the mission's graveyard reserved for distinguished members of society. Sure enough, moonlight illuminated a freshly dug grave. It was marked with a simple stone that read, *A faithful servant of the Saints and their holy mission.*

"Hey, old man," Cat said, curling into a sitting position next to the newly smoothed earth. "I always loved our late-night chats by the fire, so I guess this'll have to do."

A slight breeze rustled the rosebushes that surrounded this part of the garden. It was beautiful and peaceful, a fitting resting place for a soul such as Amos's. He'd always seemed so rough on the outside, but Cat had known him for his gentle, loving heart.

"Tomorrow is a big day," she continued. "I wish I could hear what you think about my idea. It's probably stupid. Saints, I might be joining you by tomorrow night." She laughed without humor. "But it's also a shot for me to finally do what you always told me to. I'm not running anymore. It's scary as hell, and I don't want to do it, but I know it's the right thing to do. I know I can't blame myself for what happened in the past."

Though nothing but silence answered, she could sense Amos's pride in her, as if he'd placed a hand on her shoulder and growled, "There ya go, kid." He might not be here physically anymore, but his memory and his presence would always stay with her. She reached over and plucked a rose from one of the nearby bushes.

"I'm facing the night, Amos." She laid the rose down gently atop his headstone. Several tears slipped down her burning cheeks. "And I intend to run through it. I will catch that sunrise on the other side. I promise."

CHAPTER
41

The day of the vote had finally come, and Adrian didn't think he could feel less ready for it. The city was abuzz with excitement. The streets were packed with people wanting to be close enough to hear the final news when it was announced from the top of the courthouse steps.

Adrian had only been to the courthouse on two other occasions. Once to pick up Edith's birth certificate, and once to pick up his mother's death certificate. The vote would take place in the main courtroom, overseen by the Honorable Judge Barber. He was a fair judge, from what Adrian had heard: stern, but well respected among the barons and the Ordonian Empire alike.

His father, unfortunately, had been in a horrible mood from the time they'd left the ranch, reducing no fewer than three servants to tears and nearly giving his footman an embolism.

"This is a big day, Adrian," he kept saying over and over.

As if his father would ever let him forget.

He still didn't know if he wanted his father to become governor. On the one hand, with his obsession with order and propriety, he'd clearly do a decent job of "cleaning up" the territory. But what made his father so efficient was also his greatest weakness—he lacked compassion. And while law and order were important, Adrian always thought compassion was an essential quality for someone in such an important leadership position.

He also wasn't sure what to believe about Catriona anymore. Or Cat, he guessed he should call her. Whoever she was, she wasn't the Catriona he'd known all those years ago. His heart twisted. It felt like he'd miraculously gotten her back, only to realize she was gone all over again. It was a sharp stabbing sensation, one that pulsed and throbbed each time her name flitted across his consciousness. Was what his father said about her true? Had she really lied to and manipulated him and Edith? He didn't want to think so. But he didn't know what to think anymore.

"Where will we pick up Edith?" Adrian wanted to discuss anything but the vote.

His father grunted, jerking his attention away from the carriage window where he'd been watching the bustling crowd with a strange kind of hunger in his eyes. "What? Edith? Oh, yes. The priest's letter said they have her at the mission. We can pick her up after the vote."

Adrian didn't like waiting until then; he wanted to see her as soon as possible, to wrap his arms around her and apologize for making her feel like things were her fault. That poor girl had been through enough the last few years. But his father had insisted she not come with them to the courthouse. *It was no place for an unruly child.*

Translation: I don't want her to embarrass me during the vote and hurt my chances.

Adrian fidgeted in his seat until the carriage finally pulled up in front of the courthouse. The massive clock tower was silent for now, but in about ten minutes it would shake as the bells tolled the eleventh hour of the morning. The sun was already high in the sky, nearing its pinnacle and baking the land beneath its dry, unforgiving heat. As usual for this time of year, dark thunderheads gathered on the horizon, though it was unclear how close to the capital they'd venture today.

The courtroom steps were crowded with the arriving barons and their security entourages. His father brought three privately hired guards himself, though why he needed so many, Adrian wasn't sure. It was likely an effort to show off and intimidate the other barons.

They exited the coach and made their way into the main courtroom, a large square room with wood-paneled walls. Adrian felt like he was walking into a polished wooden crate, with all the barons as sardines ready to be packaged up for shipment.

Tables with white linens, placards, quills, and bottles of ink were set up in a large inner square, all facing the raised bench of Judge Barber. His father, of course, selected a seat at the center, placing himself in prime view of all in attendance. Adrian took a seat behind his father along the outer wall, not important enough to sit at the main table yet.

Delicate crystal goblets rested beside each of the placards, already filled with a glittering white wine. Green glass bottles were placed at regular intervals between every third seat. Adrian licked his dry lips. He was tempted to ask his father if he could have some to wet his parched tongue, but knew better than to risk it. If it came from one of the local vineyards around Saint's Landing, it was sure to be exquisite. And expensive.

He watched the other barons trickle in, many of them bringing their oldest children to sit and observe as well. He caught sight of Evangeline Hernandez across the room and gave her a warm smile, which she returned. But then Cat's face flashed behind his eyes, and he flinched as his chest gave another sharp twinge. *Damn it.* He was going to have to do something about that.

"Please rise for the Honorable Judge Barber," announced one of the soldiers beside the door to the judge's chambers.

There was a great scuffing of chairs against wood as those in the courtroom rose to their feet. Judge Barber entered in flowing robes of black, his dark hair streaked with silver. His eyes, even from across the room, struck Adrian as unusually bright, a blue that shone like chips of ice. They were also incredibly sharp, as if that ice were broken into jagged shards.

The judge took his seat, and the barons all mimicked him.

"Thank you for taking the time to gather in honor of Emperor Lawrence, may his reign be long and fruitful."

"May his reign be long and fruitful," echoed the fifty or so voices of those gathered.

Judge Barber leaned over and began to read from a prepared

parchment. "We are meeting today to discuss the appointment of the new governor for Saelum Territory. Though we will vote for our recommendation, it is essential for the barons of this territory to remember it is the emperor and the emperor alone who chooses those who oversee the territories of Ordonia in his stead. Upon receipt of the recommendation of the territory's landowners, Emperor Lawrence will arrive to make the official appointment and receive tribute from the territory in question."

Adrian glanced around the room at the solemn faces of the barons and baronesses. There was palpable irritation at the mention of "tribute." The landowners were always reluctant to let go of any of their wealth, even for the sake of honoring the emperor. Especially an emperor who tended to view Saelum as an unimportant backwater territory.

"We will now accept nominations," Judge Barber continued. The barons all lifted their quills and dipped them into the small pots of ink before scratching their choices onto scraps of provided parchment. Adrian didn't have to guess that his father would be writing his own name down. The parchments were submitted and sure enough, his father was one of three final nominees.

"We will now allow the nominees to make their arguments," the judge announced.

The other two nominees, Baroness Richfield from Bolsa and Baron Wayne from Henrietta Flats, gave their arguments for why they deserved the vote, and finally, it was his father's turn.

"Baron Caldwell of Caldwell Ranch, you have the floor."

His father rose to his feet, crystal goblet in his hand. His speech was short, eloquent, and to the point. He made his arguments that he'd crack down on crime against the barons and further restrict the reach of the missions to allow for greater separation of church and state, taking away the influence of the priests who prioritized the will of the gods over the will of their emperor. He argued for increasing the barons' standing in the empire, expanding the economy and beef trade to improve their influence. Many of the barons and baronesses nodded their agreement, but many more watched him with eyes narrowed in suspicion. Most of them knew his reputation. Here he was preaching on law and order when he so rarely held himself to the standards he expected everyone else to follow. If he did win the vote, it would be by a very narrow margin indeed.

"Let us now write down our final selection for governor," Judge Barber announced in a deep voice.

A door opened in the back of the room, and Captain Freemen entered, followed by a small detail of about ten Ordonian soldiers.

The judge eyed them shrewdly as they entered, but recognizing them as members of the military, decided not to say or do anything. Something in Adrian's stomach squirmed. It was an odd sensation, as if his body sensed something was about to happen before his mind had caught up.

"Ah, Your Honor. Before we vote, I wish to raise a toast," Baron Caldwell announced suddenly.

"A toast?" the judge repeated impatiently. "For what purpose, Baron Caldwell?"

"To honor His Majesty the Emperor, of course. And to honor the process by which we fairly select the best option for governor. Even if I am not the winner, we must show respect and unity as the landowners of Saelum to congratulate those whom we choose to lead." He gave a hearty wink. "That—and my dear friend Donald Thompson has donated these lovely bottles and it would be a shame to see them go to waste."

Thompson. Thompson? Something about that name tickled the back of Adrian's memory. Where had he heard it before?

He leaned forward and plucked one of the unopened bottles off the table. Nothing about it seemed particularly threatening. It was just a bottle of sparkling white wine, a little picture of a cottage nestled among vineyards on the label, the name *Thompson Vineyard* in swirly script writing.

Wait . . . hadn't Cat said something about that name? About Thompson having something to do with his father's plan to rig the . . .

Oh my gods.

The realization hit Adrian just as every baron and baroness lifted their glasses at his father's beckoning. Sure enough, as the sunlight pouring through the windows reflected off the nearest glass, he saw it, so subtle he would have missed it if he hadn't been looking specifically for it . . .

A golden sheen swirled within the sparkling white wine.

The bottles were spiked with aurium powder. Aurium powder that was cursed with the power of Saint Pietas to force obedience—like obeying when told whose name to write down on the paper.

"No!" Adrian yelled just as they all tipped their heads back and drank deeply from the cups. But it was too late.

"Don't forget to vote for *Baron Caldwell for governor*," his father ordered, not taking so much as a sip from his own glass. He let his gaze wander around the room, his chest swelling with pride at his accomplishment.

But Adrian watched with horror as the face of every baron and baroness went strangely blank—just as Edith's had when she'd worn the aurium necklace. And then, almost in unison, they picked up their quills and began to write the same thing . . .

Baron Caldwell for governor.

Adrian wanted to scream. Cat had been right all along. His father had used aurium to *steal* the governorship. He'd cursed every one of the barons and baronesses into obedience, then he'd ordered them to vote for him under the guise of making a toast. The powdered aurium would last just long enough to get his desired result, then it would wear off before anyone could suspect what had happened. Within a minute everyone would be back to normal.

"Please hand your votes to my page as he comes around to collect them," Judge Barber ordered.

Of course, the barons and baronesses obeyed.

The judge took the parchments at his bench and began to tally the results. His brow furrowed in confusion, he looked up as though to question them before continuing with his count. He clearly didn't understand the results he was seeing, but he also had to honor the supposedly fair system.

Adrian's palms were sweating inside his gloves. His heart raced with the need to do something, *anything*. Was he going to stay silent and just let his father get away with this?

He made eye contact with Captain Freeman, who gave him a shake of his head in warning. Almost as if to say, *Don't do anything stupid, boy.*

But Adrian couldn't stay silent. He couldn't just let this happen. As soon as the aurium wore off, and he guessed it would be any moment now, he was going to disclose exactly what happened. He got to his feet, cleared his throat, and . . .

The doors to the courtroom opened again. But this time, instead of Freeman and his soldiers entering . . . *it was Cat.*

And she wasn't alone.

She was followed by a small contingent of priests, about five or six in total. While they were dressed in their traditional brown robes, Cat herself wore a simple yet tasteful dress. Her short black jacket was proper and flattering over her black-and-red-striped skirt, and from her waist hung double gun holsters. The heels of her boots tapped against the hardwood floor as she tipped back her black hat.

"Excuse me, Your Honor, but I believe we need to redo the vote."

Judge Barber's cold blue eyes seemed to harden even more. "And who, might I ask, are you?"

"I am Baroness Catriona Macgregor, the rightful heir of Macgregor Ranch. I am here to claim not only my birthright but to vote in the proceedings of who to recommend for governor."

Adrian froze, unsure how to proceed beyond watching what was unfolding before him. He felt a mixture of awe and horror. But mostly awe.

"This is outrageous!" his father bellowed, rushing into the center of the room. "We've already voted. And there is no evidence that this young woman is who she says she is."

"I do have evidence, actually," Cat said, lifting her hand and displaying the ruby-and-gold baron's ring for all to see. Adrian couldn't see from where he stood, but he imagined it was engraved with the Macgregor family crest.

"Stolen," his father scoffed.

Father Ephraim stepped forward. "We, the priesthood of the mission in Saint's Landing, verify that according to church records, Catriona Macgregor was Blessed at her baptism as an infant by Saint Prudentia with the gift of foresight. We have confirmed her identity and believe the young woman to be who she says she is. The six elders of the priesthood are in unanimous agreement and offer our personal recommendation on her behalf."

Judge Barber's eyes widened. "If this young woman is indeed *the* Catriona Macgregor, the rightful heir to the Macgregor homestead, that means—"

"Nothing. It means absolutely nothing," Captain Freeman said, his tone cool and collected. He motioned with a white-gloved hand to the soldiers behind him, and they immediately rushed forward.

Adrian cried out as the guards surrounded Cat, knocking her to her knees and holding her in place.

Judge Barber jumped to his feet. "What is the meaning of this, Captain?"

Freeman clicked his tongue. "Unfortunately, Your Honor, she failed to mention that in addition to being Catriona Macgregor, she is also Black Cat Whitfield, adopted daughter of Amos Whitfield and notorious outlaw. She is wanted for a list of crimes that would easily extend out the door were I to unfurl them all."

Judge Barber looked down at Cat, his lip curling. "Is this true?"

Cat took a deep breath, still on her knees before him. "Yes, it's true. But I still demand a revote, as it is my right as a landowner of Saelum Territory."

The judge's mouth thinned as he pursed his lips together. "Then tell me why I shouldn't have you arrested right here and now? Why would I allow a revote?"

Adrian glanced around. Already the gold was fading from the barons' and baronesses' eyes. If Cat succeeded in securing a revote, his father would lose his manipulative advantage. His father seemed to realize this as well.

"The vote is complete, why waste any more time with this? Arrest her and be done with it!" his father cried.

"First tell them about the aurium you put in the wine," Adrian called, stepping forward now too. "Your Honor, I have reason to believe my father tampered with the vote by spiking the wine with aurium cursed with the power of Saint Pietas. The barons have all been influenced to cast their votes for my father."

The judge's eyes first went wide with shock but then narrowed with suspicion. He was a smart man, and Adrian hoped he saw the evidence as clearly as everyone else seemed to. There was a sudden murmuring that swept through the courtroom. Barons and baronesses were shaking their heads and holding hands to their temples as if trying to dispel headaches. They felt something had happened as well.

"An unfounded accusation!" his father retorted.

"No, I feel strange," Baron Higgins said. "I never would have voted for a man as corrupt as Caldwell of my own volition. I demand to see what was written on my vote."

There were shouts of agreement as chaos threatened to take over the room.

Judge Barber must have sensed the building unrest as well because he slammed his gavel on the podium, demanding everyone's attention. "Order! Everyone, please remain in your seats!" It took several more bangs of his gavel to gather everyone's attention.

Freeman's men continued to hold Cat on her knees before the judge's bench. Adrian's heart twisted at the sight. He wanted to jump up and rip their hands off her.

"Your Honor. Permission to take this outlaw into custody," Freeman said casually. He was struggling to contain a smile, which just made Adrian want to smash one of Thompson's bottles of cursed wine over his head.

There was no way the judge would just allow that . . . would he?

Judge Barber considered Cat with his shrewd eyes, and his lips thinned once again.

"Miss . . . Macgregor. I do believe you are who you say you are, and as the ten-year limit has yet to expire, I do believe it is within your right to claim ownership of your family's land."

Adrian's heart leaped into his throat. Was it possible he would allow Cat to vote and serve as baroness after all?

"But I cannot just dismiss your past actions either," Judge Barber continued, sending Adrian's heart plummeting. "You have committed many crimes against not only the barons and the territory, but the empire itself. Unfortunately, there are consequences to our actions, Miss Macgregor."

Cat's face blanched as if this was not the result she was expecting at all.

Judge Barber continued. "For that reason, I must allow you to be taken into custody and tried for your crimes."

"NO!" Adrian said. He wasn't a fool. And neither was Cat. The penalty for her many—*many*—crimes was sure to be death.

"Yes," Baron Caldwell said, stroking his mustache. "Take her into custody, Freeman."

"I am not finished," Judge Barber snapped.

His father's hand fell away from his mustache and flopped pathetically at his side.

"I will still allow her to vote, as is her right as a baroness. Because she did not participate in the original vote, we will be doing the entire vote over again," Barber announced.

This time, it was his father who yelled "NO!"

And every soul in attendance knew the reason.

"I mean, the legal process has already been carried out," Baron Caldwell said, trying to cover his misstep. "It is a binding legal process—"

"Which is true, when the winner is not also suddenly taken into custody." Judge Barber angled his head at Adrian's father, a half smile pulling at his hawklike features.

"Into custody?" his father repeated, taking a step back.

"Yes, unfortunately. I am also ordering Captain Freeman to take Baron Caldwell into custody under the charge of conspiracy to interfere with an election. He is no longer eligible as a candidate for governor."

Adrian felt as if the breath had been sucked from his lungs. He collapsed back onto his seat, his legs shaking with the shock of watching his father about to be arrested . . . alongside the girl he'd always loved, who might or might not hate him right now. He had no idea what to do. He looked to the priests, hoping they had an answer, but they seemed just as shocked and confused as he was. He told himself he needed to move, he needed to do something.

Freeman's men closed in around Baron Caldwell. Cat cried out in pain as someone tightened their grip on her. The sound of her cry jolted through him like a bolt of lightning, jarring him into action. Adrian reached for the Crockett gun in his coat . . .

BANG.

There was a sudden shot from a pistol, and then a scream. More screams, as the room realized what had happened. What the hell? His fingers hadn't even touched the barrel of his gun yet.

Adrian's eyes shot to the bench, where Judge Barber now slumped face-first onto his court documents. Bile rose in Adrian's throat. A gaping wound oozed blood from the judge's temple.

And behind him stood Captain Freeman, his gun outstretched.

"Yes, *unfortunately*, that arrangement isn't going to work for myself or Baron Caldwell," he said, sucking in a breath through his teeth as though disappointed.

Cat fell forward onto her hands and knees as the grip holding her loosened. The sound of the gunshot had made her jump, rattling her nerves so much that it took her a moment before she dared to look up. And what she saw froze her insides.

Judge Barber was dead.

Of all the developments to happen after the judge told her she was going to be arrested . . . this was one she would not have put money on. Especially to have *Freeman* be the one who shot him. It just didn't make sense. Freeman was an Ordonian captain, charged with upholding the law and supporting the judge of the territory—not murdering him in cold blood.

"Freeman! What the hell?" Baron Caldwell demanded, which only further jumbled Cat's thoughts. Caldwell appeared as genuinely shocked as everyone else. Whatever Freeman was doing, it hadn't been part of their plan.

That would have been the most surprising thing that happened to Cat that day, more than even the surprise of Judge Barber announcing he was going to have her arrested . . .

Until she watched as golden wings unfurled from Captain Freeman's back.

Cat skittered onto her backside, wanting to put as much distance between herself and . . . whatever the hell Freeman really was. Because clearly, he was more than human.

His dark eyes glowed into iridescence as the golden wings—sparking with otherworldly energy—stretched outward. His features grew sharper, more handsome in a harsh sort of way. He was . . . beautiful. But *too* beautiful. Beautiful in a way that almost hurt Cat's eyes to behold.

"You humans always have to do things the hard way, don't you?" Freeman's voice echoed around the thick silence of the room. "So I will make this simple. The votes will remain as they are."

"What . . . who are you?" a tremulous voice called from somewhere behind her. Cat didn't turn around to see who had spoken. She seemed unable to move as if she'd frozen, transfixed like a deer caught in the gaze of a hunter.

"Who am I?" Freeman laughed. "That you even have to ask is an insult. I am Gravitas, patron saint of responsibility and significance. Before I was punished, I would grant the Blessing gift of problem solving. It is I who gave humans the greatest problem-solving gift of all."

Punished? He *used* to grant Blessing gifts? The name Gravitas was not included in the pantheon of the Saints, which meant . . .

The winged figure drew itself up. "I suppose you know me now by another name, or lack thereof. Ironic, given my particular patronage."

Holy Mother above. Gravitas was the Fallen Saint.

Cat's arms began to tremble. She'd sat in a train car with him, eaten dinner with him, seen him *bleed*—it just didn't make any sense.

Unless . . . unless . . . he'd somehow possessed this human body he now resided within. That he wasn't completely divine, but somehow a mixture of the two. And if he wasn't fully divine . . . did that mean he was still mortal? Cat didn't know. But she knew she had to find out— once she could force her muscles to start working again.

"I will make this easy and plain for all of you. Caldwell is now the new governor," Gravitas continued. "And as such, he has an important announcement to make about the future of the territory. A territory that will become independent in every way. It will immediately tear down any trace of my brothers and sisters and replace them with images of their *true* god. Isn't that right, William?"

But Adrian's father didn't respond. He continued to stare at the Fallen Saint with his mouth half-open. After a moment of stunned silence, he finally cleared his throat and straightened his spine. "No." It was a single word, but Cat had to give him credit. His conviction was strong like a million voices were speaking that one word. "No, not like this."

"And what's so different about this, Caldwell? You've shown before you don't mind killing to get ahead. That's what happened to this girl's parents, is it not? You killed them in cold blood to steal their daughter and her land just to get the aurium I placed there?"

Cat's heart squeezed at Gravitas's matter-of-fact description of the darkest moment of her life. All around the room there were gasps. But Caldwell didn't even attempt to deny it.

"I will not serve as a puppet of the Fallen Saint. I wanted to rule my own nation, yes. I planned to use the aurium on her land to do so, but I will never bow to another, Saint or no. I am a man of my own making, and I will certainly not bow to you."

Saint Gravitas angled his beautiful face as he considered the baron. "That's really too bad, Caldwell. That aurium was my answer to your prayers, and now you want to back out. I had high hopes for you. But if that is truly your desire, then I cannot force you."

Cat wanted to scream a warning, but she wasn't fast enough. She watched in horror as Gravitas lifted the gun he'd used to shoot the judge. She prayed Adrian's eyes were closed—no child should ever have to watch the death of a parent . . .

BANG.

Caldwell's body hit the floor with a sickening thud. It was a fate he deserved, but it didn't make it any less brutal in its execution.

Gravitas rolled his neck. "These human bodies are unbearable. I can't believe I was human myself at one point . . ." He turned back to the crowded courtroom, where almost everyone now cowered in their seats or hid beneath the tables. Cat was still stuck flat on her backside in the center of the room before him.

He turned to face her. "Ah yes, the Black Kitten or whatever it is they call you. Blessed by my sister Prudentia. Foresight is the gift, is it not?"

Her vision flashed a warning as he lifted his gun and fired at her. Cat barely dodged the bullet and rolled to the side.

"Oh, come now, little kitty. Don't you want to play? My sister planned for you to be the one to stop me, you know. So I think I shall destroy you first just to spite her."

He fired again, and again her vision flashed. But she wasn't fast enough. This time the bullet ripped through the arm of her jacket, grazing her arm. Thank the Saints it was a normal bullet and not aurium . . .

It still didn't stop the searing pain that burned across the flesh of her arm or the warm blood that followed in its wake and soaked her sleeve. She screamed, her opposite hand darting to cover the wound.

Gravitas laughed. "Her little gift is not as useful as some of the others, is it? Is being one of the Blessed all you hoped it would be?"

But then it was Gravitas's turn to scream. The six priests, including Fathers Iggy and Ephraim, had surrounded him from behind. They removed small vials of holy water from around their necks and tossed their contents toward him.

Where the water met his flesh, smoke rose and skin boiled. Gravitas roared in pain, his wings thrashing like those of an injured bird. One wing caught one of the younger priests in the stomach and sent him flying. He crashed into a wall, fell to the ground, and did not move.

"Run!" Father Ephraim yelled at her before turning to address everyone else. "*Run to the mission!*"

Cat's head felt full of cotton. She needed to move, to get out of his line of fire, but shock kept her frozen in place. The other priests continued to surround the Fallen Saint, holding him back with vials of holy water they were producing from the pockets of their robes. They lobbed the fragile glass bottles at him, like children throwing rocks at a beast. It was keeping him distracted, but it wouldn't for long.

Most of the barons and baronesses didn't need to be told twice. There was a mad scramble toward the door as the nobility of Saelum tripped over themselves—and each other—to escape. Cat couldn't see

Adrian in the chaos of bodies shoving against each other. But then she felt arms around her, lifting her to her feet.

She looked up to see Father Iggy, his watery eyes alight with concern. "Come, my dear. Let's get you out of here, shall we?" Cat allowed herself to be dragged forward. She shook her head, trying to dislodge the shock that seemed to slow everything down like molasses. When her senses finally returned, they rushed back in a sudden overwhelming volley of color and sound.

Another priest went flying in a sweep of golden wings. She had to do something, she had to help everyone escape. Once she was steady, she pulled out one of the guns Father Ephraim had given her that morning and took aim.

Gravitas must have sensed it somehow because he turned his starbright eyes to her and bared his teeth just as she fired. The bullet tore through the air, but the Fallen Saint smirked as he avoided it easily. She lifted her second gun and fired, but again, he dodged. This time, he lifted his own gun, pointing it at her.

Father Ephraim appeared out of nowhere, throwing himself on Gravitas's arm. The gun fired, missing Cat by a few inches. Arms wrapped around her again, and she heard Adrian's voice yelling in her ear.

"Cat! Move!"

But she had to stop Gravitas. Somehow, someone had to stop him. And what they were doing now was not working. She looked around. They were the last ones left in the courtroom aside from the other priests still standing.

Gravitas threw Father Ephraim's frail form, and the older man landed hard on his back. He cried out in pain. Cat's stomach dropped. But then he pulled aside his robes and withdrew a beautiful Dalton pistol. He fired so quickly that Gravitas didn't have time to register what was happening. The bullet hit the Fallen Saint in the shoulder, making his wings curl in pain.

Gravitas roared as blood soaked through his Ordonian guard uniform.

He was still mortal. Or at least his host body was, which meant if Cat could get a shot in too . . .

But Adrian and Iggy dragged her out the doors before she got the chance. Her last sight before the doors closed was Gravitas advancing on Father Ephraim, who was still lying on the ground, his pistol raised in defense.

"No!" she screamed. "We need to help! We need to stop him!"

"Father Ephraim is giving you a chance to escape, Catriona. You need to take it."

"But he'll kill him!"

Surprisingly, Father Iggy chuckled. "You clearly don't know Father Ephraim as well I do."

Adrian's arms were warm and strong around her as he led her down the front steps of the courtroom and into the plaza out front. A small patch of grass housed a large fountain and the wooden gallows where executions took place. The dirt streets were clouded with dust as the crowds waiting for news of the vote now dispersed in pandemonium. Everyone had taken shelter in the surrounding shops and in the mission or fort on either side.

"We need to get into the mission. The Fallen Saint can't cross its threshold," Father Iggy instructed.

They had just reached the bottom of the stairs when the front doors to the courthouse blew open as if in a great wind. One of the thick wooden doors flew off the hinges completely, snapping in half as it crashed into a stone pillar. Above their heads, the clock tower began to toll high noon. Each knell seemed to rattle Cat's teeth.

They took shelter behind the raised wooden dais of the courthouse gallows. Saint Gravitas materialized amid the wreckage, his beautiful face contorted in rage.

"Let me face him," Cat said, pulling Adrian's fingers off her arm.

"No way, you're injured," Adrian growled through gritted teeth.

"I can do this. I think . . . I was meant to do this."

"What do you mean?" Adrian's eyes swam with concern.

"Her gift," Father Iggy said. "It gives her an advantage to avoid his attacks. This may be the very moment your gift was given to you to use."

"Don't encourage her!" Adrian shouted.

"That is my job. To encourage her in her holy mission. I feel it as you do, my dear. You are meant to face him. This is the time."

"No!" Adrian's grip tightened on her arm.

"Adrian." Cat reached up and placed her hand on his cheek. Then, she leaned forward and kissed him gently.

A single tear tracked down his cheek. "I know it's the right thing to do, but I'm so afraid to lose you again."

Cat smiled, pressing her forehead against his. "You *never* lost me."

He kissed her again, with a fierce intensity that Cat felt burn all the way to her toes. And then she pulled back, knowing it was time.

But before she got the chance to step out from behind the dais and face her destiny, there was another scream.

The scream of a little girl.

It was Edith.

CHAPTER

44

"Edith!" Cat yelled.

Cat rushed around the dais to find Gravitas at the foot of the courthouse stairs. Edith struggled in his arms, her dress stained with the blood still pouring from his shoulder wound. At their feet lay a small wooden slingshot, and a welt was forming on Gravitas's pale cheek.

Cat wanted to laugh and curse at the same time. Edith had apparently rushed out of the mission where she was supposed to be waiting, thinking she could help with her slingshot. And by the look of the Fallen Saint's cheek, her aim had been pretty close. But terror quickly replaced Cat's pride as Gravitas lifted his gun to Edith's temple.

"Let her go!" Cat stepped out and presented herself before him. She lifted both her guns and pointed them directly at his face.

"Oh, I have no desire to harm the girl if I don't have to. I am a *Saint*, after all," Gravitas said calmly.

"What do you want then?" Cat did not lower her guns, but she knew she couldn't shoot him while he held Edith in front of him like a shield. A fact he was clearly exploiting.

"Help me free this land," Gravitas said simply. "It is captive to the will of my brothers and sisters. I wish for a place where I may be worshipped freely, recognized for the gift I have given to all of you. The gift of choosing what is right for yourselves!"

"Aurium isn't a gift, it's a curse."

Gravitas shook his head. "Power, influence, *significance* is not a curse! You have the power to make your own destiny, to choose for yourself what is right or wrong. No matter what anyone else thinks!"

"But that's selfish," Cat said. "I can exert what is right for me, and it has ripple effects on those around me. What is right for me may not be right for another. Look at Caldwell, look at what he did to my family. It was right for him, but not for me. Not for my *parents*. Power like that is an illusion. Nothing more."

"So you won't take your power into your own hands? You choose to leave it with your precious Saints?" Gravitas laughed.

Edith whimpered in his grip.

"I won't hurt others for the sake of doing what's best for myself. All I wanted to do was run from the truth, no matter what it cost those around me. I only cared about myself. I certainly wouldn't be where I am now if I'd listened only to my own selfish desires. I'd be across the Dark Sea by now, instead of doing the hard thing of facing my past and doing what's right. Saint Prudentia didn't give up on me, no matter how many times I begged her to take my gift away."

"Well then, if you will not help me, I have no choice but to remove you from my path. Prudentia should have chosen a better option to stop me." He lifted his gun.

Cat's vision flashed. And she knew exactly what to do.

"Edith!" Cat yelled. "*You don't ever have to let someone take your will from you again.*"

They were the same words she'd told her after removing the aurium necklace, after her father had exerted his will over his daughter for his own selfish purposes. She'd given Edith the necklace of holy water Father Ephraim had given her, and if her vision was right, it was a necklace Edith still had around her neck.

Edith's eyes went wide with understanding, and she nodded. Cat gave her a small nod of encouragement and mouthed, *Trust me*.

Edith moved as fast as the strike of a rattlesnake. She yanked the necklace out from beneath her dress—and smashed the vial between Gravitas's eyes.

The Fallen Saint screeched in pain as the skin on his face blistered and smoked. In his shock, his grip loosened on Edith, and she wiggled out of his arms.

And Cat pulled both triggers at the same time.

The shots rang out across the plaza, echoing through the empty streets.

Saint Gravitas's neck snapped back as the bullets hit him squarely in the head. His outstretched golden wings went suddenly slack, and the light faded from his eyes as he slowly tipped backward. Edith scrambled away from him and ran to Cat. She wrapped her arms around Cat's waist just as Gravitas's body hit the ground in a cloud of dust. A burst of wind swept across the plaza, swirling above Gravitas's fallen body like a dust devil that glittered with golden sparks. By the time the dust devil cleared, all that was left behind was the fallen body of Captain Freeman, the unfortunate victim of Gravitas. Relief swept through her, refreshing as a cool stream in the dead heat of summer. Cat didn't know where the spirit of the Fallen Saint had gone, but it was clear he was no longer *here*.

Well done, my child, a woman's voice said in Cat's mind. *I knew I chose well.*

Cat turned to see who had spoken, but there was no one else there aside from Adrian and Father Iggy, who were now rushing out to meet her and Edith. But soon they weren't the only ones.

The doors to the mission flew open, and people poured back into the streets to celebrate. The body of Freeman was removed; the priests would sanctify and cleanse it before ensuring he was properly buried. She wondered who Freeman had been before Gravitas had taken him over. According to Father Iggy, she didn't need to feel too sad about it. He would have had to invite Gravitas into himself in order to be possessed like that.

"It was his choice, Cat," the priest told her. "Don't let the guilt of killing him eat away at you. Again, an example of how our own choices affect those around us. Whoever he truly was, he *chose* this."

But Cat had seen enough death to last her a lifetime, especially at her own hands. A few people pointed at her and whispered behind their hands to one another. Her stomach squirmed at the judgment in their eyes. She didn't want to be an outlaw anymore, but what choice did she have now? She knew exactly what the people of Saelum saw when they looked at her.

The crowd in the plaza of both citizens and barons had grown so large that it was getting hard to hear and see. Her feet tingled with the need to move, to get out of the plaza before someone remembered what the judge had said and she was arrested again. Perhaps now was her time to escape, to run while she still had the chance. But Baron Hernandez suddenly appeared at her side.

"I have a proposition to make," Baron Hernandez announced, placing a hand firmly on Cat's shoulder as though he could sense her skittishness. "Please come inside the courthouse, Miss Macgregor, before you leave? I promise to make it worth your time."

Run? Or stay? The two options warred within her. She glanced over her shoulder toward a gap in the mass of bodies pressing together, but then Adrian's hand slipped around her own and squeezed.

He leaned in and whispered, "Stay. Please."

Edith gripped her other hand as she implored Cat with puppy eyes.

"Fine. I will hear whatever this proposition is, but I can't promise I can stay after that."

"We'll see," Adrian said, his eyes twinkling. Did he know something she didn't?

The barons and baronesses all filed back inside the courthouse. Cat turned her head as the judge's body was borne away. The priests who had been injured during the attack, including Father Ephraim, were already recovering at the mission's infirmary. Cat smiled. Father Iggy had been right; it apparently took more than the Fallen Saint himself to bring down Father Ephraim.

This time there were no formal tables, no glasses of cursed wine waiting to toast, just a collection of landowners standing together and waiting for someone to stand up and take the lead.

Baron Hernandez stepped forward and cleared his throat. "As you all know, the barons are the ones who vote to appoint the territorial judge. As we have not yet selected Judge Barber's replacement—may he rest in peace with the Saints—I believe it is within our jurisdiction to vote on the choice of one of our peers."

There was a general rumble of agreement.

Cat sucked in a breath as she realized what he was saying. A warm, swelling sensation filled her chest as if she'd taken a sip of whiskey.

"I am aware that Catriona Macgregor has a criminal record," he continued. "However, as we heard from the cursed Saint himself, that would not have happened had Baron Caldwell not murdered her parents. Given the circumstances and her role in saving all of us from the Fallen Saint, I motion that we clear her of her crimes and reinstate her as the rightful baroness of the Macgregor Ranch. Those in favor?"

Tears burned behind Cat's eyes as she watched hand after hand go up. Of course, there were several reluctant *ayes* and several *abstains*, but in the end, all that mattered was the outcome.

"Cleared of all crimes!" Baron Hernandez announced. He motioned for her to join him at the head of the room. She stepped forward, her legs shaking.

Baron Hernandez held out his hand. "It is a pleasure to welcome you home, Miss Macgregor."

Cat finally let her tears fall. She reached out and shook his offered hand with a firm determination. "I promise to make you and the rest of Saelum proud."

Baron Hernandez winked. "I'm sure you will."

She turned to find Father Iggy rushing toward her. He threw out his arms and pulled her into a bone-crushing embrace.

"I told you, my dear," he whispered in her ear.

Cat pulled back and squeezed his hands. "Thank you, Father Iggy. I couldn't have done this without you."

"Oh nonsense," he said, wiping a tear from his eye. "This is my job."

"A job which you excelled at," she reminded him. "And if you ever want to start your own vineyard—a *proper* one, I would love to be a financier for such an endeavor. Apparently I am a landowner now."

Father Iggy patted her cheek and winked. "We will definitely stay in touch."

Next, it was Edith's turn to embrace her. "Does this mean you aren't going to be hanged?" she asked.

Cat laughed. "Yes. I'm not going to be hanged."

Edith squealed with delight.

She looked up, and her eyes locked with Adrian's, a thousand words hanging unsaid between them. She didn't know where to start, and neither, it seemed, did he.

"There is a lot to figure out now, isn't there?" he said.

Cat nodded, a lump forming in her throat.

He was right: there was still so much to figure out, to mourn and rebuild. But she didn't fear the future anymore. She wished Amos could see her now, but she knew that somewhere, he was smiling down on her alongside the Saints.

Alongside her parents.

"No offense, Cat, but this looks like a piece of—" Soap started to say before Cat elbowed him in the stomach.

"Paradise? You were going to say paradise, weren't you?" She arched an eyebrow at him.

Soap wheezed as he bent double, trying to catch his breath. "Yup," he coughed. "Paradise. You took the words . . . right outta my mouth."

Cat tilted her head as she considered the sight before them. Unfortunately, Soap was probably right with his initial unfinished assessment. What was left of the Macgregor homestead was the farthest possible thing from a paradise.

"It has . . . excellent bones?" Pedro offered, stuffing his hands into his pockets.

Cat let a heavy breath escape from her lips. It had been almost a decade since the fire had destroyed most of the main house. Though some of the original structure remained intact, what framing remained was charred black and overrun with sagebrush. A lone coyote scampered out from the ruins of the kitchen and into the hills upon their approach.

"That used to be my room," Cat said flatly, pointing to a section of the second story that was still standing.

"How can you tell?" Pedro asked.

"I can't really. I'm just going based off my memory, to be honest."

"Well." Soap finally caught his breath and clapped his hands together. "We got a lot a work ahead of us, but a right rich sponsor now, don't we? *Baroness* Macgregor?"

"I'm not going to be your sugar mama, Soap."

"What about mine?" Pedro asked, the corners of his mouth twitching.

Cat swept off her hat and beat it against Pedro's shoulder. He actually smiled and took his beating with exceptional grace.

"What am I going to do with the pair of you?"

Soap grinned. "Take care of us for the rest of our long, lazy lives, of course."

"Hell no. I'm putting you both to work. Immediately."

They both chuckled. She hated to admit it, but she was so grateful to have them with her. If her birth family couldn't be here with her, the family she chose for herself could be.

"Find anything worthwhile, priest?" Soap called over to where Father Iggy was digging his hands into the dirt several yards away.

The priest lifted some of the soil and rubbed it between his fingers. "Yes, I think it will do nicely. The earth is rich enough, and if I can import some different varieties, we can have some fine vineyards planted by spring."

"What about cattle? Rebuilding the house?" Cat worried her lower lip between her teeth. She didn't even know where to begin on such matters. Her parents had left behind some substantial funds tied to the Macgregor estate, another reason Baron Caldwell had likely been eager to get his hands on it. She would never allow the aurium on her land to be mined. But even without it, she had enough money to reestablish the ranch and get it running again . . . with a few improvements. Such as Father Iggy's new vineyard. He planned to sell his own wines—as a private endeavor not in any way tied to the church, of course.

"We will need to hire some builders from Saint's Landing to help with the main house, and that will take a while. I suggest putting up a smaller establishment for you to live in the meantime. As for cattle, we need to begin purchasing a herd and preparing the pastures."

"Will you help me?" Cat implored the priest with wide, desperate eyes.

"Of course, Catriona. I have been with you every step of the way and I don't plan on letting you down now." He waved a hand as though the thought of him *not* helping was preposterous.

Cat's throat tightened, and she gave him a watery smile.

"What happened to your fancy boy?" Soap asked, kicking at the dirt. "I thought he'd be here by now, begging at your feet for you to marry him."

Cat shrugged and tried to pretend she didn't care, but the reality was, it had been almost a week since the events of Saint's Landing, and she hadn't so much as gotten a letter. And it wasn't like they lived all that far away from each other now. Adrian could come over anytime he wanted, but he clearly didn't want to. The last time she'd seen him was back in the courthouse. After her charges had been cleared, the barons had started over with the vote—Cat and Adrian both speaking for their respective ranches—and selected Baron Hernandez as their recommendation for the new governor of Saelum Territory. It was a role Cat believed he'd serve in well. She'd watched as he and Adrian spoke at length after the vote. They'd been too far away for her to hear their conversation, but she could have sworn she saw Adrian say "Evangeline" more than once.

Could that be why he'd distanced himself? She knew he had his own matters to sort out as the new Baron Caldwell, managing the cattle ranch, settling up his father's substantial debts . . . debts that might require him to marry another wealthy landowner's daughter to cover. A wealthy landowner's daughter like Evangeline Hernandez. Perhaps he was doing what he had to, or perhaps he'd come to actually care for her. Evangeline was well bred, beautiful, and had a genuinely kind heart. She had seen that for herself. And Cat . . . well . . . Cat had lied to him for weeks about who she truly was. Just because they had a history together, it didn't mean he owed her any kind of future. She was a little rougher around the edges and came with more vinegar than honey when it came to her personality. Adrian probably felt guilty or wanted to protect her feelings by staying away. Cat crossed her arms across her chest and squeezed, pretending the empty, aching feeling was just about what had become of her once fine home and nothing whatsoever to do with Adrian.

"He's probably just busy taking care of things." Her tone was casual, but she didn't miss the way Soap eyed her with disbelief. "If he wants to come see me, he knows where to find me," she added for good measure.

"You know, I am proud of you, my dear, for no longer running from your past. But Adrian is part of that past too, you know. You don't have to run from him either," said Father Iggy, jumping into their conversation.

Cat rolled her eyes. "You still have the bet going on with the other priests, don't you?"

Father Iggy sputtered. "That—that is neither here nor there!" He became suddenly very interested in the state of the soil again.

"I dunno. If I were him, I'd have swept you off your feet by now and ridden off into the sunset," Soap said.

Cat snorted. "Well, we aren't all hopeless romantics like you, Soap."

"Emphasis on the hopeless part," Pedro added.

"And who says I even want that?" Cat fiddled with Almond's reins. "If that's what he wanted, he would have made that known by now, which means he must want something else." She'd heard rumors of "preparations" for an event happening at the Caldwell Ranch from one of the riders delivering supplies, and preparations clearly meant one thing. Why else would he be keeping such a careful distance between them?

"Oh, don't pretend you aren't in love with him, Cat," Soap teased. "I know love when I see it, and you've got it bad for Mr. Fancy Pants."

"Don't call him Mr. Fancy Pants," Cat snapped. But she didn't contradict him about loving Adrian. She knew she did, but a fat lot of good it did her if he was going to end up marrying Evangeline.

So instead of dwelling on it, she threw herself into her work, sparing only an occasional glance toward the river that marked the boundary of their lands. Each horse that rode up with news from Saint's Landing or with supplies made her heart leap until she saw that none of them were Adrian.

By the last morning of that week, they had a decent camp set up that would serve as a home base during the rebuilding phase, and Cat had given up any hope of hearing from him. She was pouring herself a cup of hot coffee from the pot hanging over the fire when the sounds of hoofbeats reached her ears. Soap and Pedro were still asleep in their tents, and Cat didn't even look up, expecting it to be another delivery for Soap or a messenger with another bid on pricing for lumber. But the sound of a little girl's voice snapped her attention to the newcomer.

"Cat? Are you here?" came Edith's familiar tone.

"Edith?" Cat jumped to her feet. "What are you doing here? Are you . . . on a horse *by yourself*?"

And so she was. Cat's jaw nearly dropped to the dirt, especially when she noticed the carpetbag Edith had tied to the saddle.

"Yes. I came by myself. I decided I am moving in with you." Edith tossed the small bag onto the dirt and then dismounted, spreading her arms wide as though proud of herself.

Cat nearly choked on her coffee. "Moving in? With me? Why?"

"Well, Adrian is so busy and he's trying to get me another governess, but I absolutely refuse. You were the best one I ever had. He told me you had your own place to live now, though, so I decided that if you can't come to us, then I would come to you."

Edith's words lanced through Cat's chest like an arrow. She "had her own place to live" now, did she? So much for offering her a place to call home with him. Perhaps Evangeline wasn't comfortable with their past together. Considering the feelings Cat had for Adrian, that was probably for the best anyway.

"Yes, I have my own place now, but I'm pretty sure Adrian will mind you leaving." Cat quirked the corner of her mouth into a half smile. "Not that I would mind having you here."

"Then why can't you just come back and live with us?" Edith pressed. "You haven't even come back to visit! Do you not like us anymore?"

"Edith, you know that's not true at all. I've just been really busy."

"That's what Adrian says. That I just need to leave you alone and let you get settled. But it's been a whole week! Are you settled yet?"

Cat glanced around at the canvas tents she, Soap, and Pedro had erected along with the campfire that was serving as their kitchen until the main kitchen was in better shape. "Not exactly settled. But we should probably get you back home, sweetheart. Does Adrian even know you're here?"

"I don't mind sleeping in a tent. I promise. And I can be a very hard worker if you need me to! Please don't send me back yet!"

Cat pulled the little girl into a hug. "I'm sure you are a very hard worker. You are more than welcome to visit me anytime. Tell you what. Why don't you stay for breakfast and then we can get you home, okay?"

Edith grumbled but situated herself by the fire while Cat baked some drop biscuits in a skillet. They munched in silence, listening to the gentle rhythms of Soap snoring in his tent until the sound of more hooves approaching caught Cat's attention. This time, she did choke on her coffee.

Adrian rode up, his face frantic with concern. His hair was disheveled, and he'd missed a button on his wrinkled shirt. He practically jumped off his horse in his haste to approach them.

"Edith!" His voice was low and dangerous. "Where. Have. You. Been?"

Edith gave her brother a sheepish smile. "I told you I don't want a new governess. I want Cat. So I came to live with her."

Adrian ran a hand through his hair, making the ends stick up even worse than they already were. "Edith, we talked about this."

"She's settled! Look! They have tents up and everything!"

Soap chose that particular moment to stumble out of his tent, completely shirtless. Adrian looked between him and Cat, his cheeks turning crimson.

"Well, they obviously seem very settled, so let's leave them be, Edith . . ."

"Ah, Mr. Fancy Pants finally returns," Soap proclaimed, helping himself to a biscuit. "You gonna propose now, or what?"

Adrian's eyes went wide. "I—What? What do you—"

Cat shoved Soap back toward his tent. "Nothing. He doesn't mean anything."

"Cat! Aren't you going to tell him you love—"

"Time to get dressed now, Soap!" Cat said very loudly.

Adrian looked at Cat, his eyebrows pulling together in confusion.

"Sorry. It's nothing. I'm sure you need to get back home. I'm so sorry about Edith, I told her she's welcome to visit anytime, but she definitely needs to ask first." Cat lifted Edith by the elbow from where she sat on a log by the fire.

Edith yanked her arm back. "I don't want to go back without you!"

"I don't really have a place there anymore, Edith." Was it her, or did Adrian flinch when she said that? It was true though. If he was going to marry Evangeline, it wouldn't be proper for her to be at their house.

"It's, um, good to see you, at least, Catriona. I mean Cat." Adrian cleared his throat as though he was uncomfortable.

Soap groaned from somewhere inside his tent. Cat's face was on fire. Despite how badly she had wanted Adrian to come visit, now she wanted nothing more than the Caldwells to go home before she burned to a crisp in embarrassment.

"Yeah, it's . . . good to see you too. How is . . . everything?" Why did it feel like she'd swallowed a swarm of moths instead of coffee and biscuits for breakfast?

Adrian shrugged. "Just familiarizing myself with my father's affairs. Making preparations. That sort of thing."

"Oh." Cat paused. "How are the wedding preparations going?"

Adrian blinked at her. "Wedding preparations?"

"For you and Evangeline, of course."

To her surprise, Adrian started *laughing*.

A flicker of irritation sparked inside her. "What's so funny?"

"I'm . . . not marrying Evangeline. Is that what you think?"

"I saw you talking to her dad after the vote! You haven't so much as said hello since everything happened, and one of the supply runners said you were busy with preparations!"

"Preparations for my father's *funeral*, not for a wedding," Adrian said, catching his breath. "Is that why you haven't come to visit? You thought I was marrying Evangeline?"

Cat crossed her arms across her chest. Now she felt like a fool. Anger prickled hotly along her cheeks now, burning away the embarrassment. "Well, you could have come to visit too, you know."

"That's what I said," Edith grumbled.

"I didn't want to impose, especially if you were getting settled. I just wanted to give you time to . . . you know, figure out what you want."

"She wants *you*," Soap called from his tent.

"Oh my Saints." Cat covered her eyes with her hand.

"Is that true?" Adrian asked, taking a step closer.

The burning in her cheeks intensified to an almost unbearable level. But she couldn't find it in her to admit the truth.

"We never made any promises to each other, and we didn't get much time to talk about things after what happened."

"But is what he said true?" He took another step toward her, so close she could smell his sandalwood soap.

Cat sighed heavily, not making eye contact with him. She had the sudden urge to run away like a desert antelope. "Maybe . . . I don't know. Yes? I guess."

Adrian cleared his throat again, his tone sounding suddenly very businesslike. "Then, perhaps, if you are amenable, Baroness Macgregor, we might still discuss joining the Caldwell and Macgregor lands?"

"Oh? Really?" Cat said, finally looking up and fighting to contain her smile. Her chest felt like it was expanding, blooming with something that felt an awful lot like hope.

"Yes, as I am legally Baron Caldwell myself now. There is a lot to figure out, but I would propose an agreement that the aurium on your land remain exactly where it is as long as we're both alive. Do you think Soap and Pedro could help us manage such a large homestead?"

"Wait," Cat said, grabbing the front of Adrian's jacket and pulling him close. "Are you proposing *marriage* to me, Baron Caldwell?"

"Finally!" Soap yelled from his tent. "Can I come out now?"

Cat ignored him.

"What if I am proposing marriage?" Adrian said, arching an eyebrow.

"She says yes!" Edith yipped from somewhere to their left as her arms wrapped around their waists.

"Well, I guess I don't have a choice then," Cat laughed. "We don't want to disappoint your sister."

And Adrian pulled her in and kissed her.

It looked like Father Iggy was going to win his bet after all. And Cat didn't care because, for the first time in her life, the future was brimming with possibilities and untainted by the shadows of her past.

Because she'd done it. She'd faced the night instead of running from it, and as painful and terrifying as it had been, she *had* come out on the other side and found the rising sun. As she looked around at Edith and Adrian, and even Soap and Pedro, she realized the sun she had been chasing had been here all along, in the love and support of those who cared about her.

And she couldn't wait to bask in its warmth for the rest of her life.